WAKING
FIRE

WAKING FIRE

JEAN LOUISE

ISBN-13: 978-1-335-42857-8

Waking Fire

Copyright © 2023 by Jean-Paul Bass

For questions and comments about the quality of this book, please contact us at CustomerService@Harlequin.com.

Inkyard Press
22 Adelaide St. West, 41st Floor
Toronto, Ontario M5H 4E3, Canada
www.InkyardPress.com

Printed in U.S.A.

This one's for Sara, Barbra, and Shyla,
who've been on this journey with me since our Whittier days.

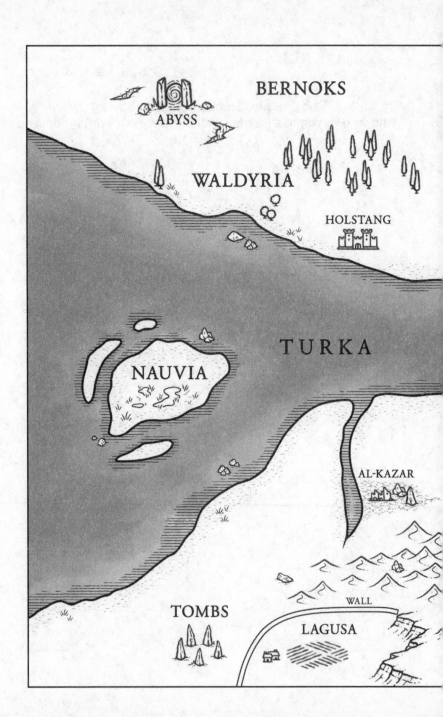

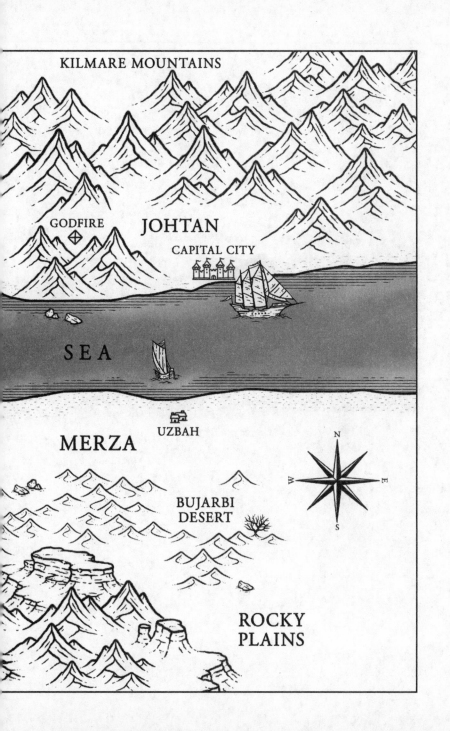

PROLOGUE

Everything that happened before will happen again.

The names will change. The faces will be different. The kinships and experiences will be unlike those of their historical counterparts.

But the betrayals will be the same.

The hurt, the anger. The love and ecstasy. The greed.

The desire for power, the need to obtain what's owed.

Those never change.

Let me tell you a story.

I was once a prince, my father the King of Volsgaria. He was a cruel man, and his cruelty tore our country apart. As my father lay dying, he called my older brother Wallen and me to his bedside and warned us about a bastard he had fathered before the birth of his first *true* son, Wallen. The mother was a lowly scullery maid—her name not important enough for my father to remember. To him, she was simply an obsession that had turned into annoyance, a plaything to be discarded when something shinier caught his eye.

Except his plaything refused to accept her fate and fade away.

When Wallen was born, she confronted my father and tried to claim the throne for her son Soras. In return, my father banished them both to the Bernoks. He called the banishment a kindness—he felt pity at the rotten hand dealt to her by the Three-Faced God, so he sent them away instead of killing them. When I reminded him that banishing a mother and child to a frozen wasteland of ceaseless night was essentially a death sentence, it was his illness that saved me from his wrath. He was too weak to smack me across my mouth, knock my head against a table, or slam me into a wall for my insolence as he had done many times before. This illness had come upon him swiftly, rendering his legs useless within days and filling his lungs with thick, dark phlegm that crowded every hall and room with the sound of his hacking. Even when dying, he refused us peace.

His last words were a warning: the kitchen wench's son was now calling himself the Bastard King, and he was coming to get what was owed.

Soon thereafter, the old king was dead and Wallen was crowned the new King of Volsgaria. But my brother was too kind for the throne my father had molded into a seat of treachery, suspicion, and faithlessness. Wallen saw his reign as the start of a new age—one of peace and enlightenment—and didn't heed our father's warning.

We had hardly finished Wallen's coronation, the throne barely warmed beneath my brother's ass, when the Bastard King arrived at our gates.

Soras came bearing gifts for the new king, and Wallen trusted him. Believed him when he called himself a friend. As I said, Wallen was too kind for the throne our father had built.

I tried to warn him. You must remember that I tried.

I walked into the throne room one morning, expecting it to be empty, only to find my father's bastard sitting in Wallen's place.

Sitting in the place reserved for kings.

"Don't get too comfortable up there, Soras," I said. "The throne will never belong to you."

Soras grinned, his teeth yellow and sharp. "If there is something I want, then there is nothing that can stop me from obtaining it. Especially someone as weak as you."

Like I had done with my father, I saw the true intent behind Soras's words. "So you admit it—you're not a friend. You're only here to unseat my brother."

"*Our* brother, young Gamikal." Soras motioned for me to come closer, and when I remained where I stood, he rose from the throne and approached me. "I know you've been whispering in Wallen's ear, telling him I'm going to betray him, that I'm pretending to care for him when I'm really only after the throne." Soras leaned close. "You're right, of course. Too bad no one else will ever know."

Before I could react, Soras knocked me out with a blow to the head and I awoke in the dungeon beneath the castle. For years, I had to learn about what was happening above through offhand comments by his guards, by begging for information from the servants who brought my meals, and from imprisoned courtiers who had crossed Soras in one way or another. And what I learned only confirmed what I had suspected of Soras since the day our father told us his name.

Soras quietly replaced most of the castle guards with his own men before striking Wallen and those loyal to him. Only one knight, Theda, survived the slaughter to defend Wallen. Together, Wallen and Theda escaped the castle and fled to the Bujarbi Desert to reach safety at her estate.

With that, war erupted in Volsgaria. Those who supported the Bastard King thought Wallen to be nothing more than a newer version of the dead sovereign, while others followed Wallen, the Rightful Heir, in his quest to free Volsgaria from Soras.

Many, though, waited for a sign from the Three-Faced God, who during periods of deep unrest, when humanity had lost its way, would favor us with dragons to set us on the right path. Over the course of history, there had been twelve dragons of benevolence to walk among us, guiding us, protecting us—starting with Maganor the Never-Ending and most recently Zulgaron the Curse-Taker. If there was ever a time to send another dragon, it was during the war.

And then Soras revealed the dragon Ergenegon, loyal to his cause.

The dragon's very existence seemed as if the Three-Faced God had taken Soras's side and abandoned the rest of us. No army could defeat a dragon, and I knew my kindhearted brother's end was near.

I cried when they told me Wallen had died on the battlefield, engulfed in Ergenegon's blue flames. But the Three-Faced God hadn't forsaken Wallen's cause after all, for a few days later, Theda emerged from the Kilmare Mountains with a dragon of her own. Like the dragons of legend, Crafulgar was born in the godfire, a sacred lake of fire that had been tended to for centuries by the Hands of God, a band of secretive warrior monks devoted to serving the will of the Three-Faced God.

Not since the twin dragons Enog the Sorrow-Ender and Nurega the Joy-Provider had there been two dragons alive at the same time, and never had they fought against each other as Ergenegon the Chaos-Bringer and Crafulgar the Fiend-Slayer did.

Despondency settled into the vacant throne of Volsgaria as Crafulgar chased Ergenegon through the skies, battling him over the villages Theda had sworn to protect, shielding with her wings the people who still loved Wallen. The world was a place of confusion for believers of the Three-Faced God, left to question why it had seemingly sent one dragon to destroy and another to defend.

I remained in the dungeon for months as the war between the dragons raged on the surface, wondering why Soras hadn't killed me yet. Whispers that the tide was turning, that Crafulgar was forcing Ergenegon to retreat to the Bernoks, grew louder and louder, until the castle itself was abandoned. Theda was coming to avenge Wallen, and anyone who had aided Soras would be killed in Crafulgar's righteous flames.

Locked away in my cell, I was forgotten. Days passed with no one to talk to, no one to bring me news, no one to tell me if Soras was finally dead. I figured I had been left to rot, but I was wrong.

One night, two of Soras's soldiers unlocked my cell and dragged me outside to a waiting horse. We galloped into the night, heading north toward the Bernoks, the air growing crisp and then cold, until the exposed skin on the tips of my nose and fingers turned blue, then purple, then a deadly black.

In the Bernoks, time means nothing. There is only cold and dark. I don't know how long we traveled. My waking hours were filled with as much darkness as those I spent sleeping. But eventually we stopped, my captors anxious as if waiting for something.

Before my eyes, the snow on the flat, frozen ground began to swirl, growing and growing, until the sky was filled with a whirling vortex of ice and wind. And in the middle of the vortex, a dark void appeared. As we moved closer, a coldness I had never felt before seeped into my bones. My ears filled with the howls of something ancient, something voracious, something deadly, and my horse reared back, throwing me off.

Rough hands dragged me to the void, where the wind stole my breath and an invisible power tried to pull me into the blackness. A roaring noise of human screams and monsters shrieking filled my ears until blood trickled from them. I dug in my heels, grasped at the frozen ground with my frostbitten fingers as the abyss tried to pull me into its ravenous embrace.

I would have understood if Soras had killed me in front of everyone like he had killed my brother—but why bring me to the Bernoks only to have me disappear into an abyss in secret?

It didn't take long for my question to be answered.

Ergenegon swooped down out of the sky, landing next to me at the edge of the vortex.

I expected him to look like the twelve dragons of yore: human in shape with large leathery wings and a chest that glowed before fire burst from its mouth.

The swirling, crackling energy of the abyss revealed Ergenegon's true form. He had no lips, only sharp yellow teeth that were too big for his mouth, and he stared at me with black lizard-like eyes. Emaciated and hairless, his body was covered in scales the color of night. His sharp bones stuck out at odd angles, his wings tattered and thin. Thick, black claws erupted from the ends of his fingers and toes, and a long, whip-like tail snaked behind him.

Ergenegon was a dragon of nightmares. An abomination clearly not created by the Three-Faced God. He came from something darker, something older, something best forgotten and undisturbed.

He dug his claws into my shoulders, wrapped his tail around my waist, and beat his wings, keeping the both of us from being sucked into the abyss. But instead of flying away, he hovered above the vortex.

"O you ancients of the abyss," he called into the whirling blackness, "bind us together soul to soul. Make his life mine, and make mine his, and through him I shall be immortal."

Immortality for a creature like him would only mean ruin for the rest of us. But he was a powerful and dangerous simulacrum of a dragon, and I was a mere man. There was nothing I could have done.

When the ritual was complete, the abyss faded and Ergenegon tossed me aside. He got what he wanted, and I was left in the Bernoks without food, water, or shelter. But I did not die. I could not. Ergenegon and the ancients had made it so. My wounds healed, life returned to my frozen extremities, and I survived months in the Bernoks with nothing but the clothes on my back.

By the time I returned to civilization, Ergenegon and Crafulgar were both dead. She had chased him to the godfire in the Kilmare Mountains, where he struck a mighty blow. She threw him into the godfire before dying herself, trapping him in the ever-burning lake of flames.

And yet, I was still alive. Which meant Ergenegon was not dead.

He is down there, in the godfire, waiting.

As the years passed, chaos rampaged through what was once Volsgaria. Anyone with the ability to raise an army fought for control of the throne. After more than a century of fighting, those who remained agreed to break Volsgaria into four distinct nations: the islands in the west formed Nauvia, the forests of the frigid north became Waldyria, the vast countryside ringed by mountains in the east was named Johtan, and the arid lands to the south below the Turka Sea were designated Merza.

Each country formed its own distinct culture and language until Volsgaria was no longer even a memory. Time had taken everyone who lived through those decades of fighting.

Everyone except me.

But as I said, everything that happened before will happen again.

Unrest will brew. Complacency will lead to the deaths of thousands. Trust will lead to love, which will lead to betrayal.

I've seen it all with my own eyes.

Everything that happened before will happen again.

In fact, it has already begun.

—from *The Foretold*, by the prophet known as
Gamikal the Long-Lasting

CHAPTER ONE

"FIVE SILVERS FOR TWO KUFFAS OF RICE?" I SHAKE MY head at the exorbitant price and back away from the grain merchant's stall. "My mother would kill me. I'll give you two silvers."

The merchant's eyes widen in shock. "Two silvers? I can't do that. My children have to eat too!" He holds out the sack of rice. "I'll give it to you for four." When I don't immediately agree to his offer, he shakes the bag. "The market's closing. You won't find a better deal anywhere else. Here, take it."

He's right that my options are limited. The stall my mother usually purchases grain from has already closed and most of the other merchants are putting away their wares and boarding up their stalls. But four silvers is still too much.

"Two and a half."

The merchant grimaces as if my counteroffer hurts him. "Three, and I won't go any lower."

I can tell he's finished haggling, so I have no choice but to agree. "Fine."

While he fastens a rope around the opening of the sack, I fish out three silver rubes from the leather money pouch tied around my waist. Omma's not going to be happy. She sent me to the market to buy spices and rice for dinner when the sun was six hands from the western horizon, but I took so long picking out incense at my favorite shop that by the time I got around to the errand my mother sent me on, the market was shutting down for the evening.

I hand the merchant the money and he passes me the sack of rice.

"Thank you for your business, samida," he says with a smile. "See you again!"

The merchant bows and I roll my eyes as I return the gesture. I'll never come back to his stall even if he were the last grain merchant in all of Lagusa. We both know he's ripped me off, and his satisfied grin makes me scowl even more.

I only have three silver rubes and four coppers left to buy the rest of the ingredients on Omma's shopping list: cumin, ground red chilis, honey, and dried orange peels. The chilis will be the most expensive, so I'll buy them first and then see what I can get with whatever rubes are left.

Even though the market's closing, the roads squeezed between stalls and mud-brick buildings where one buys spices and cloth, jewels and swords, livestock and produce are still busy enough that I can't run to the next open spice shop. The remaining merchants and customers haggle over prices while dirty children hold out their hands for scraps and coins. The savory aroma of charred meat cooking on a grill makes my stomach grumble as I pass the crowded food stalls, but that's quickly replaced by the flowery scents coming from up ahead. Perfumed air engulfs me as I cross Honey Street: the place where those who can afford it go to soak their bodies in cleansing oils and fragranced water.

I find an open spice shop with a bowl of ground chilis right out front. I motion to the owner, but she ignores me, her eyes on something farther up the road.

"Excuse me, samida," I say, trying to get her attention. "I'd like—"

The owner shoos me away with a wave of her hand without even giving me a glance. Annoyed, I follow her gaze to see what could be so important.

A few stalls down, a plume of black smoke rises above the open market.

"Is that a fire?"

The woman nods. "I think so."

As we watch the pillar of smoke grow, more and more people gather in the street, their eyes transfixed on the dark clouds bisecting the sky.

"It's those Haltayi," a man next to me says, a sneer in his voice. "They brought in one of those mangy desert animals, what do you call it?"

"A maugrab?"

"Yeah, the damn thing went berserk. There was some kind of scuffle and a lantern got knocked over and set their tent on fire."

I stand on my toes to peer over the heads of those in front of me, but it's no use. I can't see anything except the smoke. "What happened to the maugrab?"

The man shrugs. "Burned to death, I guess. There's no way it could have survived those flames."

A frenzied roar fills the streets, quieting the crowd with its intensity. The maugrab isn't dead yet.

I've always felt sorry for maugrabs—they're sickly creatures that the Haltayi nomads capture out on the plains beyond the village and charge parents a few rubes to let their children tug on their matted manes or ride on their bony backs. Selling maugrab rides is one of the few ways Haltayi make money to buy supplies so that they can survive the Rocky Plains, but the maugrabs always look so sad, so beaten, as if the rope that keeps them tied to a stake in the ground is sapping all of the life out of them.

I can't turn my back on a creature in pain, not if there's something I can do to help. I forget the orders from my mother to not dally and push my way through the crowd toward the fire.

The smoke thickens as I get closer, stinging my eyes and making me cough, but I trudge ahead. I finally burst through the crowd and see the Haltayi nomads tossing buckets of water onto the flames, which rage like a beacon in the night. Merchants with stalls on either side of the fire are clearing out their wares while using wet cloths to beat away the flames that lick their wooden structures.

The maugrab roars again. A wall of flames separates the animal from safety. Through the fire, I catch glimpses of the poor beast, its mouth open wide, its heavy paws pacing back and forth. Its short snout contains massive, sharp teeth, and anxious muscles ripple beneath the rust-colored fur covering its broad shoulders and hindquarters. Waves of heat prevent anyone from getting too close and helping.

Someone has to do something, or that maugrab is going to die.

Dropping my purchases on the ground, I run toward one of the stalls and climb on top of the structure, my feet sinking into the cloth awning. A merchant grabs at me, yelling for me to get down. I kick his hands away and jump onto the next stall, then the next, until I'm on top of the stall closest to the crackling flames.

I can hear more people hollering for me to come back, but I ignore them. Looking down, all I see is fire and smoke. The sides of the tent have burned away but the crates and furniture that lined the walls are still on fire. What remains of the top of the tent is in flames, but the section closest to me has already burned away. I'm about to turn back—the foolishness of my actions has finally caught up with me—when I catch sight of the maugrab through the haze.

I look into the maugrab's eyes, and I see that it wants to live. There are so many people standing around, watching, some of them crying, but no one's doing anything to help. The maugrab's going to die unless I do something.

I have to act fast if I'm going to save the maugrab.

Luckily the roof of this stall is made of wooden planks and not fabric. I cover my face with my arms, grit my teeth, and pray to the gods that I land on the other side of the fire and not within the flames.

A gasp erupts from the crowd as I leap over the flames. The heat briefly singes my skin before I hit the ground with a thud. My pants are on fire, the hungry blaze eating the thin cloth. I beat out the flames with my hands and get on my hands and knees.

The only sound is the roaring fire, and acrid smoke coats my lungs with every breath. I've never felt such heat and I'm instantly drenched in sweat. It's difficult to see, so I crawl to where I last saw the maugrab and cry out with relief when my hand brushes a furry paw.

The maugrab is lying on the ground, its breaths shallow. I climb to my feet and tug on the beast's rough mane.

"Come on," I say between coughs. "Get up!"

Slowly, the maugrab gets on all fours and I rub the sleek reddish-brown fur on its powerful shoulders.

"There's only one way out of here," I tell the animal, pointing at the top of a stall, barely visible over the wall of flames. "And I can't make the jump. Can you do it?"

The maugrab starts forward but is held back by the rope around its neck tied to a stake in the ground. I make quick work of the knots, and the maugrab shakes its mane and roars when it's free.

I climb on the beast's back and grab hold of its mane, my mind racing with prayers to the gods that I can actually pull this off. With a powerful lurch, the maugrab leaps and clears the fire, landing on top of the wooden stall with a skid and digging its claws into the wood to stop us from sliding off.

A cheer rises up among the crowd. I'm grinning, reckless but triumphant.

"You did it," I tell the maugrab.

The rickety stall wobbles beneath us and the maugrab jumps onto the ground as the roof crashes down.

We're immediately surrounded by onlookers, many of them clapping me on the back and congratulating me as I slide off the maugrab. A Haltayi woman runs up and wraps her arms around the animal's neck, as a Haltayi man bows deeply before me. "Thanking you, samida," he says in his thick accent.

My cheeks flush from the attention and I return the bow. Before I can get caught up in all the smiles and excitement, the structure that enclosed the maugrab finally collapses. Swirls of fiery ash and smoke ride the gust of wind released by the falling structure before descending on the crowd. Cries ring out as hot embers fall on bare skin, and I'm jostled aside by elbows as those around me slap at the little fires clinging to their clothes.

Coughing and stumbling, I move aside to clear a path for more buckets of water to douse the flames and find myself shoved into an alley. I take a moment to collect myself, my heart still racing, when I realize I tossed the expensive rice aside to save the maugrab. I still need to buy everything else on Omma's list, but with the market in such disarray and with most of the shops already closed, I don't know if that's possible. And now that all the excitement has waned, exhaustion has taken over, and I just want to go home.

I wipe the sweat from my face with the hem of my scarf and groan when I see the streaks of black on the light blue fabric. Maybe if I explain to Omma what happened with the maugrab, she won't be disappointed that I didn't buy any of the things she asked for and why I returned in such a state.

Deciding I'd rather be scolded by Omma than deal with the market again, I head down the alley, toward the main road that will take me home. I pass boxes of refuse filled with rotting vegetables, discarded sacks of mealy grain, and rolled-up rugs with frayed edges and covered in stains. I'm halfway

through the alley when I hear a group of voices coming from
the shadows on my left.

"You're such an idiot!" a girl yells and I stop in my tracks.

She's shrouded in shadows, but I don't need to see the girl
to know who's yelling.

Hamala Mugabe is the last person I'd want to meet in a
dark alley.

Not because I'm scared of her. But because she makes my
blood boil.

At school, Hamala seems to get all her pleasure picking
on younger students, and anyone who tries to stop her gets
it worse. I've had no choice but to step in a few times to defend someone against her bullying and that's made me one
of Hamala's top targets. Now, every time we encounter each
other, we're both on guard, waiting for the other to strike
so that we have an excuse to strike back. It's as if a lifelong
bond has formed between us: one that pits one girl against the
other, always in conflict, resolution residing in the strength
of our fists.

"By the Fires, I swear I ought to bash your head in," Hamala
continues. "It was supposed to be a quick grab. We had the
hard part—we were the distraction! All you had to do was
sneak in, steal his purse, and sneak out, and you couldn't even
do that."

So now Hamala's stealing too. I thought I had reached
the limit of how much I could loathe another person, but
Hamala always finds a way to push me. She doesn't even need
the money—everyone knows the Mugabe family has plenty.
She only gets away with terrorizing others because her family always buys her way out of trouble.

The last thing I feel like doing right now is confronting her, so I try to sneak by. But I can't help overhearing their conversation as I pass the darkened alcove where they're hiding.

"How was I supposed to know that maugrab was there?" another girl whines. She sounds like Jalaan, one of Hamala's lackeys. "You know I'm scared of those things, and you said the tent was empty!"

I pause midstep, one foot barely touching the ground. They can't be talking about what I think they're talking about, can they? Did Hamala and her goons try to steal from the Haltayi, who are some of the poorest people in the village? Stealing from them is like snatching a beggar's cup of change.

"You're blaming me for this mess?" Hamala says, her voice menacing.

"Well," a third girl chimes in, "no one told you to start a fire."

I stiffen in shock, my eyes wide. My feet are rooted to the ground. I knew Hamala was dangerous, but now she's gone too far. So many people lost their livelihoods in the fire, not to mention the Haltayi losing their tent. And that poor maugrab would have died if I hadn't jumped in to save it.

I have to confront her. If I don't, no one will know what she's done, and then there'll be nothing preventing her from doing something even worse next time.

Behind me, the market is emptying as the last fires are dampened. A group of watchguards inspect the smoldering remains of the maugrab's tent while a few stall owners linger, many of them distraught over the damage. Hamala did this—she caused all of this destruction.

"You've gone too far this time, Hamala," I say, stepping

into the brightest section of the alley. "Picking on kids in the schoolyard is one thing, but stealing from Haltayi? Arson? Either you turn yourself in, or I will."

Slowly, as if she is the hunter and I am the prey, Hamala emerges from the shadows with three of her friends behind her.

"You bitch," she growls as she moves in front of me. Her lackeys stand behind me, blocking the only other exit. I wish I had my twin brother, Nez, with me to make this fight more even. But then again, he's always telling me not to fight. "I'm getting so tired of seeing your ugly face. Everywhere I go, there's Naira Khoum sticking her nose in places where it doesn't belong."

I don't clench my fists even though I want to. But if Hamala takes a swing at me, I'll have no choice but to defend myself and deal with Nez's disappointment later.

"If you weren't always causing trouble, I wouldn't be here. I'd be home right now eating dinner. It's because of the fire *you* set that I'm here among all this garbage trying to convince you to do the right thing."

Hamala puffs out her chest. "Did you call me garbage?"

My stomach sinks. I should have known trying to reason with her would be a waste of time. She twists everything I say into an insult.

"I think she called all of us garbage," Jalaan says from behind.

A fight is coming—a big one. I can feel it in the charged air between us, hear it in the way Jalaan and the others snicker nastily behind me, see it in Hamala's clenched fists. I turn to the side so that I can keep my eyes on Hamala and the others.

Hamala curls her lip in a menacing snarl and looks down at me. "I think so too. And I know exactly what to do to someone who calls me names and can't keep her nose out of my business."

Hamala reaches out to shove me, but I'm too quick. I knock her arms aside and plant my foot squarely in her stomach, kicking the air out of her lungs and sending her flying backward. She lands sprawled out on the ground, stunned. The other girls look at each other, not sure what to do, waiting for their leader to guide them, but Hamala can barely talk. Tears run down her cheeks, catching the dust that clouds the air from her fall.

"Get her!" Hamala wheezes at last.

The next thing I know, the other girls are on top of me, pulling my hair, trying to scratch my face and knock me to the ground. One yanks me by the arm while another tries to kick my feet out from beneath me.

I have no choice but to fight back. My father started training me in combat as soon as I was big enough to hold a sword, so I try to end this fight quickly. I punch the tallest one in the chest, knocking her breathless, and grab the arm of another girl and twist it behind her back. She whimpers in pain.

By now, Hamala has recovered her breath and is standing. She charges, knocking me and the whimpering girl to the ground. I push the girl off me and try to get on my feet, but Hamala kicks me in the stomach once, twice, three times. I can't breathe, my abdomen throbs with pain, and I lie on my side gasping for air. Then Hamala grabs my arms, wraps her legs around my waist, and holds me down. I thrash around in an attempt to free myself, but her grip is tight.

Hamala yells out something to her lackeys, but I'm so focused on our struggle that I barely register what she's saying.

She yells again: "Do it! Do it now!"

I glance at the other girls, afraid because whatever she has planned, it's going to hurt. I only catch a glimpse of the heavy rock in Jalaan's hand right before she cracks me in the head with it.

The entire side of my face explodes with pain and my head lolls to the side. Hamala releases me from her grip with a laugh. I crumple to the ground, dizzy and nauseous, and touch shaking fingers to my forehead. They come away bloody.

Hamala kneels in front of me and grabs the collar of my tunic, bringing us face-to-face. She's so close I can see the crust in the corners of her eyes.

"This is what happens when you keep getting in my way, Khoum." She shoves me and I fall against a broken pot, the jagged edges scraping my back.

"You think she's learned her lesson?" Hamala asks the others. She turns to me. "Well, you little snitch, did you?"

I can barely see straight, stabbing pains radiate throughout my skull, and I feel like I'm going to retch. But I still can't let Hamala win.

I spit in her face and she jumps back in disgust.

"You rotten bitch!"

Hamala snatches the rock from Jalaan and towers over me. I'm trying to get up, get out of the way of what I know is coming next, but I can't seem to get my balance. The giant rears her hand back. I notice a dark spot on the rock and it occurs to me *That's my blood*—and then the world goes black.

CHAPTER TWO

MY EYES FLY OPEN AND I JOLT UPRIGHT, MY HANDS BALLED into fists and my head throbbing. I'm ready to fight the next person who comes at me.

But there's no one. And I don't even know where I am. My breath quickens, the darkness settling around me like a pool of water, drowning me in its thick blackness. To stop the panic from flooding my chest, I do as my father taught me: sit cross-legged on the ground and take a few deep breaths. I need to stay calm to figure out what's happened.

The ground is yellow sand, the walls encircling me cone shaped. Faint markings line the walls and a pillar of light shines down from a hole above me. There's an unlit torch on the ground, an old fire-strike beside it. Urns are stacked atop each other across from me.

I squint at the markings, but I can't make out the words because of the darkness. I pick up an urn and carry it to the shaft of light, where I open the lid and find that it's full of ashes. I quickly shove the lid back on the urn, place it on top of the stack, and put as much space as I can between myself and it. I don't want to disturb the remains of whoever is resting in there. The markings on the walls must be the names of the dead in the urns.

I know where I am, if not why.

I'm inside one of the hundreds of tombs outside the village—unprotected from raiders, from the desert sands, from the monsters that prowl among the conical clay structures—but how did I get here?

I remember the fight in the alley, Hamala holding me down and hitting me with the rock. That second blow to my head must have knocked me out, and they somehow got me out of the village and dumped me in a tomb. I don't even know how they did it—there are always watchguards and rangers patrolling the village.

I touch my aching left temple and my fingers come away sticky with blood. Rage fills my body and I punch the wall in anger. I breathe in and out through flared nostrils, my stomach still sore from being kicked, as dust crumbles to the floor. Now my knuckles ache as well as my head and abdomen. Hamala will pay for what she's done to me.

But first, I have to get out of here.

I find the stone shoved into the entrance and push. It doesn't budge. I push with my shoulders, press my back against the stone and push with my legs, even get on the ground and push feet-first with a loud grunt, but the stone refuses to move. Hamala must have put something in front of the stone to block it.

I give the stone one last kick before giving up.

I'm trapped.

As I sit on the floor, the events of the day running in my

mind, my throat tightens and I use the heels of my hands to rub away hot tears. I know I shouldn't have provoked Hamala by spitting on her, but that doesn't excuse her from imprisoning me in a tomb. She's gone too far, and when I get out, I'm going to—

Stop. Thinking about retaliating only makes me angrier. I need to concentrate on surviving, not plotting revenge.

Get it together, Naira, I tell myself. *Focus on what matters.*

The faint light trickling from the hole in the ceiling tells me it's getting dark outside. And I'm stuck in a tomb, outside of the protection of the thick stone wall surrounding my village.

It's whispered that there are Vra Gool Dambi hunting in packs around the tombs. They rove the desert, appear in the blink of an eye, steal Haltayi nomads from their camps while they sleep at night. They'll feast on any who dare to venture beyond the protective border of Lagusa's wall. Some say they can hear Dambi shrieks on the night air, chilling the listener to the bone.

I haven't heard anything yet, but my father says there's always a grain of truth behind rumors. Up north, beyond the desert, Dambi have been terrorizing the people in what remains of the Merzan empire for almost twenty years. War hasn't reached Lagusa—yet—but that doesn't mean a few stray Dambi couldn't have made their way down to our village.

I shiver, trying not to think about facing a Dambi while stuck in a tomb with no weapons except my fists. The only thing that gives me comfort is knowing that my parents will get me out. They're probably at the market right now looking for me, and as soon as they find out what happened, my omma and obba will come set me free.

Until then, there's nothing left for me to do but lie down and wait, even though everything inside me aches to do something, to fight back. But there's nothing I can do, no one I can fight.

I sprawl out on the sand directly under the opening in the ceiling and watch the stars. According to the teachings of the Temple, each star represents one dragon. Eventually, all will fall and the sky will turn black, signaling the end of this world and the beginning of the next. But there hasn't been a dragon among humans since Crafulgar the Fiend-Slayer, who fell from the sky and was reborn in the fires deep within the caves of the Kilmare Mountains almost five centuries ago.

With millions of stars in the sky and only one star falling every five hundred years, I reckon the next life is an eternity away.

I drift off imagining dragon fire. Boredom drives me to a dreamless sleep, but a loud shriek wakes me. Already I'm crouched, listening carefully.

It's still dark out—I haven't been sleeping long—and for a moment I think I dreamed the sound, until it rings out again from somewhere in the night. It's the cry of an animal that shouldn't exist in this world, one whose howl carries across the dunes and up my spine, scraping my bones and stealing my breath. Another inhuman screech, then another, and I wish I wasn't so sure of what I'm hearing.

Vra Gool Dambi.

Nothing living makes a noise like that.

Slowly and quietly, I crawl out of the pale moonlight shining in through the chimney. The chances of the Dambi climbing on top of my tomb and seeing me inside are slim, but I don't plan to risk it. I lean my back against the wall, pull my legs to my chest, and wait.

The Vra Gool Dambi continue to screech into the night. Why are they making those noises—are they talking to each other? Where are the rangers who patrol the wall? If I can hear the Dambi, shouldn't the rangers be able to hear them as well? Why aren't the rangers beating the drums?

But silence follows in the wake of their shrieks—a long, deafening silence that is only broken by my heart pounding loudly in my chest. I must be so far from the village that the noise hasn't traveled to the wall.

I'm on my own.

After what feels like an entire hand has passed, but was probably only less than a quarter, I let out a long exhale. The Dambi must have moved on. Or maybe the rangers heard them and took care of them. Either way, it's finally quiet.

When the next shriek tears through the air, the ear-piercing sound feels like it's right next to me, and I cover my mouth to keep from screaming. But then scratching starts on the other side of the walls and I move to the center of the tomb, putting as much distance from the noise as possible. The shaft of moonlight coming from above abruptly disappears. I force myself to look up—and meet a cloudy pair of eyes. The Dambi above me opens its scarred maw, thick saliva dangling from its crooked teeth, and shrieks. I fall to my knees, my hands covering my ears, the force of that horrible sound vibrating through my bones.

The scratching intensifies as the Dambi on top of the tomb shoves its arm down the chimney and swipes at me, trying to grab me. The stench of rancid meat fills the room and I gag. Black claws swipe at my braid, but I yank it away before they catch hold. Leaning against the wall, I wrack my mind for a plan.

Nothing. I have no weapons and nowhere to go.

If I stand too close to the walls, the Dambi are on the other side, scraping and scratching to get at me. If I move too close to the center, another Dambi is there to claw my face off. I'm going to die tonight and Hamala will probably be happy about it.

But that's only if I give up.

With a new resolve to survive no matter what, even when so many others want me to quit, I realize I'm not defenseless.

I have fire.

I ignore the scratching, grab the torch off the ground, and light it with the fire-strike that was lying beside it. The next time the Dambi plunges its arm into the chimney, I shove the torch into its too-long limb. The ragged cloth covering the creature's arm erupts in flames and I jump back to get away from the fire dripping onto the ground. With a screech of pain, the Dambi retreats and disappears. I smother any residual flames with sand and hope the creatures won't return.

Or bring reinforcements.

Crouching on the ground, holding tight to the torch, I make a bargain with the dragon gods.

Make them go away and I promise to pray to the Thirteen and renounce the fallen dragon Ergenegon every day.

I wait in silence for what feels like an eternity. I'm covered in sweat, my muscles trembling from holding still and alert for so long, my heart beating faster than the quick, short breaths I pull in through clenched teeth.

I will not die tonight.

Those bastards thought they could break me.

I can't be broken.

Not like this, not by them.

"I will not die tonight," I say aloud once, then again and again, my voice getting stronger and louder until I'm shouting. I turn my face toward the night sky, hoping my words carry across the tombs, over the wall, and into the ears of Hamala and anyone who's ever helped her hurt others. "I will *not* die tonight!"

I refuse to.

Fresh scrabbling at the walls, this time on all sides, forces me to move beneath the open chimney. The walls start to crumble amid shrieks and scratches so loud I want to shout at them to be quiet. The scent of death permeates the clay structure.

I grip the torch with both hands and wait for the first claw to break through, the first eye to peer down the opening. I'll set them on fire, even if it means I'll burn too. I plan on taking as many Vra Gool Dambi with me as I can.

Suddenly, the world goes silent.

Out of that silence comes a woman's voice. Clear. Human.

"I've been looking for you, my wild ones." She has a strange accent that seems to make her words come from far away. "Like a shepherd searching for her lost lambs, I've come to bring you back into the fold."

The word *Help!* forms on my lips, but I don't release it. Something inside tells me to stay quiet—that this woman isn't here to help *me*. The only sounds are my own pounding heartbeat and soft footsteps as the woman circles the tomb, shushing the creatures as if they are naughty children.

"What have we here?" the woman continues. "What has aroused my curious children so savagely?"

Why aren't the Vra Gool Dambi attacking the woman?

Something soft-footed scrambles up the walls of the tomb. Slowly, I creep over to the wall and press my ear against it.

"I see you," the woman says, this time her voice coming from above.

My breath catches in my throat as I whip around to look up. I catch a glimpse of a masked face, only the eyes and mouth visible, staring at me from the hole at the center of the ceiling.

"You are so fresh and my children are so hungry."

Her *children*? The Dambi?

I hold the torch up high, the brightness forcing the woman to shield her black eyes.

"I'll burn every single one of those Dambi." I try to make my voice as threatening as possible. "And you, too, if you don't leave me alone."

The woman studies me, her eyes cruel. "You speak Waldyrian, the language of conquerors. How interesting. We were told there was nothing south of the desert except trifling nomads. But I found a village, a large one, and a girl who speaks a language not her own."

I have no idea what the woman is talking about—the only language I speak is Merzan. But I'm not going to ask her to explain.

"I'm warning you." I make my way toward the center of the tomb with the light held high. "You'd better get out of here—"

"Or what? Will you hurt me with your little fire? My children will tear you to pieces first."

"Who are you?"

The woman backs away from the chimney until only her eyes are visible, reflecting the light of the torch. "My name does not matter. Besides, you already know the name of my master."

A woman who pacifies Dambi would swear fealty to only one person: *Sothpike*.

The Waldyrian warlord Sothpike rips the dead from tombs and graves, steals bodies from battlefields and sleeping villages, and reanimates them into monsters that are notoriously difficult to kill. All traces of humanity are stripped away until there is nothing but an unthinking beast, controlled by a savage thirst for blood, running on its hands and feet, digging ragged, black claws into the soft bellies of those still alive and feasting on what it finds inside.

Vra Gool Dambi are the creatures mothers use to scare their children into behaving. They are the reason the rangers patrol the massive wall of wood and stone between the village of Lagusa and the Bujarbi Desert. The Vra Gool Dambi are the reason Sothpike is winning the war that ruined Merza, the homeland of everyone who now resides in Lagusa.

There's only one thing my people hate more than the Dambi, and that's Sothpike—the man who created them.

Something in my expression must change as soon as Sothpike's name enters my thoughts. The woman smiles.

"I told you. Everyone knows my lord Sothpike. Even in this wretched little village, you know the name of your true master."

"My *master*?" I spit on the ground. "Sothpike is nothing but a traitor!"

"You will regret spewing such lies," the masked woman says, her black eyes turning cold and sharp.

"Make me." The words come out before I can stop them. Is my bravery due to pride, or just plain foolishness? Either way, I can't back down now. "I've already burned one of your children. I have no problem burning the rest of them—and you too."

The woman's eyes bulge. "You what?"

She disappears. I hear her sliding down the walls of the tomb. Silence reigns for only a few moments, long enough that I want to kick myself for antagonizing someone who controls monsters that would love to crunch on my bones. I crouch in the darkest part of the tomb, the flickering torch casting long shadows in front of me. A scream from outside, this time human, sends chills down my spine—and lets me know the woman found the Dambi I burned.

Again, the scratching starts directly behind me, then surrounds me on all sides. Cracks form in the structure and my heart beats so fast I'm afraid it will burst. Both hands are wrapped around the torch—I wield it like a weapon, ready to strike the first Dambi that breaks through.

A Dambi sticks its head in and I shove the torch in its face. The creature screams and backs away from the flames. But I have no time to enjoy my triumph, as the wall behind me collapses and a Dambi bursts out of the rubble.

CHAPTER THREE

THE THING THAT'S HARDEST TO REMEMBER IS THAT THE creature in front of me was once human. But after Sothpike turned it into a member of his dead army, it's nothing more than a monster.

Its arms grew too long, its head misshapen and bald save for the scraggles of hair still clinging to its scalp. Its teeth are sharp as knives, its fingernails blackened and hooked like a bird of prey's talons. Its shredded clothes trail behind it like the afterthoughts of the person it once was as it swipes and snarls at me.

I swing the torch, hitting it on the shoulder and lighting the rags it wears on fire. The Dambi writhes on the floor in pain as its body is engulfed by flames. Black smoke pouring off the creature clogs my throat, and I choke.

Another side of the tomb comes crashing down, dust and debris clouding the air even more. In the chaos, I stamp out the torch and flee into the night through the maze of tombs, the massive wall of the village a long dark shadow against the night sky—but every turn I take leads me farther from Lagusa. The paths curve and twist, and I'm lost.

"Bring her to me!" the woman yells, her voice bouncing from tomb to tomb, surrounding me in the moonlight.

Dambi chase me, their claws scraping the tombs as they turn corners. One blocks my path and I skid to a stop, my heart thumping hard in my chest. The Dambi faces the opposite direction, its face turned toward the sky, sniffing the air as if searching for my scent.

I sidle around the tomb, my body pressed against the hardened clay, keeping to the shadows. When the Dambi shrieks, I take off running. I pass tomb after tomb, the Dambi so close I can smell it, its rancid stench of rotting meat making me want to vomit but I swallow hard to force it back down.

A Dambi leaps out at me from between two tombs but I dodge, smacking its claws with the unlit torch using a move my father taught me in our sparring sessions. The stick cracks in half, so I jab the splintered end in the Dambi's neck. While the Dambi grasps at the wood, I scramble out of the way. Another Dambi shrieks. It's close.

I don't know what to do except to keep moving. I snatch up the other half of the torch and get back on my feet. Thick, black blood is pouring out of the Dambi's neck, but that doesn't stop it from chasing me as I flee.

The tombs around me grow older and more decrepit, their shapes less defined, some of them nothing but piles of rubble. The ones still standing have gaping holes where stones used to cover their entrances, now resembling the maw of a creature that wants to eat me alive, suck me into its blackness, crush me with its teeth of broken stones. Nothing looks familiar. I crawl over rubble toward where the stars above meet a swath of blackness, the towering wall protecting Lagusa abruptly cutting the sky in half.

A Dambi screech penetrates the air—and my ears—like an arrow hitting the center of a target. I look over my shoulder, but there's nothing behind me. I don't want to take any chances of being spotted, so I duck into a tomb whose entrance has crumbled away to hide.

It isn't long before the Dambi race past. I count three.

I let out the breath I was holding when I'm sure they're gone. There's nothing I can do but wait. The woman could be anywhere.

Soon, soft footsteps approach the tomb I'm hiding in, and I move deeper into the shadows. The woman is humming as if singing a baby to sleep. The hairs on the back of my neck rise.

"Come to me, my wild ones," the woman murmurs. I smell the Dambi before I hear them, the tomb filling with their stench as they shriek. I cover my ears and breathe through my mouth.

I catch a glimpse of her approaching the Dambi I stabbed, rills of blood flowing down its neck glistening in the moonlight. "We will find her, and she will pay for what she has done to you. But first, we have other business we must attend to."

Then the woman faces me and my heart stops. I know she can't see me from my hiding place in the shadows, but her gaze is so intense from behind the mask it seems as if her eyes can penetrate the darkness and stare right into my own. I hold my breath and remain as still as possible.

"You can't hide forever," she says into the night. "I will find you."

When she looks away, I slowly exhale.

The Dambi follow the strange woman, shrieking as they go. She leads them away from me, away from Lagusa, deeper into the desert.

And then, once again, quiet. No screeching. No snarling. No distant, sing-song voice of a strange woman who lulls Dambi and calls them her children.

In the silence, I finally have a chance to think. Who is that woman? Why is she in Lagusa? Does this mean Sothpike has finally crossed the Bujarbi Desert?

In the end, all I have are questions without answers.

I grip the broken torch. As soon as the sun rises, I'm going to find my way out of the tombs. It's going to take a lot more than Hamala and a few Dambi to get rid of me.

My muscles ache from crouching in the dark for so long. Blood flows from a cut on the knuckles of my right hand, and the wind whistling through the cracks of the tomb walls sounds like the scrape of a thousand swords being sharpened. A thin blade of a headache pierces my thoughts, the pain slicing through my skull like a well-honed sword through sheaves of straw.

I breathe in sharply through clenched teeth as I dab at the cut on my hand with the hem of my tunic. After a few tentative pats, I become used to the pain and press down on the knuckle, my headache also dissipating as I increase the pressure. The pale blue cloth soaks up the blood; a dark stain forms around the fabric covering the wound.

My relief doesn't last long. The pain in my head roars

back to life with such a force that I realize something must be wrong. This pain isn't normal. I curl up in a ball on my side and pray to the thirteen dragon gods to end my suffering. But they don't listen.

My eyes squeeze shut as I grimace from the pain and white spots appear at the edge of the darkness. I blink, rub my eyes, open them wider, shut them tight.

Still, the spots remain.

A high-pitched whine—like the sound made when a mosquito buzzes about my head as I lie in bed trying to sleep—rends my thoughts. I cup my hands over my ears and fall on my side with a loud moan. My vision clouds over completely, casting me into deeper darkness, only moments before I black out.

But I'm not lucky enough to sink into unconsciousness.

Flashes of fires burning bright, of whole villages aflame, fill my vision. I'm witnessing a war, but not from the ground. I'm above it, among the clouds, while a battle rages below.

I'm dreaming.

In this dream, my attention isn't on the battle. I'm chasing something. Something dark and long, twisting through the air.

Fire erupts from the clouds, blue, burning hotter than anything I've ever felt. It blisters my skin, singes my hair. But I keep pushing forward.

The creature in front of me turns to face me. As it hovers in the air, I see it for what it is: Ergenegon, the fallen dragon.

While the thirteen dragon gods protect those who believe in them, Ergenegon is the Chaos-Bringer. His sole purpose is to sow turmoil and bring about ruin.

Ergenegon is not like the other dragons, not in shape nor in behavior. He's more animal than human, more monster than god.

He beats his wings fiercely, his claws and teeth bared, his chest glowing blue. His maw opens to deliver another burst of flames.

I'm headed right toward them and I can't stop or move out of the way. It's as if my actions have already been decided, and I must see them through. All I can do is cover my face with my arms as I plow through the fire.

Engulfed by blue flames, I scream out in pain.

I'm falling, falling, falling...

A strange voice—or many voices, I can't tell—calls my name. I search for the source but see nothing except flashing lights in the distant sky.

Awaken, the voices say, each of them dry and raspy, like the kindling used to start a fire.

And then I wake up.

CHAPTER FOUR

COVERED IN SWEAT, MY BODY SHAKING, I PUSH INTO A seated position and shield my eyes against the sunlight streaming through the cracks in the tomb. I poke my head out of the entrance and my heart sinks when I see that the village wall is far, much farther away than I expected.

I force myself to step into the hot sand, turning to take in the view beyond the tombs, where there's nothing but sand and sky, the swelling dunes stretching all the way to the horizon. It's easy to forget there's more to the world than just my village when I hardly ever see the Bujarbi Desert. The last time I went beyond Lagusa's protective wall was when the mother of my childhood best friend died. Back then, I was too young to pay attention to my surroundings, so I have no memories to draw on to help me now.

The world hasn't changed much since then, but the same can't be said for me.

Far away to the north, across the great sandy expanse, a war is still being waged.

In the secluded village of Lagusa, the only battles that affect me are the ones I keep throwing myself into.

I sigh and begin my trek back to Lagusa. Footprints from the night before mar the sandy ground. I sidestep long trails where the Dambi's claws raked through the sand, keeping my distance from anything they touched.

It's not long before I'm sweating, though I try my best to stay in the shade, darting from tomb to tomb. The heat doesn't bother me as much as the thirst; I haven't had anything to drink since the day before, and I spent the whole night running from Dambi.

I'm so thirsty it's all I can think about, and my steps falter. The world swims in front of me and I lean against a tomb until I regain my balance. The clay, hot from baking in the sun all day, sears my skin.

I know I won't last long in the stifling desert heat without water, so I decide to avoid the sun and take a rest. I crawl into an open tomb and lie down, hoping to sleep through the worst of the unyielding thirst until the sun passes its zenith. But the air is too dry.

Time stands still. With my eyes closed, I imagine all the things I'll do once I'm back home. First, I'll swim in the river to wash away the sweat and grime sticking to my skin. Then I'll drink every glass of water I can get my hands on. Or maybe I'll drink, then swim. Or I'll do both at the same time.

With nothing left to do but wait for the afternoon sun to fade, I let myself fall asleep once more. When I wake, the air is slightly cooler than before, which means the sun must be setting.

I try to sit up, but the whole world shifts. Dizzy with the

sound of rushing water in my ears, I try again, but my elbows buckle and I topple over.

I need something to drink. I try to sit up one more time and, though I'm still woozy, I'm stable.

Am I really that out of it?

Someone has to be looking for me. My parents must have found out where I am by now. I lie back on the ground and wait, hoping whoever finds me brings the biggest jug of water ever made.

The sound of something scraping against a tomb jolts me to my feet. In a panic, I grab the broken torch. If it's a Dambi, I'll stab it again. If it's the woman, well...

I'll stab her too.

I wait, my breath heavy, my eyes wide, as voices faintly carry through the tombs to my ears. I stumble to the entrance and cock my head to hear better.

"Naira, where are you?" my mother's voice calls out. "If you can hear me, answer!"

I let out a loud, long sigh and drop the torch. The piles of rocks that had been building in my stomach, weighing it down with fear, are gone.

"I'm over here, Omma!" I stagger out of the tomb and look around, but I don't see anyone. "Where are you?" I yell, my voice hoarse.

"Stay where you are," my mother calls back. "We'll find you!"

The pounding of feet approaches and I stiffen in fear, a reflex after the night I had. A tall, lanky shape rounds the corner.

That's no Dambi. It's my brother.

I run toward Nez and tumble into him, my legs wobbling, and he keeps me from falling to the ground by gripping my arms.

"I found her!" Nez yells over my head. More footsteps approach, and over Nez's shoulder, I see my parents heading toward me. Behind them is Captain Farouk with a retinue of watchguards.

I have to concentrate on keeping my legs from shaking. Once I'm steady, Nez envelops me in a hug that threatens to squeeze out all the new air I just breathed in.

"Nez," I wheeze. Even though I struggle against his bony arms, I missed my brother and I can't stop grinning.

"She can't breathe," Omma admonishes, pulling Nez and me apart. Then she pulls me into an even tighter hug. This is what I've been waiting for—my mother to hold me tight. I feel like a small child in her arms, even though we're the same height. For the first time in hours, I let myself relax.

"Farina, you're as bad as Nezra," my father says and, with a little laugh, Omma releases her grip. I'm a little disappointed that she lets go.

"I'm so happy we found you." With tears in her eyes, Omma rubs my hair and cheeks, her dark brown hands finally resting on my pale brown shoulders. "My headstrong girl." Then she pulls me in for a gentler hug and kisses my forehead. I rest my head on her shoulder and inhale.

Cinnamon and soap. That's what my mother always smells like, the scent reminding me of happier times.

When Omma finally releases me, I turn to face my father. Obba stares at me with piercing, dark eyes, which are settled deep into his face beneath bushy brows. Tall and broad-shouldered, with skin the color of night and hair like lamb's wool and just as white, Obba cuts an imposing figure, one that makes me wary. I can't tell if he's upset with me—if he blames me for getting myself trapped in the tombs.

But then Obba hands the ceremonial staff he always carries to Nez and takes me into his arms. I wrap my arms around Obba's waist in return.

"I was so worried about you." His deep voice rumbles in his chest.

With my cheek pressed against his heart, I feel every word.

"Farina and I talked to everyone at the market when you didn't come home," Obba says as he releases me. "We heard about the fire—"

"What were you thinking, running into an inferno?" Nez interjects.

"It wasn't an inferno," I reply, my voice not as strong as I want it to be. Even though I know what I did was foolish, I'm not going to let Nez get the better of me. "And I didn't run, I jumped."

Nez opens his mouth to chide me even more, but this time Omma cuts in.

"Whether you ran or jumped doesn't matter!" Omma's hands inspect the burned fabric at the hems of my clothes, the cut on my temple, then wipes the soot and sand off my face. "What you did was dangerous. Do you want me to have a heart attack?"

"I had to, Omma," I say. "No one else was going to. And if I hadn't, that maugrab would have died."

"And what about you? *You* could have died!"

My eyes drop to the ground. "I didn't think about that."

"Of course not," Omma says, pulling me in for another hug. "You never do." She places her hands on my cheeks. "Oh Naira, what are we going to do with you? You've got to start thinking before you act, especially when dealing with people like those awful girls who left you here."

Thinking about Hamala makes me tense and my father notices.

"Naira, you must stay calm." Obba stares into my eyes. "Especially when dealing with known troublemakers. Do you have any idea what it feels like to hear that your daughter was seen fighting in the alley like a stray dog? Haven't I taught you better? We fight for what is right, not because of some petty grudge."

"But I wasn't fighting because of a grudge! They stole from the Haltayi and started the fire in the market to cover it up. I overheard them talking about it. When I tried to tell the watchguard, Hamala and her goons attacked me and then…" I motion at the tombs, not needing to explain what happened next.

"*They're* the ones who started that fire?" Nez's eyes widen in disbelief. "People are saying it's going to cost thousands of gold rubes to rebuild. I wonder if her family's going to pay her way out of this one."

Omma shakes her head and rubs my back. "Those girls are trouble, Isrof. Something needs to be done."

"I'm sorry, Naira," Obba says, his hands on my shoulders. "I should have waited to hear your side before passing judgment. After we spoke to the merchants, we tracked down that Mugabe girl and some of her friends. All she would say is that you were the instigator. The others backed up her story and told us what happened to you."

All I want to do is kick Hamala in the chest all over again. As per usual, she tried to weasel her way out of facing the consequences of her actions and put the blame on me. The next time I see her—and I pray that there's a next time—I'm going to—

Nez waves a hand in front of my face, interrupting my thoughts of revenge. "Hey, are you still with us?" he asks.

I blink a few times and realize my parents are watching me, as if waiting for me to say something.

"Yes, of course." My tone is sharper than I intended and I feel bad for snapping at my brother. I'm not annoyed at Nez— I'm annoyed at myself for once again letting Hamala get into my head. I take a quick breath and try again. "Yes, I'm here."

"Glad you're back," Nez says. "Now do you want a drink of water or what?"

Nez's playful tone wipes away the anger that had been building inside me and I nod desperately. Omma shoves a jug full of cold water into my hands. I would cry if I had any moisture to spare.

"Drink up," she says as I guzzle the water. Cool liquid slips down my throat, through my chest, and settles in my belly. It's the sweetest water I've ever tasted.

"She'll be sick if you let her drink all of that now," Obba warns, his staff back in hand.

"I don't care." Water spills out the sides of my mouth, coating my skin, as I swallow another gulp.

"Let's just thank the gods our daughter is safe and take her home." Omma continues to rub my back while I drink.

Obba approaches Captain Farouk and says, "Now that we've found my daughter, you must do something about Hamala Mugabe and those other girls. They're dangerous, not only to my daughter but to everyone else in Lagusa."

"We've already got men rounding them up, Qal'at Subaan Khoum," the captain says. "We'll stop by your house tomorrow afternoon so that your daughter can make a statement and we'll present everything to the judge."

"Can't you lock those girls up right now?" Omma's voice shakes with anger. "You have all the evidence you need—just look at my daughter. Look where they left her. This alone is attempted murder, not to mention what they did to the market, and I don't want those girls coddled by the law."

Captain Farouk nods his head. "I promise, Samida Khoum, we will pursue this matter with all of our might. Those girls will be investigated and justice will be served for your daughter and everyone else."

I'm tempted to ask how they managed to imprison me in a tomb, but I don't have the energy. For now, it's enough that Hamala and her friends will get what's coming to them.

Obba and the captain bow to each other, then Captain Farouk turns to me.

"I'm glad we found you, young samida," he says. "May the gods watch over you. Until tomorrow…" He bows in respect, then motions for his men to follow him out of the tombs.

Stone scraping on stone makes the hair on the back of my neck rise. I turn around to see Nez kicking rubble aside as he walks into the tomb I was hiding in. The day that sound doesn't cause my heart to race will be the day I know I'm free

of the nightmares I'll carry from being trapped while Dambi
claw their way through walls to get me.

I hand the jug of water to Omma, my hands shaking.

"Obba, last night when I was in the tomb, I was attacked.
By Dambi." My words tumble out of my mouth almost faster
than I can say them.

Obba's eyes widen. "What?"

"They broke into the tomb and I managed to escape but
they chased me," I continue. "And there was this woman with
them—she was so strange, Obba, it was like she controlled the
Dambi. I thought they'd never quit chasing me, but then she
made them stop. I don't know how, but she walked among
them and they didn't touch her. They were silent."

By now, Nez has crawled out of the tomb, and everyone
is hanging on to my every word.

"The woman told me she has a master," I finish, "and his
name is Sothpike."

Omma gasps and looks to Obba. Nez and I do the same.

"We'd better get back inside the village," Obba says, his
eyes piercing the encroaching darkness as if searching it for
the woman I described. "I need to talk to the Council about
this immediately. We have to capture this woman and find
out why she's prowling around Lagusa."

Obba leads the way through the maze of tombs. My memories of being lost in the labyrinthine twists and turns the
night before flare, but my father's strides are sure-footed and
confident. He deftly guides us back to the village, the wall
growing larger as we get closer.

Water sloshes in my near-empty stomach with every step,
but I ignore the discomfort and follow my father. I just want

to be safe, and I know I won't have anything to fear if I'm
with him.

"I don't know how you did it," Nez says, walking beside
me. "Being surrounded by the ashes of the dead is bad enough,
but to survive the Dambi and that strange woman chasing
you all night... You're amazing, little sister."

I grin at his unexpected compliment.

We reach the gates and the rangers on duty bow to my
father, who returns their respect with a curt nod. A wagon
waits for us, the driver snapping to attention when he sees
my father. We climb inside, my father helping me up with a
strong hand.

The driver sets the horses at a trot and the rangers stand
aside to let us into the tunnel cutting through the stone and
wooden beams of the wall that separates the desert from
Lagusa. Even though the vast Bujarbi Desert acts as a natural
barrier between our quiet village and the rest of the world,
we can never be too careful. Centuries ago, the dragon Crafulgar founded Lagusa as a refuge for those fleeing the Volsgarian War. Anyone who survived the journey across the
desert was welcomed here. But after the war ended, there
was no need for a hidden refuge, and the people north of the
desert slowly forgot about Lagusa. It became a mythological
place, like the godfire tended by the Hands of God in the
Kilmare Mountains. Even if people still believed in its existence, they'd never seen it and they didn't know where to
find it. Over time, Lagusa was lost to those who lived outside of its protective walls—until Sothpike betrayed the Ur
Atum Asim Avari of Merza and her royal consort, the Asimra
Yafeu. He killed them both, destroyed the capital, Al-Kazar,

and set his Dambi loose in an attempt to conquer Merza and claim the country as his own. Once again, people needed a refuge, and the myth of Lagusa lured them into the desert in search of Crafulgar's haven.

At the start of Sothpike's war, hundreds of people made the perilous desert crossing, but for the last few years, months have gone by without even one soul making it to our gates. Being cut off from the rest of the world is a blessing and a burden. The Bujarbi Desert protects us from Sothpike, but it also makes us vulnerable. We relied on refugees to provide us with information about Sothpike and the war, and without any new people arriving, we won't know if Sothpike is on his way until it's too late.

Thinking about the war and Sothpike only reminds me of his Vra Gool Dambi chasing me through the tombs. I shiver when the darkness of the tunnel envelops us and Omma wraps her arm around my shoulders. Behind us, the rangers crank the lever that releases the heavy metal gates. Two of them fall into place with a loud clang that echoes throughout the tunnel and makes my teeth rattle, blocking the entrance.

"You must be starving," Omma says to me in the dark tunnel. "Tell me, what would you like to eat?"

My stomach growls at the thought of food.

"Everything, from the sound of it." Nez's laugh bounces off the stone walls.

"Nez is right," I say. "I'll eat whatever you have."

As we exit the tunnel, another pair of gates slam shut, and I take a deep breath. We're almost home. The nightmare is behind me. If the woman and her Dambi are still out there, they aren't getting into Lagusa tonight.

We pass mothers calling their children home to eat dinner, a group of girls my age running to buy one last trinket from a shop before it closes, a man leaning forward to steal a kiss from a woman only to have her turn away with a laugh.

Down one road, an overly laden cart pulled by a tired donkey rumbles by. On the corner, some children crouch in a circle playing ritska, placing bets on who can flick their small clay disk in the center of a row of circles the most times without going out of bounds.

To our left, the Temple of the Thirteen presides over the village. Atop the highest hill, visible from almost everywhere in the village—even from across the river—the domed Temple made of sun-bleached stone gleams white in the low light of the fading sun. Painted statues of the Thirteen, like the wooden ones in our family mazan at home, stare at me with empty eyes.

Of all the dragon gods, Crafulgar is the only one I feel any connection to even though it's been five centuries since she returned to her place among the other dragons in the heavens. Crafulgar is the mother of the dynasty that ruled Merza after the Volsgarian War and the founder of our village. It's said that she once lived among the Lagusans. During her time here, she learned what it's like to suffer, to cry, to dance, to sing. She learned what it means to be fully human. Everyone in Lagusa owes their life to Crafulgar and so the sacred Mother of the Temple makes regular sacrifices to our protector to show our gratitude.

As we pass the Temple and the statues keeping watch over the village, everyone in the wagon, including the driver, makes the motions of respect depicted by the statue of the dragon god Purganor: arms crossed, fingers touching our shoulders, heads dipped low. But before we turn off the main road, Obba has the driver slow to a stop and jumps down from the wagon.

"Where are you going?" Omma asks.

"To the meeting house," Obba says. "As the Qal'at Subaan, I have to tell the Council what Naira saw." Obba turns to Nez. "Go to the Temple and request a scribe. I'll have a messenger round up the other Subaans."

"Yes, Obba." Nez hops down from the wagon. "Naira, you'd better save some food for me!" I make a face at him as he runs up the steps to the Temple.

Obba takes Omma's hand. "I'll be home late. Take care of our girl."

"You know I will," Omma says with a smile.

Obba winks at me. I smile back as a warmth I had been missing since my fight in the alley settles in my core and spreads throughout my body.

A wink is something Obba and I have always shared. When I was young, we created an entire secret language through winking, but over time, we've forgotten all of the various winks and their meanings except one: a single wink means *I love you.*

I wink back at Obba and a warm smile spreads across his face. He kisses Omma's cheek before walking off toward the meeting house with his staff in hand. The wagon driver looks to Omma and she nods. He flicks the reins and we're off.

Any other day, I'd have argued with my father about being sent home instead of given a task like Nez. But not today.

There's nothing I want to do more than eat and take a bath. Maybe afterward I'll ask Omma to rebraid my hair.

We round the corner onto our street, where stone and mud-brick walls line the road. Behind each wall are families like my own, returning from work, preparing dinner, finishing chores before the sun sets for the night. The wall surrounding our house comes into view, the stones scrubbed clean, the bright blue wooden door freshly painted. Omma taps the side of the wagon to signal the driver to stop. We both climb down onto the dirt-packed road, and Omma opens the heavy door.

"Welcome home."

I let out a relieved sigh, cross the threshold, and leave the terror and anxiety I've been carrying since the night before outside of our safe, familial walls where it belongs.

CHAPTER FIVE

I'M LYING IN MY BED, SILENTLY THANKING THE THIRTEEN I'm home and not back in the tombs, when the morning quiet is broken by the sound of footsteps shuffling past my room.

It must be Obba going to the mazan to do the morning prayer for the family. The rest of us join him on special holidays, but Obba does it every day. I haven't prayed with Obba since the harvest festival two moons ago.

Rubbing my eyes, I crawl off my pallet and pull back the curtain covering the entryway. The sky above the courtyard is streaked with dawn pink and morning blue. To my right, Obba is heading to the alcove that houses our altar with wooden statues of the thirteen dragon gods.

Yawning, I join Obba at the mazan. He smiles and hands me twelve sticks of incense, keeping one for himself.

"By the Fires we honor you, Maganor the Never-Ending," he says as he places his stick of incense in front of the first dragon to walk the earth. "Continue to give rest to the weary and burdened." The smoke from the incense swirls around the figure of the dragon god.

Obba reaches for the next stick and I light it before handing it to him. "By the Fires we honor you, Thregor the Light-Maker." Obba blows on the incense, extinguishing the flame and releasing the heady smoke, then places the stick before the god who brought light back to the world after a period of darkness. "Continue to guide us on the path to grace."

Once again, I light the incense and pass it to my father.

"By the Fires we honor you, Dynago the Pride-Breaker," Obba says, repeating the ritual. "Continue to reward the meek and humble."

We move on to the fourth god, Xergas the Strength-Giver, who inspires integrity and perseverance. Then it's Enog the Sorrow-Ender, the god who comforts those who mourn or are suffering, and his twin, Nurega the Joy-Provider, who blesses the innocents. Albedego the Heart-Saver heals the sick and dying, while Uega the Life-Bringer fills those who hunger and quenches the thirsty. Obergon the Never-Waver strengthens the generous and dutiful among us; Purganor the Bane-Forsaker redeems those who seek forgiveness; Galga-mex the Peace-Bearer protects the hearth and home of the faithful; and Zulgaron the Curse-Taker shields the benevolent from harm.

Obba reaches for the last stick of incense.

"By the Fires we honor you, Crafulgar the Fiend-Slayer." Obba places the stick in the bowl of sand before the final god, the one who saved us from the tyranny of Ergenegon, the fallen dragon. "Continue to avenge the persecuted."

Once all the sticks are placed and the mazan is hidden by

clouds of thick smoke, Obba and I cross our arms over our chest and place the tips of our fingers on our shoulders. We bow our heads in respect for the gods.

"By the Fires we live, by the Fires we are blessed, and by the Fires we die," we chant together.

When the prayer is finished, I drop my hands to my lap and Obba gives them a pat.

"I'm glad you joined me today," he says. "It's important we have these moments together while we still can. You're growing up. Soon, you'll be off having adventures of your own, and you won't have time for your old Obba."

I roll my eyes. "Adventures? Nothing exciting ever happens in Lagusa."

Obba wraps an arm around my shoulders. "Let's hope it stays that way." Then he smiles. "How about a sparring session? We haven't had one in a while."

I grin. "Should I wake Nez?"

A snore tears through the courtyard and Obba laughs. "It's time that lazy boy got out of bed anyway."

I run to Nez's room and shake him by the shoulder. "Wake up, sleepyhead."

Nez groans and pulls the blanket over his head. I yank the fabric away and continue shaking him.

"Come on! Obba wants to do some sparring."

Nez stares at me with slitted eyes. "Why? Is the sun even up yet?"

I cross the room and throw back the curtains. Golden light floods the room, making my eyes sting and highlighting the piles of dirty clothes on the floor.

"The sun is up, and you should be too."

Nez flings an arm over his eyes and groans again. I tug on his arm, pulling him to his feet.

"Let's go, big brother." Although we're twins, Nez was born first, so technically he's the oldest, but he doesn't act like a big brother. He's not bossy or annoyed to be seen with his younger sister. In fact, I'm usually the one bossing him around.

With much grunting and groaning, Nez follows me to the back of the house. I lead him to the jirkana, where we've spent years practicing stances and lunges, twists and flips, under the critical eyes of our father.

My skin prickles with excitement as I cross the threshold. I love training. It's a chance for me to forget what's happening outside of the jirkana and concentrate on improving myself.

Obba is waiting for us. He leads us through a series of warm-ups before doling out weapons—wooden poles. When Nez isn't paying attention, I quickly tap his left arm with the pole.

Nez gasps and pretends to be mortally wounded, grabbing his arm and dropping down to his knees on the floor.

"I barely even touched you!" I laugh.

Nez reaches out to me. "Help me, little sister." I shake my head and Nez turns to Obba. "Save me!"

Obba crosses his arms, his mouth a thin line and his brows furrowed. But I can tell he's not upset. The corner of his mouth twitches as if he's holding back a smile.

Obba pokes Nez in the chest with his foot. "If you're going to die, then do it so we can move on."

Nez shudders, sticks out his tongue, closes his eyes, and dies with a loud wheeze. Then he opens one eye. "Since I'm dead, does that mean I can skip training?"

"You're so lazy," I say with another laugh. "Even worse than those cowardly Hands of God. At least they pretended they were going to fight Sothpike before abandoning the Asim."

"Well, if you're going to insult me..." Nez crosses his arms and closes his eyes, feigning sleep.

"Get up," Obba says, poking Nez with his foot again. "I want you and Naira to spar." Obba turns to me. "And no more talk about the Hands. I don't want to sully the integrity of our jirkana by speaking of those who have none."

Obba is right—just mentioning the Hands of God is enough to anger most Merzans, and for good reason. They vowed to protect the Ur Atum Asim Avari, but when Sothpike was tearing down the gates of Al-Kazar, they fled like cowards. No one's seen them since, although there are many Merzans who'd love to tell them what they think of their betrayal.

When Nez is on his feet, we face each other and drop into fighting stances, holding our poles with both hands. Whenever he has a weapon in his hands, my brother becomes another person. His eyes darken, his jaw clenches, and his focus is razor-sharp. It's easy to underestimate him when he's clowning around, but I'd be a fool to not take him seriously when we spar.

Obba clasps his hands behind his back. "Never let your weapon fall to the ground unless you are ready to admit defeat." Obba's spoken these words so often that I can recite them in my sleep. "And Khoums never admit defeat as long as we have a weapon in our hands and breath in our lungs. We fight until the end. Why do we fight?"

"We fight not for honor, not for riches, not for glory," Nez and I reply without hesitation. "We fight for what is right. And what is right will always win."

"Good," Obba says. "Now begin."

Nez steps toward me while spinning his pole in front of him, blocking any attacks from the front. I know he isn't going to go easy on me, so I take a deep breath and dart to his side. Nez readies his pole for a hit. I dodge his strike and whack him across the back with my pole. Nez stumbles first, but counters by using his pole to sweep my legs out from under me. I fall on my back and quickly roll to the side to avoid the end of his pole plunging into my stomach. I rap Nez's ankle with the wooden pole and he yelps in pain. While he's distracted, I jump to my feet and land another blow on his left arm, this time using force. At the same moment, Nez strikes me across the thigh, making me gasp in pain.

That's going to bruise.

Nez thrusts and I dodge. He pivots and I hold up my arms, deflecting a blow aimed at my neck. The wood smacks my bones and I clench my teeth. I barely have time to register the pain before Nez is behind me, the wooden pole coming down in an arc across my shoulder blades. I lurch forward, my hand out to break my fall, and I drop to one knee, my back burning.

Come on, Naira, I tell myself. *You can do better than this.*

I grit my teeth and get back on my feet.

Nez is expecting me to hit him with the pole, so I surprise him with a clenched fist to his stomach. A whoosh of air escapes his mouth, and he doubles over. Nez hates hand-to-hand combat and is always slow to react with a fist of his own. I know this, so I exploit it. While Nez is still recovering, I throw random punches, disorienting him so that I can jab the end of my pole in his chest.

The next few moments are a blur of strikes and parries, precise blows to the shin and back. I spin to avoid Nez's pole and bash him across the chest. He stumbles backward, and I swiftly knock his feet from under him. Nez falls on the floor, hard, and gasps for air. While he's stunned, I stomp on his wrist. His fingers fly open and I kick his pole across the room.

Breathing heavily, I hold the pole in the air, poised to deliver a blow to Nez's head. He groans and closes his eyes when he sees my stance. He knows that if this were a real fight, he'd be dead.

"Stand down," Obba says. I lower my weapon.

I let up off Nez's wrist and another groan escapes his lips as he crawls to his hands and knees. My shins and forearms ache, my knuckles are red and raw, and my ribs are bruised, but I ignore the pain to help Nez.

"Come on." I grab his arm but he shrugs me off.

Nez flops onto his back and glares at me. "You know what I hate most? The fact that my little sister can kick my butt."

I smile and offer my hand. Nez rolls his eyes but lets me help him get back on his feet.

"You both did well," Obba says. "Nez, you need to keep your eyes on your opponent at all times. That's how she was able to get you in the end. You let the pain overcome you and you lost your focus."

"Yes, Obba," Nez says with a bow.

"And Naira, you could have taken him down much earlier if you had followed through with your attack."

Obba grabs a pole and shows me the finishing move I

should have executed to end the fight earlier. It's efficient—
a quick jab to the chest, like the one I'd done to Nez, then a
flick of his wrist brings his pole on my forearms. The surprise
blow weakens my grip and makes it easy for him to knock
the pole out of my hands, leaving me open for a takedown.

"Go, Obba!" Nez cheers and I shoot him a nasty look. He
laughs in response.

"Alright, we've practiced enough for today," Obba says.
He hands his weapon to me and I place it on the rack along
with ours.

As Nez and I limp out of the jirkana, Obba calls my name.
I turn, and he says, "You did well," giving me one of his rare
compliments. All the pain melts away under his approval.
"You have a true fighting spirit—which is something that
can't be taught. You must embrace that part of yourself. It is
who you are. I expect great things from you."

My face flushes with pride. "Thank you, Obba," I say with
a bow. "I promise I won't let you down."

"But a great fighting spirit isn't enough," Obba says. "Why
we fight is just as important."

"We fight not for honor, not for riches, not for glory," I
say, repeating the credo Obba has said to me and Nez hundreds of times. "We fight for what is right."

Obba pats my shoulder and guides me out of the jirkana.
He walks me to the dining room, where Omma is serving
a breakfast of lentil stew and flatbread, before heading to his
study.

Nez is recounting his injuries and Omma clucks her tongue
in sympathy.

"You poor, poor boy," she says, ruffling the soft curls on top of his head.

Nez points at me as I enter the room. "There's the hellion who beat up your favorite son."

As I take my place next to Nez, I make a fist at him and he pretends to cower before batting away my hands.

Obba returns to the dining room with his staff in hand. He watches but does not sit down.

"Aren't you joining us?" Omma asks.

Obba shakes his head. "I have to go to the meeting house. We're expecting reports from the rangers we sent out last night to track down that woman and those Dambi. I'll be back before Captain Farouk arrives to have Naira give her statement."

Omma grabs a stack of flatbread and presses them into Obba's hand. "Take this with you, at least."

The sound of the war drum punctuates the morning air and a shiver runs down my back, as if a Dambi traced its claws along my spine.

Boom. Boom. Boom.

Boom. Boom. Boom.

Boom. Boom. Boom.

Vra Gool Dambi are coming.

Obba is the first to act. He drops the flatbread on the table and turns to Omma.

"Nez and I are going to see what we can do to help. Naira isn't fully recovered yet, so you should take her with you to the Temple."

"What?" Nez and I say at the same time, but for different reasons. Nez looks incredulous while I'm annoyed. I don't want to be sent to the Temple, hidden behind a locked door like I'm in need of protection. If Obba is going out into the fray, I want to be right there with him.

"Obba, I just got the living daylights kicked out of me." Nez's face is contorted in pain. "Shouldn't Naira be the one to—"

Obba bangs his staff on the tile floor and Nez shuts his mouth. But I'm undeterred.

"Don't send me to the Temple," I beg Obba. "I want to fight."

Obba shakes his head. "I want you to go with your mother to the Temple. That's where they'll take the injured. I'll send word when it's safe to leave."

"You told me I have a fighting spirit," I say. "So why can't I go with you?"

"Wait, why does Naira get compliments? I would have won if she hadn't sucker punched me in the gut."

I glare at Nez. "You lost because I know how to keep my focus and you don't."

Nez holds up a fist. "How about you focus on this?"

"Enough!" Obba barks, banging his staff again, this time with enough force to send cracks through the tile in the shape of a spider's web. "Nez, go to the jirkana and get my sword and your bow."

Without another word, Nez runs out of the room.

Boom. Boom. Boom.

Omma shudders and Obba kisses her forehead.

"Good," Obba says as Nez returns with the weapons. Nez wears his bow and a quiver of arrows slung over his shoulder. He hands the sword to Obba.

Obba passes his staff to Omma and takes the sword in hand. He flexes his wrist a few times, the light dancing on the curve of the blade, before tucking it into his waistband.

"Isrof, are you sure this is a good idea?" Omma glances at Nez with concern in the crease of her brow. "Shouldn't you both stay here where it's safe?"

"If the Vra Gool Dambi break through the gates," Obba says, "then nowhere is safe."

CHAPTER SIX

AFTER NEZ AND OBBA LEAVE, I REMAIN AT THE TABLE. Omma fills my bowl with stew and passes it to me. When I don't take it, she places it on the table before me.

"You still have to eat," she says, handing me the flatbread my father left behind.

I can't believe what I'm hearing. "Omma. There are Vra Gool Dambi at the gates. How can you expect me to eat at a time like this?"

"Do you hear that?"

Besides the trill of some birds in our garden, there is only silence. "Hear what?"

"Exactly." Omma grabs my hand and presses the flatbread into it. "No war drums, no screams. If the village is being overrun with Dambi, don't you think we'd have heard it?"

I'm too defeated to keep arguing, so I rip off a piece of bread and dip it in my stew while Omma clears Nez's and Obba's dishes from the table. How can Omma be so calm at a time like this? Are my father and brother in danger? Are

Dambi destroying the village? Maybe the rangers stopped beating the drums because they're all dead. I have no idea what's happening and every passing moment only brings more questions without answers.

I shove the half-eaten bowl away, get up from the table, and head toward the jirkana.

Nez favors bows, Obba his scimitar, but I feel strongest with a pair of daggers in my hands. I grab the sharpest set off the shelf and wrap the leather gauntlet sheaths around my forearms.

Taking a deep breath, I go back outside, where Omma approaches me in the garden. She carries a basket filled with her medicine kit and rolled-up bandages.

"If you're ready, we should get going," she says.

"I thought we had to wait for word from Obba?"

"He's taking an awfully long time, don't you think?" Omma starts walking toward the front door. I follow her and sit on the bench near the entrance to put on my shoes. "I can't wait any longer. I have to see if they're alright."

I steal a glance at my mother. Just when I think I have her figured out, she always surprises me. Omma had probably been planning on going after Obba and Nez all along; she just needed to be sure I was taken care of first.

I wrap my arms around Omma's waist and she lets out an "oh" of surprise.

"What was that for?" she asks when I pull away.

"For you being you," I reply.

Omma pats my cheek and smiles. "I see you've already got your tools," she says, pointing at the daggers in their sheaths on my arms.

I gesture at the basket. "And you've got yours."

Together, we step out into the street. No longer within the quiet safety of the stone wall that surrounds our home, shouts and shrieks greet us when we turn the corner. Omma grabs my arm. I think she's going to pull me back, force me to go home, but instead, we keep moving forward past hastily boarded up homes and storefronts.

In the market, a fire like the one from the day before rages, drawing onlookers toward it. Flames lick at overturned stalls and burn fruits and vegetables, spices and fabrics into blackened, unrecognizable piles of ash—but that doesn't stop some people from looting whatever they can get away with.

A scream rings out from the looters. I don't understand why until the inhuman shrieking begins. A group of rangers on horseback thunders by, causing the people to scatter. The rangers stop at the fire, their horses snorting and stamping their hooves, and dip the tips of their arrows in the flames.

A Dambi leaps into the market, its back covered with arrows, and charges the rangers.

I feel like I'm lost in the tombs again and my heart pounds in my chest.

The rangers let their fiery arrows fly, each one striking the creature. The Dambi paws at the flames and a shrill scream bursts from its blackened lips. One of the horses bucks, its hoof striking the Dambi in the face, and the monster crumples to the ground. The rangers waste no time plunging their swords into its flesh again and again. Thick, black blood gushes like water through a crack in a dam from every strike, coating the monster's hardened skin and running down the street in rivulets.

Once it ceases its grasping movements and is totally still, my mother and I step around the killing. Omma's face is ashen but determined, ready to put the Dambi behind her. But I can't let go that easily.

This has never happened before. Dambi have never broken through the gates. Lagusa is secluded, far away from the war up north, with a desert separating us from the rest of the world. This isn't supposed to happen in our streets. We're supposed to be safe here.

Omma tugs on my arm. "Come on, Naira," she says gently.

I take a deep breath. The shouting up ahead intensifies and I quicken my pace, Omma doing the same. In the distance on our right, the Temple looms large and a frenzied mass of people climb up the hill to find safety within the stone building. The statues of the Thirteen look down on the chaos happening at their feet. Many of them hold weapons in their hands, but I know I can't count on them joining in this battle. It's been five centuries since the last dragon fought alongside us.

The only ones who can help Lagusa are the people living in it.

A group of watchguards run past, their swords drawn, and one of them shouts at me and Omma to return home.

"There are Dambi everywhere!"

Omma tightens her grip on my arm. "We'd better hurry." She pulls me in the same direction as the watchguards— toward the village wall instead of toward the safety of the Temple. I'm filled with admiration for my mother. Whenever I imagined myself facing a dangerous foe, I'd always picture my father or Nez at my side since they're both such good fighters, but now I realize that facing danger takes more than physical strength. A fighter also needs strength of will, and my mother has more than enough for both of us.

I increase my pace to a jog, Omma running alongside me. The closer we get to the wall, the more watchguards and rangers surround us. They're busy blocking off roads by erecting makeshift barricades of overturned wagons, planks of wood, crates, and barrels. Rangers climb ladders to the tops of buildings, where they wait with their bows drawn. Villagers are also among those preparing for a battle, ready to give their lives for Lagusa.

Dozens of dead and wounded line the streets, the Mother from the Temple and the Daughters who serve her walking among them. I'm familiar with many of the Daughters—although they usually work in the Temple feeding the poor, praying for the dead, and maintaining the altar fires, they also come into the village to tend to the sick. But I've never seen the Mother outside of the Temple, where she leads the village in praise of the gods. It's strange to see her kneeling on the dusty road with the Daughters, giving healing draughts to those who need them and patching up wounds.

I try not to stare into the faces of the dead, their eyes wide with fright even in death, but my gaze is drawn to their final suffering. Many are missing limbs, their legs and arms ripped from their bodies and tossed aside like trash. Claw marks mar their faces, gashes across stomachs pull back the curtain of skin that once hid inner workings that were not meant to be revealed. Bones protrude from skin. Lower jaws are missing, strips of skin hang like ribbons, and blood flows down the street in rivers.

The Dambi are brutal, created to inflict the most damage

in the most savage way possible. Perhaps because they've already tasted death, they relish bestowing it on others.

I tear my eyes from the dead and see onlookers huddled in doorways or hiding behind half-closed doors and curtains, watching those who braved the destruction but not daring to be part of it. Others kneel on the ground, their faces upturned toward the Temple, prayers to Galgamex falling from their lips.

For a moment I wish that prayers worked—that the pleas of the faithful could save us, could bring life to the fiercest dragons like Obergon, Galgamex, Zulgaron, and especially Crafulgar. Or if Albedego saw our pain and swooped down with his medicines and healed the injured. I'd even settle for Enog's grace to comfort the suffering. If the gods showed us just one sign that they cared, I'd fall to my knees and pray with the other believers.

I look to the gods, and they stare back at me with blank eyes, their figures covered in soot and ash. Many prayers will go unanswered tonight.

What else could I expect from gods made of stone?

Beyond the barricades, the massive wall finally comes into view, and with it, the rest of the fighting.

In front of the metal gates, a handful of Dambi are surrounded by rangers and watchguards. A host of men and women attack the beasts with arrows and swords, poles and spears. The stench emanating from so many Dambi makes me want to gag.

Dambi don't belong in Lagusa. I hate seeing them in our streets, bringing the war to our doorsteps.

"By the Fires," Omma whispers as her eyes take in the

scene. Then she approaches one of the Daughters. "I've brought supplies," she says, her voice strong, calm, and clear. And beautiful too, I think. "How can we help?"

The Daughter kneels beside a man with a laceration across his thigh. "Do you know how to stitch a wound, samida?"

"I have a rambunctious set of twins who love nothing more than to cause trouble." Omma kneels next to the man and inspects the cut. She pulls a bit of leather from her medicine kit and places it between the man's teeth. "I've had to stitch quite a few wounds in my day. I can handle this."

The Daughter nods her thanks and moves on to the next patient.

While Omma goes to work, I scour the faces of those still fighting and find Obba, his height making him stand out among the others. Obba raises his sword and drives it deep into the belly of one of the Dambi. Relief floods my body and I let out the breath I hadn't even known I was holding. Of course, my proud, tall father, the man who taught me and my brother to fight, is untouchable, scattering the Dambi like a true soldier.

"There's Obba." I point him out for Omma as he readies his stance for another thrust.

"Praise Zulgaron and his shield." A length of thread in one hand and a needle in the other, Omma's eyes skim the wounded and those still fighting. "And Nez? Do you see him?"

I look around but I don't see Nez anywhere. A group of rangers atop the wall rain arrows down on the Dambi and I hope Nez is safe up there with them. I'm sure Obba would have wanted Nez up there to keep him out of danger.

At least, I hope that's what happened. But what if Nez went off on his own?

"I have to talk to Obba," I tell Omma, tamping down the panic from not knowing if Nez is safe that threatens to overtake my senses. "He'll know where Nez is."

Omma shakes her head. "No, you can't go there." She drives the needle into the gathered bunches of skin to stitch up the man's thigh. He cries out in pain and bites down hard on the leather. "It's too dangerous. Stay here and help me."

"I'm sorry, Omma, but I have to do this." I take off running, Omma's voice following me down the street.

I ignore her pleas and keep going, my head down, my jaw tight, my heart racing. A Dambi screeches, its inhuman voice reverberating throughout my body. Now that I've decided to face the Dambi, the fear I'd felt in the tomb, the walls crumbling around me as those abominations tried to claw their way in to tear me apart, hits me with such a force that I stop in my tracks. There is nothing shielding me from their hunger. If I take one more step, I'll be caught up in the battle, and I'm not sure I can survive a fight against a Dambi. I'm not stronger. The only thing I can do is be smarter.

I push my fears aside, take a deep breath, and run forward, right into the thick of the fray, toward where Obba was fighting. With my daggers unsheathed, I dive in.

Immediately, a Dambi rears back to strike me, my daggers poised to jab it in the side, when the creature howls in pain. I look up to see Obba slice off its hand at the wrist. He grabs me by the collar and yanks me away from another swipe by the Dambi, its ragged claws coming dangerously close to my face.

"What are you doing here?" Obba drags me out of the fray.

"I'm helping you!"

"You're supposed to be at home." Obba's eyes roam the streets. "Is your mother here, too?"

"Of course." I try wrenching my shirt out of Obba's grasp and fail. "I wouldn't leave her at home by herself. It was her idea to come here."

"Of course," Obba repeats. He finally releases my tunic. "Where's Nez? Is he alright?"

Obba looks to the top of the wall. "I sent him to join the archers where he'd be away from the worst of it. And that's where you should go, as well."

"Bows and arrows are Nez's thing." Now that I know Nez and Obba are both safe, I'm eager to fight. "I'm better with my daggers."

A hint of a smile plays across Obba's lips. "And I'm best with my sword."

I grin and head for the battle with my father at my side.

CHAPTER SEVEN

"REMEMBER YOUR TRAINING," OBBA REMINDS ME AS WE approach the fighting.

Five Dambi remain. One of them is missing a hand, the others bloody and covered in arrows and stab wounds, but they refuse to go down for good. A Dambi bursts through the attackers and runs toward me and Obba with an unnatural loping gait.

Back hunched, too-long arms scraping the ground, legs bent sharply at the knees.

I don't think. I act.

The Dambi claws at me. I duck and stab it in the abdomen one, two, three, four times before rolling out of its way. The creature tilts its head back and howls. Obba slices his sword across the Dambi's throat but even that isn't enough to kill it.

I finally understand how Sothpike defeated the Merzan empire in a matter of months. The Dambi are stronger than any animal I've ever seen.

Which only means I have to fight harder.

Now behind the Dambi, I cut the tendons on the back of its legs. The beast falls on all fours, Obba tries to hack off its head, but his sword is stopped by the thick cords of muscle in the Dambi's neck. I plunge both daggers deep into the hardened skin, going for the kidneys. The Dambi rears, its long arms reaching for me, and I back away.

I find a discarded spear on the ground and shove the tip into the Dambi's milky white eye and twist. The Dambi screams. When I pull the spear free, the eye pops out with it.

But still the Dambi isn't finished. It snarls and snaps its black teeth at Obba then leaps forward, too fast to be human, pinning Obba to the dusty ground. With one clawed hand around Obba's neck, the Dambi raises the other to tear Obba's face off. I block the attack with the spear—and the creature uses both hands to yank the weapon out of my grasp, breaking it in half.

Obba scrambles from beneath the beast, trickles of blood running down his throat. "Naira, get away!" he shouts. This monster is indestructible.

How could anyone hope to defeat Sothpike's undead army?

Obba and I step back from the Dambi as it stalks closer on all fours. I'm so focused on the Dambi that I almost bump into a metal basin full of burning embers resting on a column of stone, used to light the streets of Lagusa after dark. There's a fiery arrow sticking out of the coals. A memory of that night in the tomb flashes in my thoughts—how fire made the Dambi retreat.

As soon as the creature gets close enough, I shove the blade of one of my daggers between the stones and the basin and, using the hilt as leverage, I push down with all my might. I almost snap the blade in half as it tips the basin to one side, scattering the fiery embers in the direction of the oncoming Dambi.

The Dambi howls as the sparks set its ragged clothes alight—whether it's roaring in pain or anger, I can't tell. This close to the creature, I see nothing but blackness behind its teeth.

Its tongue has been ripped out.

Thick smoke pours off the creature as it burns. The acrid stench of burnt skin fills my nostrils as the Dambi rips at its clothes and skin, trying to get rid of the flames that lick its body. Screeching, the Dambi turns and plows into the fight, people jumping aside to avoid it. By now, there are only two Dambi left. Only two of them were defeated while Obba and I fought ours, while many more men and women lie injured or dead. For every Dambi killed, it takes ten times as many humans with it.

As I watch, a Dambi crushes a man's skull with its hands while another rips apart the soft belly of a woman. Her screams fill my ears.

Even the one I set on fire is still fighting. I don't know what else to do. We stabbed it, slashed it, and lit the damn thing on fire, but still it continues to move.

Well, if the Dambi isn't going to back down, I won't either. I ready my daggers.

"Are you ready for round two?" Obba asks. I nod. "Good girl."

As Obba and I run to dive back in, the remaining Dambi rear back on their hind legs and shriek, stopping us in our tracks with their deafening cries. All the fighters pause to cover their ears.

The Dambi drop down on all fours and run to the tunnel

carved into the wall, barreling past anyone who gets in their way. Fighters are flung left and right as the monsters retreat through the mangled gates. Rangers on horseback chase after them while a cheer rises among the living as the last vile creature departs.

The drums take up a new chant: *Ba-boom. Ba-boom. Ba-boom.*

The Dambi threat is over.

"Is that it?" I ask Obba.

"It seems that way." He sounds as unsure as I feel. Then he pats me on the shoulder. "You did well."

"Thanks, Obba." I can't stop myself from grinning—and I don't want to anyway. A compliment from Obba is rare, and this is the second one I've received from him today.

"We'd better check on your mother and brother."

I face the wall. "I'll find Nez," I say. I start forward when Obba calls my name. I glance over my shoulder and he smiles and winks.

I return the wink, then make my way to the steps leading to the top of the wall. I maneuver around fighters helping their comrades to their feet, some of them carrying the injured in their arms. Daughters move among them to treat wounds, say prayers for the dying, and place red cloths over the faces of the dead. Someone already set the dead Dambi on fire and a crowd surrounds the bodies to watch them burn.

Up the stairs, I reach the top of the wall. Many rangers still have their bows in their hands and are shooting arrows into the desert at the departing forms of the Dambi. I steer clear from them as I search for my brother, stopping a few other rangers

I pass to ask if they've seen Nez. Most of them ignore me, but I press on. Finally, one asks, "What's your brother look like?"

"Tall and skinny, with light brown eyes and curly hair," I say.

"Can't say I spend a lot of time looking at young men's eyes, samida." She turns away, but I grab her by the arm.

"Please! He's light-skinned! Like me."

"Oh, him I've seen." The ranger points toward the southern end of the rampart. "Check over there."

I thank her and run past warriors clapping each other on the back, some of them laughing while others sit on wooden crates, their hands shaking, their eyes blank. There's a flash of light brown skin but it's not Nez. I approach the man anyway, in case he knows where Nez might be.

As I get closer, the man steps aside and a familiar face appears.

"Nez!" I race toward Nez and throw my arms around him.

"Naira!" My brother pats me on the back, then pulls away. "What are you doing here?"

"Oh, picking flowers." I punch Nez in the shoulder and he laughs.

"Where's Omma? Don't tell me you left her behind to make a bouquet."

I laugh too. "She's down there." I point at the road leading from the gates. "Tending to the wounded."

"Did you see the fight?"

"Did I see it? I was part of it. Obba and I took on a Dambi all by ourselves."

"Really?" Nez sounds envious. "Obba made me stay on the

ramparts. I wanted to go down there and help, but I did do some damage from up here."

"Really?"

Nez points to a dead Vra Gool Dambi in the empty space between the tombs and the wall.

"There, that black arrow in its back. I shot that one. After that, the thing was dead."

I lean over the rampart and squint. "There must be at least twenty arrows in that Dambi, not counting the ones sticking out of its head." I turn toward Nez. "How do you know your arrow is the one that killed it?"

"Because," Nez says, drawing out the word, "it did not fall until *I* shot it."

I smirk. "Right, of course."

Nez glares at me. "You know, you shouldn't even be up here. You're terrible with a bow. I could get in trouble—"

"Alright, alright." I hold my hands up to appease Nez. "You are a powerful warrior. You felled a Dambi with one arrow. Woe to those who doubt your terrifying strength." I give Nez an exaggerated bow. "Happy now?"

"I would have said dazzling strength, but that'll do." Nez slings his bow over his shoulder and rests his arms on the ledge. He stares out over the wall, toward a blue afternoon sky, the sun warming the tops of our heads. Nez's eyes are on the rangers chasing after the last of the Dambi. "Do you think they'll catch them?"

"I hope so." If a handful of Dambi can do so much damage, what would a true army of the creatures manage? I think about the strange woman who seemingly controlled the Dambi the night in the tombs. Was she a part of this? Where is she now?

I shake my head and turn away from the horizon, tugging on Nez's arm. "Come on. Omma was really worried about you. Let's show her you're still alive."

Once we reach the bottom of the steps, I guide Nez toward where I last saw Omma, but I'm not surprised to find her gone. There are so many wounded people that Omma couldn't be expected to stay in one place for long. In fact, many of the injured are being put on stretchers and carried up the hill to the Temple, which is being turned into a makeshift healer's house. It's the only building large enough for all those who need medical attention.

"Who are all these people?" For the first time, I look at the faces of the injured—and realize I don't recognize any of them. Their clothes are too heavy for the desert, and they speak to each other with strange accents, in a language similar to mine, but still different. They draw out certain words and add extra sounds to others. I've never heard so many varieties of Merzan. One woman's accent is so thick I barely understand what she's saying. It's Nez who realizes she's asking for help to stand up.

"Refugees from up north," Nez grunts as he lifts the woman to her feet. He wraps one of her arms around his neck; she groans and leans heavily against him. I take the woman's other arm and we help her to the stairs leading up to the Temple.

It's tough work climbing all the steps with an injured woman between us, and neither of us speaks until we make it to the top, where a pair of Daughters takes over. Nez flops onto a bench and lets his feet dangle in the pool meant for washing one's feet before entering the Temple, but with so much going on, no one finds time to stop and perform that ritual.

"They're fleeing the war," Nez says, continuing the con-

versation we started at the bottom of the Temple steps. I sit
on the bench beside him. "I guess things are getting worse,
though I don't see how that's possible. Sothpike already ruined
everything, even Al-Kazar."

Everyone knows about the fall of Al-Kazar, where the citadel of the last Ur Atum Asim lies in ruins. After Sothpike
killed Asimra Yafeu and let his Dambi loose on the Merzan
army, the Asim's allies—the Hands of God and the Emperor of
Johtan—failed her. The Hands of God vanished while the Emperor isolated Johtan from the rest of the world. Their betrayal
meant there was no one to stop Sothpike from ransacking Al-
Kazar and killing Asim Avari. For almost two decades, Merza
has been without a ruler. And since the Asim died without
any heirs, the throne of Merza has been vacant all this time.

"But what about the Dambi? Why'd they attack now?"

"I heard the rangers talking. Sounded like the Dambi were
chasing the refugees. We opened the gates to let them in, and
some of the Dambi got in, too."

I look at the wall. Although we drove the last of the invading Dambi away, I still want to be up there, watching the
horizon, on guard with the dry breeze on my face and sun in
my eyes. Sothpike is out there somewhere, and the thought
of him and what he can create terrifies me.

A person who makes creatures that creep up on humans
in the night to steal away their lives and feast on their flesh
shouldn't be allowed to exist.

CHAPTER EIGHT

I WALK AMONG THE INJURED AND THE TIRED, DIPPING A wooden ladle into the bucket of water I carry and holding it up to parched lips. Parents cradling little ones in their laps thank me as their children greedily drink. I can't stay in place for too long; there are many others who need my help.

I prefer being out here in the plaza. These refugees are weary, but they aren't dying.

Not like the ones inside the Temple.

I wish I was on the ramparts with my father and brother, both of them filling in for the rangers who died during the battle, but Omma asked me to help at the Temple instead.

With the empty bucket in one hand and the ladle in the other, I gingerly make my way back to the Temple for more water. I step over sleeping children, around the battered baskets and threadbare sacks that contain everything these people own, past men and women sitting on the ground, their heads hanging low or their eyes wide open, staring at something only they can see.

As I make my way past the statues of the Thirteen, I steal a glance at the gods I spend so much time worshipping and wonder how they allowed this to happen. How can they let so many people suffer and do nothing? Why is Sothpike still alive when so many others are dead?

And does the arrival of the refugees mean that Sothpike is getting closer to finding Lagusa? He's never attempted to cross the desert before, but something bad must've happened to bring so many to our doorstep at once.

It takes a moment for my eyes to adjust when I enter the Temple. But even though it's dark, I still see the dead and the dying. The once-spotless stone floor is smeared with blood from gashes and torn-off limbs, ripped skin that hangs like flaps of cloth. I notice a man whose intestines are piled up on his chest.

The hems of my trousers are completely ruined by splatters of blood.

While the people outside are mostly quiet, those in the Temple wail in pain and plead for help. A woman lying on the floor grabs my ankle as I walk past, her grip surprisingly strong even though her face is ashen and her fingers cold.

"My son," she whispers through cracked and bloodied lips. "Where is my son?"

I bend down and place the bucket on the floor. "I'll look for him, samida," I say as I peel off the woman's fingers. "What's his name?"

The woman takes my hand and holds tight. She moves her lips as if she is speaking, but no sound comes out. Only a trickle of blood drips onto the white stone floor. And then, as if drifting off to sleep, she is gone.

"Samida?" I squeeze the woman's hand, shake her by the shoulder. "Samida!" I call out even louder this time, panic rising in my voice. When the woman doesn't respond, I sit on the ground next to her, unable to move.

The woman is dead.

Someone needs to find her son and tell him.

But I don't know their names.

Motion on my left catches my attention, and I look up to see Omma standing over me.

She kneels and gently removes the woman's hand before closing the woman's eyes.

"She wanted her son," I say to Omma. "I don't know her name or his. How will we find him? What if he's dead too? How will we place them in the same tomb?"

"We will." Omma rubs my hair and wipes the tears from my eyes.

I've seen death before. Yesterday was filled with it. But not like this. Never have I held hands with the dead.

Omma stands, pulling me up with her. She picks up my bucket and hands it back to me. "Here. You have a job to do. These people need you."

I wipe my eyes with the heel of my hand. Omma kisses me on the cheek and sends me on my way. I only turn back once to see Omma and a Daughter covering the woman with a red cloth.

Back outside, I sit on a bench and dip my feet in the pool of cold water. But there is no peace to be found at the Temple today.

An old man sitting on a bench on the other side of the pool keeps waving his arm to get my attention. When I look his way, he points at my feet. The hem of my trousers has drifted into the pool and turned the blessed water red.

"By the Fires," I growl as I gather my trousers out of the water, startling the woman who shares my bench so much that she gets up and moves two benches down. I tug and pull on the hems of both legs, ripping them completely off, and throw the wet fabric into the nearest fire cauldron, where it hisses and spits steam until the flames consume the fabric. People are staring, but I don't care. I watch the bloody fabric shrivel and burn until there is nothing left but black ash.

As much as I want to sit at the pool and never have to walk through the Temple again, I can't stay away forever. I grab the bucket and ladle and make my way over to the stone fountain in the shape of a water pitcher held by Uega the Life-Bringer, where I wait in line to refill the bucket.

Once it's full, I inhale deeply before going back into the Temple. I take a different path this time, far away from where the woman died holding my hand, the red fabric covering her face visible from across the room. Everyone is too busy to clear away the dead.

"Excuse me, samida," a voice calls. "Can my father have some water?"

I turn toward the sound without thinking—I've been responding to requests like that all afternoon—and am surprised to see a boy not much older than myself. The stranger's fallow-colored skin is only a shade or two darker than my own, and thick, wavy black hair spills out of the dusty blue scarf wrapped around his head. He waves me over to where he sits on the floor beside an older man wearing a bloody patch over one eye. Poultices cover one side of the man's face and bandages sticky with dried blood are wrapped around his chest and left shoulder.

"Oh—of course." I hurry toward them, dipping the ladle into the bucket as I kneel. The boy grimaces when he lifts his father's head so that he can drink. When he's finished, the boy gently rests his father's head on a bundle of cloth they're using as a pillow.

As soon as the old man closes his remaining eye, his son winces in pain, clutching his right arm. He sucks in a mouthful of air and slowly exhales.

"Are you alright?" I lean forward to look at his arm but he turns away. Up close, his eyes are a strange combination of green and brown, as if the gods couldn't decide on a single color.

"I'm fine," the boy says. "My father is the one who's hurt."

I don't believe him for half a heartbeat. Fresh blood blooms across the fabric of his sleeve.

"You need to have that looked at." I point at his arm, but the boy only draws away farther. "You won't be able to help your father if it gets infected."

"Listen to the young samida, Kal." The old man's voice is raspy and weak. "One of us has to survive this, and I'd rather it be you."

"Baba," Kal begins, but his father waves away his protests.

"Get him fixed up, will you?" The old man focuses his one good eye on me. "And make him go outside for some fresh air. He's been with death for too long."

"I'm not leaving," Kal says, but once again his father shoos his words with a wave of his hand.

"Go away. I want to sleep, and I can't do that if I'm worried about you."

Kal sighs but doesn't argue. He looks at me with a face of resignation. "I can patch myself up. All I need are bandages and some bitterroot for the pain."

"I can get them for you." I rise to my feet. "You stay here and rest."

Kal shakes his head. "No, the old man is right. I have been in here for too long. I'll go with you." He looks at his father and reaches his good arm over to feel his father's forehead with the back of his hand. "He was burning up a hand or so ago, but now he's cool. It seems like the worst is over."

As soon as Kal gets on his feet, he sways and stumbles toward me. I grab his uninjured arm to hold him steady, and when his knees buckle, I wrap my arms around his waist to prop him up.

"Are you alright?" My arms shake with the strain of keeping Kal on his feet. His eyelids flutter and his head lolls forward. "Kal!"

He rests his chin on my shoulder and mumbles something in my ear. As my hands slip and my knees bend under his weight, Kal's head snaps up and he inhales sharply.

"What...? What's happening?"

"You almost passed out," I say as he regains his balance. "Actually, I think you did pass out."

"I'm sorry. I didn't mean to—"

"No one ever means to pass out." I pick up the bucket, and when Kal takes a shaky step forward, I grab his uninjured arm and put it around my shoulders. "Lean on me if you have to, alright?"

Kal lets me lead him to the far side of the Temple, where I find Omma helping hold a patient steady while a Daughter resets his broken bone. A piece of leather is wedged between the man's teeth and tears stream from his eyes.

"Ready, samida?" the Daughter asks my mother. When Omma nods, the Daughter hits the man's shin with the flat of her hand and the bone pops in place with a wet crack.

My lips curl up in disgust. The man's eyes roll in the back of his head and he faints. When the Daughter starts wrapping the man's leg to a wooden splint, Omma pulls the leather out of his mouth and rises to her feet.

"Omma," I call, pulling Kal toward her. "This is Kal. He's hurt. Can you ask the Daughter to look at his arm?"

Omma's eyes widen when she sees the injured young man holding on to me, but she quickly gets over her surprise. "We'll do what we can." She motions for us to follow her to a less crowded spot, where she has Kal sit on the floor.

"Pull up your sleeve," she says, "so I can see what's wrong with you."

I kneel on the floor beside Omma, curious to know what happened. Slowly and with great care, Kal rolls up his sleeve to reveal three bloody gashes on his upper arm, each of them as wide as my finger.

Omma dabs at the wounds with a cloth. "You're going to need stitches, I think. But let me get a Daughter to be sure." She cups Kal's chin in her hand and looks in his eyes. "I'll bet you haven't slept. And you've lost so much blood. It's a wonder you're able to walk at all."

"It's really not that bad." Kal attempts to pull down his sleeve, but Omma slaps his hand away.

"The Daughters will be the judge of that." Omma climbs to her feet. "Naira, stay here and make sure he doesn't move."

With Omma gone, Kal and I sit in uncomfortable silence. I don't know what to do, so I fill the ladle with water and hold it out toward him.

"Are you thirsty?"

"Sure." Kal takes a sip. "Thanks."

"You don't have to thank me. It's my job." Immediately I regret my terrible response to someone showing gratitude, but I can't take it back now.

Thankfully, Kal breaks the uncomfortable silence after a moment.

"They said this place wasn't real." His eyes travel around the Temple, taking in the brightly painted murals on the walls, the pillars covered in tiles arranged in colorful patterns, the windows made of tinted glass. They cast mosaics of light on the wounded lying on the floor, obscuring their injuries. "The hidden village beyond the desert. The mythical refuge for those fleeing from Sothpike." Kal turns his gaze on me and my skin grows strangely hot where his unique eyes land. "I was afraid that even if this place did exist, they'd turn me away at the gate, but my father made us come anyway. *'It has to be better than waiting for Sothpike to kill us,'* he said. But I guess I was worried for nothing. They let me in without a question, and so far, no one's said anything about the way I look." He smiles at me. "I guess even people like us are safe in Lagusa."

"What do you mean?"

"You know, people who are only half-Merzan," he says as if I should know what he means.

I start to tell him that I'm full Merzan, not half, but the

Daughter arrives and immediately gets to work with fire-wort to clean Kal's wounds. He sucks in his breath sharply and scrunches up his face.

With all my scrapes and tumbles over the years, I've been on the receiving end of firewort many times, so I know how much it burns. I grimace in sympathy.

The Daughter threads a hook-shaped needle and dips it in the bottle of firewort.

I lean forward. "Don't you have any bitterroot? For the pain?"

The Daughter shakes her head. "We ran out three hands ago, but he's a strong lad. He'll survive."

"But—"

The Daughter drives the needle into Kal's skin and pulls it out the other side. "It's already begun."

I half watch the Daughter sew up Kal's wounds. The other half of me watches Kal, who groans and takes a lot of quick breaths, but doesn't cry out. His composure is impressive, and I have to agree with the Daughter's assessment of him.

When she's done, the Daughter rubs a salve over the wound and wraps a cloth around it. "Put on a clean bandage every day. Come back to the Temple in two weeks so we can take out the stitches. Understand?"

Before he can even answer, the Daughter is on her feet and making her way to the next patient. I help Kal to stand.

"You can put your arm around my shoulder again if you need to."

"I'm just a little light-headed." Kal momentarily places a hand on my shoulder to ground himself. "Where can I go for some fresh air?"

I set the bucket on the floor. "Come with me."

We go out the back entrance, but instead of heading toward the plaza, I turn to the left and down a short flight of steps carved into the ground that lead to the garden.

"Can we stop for a moment?" Kal asks. He's only halfway down the steps and his face seems much paler than before. Concerned he's going to pass out again and fall down the steps, I rush back up and grab Kal by the arm to keep him steady.

As soon as I touch him, Kal clenches his jaw and sucks in air through his teeth. My hands are wrapped around his newly stitched wound. I drop his arm and back away.

"I'm sorry, I thought you were going to pass out." I would give anything for a boulder to drop out of the sky so I can hide under it forever.

"I only wanted to look at the wall." Kal peeks under the bandage to inspect his wound. Satisfied it's fine, he raises his eyes back to Lagusa's protective wall, barely visible over the tops of the trees surrounding the garden. "When we were coming out of the desert and the Dambi appeared, everyone kept saying, 'We just have to make it to the wall. If we make it to the wall, we'll be saved.' Everyone but me, that is. I was tired of running and wanted to fight. But my father knew that one person against so many Dambi was suicide. He kept pushing me forward, and I made it with only a scratch, while he's in there—" Kal jerks a thumb toward the Temple. He looks ready to say more, but then he sighs. "I can't waste my thoughts on regrets. I have to make sure my father gets better."

I wonder if the Dambi that attacked the tomb were part of

the group that attacked the refugees. Did that strange woman have something to do with that as well?

A baby's cries echo across the plaza and into the garden, breaking through my thoughts. "We've had a few refugees at our gates over the years, but never this many, especially not all at once." I pluck a flower from one of the bushes lining the steps and twirl it between my fingers. "Does this mean Sothpike is on the move again?"

Kal continues down the steps and I follow. "He's mobilizing, but it's anyone's guess where he's going. Up north, the Turka Sea is crowded with Sothpike's ships, and he controls Merza from the east to the west. There was only one place left to go for the rest of us: south. I expect you'll be seeing more and more refugees in the coming months."

"You're on the other side of the wall now, and Sothpike is a desert away." I need to reassure myself as well as Kal. "You're safe."

As he reaches the bottom step, Kal turns around and smiles at me. "Thanks for saying that."

As I predicted, the garden is empty. We walk among the jasmine and lilac trees, past rows of herbs, to the pond filled with fish. I trail my fingers in the water and the fish swim up to me, expecting me to feed them.

"After weeks in the desert, I never thought something like this would await us." Kal turns one way and another, taking it all in. "I wasn't even sure we'd make it here at all. The desert was bad enough, but when the Vra Gool Dambi came after us… It's a miracle that we survived."

I want to ask him so many questions—where he is from, what it's like beyond the desert, what happened to the rest of his family—but I know this is not the time. Instead, I wipe my wet hands on my trousers and turn toward the Temple.

"I should go back. I really do have a job. But you can stay if you want."

"I should get back to my father." Kal smiles and follows me out of the garden.

Back inside the Temple, Kal seems lost, so I guide him through the wounded and dying. Halfway back to where his father was lying, I stop in my tracks, my eyes on the bright red cloth in the distance. Confused, Kal follows my gaze to the scrap of fabric covering his father's face.

Kal falls to his knees and a cry of sorrow to come escapes his lips. He rocks back and forth with his head in his hands, and I drop on the floor beside him.

I don't know what to do, so I rub his back, repeating *I'm sorry, I'm sorry* over and over until the words have no meaning. After a moment of hesitation, I pull his hands away from his face and hold him close, stroking his hair, his hands clutching at my tunic. My eyes fill with tears.

A Daughter crouches down beside us. "What happened?"

I point at Kal's father. When the Daughter sees the cloth over his face, she understands. She draws Kal away from me and holds him as he cries. Omma rushes over and once again helps me to stand.

"Come, Naira," she says, drawing me away. "Let the Daughters comfort him. It's what they're here for."

"He was fine." I sob as I let Omma escort me out of the Temple and to the statues of the gods. "Kal said his fever was gone and he was getting better."

Omma hugs me and I rest my head on her shoulder. "No, that man was dying. He knew it. The Daughters told him so."

I raise my head. "Why did he send Kal away if he knew they had so little time left together?"

"Maybe he thought it would be easier for Kal, or maybe he did it to make it easier for himself. No one can say but the gods."

When I'm finished crying, Omma gives me a bandage to wipe my nose. Then she notices my ruined trousers.

"What happened?" she asks as she lifts one of the pant legs and inspects the rip.

"They were stained with blood. I had to."

Omma sighs. "Why don't you go home and get some rest? And change your clothes."

"But—"

"No buts," Omma says. "You've helped enough. Now go, my headstrong girl."

If I wasn't so tired, I would have argued more, but instead I give Omma a kiss on the cheek and leave the plaza. I hesitate to go back in—I don't know what I will do if Kal is still crying—but he's gone. His father still lies there with the red cloth over his face, as well as the woman whose hand I held earlier.

Everyone is too busy tending to the living to take care of the dead.

CHAPTER NINE

"ONE, TWO, THREE!" THE STALL OWNER CALLS OUT, AND I grab the underside of the counter and pull, my muscles straining as I help the owner and his two sons heave the overturned structure back onto its feet. The stall creaks and groans as it's shoved upright, and with a satisfying *thud*, finally returns to its original position. The owner laughs and claps his sons on the back.

"Good job, good job." He shakes my hand. "Thank you, samida!"

I wipe the sweat from my brow and dry my hands on my pants, leaving streaks of black soot on the yellow fabric. For the last two days, I've been helping to clean up the market. It's tough work, from sweeping up piles of ash and debris to clearing away rubble so that new structures can be built. Omma is still assisting at the Temple, where the refugees wait for the Daughters to find them homes with the faithful throughout the village until they get on their feet.

I can't stop thinking about Kal. What's going to happen to

him? He's alone in a new village—I can't imagine what I'd do without my family. I hope that wherever the Daughters place him, he's able to find peace.

A tap on my shoulder breaks me out of my thoughts. I turn to see Nez handing me a mug of water.

"Thought you might be thirsty after that feat of strength," Nez says with a smile.

I grin and take the mug. "Thanks."

Before I can drink, a familiar voice joins in.

"Someone call the rangers—there's another Vra Gool Dambi loose." Hamala steps in front of me, both hands on her hips, with three other girls behind her, each of them glaring. Hearing the words *Vra Gool Dambi* out of Hamala's mouth raises my hackles. To be compared to them, so soon after the night in the tombs and the devastation they caused to the village, is infuriating. I know Hamala chose that insult on purpose, and I also know that punching her in the mouth will feel almost as good as sinking my daggers into the belly of a Dambi.

"Shouldn't you be locked up?" I stand my ground. "Or did they run out of room at the kennel?"

"You just don't know when to keep your mouth shut, do you?" Hamala steps closer, nearly touching me. "Sounds like I need to teach you another lesson."

"Only if you want me to spit in your face again." I bump my chest against hers and she stumbles backward.

"You little—" She reaches for me and I'm a breath away from shoving her to the ground when Nez pushes us apart and stands with his arms out between us.

"That's enough," he barks at Hamala. "What's your problem? Why do you keep picking fights with my sister?"

Hamala snarls at him. "Because I can't stand people like her, always in other people's business, always trying to run things. Well, guess what—I run Lagusa. And I'm tired of you getting in my way."

I'm just about to tell Hamala what I think of her when Nez doubles over in laughter, startling everyone.

Hamala recovers first. "Oh, you think I'm funny? Well, you won't be laughing when I'm through with you." She clenches her fists and her lackeys do the same.

I don't care if Hamala wants to fight me, but she's not going to touch my brother. I square my shoulders and raise my fists, maneuvering to put Nez behind me. But before it comes to blows, he finally stops laughing and straightens.

"Whew," he says, catching his breath and wiping tears from his eyes. He faces Hamala. "What are you, sixteen? And you think you *run* Lagusa?" He says the word *run* in a mocking tone and Hamala's eye twitches. "Come on, you can't be serious." When Hamala doesn't back down, Nez laughs again and turns to me. "I guess we have a real band of thugs on our hands." Nez rolls his eyes and grabs my arm. "Come on, Naira, let's get out of here before these scary thugs try to hurt us with their scary little fists."

Hamala looks ready to explode. She lunges at Nez, I lunge at her. But Nez whips out his bow and nocks an arrow aimed right at her forehead before either of us connects with our targets.

"My father always says only a dead man enters a sword fight with just his fists." Nez holds his weapon steady. "Now, this isn't a sword, but you get my drift. My father is a wise man, very wise. And if you want to run Lagusa, you'd do well to heed his advice. Or you can come after my sister again and they'll find *you* in the tombs with an arrow embedded in your skull."

Hamala narrows her eyes. "Fine. We're done. But if you stick your nose in my business one more time…even your brother won't be able to protect you."

I try to respond, but Nez clamps his hand over my mouth and shoos Hamala away. "Be gone, and take your miserable henchmen with you."

Hamala sneers, then motions to her friends to follow her. I turn in the opposite direction and start walking to put as much distance between us as possible.

Once we're out of earshot, my rage explodes through gritted teeth.

"She makes me so angry!" I stomp past workers pushing wheelbarrows and carrying buckets, past crumbling walls and scorched wooden stalls. "She left me for dead in a tomb and *she* wants to start stuff with *me*? I should be the one starting stuff with her! So what if I stick my nose in her business— someone has to! Otherwise she'll keep terrorizing people who can't fight back. She can't keep getting away with this! The people she's hurt, they deserve justice. *I* deserve justice!"

I turn to Nez, expecting some sort of reply from him, but he doesn't speak. He just keeps walking and rubbing the back of his neck like he does when he's deep in thought or confused.

"Well? Aren't you going to say anything?"

Nez drops his arm and shrugs. "What do you want me to say? You pretty much said everything already."

I stop and glare at my brother. "You could say that you agree! That I'm right and that she's wrong. That she needs to be stopped and that—"

"That you have to stop her?"

"Yes, exactly!" I let out a sigh of relief. Finally, Nez is talking sense.

But instead of backing me up, he shakes his head. "See, that's where we differ. Yes, Hamala is the worst and life would be better for a lot of people if she wasn't around, but it's not up to you to keep her in check."

I can't believe what I'm hearing and my thoughts are so jumbled I can't even speak. My brother, *my twin*, is taking Hamala's side?

Nez must sense my confusion, my outrage, my disbelief at his betrayal. He smiles and puts his arm around my shoulders. I try to pull away from this traitor of a brother but his grip is tight.

"Now, before you get angry, remember that I said Hamala is the worst. Alright? Because she truly is. And it sucks for the whole village that she's gotten away with being a bully for so long. But—and this is the truth even if you don't want to hear it—handing out justice is not your job. You won't get a medal for standing up to Hamala."

"So what do you suggest? You want me to turn away when I see her hurting someone?"

Nez rolls his eyes. "You always go to the extremes. There *is* a middle ground between going in fists flying and doing nothing. Find a watchguard, tell a teacher. And if you have to intervene, do it peacefully. Try talking instead of punching."

I push Nez's arm off my shoulders and this time he doesn't hold on. "I tried to tell a watchguard last time and look where that got me. Thrown in the tombs."

Nez shrugs. "Like I said, she's the worst. But today, why didn't you just walk away? You know she's a miserable wretch who wants everyone else to be miserable too. So why did you let her get to you?"

"After what she did to me, how can you expect me to just walk away?" Even though I'm trying to defend my actions, I know I could have handled things differently. But knowing this doesn't make me feel better—in fact, I feel worse.

I start moving again to clear out those unsettling feelings that come with admitting I was wrong, Nez still by my side. We pass a crew pouring clay into molds to create bricks. They're repairing the building next to my favorite incense shop. Surprisingly, the shop is untouched even though the surrounding buildings show signs of damage. Normally, I'd stop in to see if there are any new scents or if the long-awaited shipment of lavender oil has finally arrived, but not today.

"The choice is yours," Nez says. "You can let it go, or you can keep fighting, because that strategy's been working out so great for you."

I push Nez away from me. "Leave me alone." I know he's right, but I don't want to admit it. "She just makes me so angry!"

"You have to stop letting people like her get to you." Nez steps aside to let two men carrying a bucket of wet clay pass. "You have to get yourself in balance." Nez holds out both hands palm up. "Right now, your scales are heavy with dis-order and chaos." He tips his right hand down and brings his left hand higher. "You need to be more peaceful," he says, leveling out his hands.

I snort. "Like you?"

A smile spreads across Nez's face. "Yes, be more calm. Less prickly. More cuddly. Less *you* and more *me*."

I roll my eyes. *Cuddly.* Nez is nothing but a big-headed skeleton covered by a thin sheet of pale brown skin.

"I wish you knew what it was like to be me." I trudge around a pile of rubble while workers pick apart the pile and put the pieces in a wheelbarrow to haul it away. I wish they could gather all my anger, my quick temper, and haul those away as well. "Nothing bothers you. Everything's a joke. But I've got this awful temper that goes off at the slightest touch. The smallest prick, and I explode."

"Well, not everything's a joke." Nez grabs the tail end of my braid. "Take your hair, for instance. No joking here. It's a tragedy."

I groan and snatch my braid out of his fingers. "Can't you be serious?"

Nez straightens up. "Yes. This is my serious face." I stalk off and Nez runs to catch up with me. "Come on, Naira. Yes, you have a bad temper. But it doesn't have to control you every time Hamala rears her butt-ugly head. It's *your* temper—you can control it."

Nez is right. I've been blaming Hamala for everything, but the truth is I've been part of the problem as well. I can't let these things keep me from focusing on what's important, like repairing our village and keeping an eye out for Dambi.

The rangers Obba sent to search for the strange woman I saw haven't returned, and I'll bet a thousand gold rubes that she has something to do with their disappearance. *That's* what I should be putting my energy into, not Hamala.

I sigh and Nez walks silently beside me.

I have Obba in one ear telling me to accept that I'm a fighter, to embrace who I am. Then I have Nez in the other ear telling me to stop attacking everyone who raises my hackles. I try to listen to them both. I have to stay true to who I am, but I also have to pick my battles.

"Fine," I say. "You're right. I won't let Hamala get to me anymore."

Nez cups his hand around his ear. "What's that I hear? Did someone say that I am *right*?"

"Yes, I did," I say with a laugh.

"The world must be ending!" Nez continues his act. "Samida Always-Right admitted that me, her lowly brother, is indeed correct. What a day! I shall mark it down in stone!"

"Oh, will you grow up!" I try to look annoyed, but I can't stop the laugh that bursts forth at his antics.

Nez gives me a big grin and I roll my eyes, but he knows I'm not really angry.

"Wait, aren't you supposed to be at the wall?"

"Oh, I was supposed to report for duty—" he glances at the position of the sun relative to the horizon "—a quarter of a hand ago, but then I had to save my little sister, so…"

"Come on." I roll my eyes as I grab Nez's arm and pull him in the direction of the western wall.

Before we go two steps, the drumming starts.

Boom. Boom. Boom.

Boom. Boom. Boom.

Boom. Boom. Boom.

Vra Gool Dambi.

They're back.

Nez and I glance at each other before breaking out into a sprint toward the wall.

CHAPTER TEN

ONLY A FEW VILLAGERS HAVE THE SAME RESPONSE TO the drumbeats as ours. Many of them are running in the opposite direction of the wall, dropping their tools and materials on the ground as they scatter. Others stand completely still, their eyes wide, their hands covering their mouths, in shock or disbelief.

My own heart is racing. I'm scared of what we might find at the wall, but I can't let that stop me from running toward it.

The road leading to the wall is still blocked by the hastily erected barricades, although all the dead and wounded have been cleared away. Even the ashes of the Dambi are gone. I run beside Nez through the windy path between the barricades to the edge of the village. Dozens of rangers, many of them still pulling on their uniforms, join us as we race toward the steps, the drums growing louder with each breath.

The smell of death hits me before I even make it to the wall and a heavy stone drops in my stomach. How many Vra Gool Dambi will we have to fight this time?

Rangers with red sashes stationed at the bottom of the steps stop us from joining the rest making their way to the top.

"Rangers only. Go home and lock your doors."

"I've been working with the rangers every day," Nez says. "I belong up there!"

A ranger looks Nez up and down, taking in his height and bow. "Alright, you can go up. But not her." The ranger points at me.

I throw back my shoulders and stick out my chin. "Why not?"

"Because you're a little kid," he replies, his attention now on the real rangers jostling past.

"I'm the same age as him! I'm not a kid."

"Look, *kid*, I'm not letting you up. You'll get in the way. And you don't even have a weapon."

He's right—I don't have a weapon. He turns to Nez. "You going up? This is your last chance."

Nez shakes his head and backs away. "We're a set. Can't have one without the other."

The ranger shrugs again and goes back to ushering his brethren up the steps.

"Nez, you should go up there." Even though I'm glad Nez hasn't abandoned me, I know how much he likes being with the rangers. He's drawn to the camaraderie and sense of purpose that comes from everyone working toward the same goal of keeping Lagusa safe. He's gone to the top of the wall almost every day since the refugees arrived, doing whatever menial tasks they ask of him with pride.

"Too late now," Nez says with a smile. "Come on, let's find a place where we can see what's happening."

The only place high enough is the Temple, so we turn back around. Other villagers have the same idea, and we join the masses moving up the Temple stairs. It's slow going as many villagers stop midway to cross their arms over their chest and bow, blocking the path of those behind them.

We make it to the first landing when the war drums stop as suddenly as they started. A hush falls over the people.

Then a shout rings out among the villagers.

"The rangers! They're opening the gates!"

The people gasp and erupt in protest.

"Are they mad?"

"They'll kill us!"

"Keep the gates closed!"

I whirl around. Sure enough, the gates to the tunnel are opening. Expecting a horde of Dambi to surge through, I'm surprised to see Obba and the rest of the Subaans make their way into the tunnel. A retinue of rangers and watchguards surround them. Obba carries his staff in one hand, his other hand resting on the hilt of his sword.

"We have to get down there." I tug on Nez's arm. We push our way down the steps as hundreds fight their way up. The people shove each other out of the way, their faces filled with panic, none of them pausing now to show the dragons respect. At the bottom, we follow a more curious crowd past the first set of gates and into the tunnel. Rangers try to stop them, but there are too many villagers and not enough of them, and they are elbowed aside.

"By the Fires!" Nez exclaims when he sees what awaits us on the other side of the wall.

More Vra Gool Dambi than I have ever seen stand docile as

if they weren't raised from the dead solely to kill, their stench so overpowering bile rises in my throat and my eyes water. In front of the Dambi are six rangers, their clothes coated with desert sand, their faces haggard and their heads hanging in shame. Ropes bind their hands.

"Those are the rangers who went after the Dambi two days ago," Nez whispers.

Next to the rangers is a figure dressed in black robes, her wild, bushy hair barely contained by a hood, and a black mask covers her face. Dark eyes roam the crowd, and memories of that terrifying night among the tombs flood my thoughts.

"It's her," I say to Nez. I will never be able to forget the way the woman stared down at me like a wild maugrab watching its prey. "The woman from the tombs. The one who controls the Dambi."

"As long as you obey the Mistress, no one will get hurt," the strange woman says, a mark on the back of her hand glowing. She motions toward the abominations hunched before her and they snarl in response. Fear ripples through the crowd.

"These are my Vra Gool Dambi," the Mistress continues, her accent making her words stilted. Behind her, the tombs spread out all the way to the horizon, their chimneys still spewing black ash from the dead burning inside of them. "They are under my control. They will not hurt you."

"Why should we believe you?" one of the Subaans yells.

"Because I am what saved your lives," the Mistress replies. "Two days ago, wild Dambi came to your village. I found them and brought them under my control."

It *was* odd the way the Dambi suddenly ran away during the battle at the gates. From the way they stand now—as still as the statues of the gods at the Temple, their knees bent, their claws almost touching the ground—something is clearly controlling them. Like that night in the tomb, when the Dambi stopped trying to claw their way inside after the woman appeared. They went to her when she sang to them. I wonder if her control over them has something to do with the glowing mark on the back of her hand.

"Vra Gool Dambi can be gentle," the woman continues. "See?"

She touches one of the Dambi on the arm. In response, it grabs one of the rangers by the shoulder, its black claws piercing the ranger's tunic. Pinpricks of blood appear on the light brown cloth. The ranger trembles beneath the Dambi's clutches.

"They will do what I want, and only what I want. I can make them behave, as long as you obey my orders," the Mistress warns. "If you do not obey, then I will set these Dambi loose."

The Dambi traces its claw against the ranger's neck and a trickle of blood spills down the front of her tunic. Her eyes go wide and she cries out. Screams and gasps erupt from those watching, mine among them, and Nez grabs his bow. But the ranger remains standing—the cut isn't fatal.

"And what are your orders?" Obba asks, stepping in front of the other Subaans. A single line of watchguards is all that separates him from the Dambi.

Seeing Obba stand tall and unafraid before the Mistress and her Dambi makes me stand up straighter too.

"Give me your children," the Mistress replies. "All of them."

Murmurs of dissent weave through the crowd. I catch Nez's

eye and see that he's thinking the same thing. We're both children still, and neither of us wants to go anywhere with the Mistress or her Dambi.

A voice rises from among those watching. "She can't have our children!"

The Mistress cocks her ear toward the voice. "I can have whatever I want."

The same Dambi that scratched the ranger shrieks. In a flash, it leaps at the other tied-up rangers, sinking its claws into one's back and knocking him to the ground. The crowd screams and many retreat into the tunnel. The other hostages try to flee but more Dambi grab them by the throats and hold them still.

The first Dambi jumps on the fallen ranger and begins digging, ripping off his clothes, tearing his flesh into ribbons, pulling out organs and intestines, chewing on everything it finds. Through it all, the man screams and screams—until his throat fills with blood and he chokes to death on it, the Dambi still sitting on him and feasting.

It happens so fast I barely have time to react. My mouth hangs open wide, my eyes even wider, and I back away from the scene. Nez is rooted to the ground in shock and I have to yank on his arm to move him closer to the wall.

I glance at the Subaans. Their faces are a mixture of fear and revulsion. One of the men faints. Obba notices me and Nez among those remaining and motions for us to get back inside the village. I shake my head and Obba purses his lips before returning his attention to the Mistress.

"That's enough, my pet," the Mistress coos to the Dambi. She touches its arm again and the Dambi returns to its place among the others, its face and claws covered in blood and flesh.

The other Dambi still hold on to the rangers as the Mistress faces the Subaans. "You see what I can make them do. Disobey me—refuse me what I want—and I command all of my children to fill your pretty village with rivers of blood."

"What you're asking is impossible." Obba brandishes his sword. I want to stop him, to pull him away from the battle I know is coming—he is only one man against a horde of Dambi—but I can do nothing but watch. "These are our children. We will fight to the death to protect them."

Up above, the rangers point their bows at the Mistress and the Dambi. Nez nocks an arrow. Those who remain on the ground do the same, drawing out their weapons, readying their bows.

All I have are my fists, so I ball them and get into a fighting stance.

"Killing me would be so easy, wouldn't it? A single arrow to the head would do it." A hint of a smile plays across the Mistress's lips. "But you don't want to do that. Because without my control, these Vra Gool Dambi would become wild again—and they would eat every single one of you before my dead body hit the ground. Your precious children included."

"You will never take my children," Obba says, filling my heart with pride. And fear. Obba can't possibly take on the Mistress and her Dambi by himself, but I know he'll never back down. Family means everything to him.

A hail of arrows rains down from the wall. The Mistress holds out her glowing hand and a pack of Dambi surround her, protecting her from the onslaught. Fiery arrows embed themselves in the Dambi's backs, but this time they don't flee.

The Dambi stand their ground, even though the fire eats at
their flesh.

When the attack ends, the Mistress emerges unscathed. Four
of the Dambi are covered in fire and she watches them scream
and writhe on the ground.

"You will pay for what you have done to my children." The
Mistress clasps her hands together. A horde of Dambi descend
upon the Subaans and those who are supposed to protect them.

Obba's eyes are on me and Nez, not the oncoming Dambi.
"Hide!"

Then he winks at me.

Sunlight glints off Obba's blade before he's engulfed by the
Dambi, one of them plunging its claws into his stomach as
Obba drives his sword into the creature's chest. Both of them
fall to the ground, their bodies trampled by their own brethren.

"Obba!" I scream, running toward him. Nez grabs my arm.
I try to wrench free, but Nez's grip is tight.

Screams come from the mass of Dambi swiping and clawing
at the Subaans, many of them dead on the ground already. I
keep my eye on the horde, hoping to catch a glimpse of Obba
again, but he was in the thick of the fighting, his body hidden beneath the carnage. Rangers join in, but it barely makes
a difference.

These aren't the kind of Dambi I'm used to. They seem to
be smarter than the monsters that attacked the village two days
ago. These Dambi work together, watch their prey, and adjust
tactics based on their movements. When a Subaan breaks free,
one Dambi flanks her left while the second pulls ahead on the
right. Together, they bring her down and kill her with a slash

to her throat, dragging her lifeless body back to the slaughter. A trail of red seeps into the yellow sand behind them.

The Mistress's eyes are fixed on the attack. I know she's the reason the Dambi are fighting like trained warriors. Somehow, that mark on the back of her hand binds her to them so that she can command them. These deaths are her fault.

And she's smiling.

I want to rip her head off. But Nez won't release his hold on my arm.

"Come on, Naira," Nez pleads. "Obba told us to hide. We have to go!"

"We can't leave Obba!"

"Obba's already gone." Nez has tears in his eyes.

"No!" I don't—won't—believe him. I try to run toward the fighting, but Nez hooks his arm around my waist and drags me back despite my struggling. He wraps his other arm around my chest, pinning my arms against my sides as he pulls me away.

"Let me go!" I try to pry his arm from around my waist, but he won't budge. "We can't leave Obba!"

Nez grunts as he half drags, half carries me into the tunnel, narrowly avoiding the rangers rushing past to join in the battle and rescue any survivors. Once we're in the village, Nez locks a hand around my wrist and pulls me through the streets. Tears flood my eyes, blurring my vision until the world is a mess of colors with no definable shapes. Without Nez guiding me, I would be lost in the streets I normally can navigate with my eyes closed. But knowing where I'm going is something I no longer care about. I want to see Obba, hold his hand, *bring him home*.

Pain in my chest hits me so hard I think I've been stabbed. Unable to walk, I fall against a building and sob.

Nez sits on the ground next to me, his shoulders shaking as tears run down his face.

What are we going to do? Obba is our rock, the answer to all our problems. He is the one whose disappointment cuts me the sharpest, but also the one whose praise lifts me higher than anyone else's. Imagining life without his wisdom and guidance is impossible.

That final moment when he winked at me...that's all I have left. I wish I could go back and stop time and live in that moment forever.

But deep down, I know Obba wouldn't want that. He would want me to get up, get moving, and do something.

Shrieks fill the streets of Lagusa. I stand.

"Come on." I pull Nez to his feet. "We have to find Omma."

Nez wipes the tears from his eyes with the heel of his hand.

"I'll check the Temple," he says, his voice cracking. "You go see if she went home."

Before I go off on my own, I wrap my arms around my brother. Nez trembles as one last sob escapes his lips. Then he pulls away.

"We will make her pay," I promise Nez. Unable to speak, he nods, dries his tears, and runs off toward the Temple.

I wipe my own eyes, revealing the streets before me. I make my way home, down roads I've walked hundreds of times with Obba, and I see him everywhere. On this road, holding my hand as our family goes to a festival at the Temple. Or kneeling on that corner and dabbing the blood on my knee where

I fell and scraped it. Or in our neighbor's house, in their garden, when the neighbor and Obba sang a duet and I heard my father's beautiful and rich singing voice for the first time.

He is everywhere and nowhere. All I have now are memories.

I stand outside our house, my hand pressed against the door, and choke back a sob. I don't want to go inside. I don't want to see his sandals by the door, or smell the faint scent in his study from the oils he puts in his hair. I don't want to sit at the dinner table across from an empty seat or go to the jirkana for our regular session only to find it empty.

Sometimes you do things because you have to. What you want doesn't matter. That's called growing up.

Obba's voice is so strong I almost think he's standing beside me. I take a deep breath, unlatch the front door, and step into what looks like a healer's house. The tiled floor of the courtyard is covered with pallets for the injured, Omma walking between them, dispensing draughts and checking temperatures.

"Naira, I'm so glad you're home!" Omma takes me by the hand and leads me inside, stepping around the healing and the sick.

For a moment, I consider pretending that everything is the same. That Obba isn't gone. That he'll walk through the door a few steps behind me. But I know I have to grow up and do something I very much don't want to do.

Obba is gone. The Dambi *did* kill him. And I have to be the one to break the news to my mother.

"I need you to go in the kitchen and check on the rice," Omma is saying. "If it's ready, start filling bowls. Twenty should do it."

I attempt to pull my mother aside. "Omma, I have to talk to you."

"We can talk after lunch. Right now, we have a lot of hungry people to feed. They won't get better on air alone. A Daughter was supposed to help me, but she's late. So, I need you to—"

"Omma, listen to me. I have to tell you something."

"Is it about the drums? Well, if there's another attack, then that means there will be more injured. Which means more work for us." Omma starts toward the kitchen. When I don't follow, she turns around and puts her hands on her hips. "Don't get lazy on me now, Naira."

I don't know what else to do, so I raise my voice at my mother for the first time in my life.

"Omma, will you listen to me? Obba's dead!"

All conversation around us stops and everyone's eyes turn toward us.

Omma blinks. "No, that can't be. Isrof wouldn't do that." A fake smile is plastered on her face as if it could ward off the truth. "He wouldn't leave me alone. He promised."

I try to speak, to explain, but the words get caught in my throat and my chin trembles from holding back tears. All I can manage is, "I'm sorry."

This must finally convince her because she sinks to her knees. "No," Omma moans. I run over and hold her in my arms. "No, no, no…"

Searing pain rips through my chest and I have a hard time breathing. Loud, ugly sobs burst from my lips as Omma and I rock back and forth, each of us clinging to the other as if we have nothing else to hold on to in the entire world.

CHAPTER ELEVEN

I SIT CROSS-LEGGED ON THE JIRKANA FLOOR, OBBA'S curved sword balancing on my lap. Captain Farouk of the watchguard returned it to Omma. It was all they could find of Obba that's still in one piece. His staff is broken, just like the bodies outside the gate, disfigured beyond recognition. It's impossible to tell who is who and how many are among the dead.

I want to believe Obba is still alive, that he survived having his stomach ripped open and being trampled, but his weapon was found on the ground.

A Khoum never drops their weapon, not as long as they have breath in their lungs. That's what Obba taught me.

And that's why it hurts so much to hold his sword in my lap.

Obba always said that we must fight for what is right. But it's hard for me to believe right will win any battle against the Mistress. After commanding her Dambi to decimate the Subaans, rangers, and watchguards, those Dambi now terrorize the streets of Lagusa in their search for children. The Mistress has barricaded herself inside the meeting house, leaving scores of her Dambi outside to protect her. With the Subaans dead, the village now looks to the Mother of the Temple to lead us, but nobody knows what to do—some want to band together to drive the Mistress and her monsters out of the village, others want to pack their belongings and flee, and the rest locked themselves away.

But nowhere is safe. In the days since the Mistress's invasion, she has sent her Dambi out in batches, ten to the neighborhoods near the southern wall, a handful to the homes of the merchants near the destroyed village gates, another group to the farming estates up north. The Dambi have been invading the homes of each district, bashing down doors and scratching holes in walls to steal any children who might be hiding inside. Daughters are being ripped out of their fathers' arms, mothers are being slaughtered for trying to protect their sons, younger siblings who get in the way are being trampled and thrown aside to capture their older brothers and sisters.

Word has quickly spread throughout the village that the Mistress is after children of a particular age: fifteen to seventeen. Gender doesn't matter—she wants them all. And anyone who gets in the way of her Dambi doesn't matter either.

The villagers aren't going down without a fight. As the days pass, the people come better prepared and fight the Dambi in the streets. We cheer every time a Dambi falls, which is rare, and cry with anguish whenever a Lagusan falls, which is often. Children have been secretly shuttled out back doors to the homes of friends in neighboring districts while their families press their backs against their front doors to keep the Dambi from breaking in. Fewer children are being taken, but the searching hasn't stopped, and we have no way of knowing where the Dambi will appear next.

Some think she wants children to turn them into Dambi; others say she uses them as food for her creatures. No one really knows what her plans are, but we do know that anyone who enters the meeting house never leaves.

We've lived like this for four days. Four days without order, four days without calm and comfort, four days without Obba. Soon, she'll send her abominations to the river district where we live, and I don't know what I will do when that day arrives. Do I fight and risk getting all the refugees hiding in our house, as well as Omma, killed? Or give up, let my weapon drop to the ground, and admit defeat?

Before I can decide, the door to the jirkana opens and a shadowy figure steps inside. I quickly wipe away the tears that wet my cheeks.

"Who's there?" My voice isn't nearly as strong as I hoped it would be.

"I'm sorry, I didn't know anyone was in here." The figure pauses and I recognize him as the young man whose father died in the Temple. *Kal.* I didn't know he was one of the refugees staying with us. I've spent all my time alone in my room, or in the jirkana, since Obba's death.

"I was looking for somewhere quiet…" Kal starts to back out of the room.

I rise to my feet, Obba's sword in one hand. "It's fine. Finding a quiet spot around here isn't easy. You can stay. I'll leave." I place the sword on the shelf.

"No, samida. This is your house. I'll come back later."

"And you're a guest, so you should stay." My words are more forceful than I intend.

Kal pauses. "Are you sure?"

I nod. "Yes, please come in."

"Your name is Naira, right?" I nod again. "I'm Kal Sayeed," he says with a bow. Then he makes his way into the room, a bowl of water in one hand and a cloth sack in the other. "You don't have to leave." He stops in the center and kneels on the stone floor. "I'm going to burn some incense in memory of those I've lost. Maybe you'd like to join me?"

"You could do that at our mazan." I point in the direction of the small alcove off the courtyard where incense and candles burn for the dead. I've lit a stick of incense every day since Obba died. Sometimes when I pass by, I catch a glimpse of Obba kneeling there, praying to the gods to protect and bless our family. But when I go into the alcove to join him, Obba always disappears like a firefly into the night.

"We don't pray to dragons where I come from." Kal unwraps the cloth and begins removing objects: an incense holder shaped like a three-masted ship, a small velvet pouch, a handful of seashells.

I'm surprised. I assumed everyone worships the Thirteen. In Lagusa there is only one Temple, and it's where everyone goes to pray. I step deeper into the room.

"Who do you pray to?"

"It's not who, but what." Kal places incense into the masts of the ship. Then he opens the velvet pouch and draws out a pinch of salt, which he sprinkles in a circle around the ship. "My people pray to the stars and the sea."

I kneel beside him.

"We were traders before the war." Kal pours more salt on the ground, then runs his fingers through the white substance, creating ripples. "We lived on the edge of the Turka Sea. Once you leave our port, it takes three weeks of sailing with strong winds before the northern coast appears on the horizon. When you're surrounded by water, with emptiness as far as the eye can see, the only things you can count on are the stars."

Kal places the seashells on the waves of salt and uses a fire-strike to light the incense. Once the fire takes hold, Kal leans forward and blows it out, so that heady clouds of smoke waft from the glowing embers. Then he glances up at the wooden beams crisscrossing above us. His eyes seem to bore through the tiled roof, all the way to the empty, pale blue sky.

"At night, I keep looking at the stars, but they're different down here below the desert, aren't they?" He turns to me. "They're supposed to guide us home when we're in the middle of the sea, but I can't make heads or tails of the ones in Lagusa."

"I can teach you our stars," I say. "I'm not an astronomer, but I know enough to help you find your way if you're lost."

"Thanks." Kal gives me half a smile and I find myself half smiling back. Maybe it's because we shared our tears back at the Temple when his father died, but being here with him now doesn't feel like I'm with a stranger. "I'd like that."

"What's it like up north?" I ask before realizing he may not want to talk about his past, especially if it was a difficult one. "If you don't mind…"

He stares blankly at the smoke drifting from the incense, and just when I think I've been too nosy and he's not going to respond, he clears his throat. "Well, it's a lot different from Lagusa. Especially for families like mine."

"Why?"

"My mother was from Waldyria, like Sothpike, but my father was Merzan. When Sothpike betrayed the Ur Atum Asim, anyone with any connection to Waldyria was suspected of supporting Sothpike, even people like my mother, who had lived most of her life in Merza. I had just turned one when Merzan soldiers took everything we owned and forced my family into a camp with other Waldyrians." Kal scoffs. "It was a prison, except we didn't do anything wrong and our sentences only ended when we died. I don't have any memories from before, and now I'm haunted by the memories of my mother and brothers dying of starvation and disease in that camp."

I knew Waldyrians were shunned in Merza, but I've never seen one in Lagusa before now, and I had no idea they were being starved to death in camps. Kal's family should have been safe here, regardless of his mother's heritage.

"I'm so sorry," I say, even though the words aren't enough.

Kal nods. "Thank you." He lets out a big sigh. "I was ten when our captors abandoned the camp. Sothpike was destroying everything in his path, and resources were too scarce to waste on prisoners. My father bought a ship and we spent the next six years sailing the Turka Sea. Until Sothpike ruined that, too. Trade became impossible with Sothpike's ships patrolling the sea. They attacked our ships, stole our cargo, and we lost everything again. My father heard about some people preparing to flee across the desert and decided we should join them. We had nothing left and the risk seemed worth it. He

sold our ship for scrap to help pay for our passage to Lagusa.
Then we crossed the desert and I ended up here." For the first
time Kal looks me in the eyes. "With you."

A shock runs through me, starting where our eyes meet and
moving all the way to my core, sending vibrations throughout my body along the way. Time stands still. I can't blink—
I don't want to. I want him to keep looking at me with his
green-brown eyes, but he turns away. Time resumes—a bird
trills outside and the spigot creaks as someone turns the knob
to get water.

Kal laughs, and I tell myself to get it together. "Enough
about me. I'm sure there are others with better stories than
mine. Tell me about you."

"Me?"

"Yes, you. I want to know you."

No one's ever said they wanted to know me before, and
my stomach flutters. "I don't know what to say."

"Sure you do. Just talk. I'm listening."

I'm grateful for the dimness of the jirkana so that he can't
see the redness blossoming on my cheeks. "Well, until a little
over a week ago, my life was boring. Training, school, and
chores filled my time. On the hottest days we swam in the
river, and at the end of every harvest we attended the festival
at the Temple. Prayers at the mazan in the morning, dinner
with my family at night. That was life. And I miss it so much."

I choke back a sob and wipe a tear from my eye.

"I'm sorry—I didn't mean to make you cry."

"No, it's not your fault." I take a few deep breaths and
the pain in my chest subsides. "It just... It really hurts, you
know?"

"I know." Kal pours a bit of salt into the bowl of water and swirls it around with his finger. "I perform this ritual every day. I've done it more in Lagusa than I ever did back home."

"Why?"

"My father always said prayers to the sea centered him, made him feel at peace." Kal dips his fingers in the water and then touches them to the base of his throat. "May our words spread peace like ripples on the water." He dips his fingers again and places them on his forehead. "May our thoughts be a guide in the darkness like the stars in the sky." After another dip in the water, he touches his heart. "And may our might bear down on our enemies like a crashing wave. We pray for wind in our sails, calm seas, and a bountiful catch. The sea is our mother and our reaper and we respect her lest we die in her arms."

"Do you feel at peace?" I ask when he's finished.

Kal shakes his head. "Not yet."

I point at the bowl of water. "May I?"

Kal pushes the bowl toward me and I dip my fingers in the water, repeating Kal's ritual. He speaks the words for me when I falter. Afterward, I don't feel any different. I'm still angry and sad that Obba is dead.

"Why do you keep performing the same ritual if you still feel the same?"

"I have to do something," Kal replies. "I want to feel something besides anger and pain. I don't want to be lost anymore. I know that eventually things will change, but I can't sit back and wait for that to happen. I have to do something in the meantime, even if it feels like there's no point."

Kal's words settle in my heart like sand soaking up rain.

He's right—we have to do something. I can't sit in a darkened room and reminisce about the past. That's not what Obba would want me to do.

Isrof Khoum would have wanted me to do what is right.

The last of the incense burns out and Kal dumps the bowl of water on the floor, dissolving the rings of salt. The water seeps into the stone, into the sand beneath. I stand and go to the shelf where Obba's sword lays, reaching for my daggers and leather gauntlets from the riser below.

"What are you about to do?" Kal places the ship and the bag of salt in the cloth sack while I strap the leather around my forearms.

"I'm not sure yet. But I think it's going to involve killing the Mistress."

"If you kill her, then all the Dambi will be set loose. Do you want a wild horde roaming the streets?"

"They're more dangerous with her controlling them. She has to die."

Kal and I face each other, both of us sizing the other one up. His dark hair is cut at his shoulders and falls in soft waves, his shoulders broad, and though he's tall, he isn't rail thin like Nez. Kal looks like he can take care of himself.

"Which do you prefer—blades or bows?" I ask, breaking the building tension.

He raises a brow. "You want me to help you?"

"I don't mind going after the Mistress by myself. But you said you want to do something. Something more than performing a ritual that doesn't bring you peace. So—blade or bow?"

I move aside so Kal can inspect the weapons. There aren't

many left—most of the refugees have armed themselves in case
of a Dambi attack on our home, but there are a few weapons
still available capable of delivering mighty blows.

Kal reaches for Obba's sword, but I place my hand on his
arm to stop him.

"Not that one. You can pick any other weapon, but you
can't have that one."

He takes a sword from a higher shelf. This one doesn't
have a curved blade like Obba's, but it's sharp and made of
the finest steel.

"This one," he says, testing its weight. "I could make good
use of this sword." He ties the belt around his waist and
sheathes the sword before leaning against the wall, his arms
crossed. "Alright, now what?"

Omma forbade me and Nez from leaving the house—in
fact, she won't allow any of the children to leave. We still
don't know what the Mistress is doing to the ones her Dambi
have stolen, and Omma doesn't want to find out by having
her own taken from her. But I know we can't stay holed up
forever. The stone wall surrounding our house will fall if
enough Dambi set against it with their claws. I have to do
something before that happens. I have to find a way to stop
the Mistress and her Dambi, and hiding isn't going to help.

"Now I have to get my brother out of bed." I grab Nez's
favorite bow and a quiver of arrows. "And find a way out of
the house without notifying my mother or any of the refugees patrolling our house."

Kal smiles. "Let me work on the second one." He grabs the
bowl and the cloth sack. "I'm pretty good at getting around
undetected. I grew up under the watchful eye of the remains

of the Merzan empire. The only way I could do anything was by sneaking around."

"Alright," I laugh as we exit the jirkana, the sound surprising me. Kal made me forget for one short moment that Obba is gone. I thought I would never laugh again, that nothing could take away my sadness, but I was wrong. "I'll get my brother and wait for you in the garden."

The last rays of the setting sun beat down on me as I walk the stone path leading from the jirkana to the house. I keep an eye out for Omma and find her helping a woman with shaking hands drink a cup of water. Beside her, a Daughter lifts the woman's head.

Ever since Obba's death, Omma has thrown herself into helping the sick and wounded, barely sleeping and eating to care for them. It's as if she keeps working so that she won't have time to think about what happened to Obba, and she'll be too tired to dream about him when she finally passes out from exhaustion.

I slip quietly into Nez's room, quickly pulling the curtain closed behind myself. The room is dark, the curtains covering the windows drawn tight, and it takes a moment for my eyes to adjust.

When they do, I see Nez lying on a pallet on the floor, curled up into a ball. I want to lie down beside him, hold my brother in my arms, and cry with him, but I can't. Not anymore.

I crouch down and shake his shoulder. "Nez, get up." When he doesn't answer, I shake him harder. "Nezra Khoum, wake up!"

"I'm not asleep," Nez mumbles.

"Then get up."

"Why? What's the point? Obba is dead."

"That's why you *have* to get up." I rub Nez's arm. "Obba is gone, so you have to take his place."

Nez finally turns away from the wall. His eyes are red. "What are you talking about? No one can take Obba's place."

"That doesn't mean you can't try." I stand and pull on Nez's arm. "Come on, it's time for us to do something about the Mistress."

"What?" Nez yanks his arm out of my grasp and scoots away from me. "You know what—I don't want to know. It's too early for your nonsense."

I hand the bow and arrows to Nez but he doesn't take them. "Come on, big brother. You can't lie in bed all day."

"Fine, I'll concede that it's probably time I got out of bed, but the next step in dealing with my grief isn't going after the Mistress."

I lean the weapons against the wall. "I'm going with or without you."

He sighs. "You're serious about this?"

I nod.

"And what are you going to do to her?"

"Kill her."

Nez's eyes widen. "All by yourself?"

"I have someone to help me," I reply. "One of the refugees. He's lost everything because of this war. And I bet there are hundreds more people out there willing to die if that means they'll have the slightest chance of taking the Mistress and her Dambi with them."

"Then let them kill the Mistress," Nez says. "Let the people who are trained for stuff like this handle things. We're just kids, Naira. The Mistress is not our responsibility."

"She's all of our responsibility! Protecting Lagusa from people like the Mistress, and like Sothpike—"

"And like Hamala?"

I'm stunned by Nez's question. Hamala is nothing compared to the Mistress. Nez was right when he told me to let teachers and watchguards deal with Hamala, but they aren't enough to handle the Mistress. It's going to take everyone and everything we have to free Lagusa.

"Stopping the Mistress and stopping Hamala are not the same. This isn't some petty squabble with the village bully. The Mistress is killing people—our people—and anyone who can fight needs to do whatever it takes to stop her." I crouch next to Nez. "We *have* to do this. Not for honor, nor riches, nor glory. Not even for Obba. We do it because it needs to be done. It's the right thing to do."

I stand and hold out my hand.

Nez closes his eyes and sighs. "It's the right thing to do." Then he grabs my hand and I pull him to his feet. I pass him his bow and arrows.

"What about Omma?" Nez asks as he slings them over his shoulder.

"She'll do everything she can to stop us from leaving. We can't tell her."

"So we'd better make it back alive," Nez agrees, "or she'll kill us."

CHAPTER TWELVE

NEZ AND I PASS THROUGH THE COURTYARD, AVOIDING the eyes of those refugees on guard duty. Both of us are on the lookout for Omma, but the setting sun and noises coming from the kitchen tell me she'll be busy for a while preparing dinner.

"Should we leave her a note?" Nez asks. "So she won't worry too much?"

"Yes, but be quick about it."

Nez changes direction. Instead of going toward the garden at the back of the house, he makes his way to the opposite side of the courtyard, where our parents' bedroom and father's study are. I stop and Nez motions for me to keep moving.

"Come on," he whispers, but I stand still.

I haven't been in Obba's study since before he died. It's different than the jirkana. The study was his special space, where he spent most of his time when he was home, where I ran to find help whenever I had a problem.

Nez grabs my hand and pulls, forcing me to follow.

If Nez can face our father's study, then I can as well. Stepping around the injured slows us down, but we make it to our father's study undetected by Omma and the Daughter.

Inside, Nez grabs a metal stylus and dips it in ink. He scratches out a message on parchment, pausing to think and tapping the stylus against his chin between words.

I stand with my back against the heavy curtain covering the entryway, not ready to step all the way in. The last time I was in Obba's study, he sat at his desk poring over our family accounts, sliding the wooden disks on his counting frame from one side to the other with a satisfying click as he tallied each column. His staff rested on hooks on the wall behind him—now it lies in pieces on his desk. All of its beautiful etchings of the dragon gods are destroyed.

I step forward and run my fingers over the broken pieces of wood. I remember a normal night only months ago—Obba coming home and passing the staff to me while he removed his sandals at the front door. I followed him to his study, telling him about being chosen as one of the fire maidens, that I had the honor of tending the ritual fires at the harvest festival.

He listened as he always did, asking questions, wondering what was for dinner and being delighted to hear we were having his favorite meal: a stew of potatoes and lamb called papago, rice with cream, leeks wrapped in cabbage, and kish rafti—palm-sized squares of vanilla-flavored cake with a rosewater syrup drizzled on top and garnished with almonds—for dessert.

We had a feast on a night filled with laughter. It was hard to believe that memory was from only a few months ago, before everything changed. Before Obba was taken from the people who love him. Who still need him.

If I stay in the study for another heartbeat, I'll break down crying.

"I'm going outside," I say, my voice thick. "One of us should keep an eye out for Omma. Hurry up."

"Wait, I'm almost finished." Nez sprinkles sand on the paper to soak up the wet ink. Then he rubs the tears from his eyes and stands. "I miss him so much."

"Me too." My own eyes are welling to match Nez's. "That's why we have to do this. Obba would want us to make things right."

Nez rolls up the note, ties it with string, and follows me back into the courtyard. I wait behind a pillar while he puts the note in his room—one of the first places Omma will search when we don't show up for the evening meal. Then we make our way to the garden, hiding in shadows and doorways as we pass the mazan on the right, then the kitchen, Omma's voice giving instructions to someone assisting her.

The garden is behind the kitchen, between the house and the jirkana. Filled with apricot and fig trees and plants with dark green leaves, the garden's center contains a clay basin of water. We find Kal in the shadows by the wall separating our house from the neighbor's.

A smile flashes across Kal's face when he sees me, and my belly somersaults. I'm glad I was right about Kal, because I would have felt like a fool if he hadn't followed through with his promise to help.

"The house next door is abandoned," Kal says as we approach. "We can escape through there."

"Wait—who are you?" Nez asks Kal before turning to me. "When you said you had someone to help, I was expecting someone...with a little more experience."

"I've got experience." Kal rests his hand on the hilt of his sword. "I've captained my own boat and sailed the Turka Sea twice. I've fought off slavers and survived more storms at sea than I can count. I was stranded on a deserted island for two weeks. No food, no water. I survived on only what I could kill and find. What about you?"

Nez puffs out his chest. "Well, that all sounds very impressive, but have you ever fought this hellion?" He jerks a thumb at me.

"Nez!" I elbow my brother and he pretends to double over in pain.

"I tell you, she's worse than any of your maritime misadventures," Nez groans. Then he straightens up, his face finally serious. "Nezra Khoum." He offers Kal a bow. "But my friends call me Nez."

Kal returns the bow. "Kal Sayeed."

"Now that we're all acquainted, can we get going?" I ask, my eyes darting from Kal to Nez. "Someone will be patrolling the garden soon and Omma will be looking for us to help with the evening meal."

Nez walks over to the eight-foot-high wall. "So, I guess we're climbing over?"

"Are you ready?" Kal asks.

"Ready as I'll ever be," Nez replies, adjusting his bow and arrows. Kal gives Nez a boost over the wall, and then it's my turn. Nez pulls me up and together we help Kal.

We use a rotted tree stump to help us get down on the

other side of the wall. Kal leads the way through an over-grown garden and over cracked tiled floors, dust and leaves stirring in our wake. At the front door, Kal rattles the latch. It's rusted shut, so he jimmies his sword into the horizontal key slot and taps on the handle until he knocks the metal bar loose. The door springs open, but before I can step outside, Kal blocks the doorway with his arm.

"Are you sure you want to do this? It's going to be very dangerous."

"I know." I step forward and Kal lowers his arm. "But we can't let that stop us. We have to—"

A Dambi shriek cuts off the rest of my words, raising the hair on the back of my neck. I grab my daggers and step out-side, Kal and Nez right behind me. I look down both ends of the road but all is clear. The Dambi is close, but not close enough to see. Or smell.

"Come on, we have to get to the meeting house," I whis-per. Kal nods.

Nez takes point. "Follow me."

The streets are dark—none of the fire basins that line the roads are lit—but Nez knows the way. He leads us around corners and down dark alleys, taking effort to avoid roam-ing Dambi. It isn't easy, but we know this area of the village by heart, every nook and cranny.

The first Dambi we catch sight of is digging through a pile of refuse and eating the vermin it finds within. Quicker than a cat, it pounces on rats that try to scurry away, stabbing them with its claws and eating them whole.

"How do we fight that?" Nez whispers as we sneak past.

I don't know. The three of us going against even one Dambi

is foolish, and the Mistress has a horde of them at her command. But we have to keep going anyway.

Down the next road, we see two Dambi dragging a crying girl out of a residence. While one Dambi grips the girl around the neck, a second, smaller one attacks those trying to protect her.

"We have to help," I say, pulling out my daggers.

"Already on it," Nez replies, letting loose an arrow. It hits one of the Dambi square in the eye and it howls in pain, letting the girl go.

The smaller Dambi turns its attention to Nez and shrieks. Nez lets a second arrow fly, this time blinding the first Dambi in its other eye, and I run toward the small Dambi. It swipes at me and I slide beneath its grasp. Kal grunts and blocks an attack from the blinded one with his sword.

Once I'm back on my feet, I slash at the Dambi's stomach. My daggers are sharp, but they barely penetrate the creature's thick skin. I'll have to stab it.

But before I can try again, the Dambi slams me to the ground with bone-jarring force and grabs my ankles, its claws digging into my skin. I attack the Dambi's hands and arms with quick jabs, making the creature howl, but it won't let go.

Nez shoves the girl back inside her house and yells for her family to lock the door. Then he shoots an arrow at the small Dambi, this one embedding in its neck and drawing blood. Another arrow whizzes by, aimed at the small Dambi's eye, but it releases its grip on me long enough to knock the arrow out of the air.

I take that chance and use my free leg to swipe the Dambi's feet out from under it. The creature falls on its back, Nez pins its hands to the ground with arrows, and I jump on its chest, plunging my daggers deep into its heart. The Dambi shudders, then stops moving, black blood dribbling out its mouth.

Breathing heavily, I stand and face Nez. "We did it. We killed a Dambi."

A grin splits Nez's face. "Damn right we did."

"A little help over here?" Kal is still struggling with the blinded Dambi. His clothes are ripped from Dambi scratches and his arms tremble with the strain of holding the monster at bay. It tries to yank Kal's sword out of his hands but he holds on—barely.

"Right," Nez says, nocking another arrow. He releases, and the arrow shaves off a few of Kal's hairs before hitting the Dambi in the chest.

The creature screams in pain, but it isn't down yet. I run behind the Dambi, jump on its back, and reach around to sink my daggers into its heart. The Dambi howls but remains on its feet. It lets go of the sword to swat at me like a pesky fly, knocking me off its back. I land on the ground with a thud, banging my shoulder on the hard dirt. Something sharp stabs me in the side, and I groan in pain.

Fighting the Dambi with Obba was different. Then, I felt invincible with him at my side. But the Dambi killed my father, and now they want to kill me too. Nothing can replace the hatred I feel for these monsters, but there's something new creeping up my back: fear.

Blind and with blood pouring out of its chest, this Dambi is more angry than hurt. It charges in my direction, and I roll away as Kal slices the beast across the abdomen. Nez shoots two more arrows into the Dambi's back.

Ignoring the pain in my side and my bruised shoulder, I get back on my feet. Howls and screeches fill the street, and the smell of rotting meat grows stronger.

"We have to go." I pull Kal out of the way of the Dambi's claws. It swings its arms wildly, its blind rage making it even more dangerous.

Kal nods and I motion for Nez to follow. We run in the opposite direction of the oncoming Dambi. Around corner after corner, down more deserted roads, finally stopping to catch our breath in the doorway of a boarded-up shop. Across the street is the meeting house, a stone structure where the Subaans gather to govern the village. Usually filled with farmers and merchants waiting their turn to speak to the Subaans, the terrace outside of the meeting house is filled with Dambi instead, all of them roaming restlessly, their cloudy white eyes the same color as the rising moon.

"How do we get in there?" Kal asks, still breathing heavily.

"Why don't we rest for a moment while we figure out our next move?" I tug on the locked door. It won't open, so I try Kal's trick and shove one of my daggers into the metal lock. After a few taps, the metal bar on the other side of the door pops loose and I push the door open. From the many piles of floor pillows and cushions scattered about, I guess that's what the shop sold when it was still open. Lucky for us, the place wasn't picked clean during the looting when the Dambi first attacked the village almost a week ago and we can make ourselves comfortable while we figure out what comes next.

"You learn fast," Kal says to me as he steps inside the dark shop.

"Yes, my sister the criminal," Nez jokes and ducks when I try to pop him on the back of his head.

I close the door and put the metal bar back in place. I rest with my back against the wood, waiting for my vision to stop swirling. When the world stabilizes, I pull one of the boards off the window so I can see what's happening across the street.

"So, who are you two?" Kal asks as he settles on a pile of cushions.

Nez lounges on a stack of pillows. "What do you mean?"

"I've never seen anyone move that fast before," Kal replies. "I could barely keep up with you both. And the way you took down that Dambi… I've never seen anything like it."

I turn away from the window to see Kal staring at me, waiting for an answer. "I don't know," I say with a shrug that aggravates the wound in my side and makes me suck air in through my teeth.

"Our father's been training us since we could walk," Nez adds, not noticing my discomfort. "Maybe that's what makes us different."

The room tilts on its side. Unable to keep my balance, I sink to the floor, my hand leaving a trail of blood on the wall. Pain fills my head and I groan.

Nez scrambles to my side. "Naira! Are you alright?"

I shake my head and lift my tunic. Blood pours out of a gash in my side.

"By the Fires!" Nez exclaims when he sees the wound. "Why didn't you say something earlier?"

"It's not that bad," I say, reminding me of the first time I met Kal in the Temple. He said the same thing about the gashes in his arm that required stitches. At least I only have one to his three, so I'm doing better than he was. I try to laugh, but it comes out more like a hoarse bark that aggravates my aching head.

Nez puts his hand over the wound to stop the blood flow. The cut isn't too deep and not nearly as wide as Kal's wounds. I can probably get away with having it bandaged, no stitches necessary. But there is a lot of blood.

"I'm going to have to cauterize the wound." Kal rips a flowery pillow to shreds and dabs away the blood with fabric, turning the yellow pattern brown. "To stop the bleeding." He turns to Nez. "We're going to need a fire and something for her to bite down on." Nez gets on his feet and begins scavenging through the drawers and counters of the old shop. While he searches, Kal presses more fabric against the wound and brushes the hair away from my sweaty forehead.

"Don't worry. You're going to be fine. I've done this plenty of times."

"When you sailed the Turka Sea?"

Kal laughs, his hand resting on my cheek. "You never know what's going to happen when you're out on the water, so you have to be ready for everything."

Nez returns with the lit stump of a candle and a small pillow. "This was all I could find."

"It'll do." Kal holds the pillow out to me. "Bite on this."

I put the short end of the pillow in my mouth and bite down, a bursting pain in my head forming when I press my teeth into the fabric. Memories of my last headache flood my thoughts, and I hope this doesn't mean I'm going to have another nightmare.

Kal takes one of my daggers and holds it over the flame. When it's hot, he looks me in the eye.

"Ready?"

I nod, my eyes wide and my brow covered in a sheen of sweat. Nez holds my hand.

Kal squeezes my skin together and presses the heated metal against the wound. He holds it there for half a breath. White-hot searing pain erupts from the wound and spreads throughout my body. I bite down hard on the pillow, so hard I think I'll break my teeth and my aching head will shatter. I want to scream out but I know I can't, not with us being so close to the Dambi, so all I can do is moan.

Kal heats the metal and presses down again. Tears pour out of my eyes as I gasp for air.

When he touches me with the hot metal the third time, I pass out.

CHAPTER THIRTEEN

THIS TIME, IT ISN'T A NIGHTMARE, BUT A SOFT, LOVELY dream. It's night, and I'm at a party like the ones we have in Lagusa during special occasions like weddings and births, only grander. The walls are draped with bright fabrics, colored-glass lanterns hang from the ceiling, and tables piled high with spicy food and bottles of sweet wine are scattered throughout the room.

I step inside and am immediately surrounded by shadowy figures dancing and playing instruments. Since everything else about the scene looks normal, I'm surprised by the shadows. But even though I can't see anyone's face, I'm not scared of them. I walk among them, and in my attempt to avoid a drunken dancer, I almost bump into another shadow. I offer a quick apology, but the shadow doesn't even look at me. They continue talking with their partner, as if I'm not there. Just as I realize I can't hear what they're saying, I also realize that no one at this party notices me.

I want to explore, join in the dancing, but I have a feeling that there's something I need to see. I make my way to the far end of the room where two massive maugrabs lounge in front of three empty chairs atop a dais. A shadow man paces near the left chair.

The man seems worried. I put my foot on the first step, but something tells me that he's not the reason I'm here, so I back away. I find myself drawn to a set of guarded doors to the right of the dais. I slip past the guards and enter a sitting room furnished with embroidered pillows, low tables, and a pair of painted screens. I pass through an opening between the screens where I find two figures dancing. A shadowy man pulls a woman close, but she's not like the others. Her face is clear, her smile warm, her eyes shining, her deep brown skin shimmering in the lamplight. Everything about her looks expensive, from her finely woven clothes to the golden jewelry wrapped around her throat, wrists, ankles, and waist. She wears her thick, dark hair in braids piled high atop her head. Kohl rings her eyes and her lips are stained red while sparkling gems dangle from her ears.

Bright lights, like the ones that flashed in the sky in that nightmare I had in the tombs, flicker in the woman's brown eyes.

I immediately know she's the reason I'm here. I've never seen her before, but I know she must be someone important.

The man murmurs something in her ear and she giggles, her laugh sweet and light. She looks at her shadow partner with love and he caresses her cheek.

Then they both stiffen, as if someone has called their names. They share a kiss before the man pushes one of the screens aside and exits the room. Through the open doors, I watch him clasp hands with the man from the dais and steer him away from the sitting room. They walk away arm in arm, like brothers.

Behind me, the woman throws her shoulders back, lifts her chin, and adjusts the heavy gold ropes around her waist. I follow her into the main room. Immediately, the music stops and the partiers face the dais. The woman stands in front of the middle chair with the two shadowy figures flanking her sides—the man she kissed on her left, the other on her right. When she faces the room, the maugrabs sit up on their haunches.

She nods to each man before holding her hands out to both of them. Once they connect, she raises her arms in the air. The partiers cheer, the music swells, and the maugrabs roar.

I try to move closer to the dais—I want to ask the woman what's going on—but I can't move.

You must awaken, the many voices from my nightmare in the tomb say, the sound reminding me of a flickering flame.

And I do.

My eyes fly open. Nez is pointing an arrow at a dark shape in the shadows. Something lurks in a doorway behind the counter, and my first thought is that a Dambi must have found its way into the shop with us. I reach for my daggers but they're missing. Ignoring the scorching pain in my side, I prop myself up on my elbows.

"Give me my daggers," I bark, trying to sound stronger than I feel.

Immediately, Kal is by my side, his hands on my shoulders, trying to get me to lie back down. I swat at him but he avoids my attempts.

"Calm down, everything's going to be alright." Kal puts more pillows behind my head and turns to Nez. "Put your weapon down. Can't you see she's not a Dambi?"

Slowly, Nez lowers his bow. "Who are you, then?"

"Someone who's been looking for people like you." A young woman steps into the shop, the light of the candle reflected in her eyes but the rest of her face covered by a dark scarf. She carries a spear.

"What does that mean?" Nez asks.

"I saw how you helped that girl back there," she replies. "We need more people like you. People who aren't going to sit back and let the Mistress steal children out of their beds."

"Well, you found us." Nez slings his bow over his shoulder. "Now what?"

"Now we meet up with the others." The young woman motions toward me. "Can she walk?"

"Yes, I can walk." I'm annoyed that she didn't address me directly, as if I can't speak for myself. Kal tries to help me stand but I shrug away his efforts. Every movement seems to pull on the wound and I gasp with pain as I rise, but I get to my feet on my own. Sweat glistens on my forehead and I wipe it away, grateful that at least the headache is gone.

"Nez, where are my daggers?"

Nez reaches down by the candle to pick them up. I breathe a sigh of relief when he hands them to me and I slide them back into their sheaths on my forearms.

"Nez?" the young woman asks. "And are you Naira?"

I share a glance with Nez. "Yes, and who are you?"

The woman removes the scarf. "You don't remember me?"

I look closely. She's about my age, tall, with wide eyes and full lips, her skin dark and her hair thick. She looks almost familiar, like someone I saw in a dream.

"I'm Rima. Rima Okuba. Remember?"

"Rima," I repeat, the name bringing back years of child-hood memories. We were friends before Rima's mother died and she and her older sister were sent away to live with their grandmother. I learned to swim with Rima at my side, Nez splashing and dunking us every chance he got.

Nez grins. "Rima! How long has it been? Six years? Seven?"

Rima laughs. "Just about."

With a smile on my face, I wrap my arms around my old friend. Pain flares from the wound and I wince when Rima returns the hug.

"I'm sorry," Rima says, pulling away. "Did I hurt you?"

I place a hand over the wound to soothe the pain. "No, I'm fine."

"Good, because we've got a ways to go." Rima replaces her scarf. "Come on." She motions for us to follow her, but Nez hangs back.

"I don't think this is a good idea anymore," he says.

"What do you mean?" I ask.

"Going after the Dambi, attacking the Mistress," Nez re-plies. "We should go back home. Naira, you could have died. In fact, if Kal hadn't been here, you probably would've."

"Yes, but Kal is here and I didn't die." I rest a hand on Nez's shoulder. It's something I saw Obba do when he was trying to guide someone. It's a reassuring gesture, one that I expe-rienced myself countless times, and one that I miss. I have to be that guiding comfort for Nez now.

"We've come too far to stop now. And I'm fine."

"I saw your face when Rima hugged you." Nez brushes my hand off his shoulder. "You didn't look fine."

Mimicking Obba isn't enough. Nez doesn't seem reassured at all. But I can't take on the Mistress and her Dambi without him.

"It's a bit tender, that's all." This time, I grab Nez's hand and hold it within my own. "I promise. I won't get hurt again."

"You can't promise that." Nez doesn't let go of my hand, though. "But you can promise me that you'll be more careful."

"I promise."

"Alright, enough sentimentality." Nez adjusts his bow. "Let's see what death threat awaits us next."

Kal claps Nez on the shoulder and smiles at me. I can't help smiling back.

"Are we ready?" Rima asks and I nod. Rima once again motions for us to follow her to the back of the store. Behind the counter, through the old storeroom, there's a ladder leading to an opening in the ceiling.

"The streets are overrun with Dambi," Rima says as she starts up the ladder, "so we've taken to the rooftops."

"Who is the 'we' you keep mentioning?" Nez asks as he climbs the rungs.

I favor my right side, keeping my right arm low so that it doesn't pull on the wound as I begin my ascent. But that doesn't mean it's easy. A dull ache accompanies each step upward and I take sharp breaths through gritted teeth to keep from crying out.

"You can rest if you have to," Kal calls from below. Unable to speak and feeling light-headed, I shake my head and keep moving.

"...part of the resistance," Rima is saying when I reach the top. "We're going to take back our village and save the others trapped in the meeting house."

"How?" Nez asks. He and Rima are leaning over the edge of the building, watching the street below. I take a few deep breaths before joining them, Kal right beside me.

We're staring down at a group of Dambi snarling and biting at each other. It doesn't matter if there are no humans around. They still have the urge to attack, even if it's just one another.

"We're working on that part." Rima moves away from the ledge. "We don't have the numbers yet. That's why I'm out here, trying to find others to join. There are about three hundred of us at the Temple, rangers and watchguards, shopkeepers and farmers. All of us ready to give our lives to free Lagusa. But we need more. A lot more. We need the whole village to fight. Until then...we do what we can."

"Which is what?" Kal asks.

"Find new fighters and stop the Dambi from stealing more of us." Rima leads us to the other side of the roof, where wooden planks cover the space separating this building from the one across the alley. "Yesterday, we brought in twelve kids our age. That girl you helped—I'll let the resistance know where she lives and they'll send a team to save her and her family."

One by one we cross the planks. I have to hold my arms out for balance, which pulls at the wound. I take a sharp breath when I teeter too close to the edge, trying not to look at the Dambi roaming beneath my feet. We have to jump across a small gap to reach the next roof, my wound throbbing when I land hard on the other side, and then another bridge of planks takes us to a row of buildings that all share the same roof.

With every step, I grow more accustomed to the ache in my side, until I notice we're jogging from one building to the next. Everyone has been taking it slow because of me and that only makes me push myself harder, outpacing both Kal and Nez to run alongside Rima. I'm the shortest of the group, but I don't let that be an excuse to fall behind.

Through gardens and clothes drying on the line, across roofs where people sleep under the stars to ones where people sit huddled in corners, their eyes on the Dambi shrieking in the streets below, we make our way across the rooftops of Lagusa. The moon falls in the sky in front of us, while the horizon at our backs turns bluish white.

The statues atop the hill grow closer and closer as we progress. We'll be at the Temple soon, and I wonder how we'll get up the hill without being seen. When I'm about to ask, Rima stops running and lifts a trapdoor in the roof of the building we're on.

"Sometimes, we have to go underground." Rima drops down through the hole and I jump next. It's a short fall, but the jarring impact aggravates the pain in my side. I place a hand over the injury to calm it as I quickly move out of the way for Nez and Kal. Rima leads us down flight after flight of stairs through an apartment building where the curious peek from behind half-cracked doors, which slam shut when I catch anyone's eye.

In the cellar of the building, Rima knocks on a door, and a small cutout in the wood slides open.

"By the Fires of the Thirteen," says a male voice on the other side.

"My steps are guided by their light," Rima replies. In response, the guard removes a bolt and the door creaks open. Rima goes in first, bowing to the watchguard at the door. I do the same, as do Nez and Kal.

"You guys have secret codes and everything," Nez whispers in awe as the door is closed and bolted behind us. "This is like a real resistance. You're serious about this, aren't you?"

Rima laughs. "Yes, we're serious. We're going to take back our village."

Kal fills in the missing last words. "Or die trying?"

"If that's what it takes, yes." All traces of humor are gone from Rima's voice. "But I hope we win before it gets to that."

We enter a tunnel shored up by wooden beams. Oil lamps hang on the wall, lighting the narrow planks of wood on the ground. Rima grabs one of the lamps and holds it out in front of her.

The air grows stale as we move deeper in. Nez sneezes and I fight the urge to shush him. There is a solemnness hanging about the tunnel and I don't want to disturb it.

We finally emerge into a room filled with stone shelves carved in the wall from floor to ceiling. Long shadows from the lamp climb the walls, and pockets of light reveal bundles of cloth and knobby gray shapes on the shelves.

"What are these?" Nez grabs one of the long objects.

"The bones of someone's ancestor." Rima snatches it out of Nez's hand. The cloth unfurls to reveal a human femur.

Nez frantically dusts his hands on his trousers.

"Why?" he whines, his voice echoing in the cavernous room. "Why would someone leave their bones lying around?"

"Because this is how we used to honor the dead." Rima replaces the bone and wrapping on the shelf. "Once we learned where Sothpike was getting his Dambi from, we started burning their bodies instead."

I shake my head as I walk past Nez, still scrubbing his hands.

"Don't shake your head at me," he says. "It's not like you knew this was a secret burial ground."

"True, but I knew enough to not touch everything I see." I laugh at Nez's distress. He holds out his hands as if they are tainted by bone residue.

"Go ahead, laugh at me for being curious," Nez retorts. "You know, curiosity is a sign of great intelligence."

Kal snorts and Nez shoots him a dark look.

"Not you too," he says and Kal shrugs.

"If you're done, can we keep going?" I ask. Nez narrows his eyes at me, but he stays quiet. I turn to Rima. "Where to next?"

"To the Temple." Rima points at stone steps hugging the wall of the round room. "We're at the bottom of the catacombs, about ten flights below the Temple. We'd better get moving."

We go up the stairs, every flight bringing us to another room full of the dead. I wonder what would happen if Sothpike ever found this place. Some of the bodies have dried out pieces of flesh still clinging to their bones. Would he be able to turn them into members of his dead army, or are they too far gone? I wish I knew how he does it. How he brings the dead back to life.

That could be the key to stopping the Dambi without any more bloodshed.

By the time we reach the top of the steps, I'm ready for a rest. My legs ache from all the running and climbing, and the wound in my side spikes with pain. I'm not the only one who's exhausted. The others huff and lean against the wall for support.

"Do you do this every night?" Nez pants, wiping the sweat from his forehead.

"This was my first time out." Rima sucks in a deep breath when she steps onto the final landing. "Going down was easy. I didn't think it would be this bad coming back up."

"I'd almost rather fight a Dambi again," Nez says and I slap him on the back. "I said, 'almost.'"

The only one not completely worn out is Kal. "You've never had to repair a ripped sail while at sea. Ten flights of stairs are nothing compared to climbing the mainmast during a storm when all you have to hold on with are your legs."

"Aren't you amazing," Nez grumbles as he topples onto the landing.

I collapse on the dusty stone floor to catch my breath. The wall behind me begins to move and I scramble to my feet. I go for my daggers, but Rima holds out a hand to stop me.

"It's alright." Rima walks toward the moving wall. "We're here."

Holding the lamp out in front of her, Rima steps through the empty space left by the moving wall. There's nowhere else for us to go, so we follow her through the opening and find ourselves in the main room of the Temple, where all the injured and dead refugees once covered the entire floor.

Where Kal lost his father.

I glance at him to see if he's alright. He stands in the entrance, his eyes darting from the men and women sparring, polishing weapons, trying to sleep in dark corners. The children who run underfoot, the Daughters dishing out warm meals, the groups sitting on pillows on the floor, huddled over maps and papers.

When he doesn't move, I step toward him.

"Is everything okay?"

Kal doesn't seem to hear me—he stands in the same spot, transfixed, his brows furrowed, his eyes staring at something I can't see. I wonder what he's thinking about, what paralyzing memory has taken hold of him. I touch his arm and say his name. Finally, he looks at me.

"Sorry," he says. "This reminded me of the camps. I know it's not the same, but for a moment..."

Now I understand. I look around the Temple through his eyes, at those crammed together in the shadows, speaking in frenzied whispers. Cries from multiple children fill the room with irritation and fear, their unsettling wails echoing throughout the cavernous Temple. The room is filled with haphazard piles of baskets and cloth sacks containing the possessions of those who fled here to escape the Mistress's clutches. It's early morning and yet everyone looks tired, as if they haven't slept for days.

At first glance, the Temple seems disorganized, cramped, hopeless. But I also see the parents smiling at their laughing children, the excitement in a fighter's eyes as she perfects a move, the gentle way a Daughter helps an elderly woman stand. I don't see a people trapped, but a people who have come together to free those who can't free themselves.

"You don't have to apologize," I say, my hand still on his arm. "You spent most of your childhood in a camp. Of course it's going to affect you."

"I thought I had put all that behind me," Kal replies.

"Put all what behind you?" Nez and Rima are watching Kal, their eyes filled with concern.

Kal glances at me. I can tell he's hurting; his memories are heavy and he's going to have to carry them for the rest of his life.

"You don't have to talk about it if you don't want to," I say gently.

"I know," he says, patting my hand. "But people need to know what's been happening up north. Sothpike isn't the only one doing terrible things."

He tells them about the camps run by the Merzan army, how his family was rounded up for having ties to Waldyria. How he and his father were the only survivors from his family when the camp was abandoned and they were finally free to leave.

As he talks, Nez's and Rima's faces change expressions from shock to horror to sadness to anger. I imagine that's how I looked when I first listened to Kal's story. Like them, I'd never heard of the camps, and it reminds me how much I don't know about the rest of the world.

"How could we do that to our own people?" Nez looks ready to strike something. "You're a Merzan, just like us."

"That shouldn't have happened to anyone," Rima says.

"Waldyrian or not, no one should have to pay for Sothpike's crimes except Sothpike."

Kal takes in a deep breath and swallows. "Thanks. I don't think anyone's ever called me a Merzan. I've never been accepted before."

Nez claps Kal on the shoulder. "You're one of us whether they like it or not."

When Kal smiles, his face lights up, and I can tell he's fully in the Temple with us, his memories of the camps laid to rest. For now at least.

He turns to Rima and gestures at the room. "So, is this it?"

"Yes." Rima turns down the wick and hangs the lamp on a hook on the wall. "Welcome to the resistance."

CHAPTER FOURTEEN

"ALRIGHT THEN, WHERE DO WE START?" NEZ ASKS RIMA as he strides into the Temple, his bow slung across his chest and his hands on his hips.

Rima laughs. "You should start with some rest and a hot meal."

It's strange to walk into the Temple with unwashed feet and my shoes still on, but I push that aside and enter the cool darkness.

Rima wraps her arm around Nez's and pulls him deeper inside the building. "Come on."

"I guess we'd better follow," Kal says to me. We fall in step together and even though the Temple is filled with noise—swords clanging, children squealing, people talking—a silence settles around us. Ahead, Nez says something to Rima and she giggles. The quiet around Kal and me suddenly feels heavy with awkwardness, and I scramble to think of something to say.

"So…thanks for patching me up." My eyes are drawn to the smile that forms on his face.

"I was glad I could do it." He glances around the Temple and sighs. "I wasn't sure how I'd feel coming back to this place. Maybe angry or sad after what happened to my father, but I didn't expect to be reminded of the camps. It's almost scary how you can be going about your normal life and suddenly be hit with…things you'd rather forget."

"Or things that used to make you happy but now only bring pain." My thoughts are on Obba, how the jirkana and his study, once places of excitement and comfort, have become places filled with sorrow so overwhelming it hurts.

"No matter how hard I try, I'll never be able to put the past behind me. I'll never be free."

"You will," I say, my voice full of heartfelt assurance. "I've been so consumed with mourning my father that I thought I'd never find joy again. But you made me laugh yesterday in the jirkana. They say time heals all wounds, but I think having the right people around helps even more."

"The right people?"

"You know, people who love and support you. Family, friends…those kinds of people."

Kal glances at me. "You said I made you laugh. Does that mean I'm one of them?"

"Well, I mean…" I stammer. I don't know what to say. I like having Kal around, but I'm not going to tell him that when I have no idea what he thinks about me. "Maybe one day you could be. That is, if you wanted to."

"Maybe," he responds, setting off an explosion of butterflies inside me. "I guess we'll see."

I rub my clammy palms on my trousers, hoping he doesn't notice the way the sweat darkens the fabric. "I guess so."

Once again, I don't know what to say next. But a child no more than ten bumps into me as he's being chased by others. He falls on the floor and I help him stand. "Be careful."

"Sorry, samida," the boy says with a quick bow. He runs away laughing, the other children following with smiles on their faces.

I glance around the Temple and notice that there aren't many people my age among the resistance. A face here and there could be the right age, and I recognize a girl from school, but most are older adults or younger children. Has the Mistress taken the rest already?

We round a haphazard wall of bags and baskets piled so high I can't even see over them. Based on the patterns of the colorful cloth and the weave of the baskets, I can tell they belong to someone with lots of rubes to spare. Curious, I peer into the enclosed space. Heavy rugs and tasseled pillows cover the stone floor, and among the finery is someone very familiar.

Hamala sits cross-legged on the floor braiding the hair of someone who could be her younger sister. Half of the girl's dark, coily hair is loose and full, the other half in tight cornrows that follow the curve of her skull. In the far corner, an elderly man and a young boy are fast asleep on thick pallets while next to them another man and a woman sip tea from elegant glass cups with gold handles and gilded rims. A servant places a tray of bite-sized foods on a delicately carved low table next to them. If I didn't know better, I'd think they were spending a leisurely morning at home and not among those trying to defend our village from undead monsters.

I stare for a moment too long—Hamala notices me and curls her lip in annoyance. She huffs, drops the girl's hair, and glares at me.

"I should have known you'd show up," she says, her arms crossed. "Everywhere I go, here comes Naira Khoum."

I roll my eyes. "Not everything revolves around you. Some people actually want to help."

"And you think I don't? Why else would I be here?"

The younger girl turns to Hamala. "Because Omma made you. *You* wanted to hide in the stables."

Hamala shoves the girl. "Shut up."

The younger girl sticks out her tongue in response.

The way Hamala and the girl interact reminds me of how Nez and I tease each other. For the first time, I see Hamala as someone other than a bully, and that reminds me why I'm here. I've got to put away all that anger that rushes to the surface whenever Hamala and I cross paths and focus on what's really important: stopping the Mistress.

"Hamala!" the woman admonishes. "Be nice to your sister." She notices me standing in the makeshift entrance. "And don't be rude. Invite your friend inside for tea."

"She's not my friend!" she says.

"We are *not* friends," I say at the same time.

We lock eyes. Instinctively, even though I know I'm not going to fight her, my muscles tense. I wait for Hamala to lunge at me or say something to try to rile me up, but she doesn't. Instead, she exaggerates rolling her eyes, breaking contact. I let out the breath I hadn't realized I was holding.

A hand clamps own on my shoulder, making me jump, but it's only Nez. "What're you looking at?" Before I can respond, he sees Hamala. "Ohhh." Nez places his hand on his bow. "Is she giving you trouble?"

Hamala stiffens and her sister's eyes open wide.

I swat Nez's hand away from his weapon. "By the Fires, Nez, calm down! We were just talking."

"You sure?" He looks around and behind us. "Where are her minions?"

For the first time, Hamala's aggressive facade falters. "I don't know. I haven't seen most of them since this all started."

Hamala's sister wraps an arm around her shoulders. "They're gonna be alright, Lala. I promise."

Any other time I would have laughed at someone calling Hamala *Lala*. The cute, childish nickname doesn't suit someone like the Hamala I know, but it's obvious the Hamala at home and the one in the streets are not the same person.

Hamala shrugs off her sister's condolences. "Whatever. I'm not worried about them. They can take care of themselves." She's trying to sound unconcerned, but she's not fooling anyone.

I almost want to offer her a kind word, but then she glares at me again.

"What am I, some kind of monkey in a cage? Why don't you go do something and quit staring at me?"

I know she's lashing out because she's scared, but she doesn't want me to console her. She has her sister for that. But before Nez and I turn to walk away, Hamala gives me a terse nod, as if to say we're in this together.

It seems the death and destruction we all suffered has given us both a sense of perspective, shown us what really matters.

I return the gesture. She goes back to braiding her sister's hair and I step away from the Mugabe family in peace.

The truce holds. For now, at least.

Nez and I catch up with Kal and Rima, who are waiting for us nearby.

"Did you see someone you know?" Rima asks. "A friend?"

"Not a friend," I respond. "But yeah, she's someone I know." The others wait, as if expecting me to say more, but there's nothing I want to say. I'm not proud of how I reacted to Hamala in the past, and my shame keeps me quiet.

Nez's stomach growls, breaking the uneasy silence.

"I recall you promising us food," he says to Rima, rubbing his grumbling stomach. "Is there any chance we could have some now?"

Laughter breaks out from the four of us.

"You know, I'm feeling a little hungry, too," Kal says. "If it's not a bother."

"Of course, we don't want to be any trouble, but…" I join in, rubbing my empty stomach as well. "You did promise."

"Alright, alright," Rima says with a smile. "I'm trying to find us a quiet spot. There's usually one over in the alcoves. Follow me."

Around a group kneeling on the floor to pray, some of them with their hands raised to the ceiling; past a handful of children playing a secret game of ritska, shushing each other and hiding their clay disks whenever a Daughter looks their way; and away from a mother quieting a fussy baby, Rima leads us to an alcove containing a stoic carving of the dragon god Xergas the Strength-Giver. Flickering lamplight makes the shadows from her wings flutter, as if the statue is about to fly away.

Rima motions for us to sit on cushions strewn about the floor beneath the statue.

"Rest here for a bit and I'll see about getting some food," she says. "And I'll let the others know you're here and inform them about that girl you saved."

Nez doesn't need to be told twice to rest. He props his bow and quiver against the wall, gathers a pile of cushions, and lies down with his eyes closed.

"How can you go to sleep so easily?" I yank two cushions away from Nez's enormous pile and toss them on the floor for me and Kal to sit on.

"It's a talent," Nez replies, his arm resting over his eyes. "Now be quiet."

Kal has already moved his cushion near the wall, so I do the same. I sit down next to him, my legs crossed, and lean back against the smooth, white stone.

"How's your cut?" Kal lays the sword on the floor beside him.

I lift my tunic to check. A black blister about the length and width of my index finger stretches across the right side of my stomach. The puckered skin surrounding the wound is an angry red. Simply seeing the damage makes it hurt more and I quickly drop the fabric.

"It's healing," I say, even though it looks worse than I expected. I don't want him to think I'm weak.

"Good." Kal leans against the wall as well and gestures at a sleeping Nez. "Maybe your brother has the right idea. It's been a long night and I have a feeling we're not going to get many chances to sleep in the coming days."

But I'm not ready to go to sleep. I like sitting and talking to Kal in our alcove where it's silent, except for the sounds of Nez's deep breathing. The quiet amid the chaos reminds me of that time we spent in the Temple garden, or when we prayed together in the jirkana. The troubles of the world fade and it's just two people sharing a comfortable moment.

I want to tell Kal this, but I don't have the words. And besides, Kal has already closed his eyes, so I do the same and force myself to relax. But my mind keeps wandering to Omma—I regret not saying goodbye—to wondering what the Mistress might be doing to the children she captured. Is she torturing them? Killing them and turning them into Dambi?

Or is there something even more sinister involved?

It can't be half a hand before long, deep breaths come from Kal as well. Something heavy suddenly rests on my left shoulder. I open my eyes to find that it's Kal's head, his soft, wavy hair brushing the side of my face. I consider waking him so he can right himself but decide not to. I don't mind. In fact, a warmth creeps into my stomach, and I gently place my cheek against the top of Kal's head. When he doesn't stir, I leave it there and close my eyes.

I don't know what it is about him—I hardly know him, but we've had deeper conversations than I've ever had with anyone outside of my family. I like being near him, I like when he smiles at me, and I like hearing my name from his lips. None of the other boys in my village have ever affected me like this.

I hope Kal feels the same way.

I don't notice that I've drifted off into a dreamless sleep until I'm awakened by whispers. Nez and Rima are sitting across from me, talking quietly as they eat thick porridge out of wooden bowls.

"What happened to your grandmother?" Nez is asking.

"Te-Omma died a few years ago," Rima replies. "My sister and I have been taking care of each other since."

"I'm sorry about your grandmother," Nez says. "But at least you still have your sister."

"Thanks." Rima sighs. "It hasn't been easy, but Basheera and I are doing well. She works as a scribe so we have a roof over our heads, while I do everything else—the shopping, the cleaning, the cooking. Basheera is terrible at keeping house, and I can't work until I finish school, so it's a good arrangement for us."

Nez chuckles. "Basheera...I haven't thought about her in a long time. I'll bet she hasn't changed."

Rima giggles in response. "Yes, she's still as surly as ever. Probably even more than when we were children, if you can believe it. But deep down, she's a softy."

A breeze brings the scent of the porridge to my nostrils and I inhale deeply. My stomach responds by growling, this time even louder than Nez's did earlier. Hearing the noise, Rima and Nez turn my way.

"It's about time you woke up, lazy-bones," Nez teases. I shoot him a dirty look—everyone knows Nez is the lazy one—and he and Rima laugh.

"Here, eat up." Rima hands a bowl to me. "I have one for Kal as well."

I shake my shoulder and rouse Kal from his sleep. He sits

up and yawns, rubbing the sleep from his eyes. My body feels cold now that he's no longer resting on it.

"Was I sleeping?" Kal asks. Rima and Nez glance at each other and let out another laugh. Kal turns to me. "What's so funny?"

"Nothing, just Nez being Nez." I take the bowl, hoping my cheeks don't appear as flushed as they feel, and hand it to Kal. "Eat."

Rima passes me the second bowl, and I eagerly dig in. The food is good, but not as good as Omma's—she would have sprinkled crushed nuts on top.

As if he can read my thoughts, Nez says, "We should let Omma know we're safe. She must be worried out of her mind."

I turn to Rima. "Is there any way to get a message to our mother?"

"We have runners," Rima says. "Using the rooftops like we did, they could—"

"So, this is where you've been hiding," someone barks, startling all four of us. Basheera is short and squat, and even though she's the eldest by six years, her chubby face makes her look younger than her sister. But there's no denying they are related. She pushes her black wire glasses up her nose and huffs.

"You were supposed to report to me as soon as you returned! Instead, I had to search this whole damn Temple to find out if you made it back safely. *This* is why I didn't want you to go out."

"You shouldn't curse in the Temple," Rima says.

"If some brats can place bets on ritska in the Temple, then

I can damn well curse if I feel like it," Basheera snaps. Then she sighs and her expression softens. "I'm annoyed because I've been worried about you all night." Without skipping a beat, her brows furrow and her frown returns. "You should have known better."

"I'm sorry." Rima stands and tries to wrap her arms around her sister, but Basheera pushes her away and crosses her arms.

"I'm still angry with you," she says.

Rima smiles and plants a quick kiss on her sister's cheek. "Well, I'm here, and I'm safe. And I've brought some friends. You remember Naira and Nez Khoum, don't you? And that's Kal." Rima turns to Kal. "I'm sorry, I didn't get your last name."

Kal rises to his feet and bows deeply. "Sayeed. Kal Sayeed. Pleasure to meet you."

"Sayeed?" Basheera repeats and Kal bows again. She looks as if she wants to say more, but all she does is turn her critical eyes to me and Nez. "Well, at least someone knows how to greet their elder." We both scramble to our feet and bow.

Basheera barks out a laugh. "I was *obviously* joking," she says, even though it wasn't obvious at all. "Finish your food, then come find me in the library." With that, she turns on her heel and walks away.

"By the Fires, your sister scares me," Nez whispers to Rima once Basheera is out of earshot.

I agree with Nez, but I'll never admit it out loud. We finish eating quickly, then Rima shows us where to leave our dirty dishes with a Daughter before making our way through the Temple to the hall leading to the library. Passing through a set of heavy wooden doors, we enter a domed rotunda, the ceiling covered in mosaics of crisscrossed tiles, forming patterned arches above our heads.

Pillars surrounding the room bookend panels painted with brightly colored murals of the dragon gods, thirteen in all. The last panel, the fourteenth, is completely black, representing the dragon who attacked me in my nightmare: Ergenegon the Chaos-Bringer. Many see Ergenegon in Sothpike and pray for the Thirteen to banish him to the lake of fire deep in the caves of the Kilmare Mountains, like Crafulgar did to Ergenegon.

I'm more of the mind that we'll have to fight Sothpike ourselves if we want him gone for good. Praying to the gods only does so much.

"What are they looking for?" Nez asks as we walk past bookshelves. Carts filled with scrolls and texts are scattered about the room. Scribes and their assistants scurry between the carts and shelves as if they're searching for answers to age-old questions, scribbling on parchment, scouring texts for knowledge.

"Anything that will help us fight the Dambi," Rima replies. "Old tactics, rumors of special weapons and forgotten warriors—anything."

"Have they found any information on the Hands of God?" Kal asks.

"Why would anyone care about those betrayers?" I ask. "Why would they help now, after abandoning the Asim when she needed them the most? They're as much our enemies as Sothpike, if they're even around anymore."

"Dismiss the Hands all you want, but they may be our only hope of getting out of this mess alive," Basheera says as she approaches us, carrying a worn scroll in one arm. I open my mouth to protest, but Basheera glares at me over the rim of her glasses and I quickly clamp my lips shut. She turns to Kal. "We *are* looking for texts about the Hands of God. You should share what you know. But first—" she motions for a scribe standing nearby to join us "—this is Mandisa. She's going to record your stories."

"Our stories?" I ask.

"Yes." The scribe nods. She wears the traditional garb of the profession—black pants and black tunic. Like Basheera, braids hold back her thick hair. "We heard you fought a Dambi last night and survived. You have to tell us how."

"Actually, it was two Dambi," Nez says. He looks at me. "And *one* of us almost didn't make it."

All eyes turn to me and I wave away their concern. "I'm fine. Just a scratch. But why are the scribes searching for information about the Hands?"

Basheera pushes her glasses up the bridge of her nose. "How about this—Nez and Rima can talk to Mandisa about last night, and you two—" she points at me and Kal "—can talk to me about the Hands."

While Rima and Nez go with Mandisa down an aisle of towering bookcases, Kal and I join Basheera at a low table. We sit on pillows and tuck our legs beneath us.

Basheera unfurls the scroll and picks up a wooden stylus. She dips it in black ink, her hand hovering over the parchment. "Now, tell me what you know about the Hands of God."

I'm about to speak when Basheera shoots a glare at me again. She wants to hear from Kal, not me.

He thinks for a moment before speaking. "Well, all I know is they're very secretive and they live in the Kilmare Mountains that form the eastern border of Waldyria, Sothpike's homeland. They were supposed to aid the Ur Atum Asim Avari when Sothpike invaded Merza, but instead they closed themselves off to the world. Most Merzans call them traitors, backstabbers, liars, or fools—often all at once. A few years after they secluded themselves in their mountain fortress, word spread that the Hands had disbanded, been killed by Sothpike, or simply disappeared."

Basheera's stylus scratches across the paper, recording Kal's words. When she finishes writing, Basheera looks at Kal over the rim of her glasses. "Anything else?"

"They say there's a lake of green fire the Hands call the godfire burning in the Kilmare Mountains," Kal continues, "where they communicate with a being called the Three-Faced God."

"Three-Faced God?" I cut in. All I know about the Hands is their betrayal. I've never heard of them communicating with a special being. "What's that?"

"Exactly like it sounds—a god with three faces," Basheera explains. "Vanusha, the god of life; Kuresh, the god of death; and Uthera, the god who balances the two others. They all inhabit the same body, each of them taking control as needed, yet each of them existing at the same time. It's an old god, older than even our dragon gods. And it's one the Hands have been serving for hundreds of years, since before the Volsgarian War."

Until I met Kal, I didn't know people believed in gods other than the Thirteen. While the Three-Faced God is interesting, I feel the same way about it as I do about our dragon gods and Kal's god of the sea: praying only gets you so far. Real change depends on what *you* do.

I'm about to ask another question when Basheera cuts me off. "Don't tell me you've never heard of the Volsgarian War? What do they teach you in those useless schools?"

"I know about the Volsgarian War," I say with a roll of my eyes. But Basheera looks like she doesn't believe me, so I repeat what I learned from my teachers. "Centuries ago, Waldyria, Merza, and two other kingdoms, Johtan and Nauvia, were all part of Volsgaria. But there was a big war over who would be in control, the Bastard King or the Rightful Heir. It was so big even the dragon gods got involved. The fallen dragon Ergenegon supported the Bastard King, but they both were defeated by Crafulgar the Fiend-Slayer, and Volsgaria broke apart into the four kingdoms we have now."

Basheera sighs and I take it as a sign of approval.

"Now can I ask a question?"

"The correct word is *may*, and yes, you *may* ask a question."

I fight the urge to roll my eyes and try to remain polite. "Why is there so much interest in the Hands of God? They've either secluded themselves and won't bother to help us like they did the Asim, or they don't exist anymore. Shouldn't we be spending more time on figuring out how to defeat the Dambi without getting all of our people killed?"

"Because one of the refugees claimed to be a Hand of God," Basheera replies, her eyes on Kal. "All he could tell us was, *'Do not worry—they are coming. It is time now for us to honor our promise to the Asim.'* But," Basheera continues, sighing as if this is a personal affront, "he died before he could give us more details."

My eyes dart from Kal to Basheera. Kal looks confused while Basheera stares at him as if her eyes alone can draw more information out of him.

"Who was he?" I ask.

"He said his name was Abi." Basheera's eyes are still on Kal. "Abi Sayeed."

CHAPTER FIFTEEN

KAL SHAKES HIS HEAD. "THAT CAN'T BE. MY FATHER WAS a sailor. He was the captain of his own boat. He never said anything about the Hands of God."

"Maybe there was another Abi Sayeed," I offer.

"We have a manifest of all the refugees who entered the village since the start of the war." Basheera rests her stylus on the table. "There is only one Abi Sayeed recorded, and he listed you as his son."

"I—I don't know what to say." Kal looks as confused as he sounds. "I had no idea."

I turn to Kal. "Your father never mentioned the Hands?"

He shakes his head again. "Not in that way. If they were ever brought up, he simply repeated what everyone else said. He never let on that he was one of them. I—hmm." Kal pauses, looking deep in thought. "If he was a Hand, that may explain something that happened this one time, a few years ago. One day we were loading cargo onto our ship when a strange woman walked onboard and challenged my father to a fight. I remember she had a big sword and wore a gray cloak with three eyes embroidered on the back. My father was a sailor, not a fighter, but he accepted her challenge anyway. The woman was fast, and her sword seemed to glow as it sliced through the air. Baba held his ground against her even though he didn't have a weapon. Eventually, the woman sheathed her sword, bowed to my father, and left. I've thought about that day now and then over the years, but it was something we never talked about. I tried to ask my father about it once, and he told me it was his past catching up with him. That was it."

"You think that has something to do with the Hands?" I ask.

"Of course it does." Basheera excitedly pushes her glasses up the bridge of her nose. "That was a test, and Kal's father passed. I've read about it in my research on the Hands of God. It's called the Hakkuen Trial. One opponent attacks while the other defends without a weapon. The defender puts their faith in the Three-Faced God to protect them, and as long as they are worthy, they will survive."

"So it's true—my father was a Hand of God?"

"Sounds like," Basheera replies. "Wait here. I have to show you something." She rises from the table and disappears down a cluttered aisle, leaving me and Kal alone.

"I can't believe the Hands of God might still exist," I say.

"I can't believe my father was one of them." Kal's hands are clasped together on the table, as if he's trying to stop them from shaking. "So many people hate the Hands for abandoning the Asim, and so many still pray for their intervention. Should I be glad my father was a Hand, which means they're still around and on their way to Lagusa, or upset because so much pain and suffering could have been avoided if they'd protected the Asim in the first place? Should I be hurt that my father kept this secret from me? Or proud that he was a member of an almost-mythological band of warriors?"

"I think it's alright to feel all of those things." I place my hand on top of Kal's. "Your father must have had a good reason for not telling you. We may never know why, but now that the secret is out, it's up to you to decide what to do with it."

Taking a deep breath, Kal laces his fingers through mine. "Thank you for being here. It helps having someone who cares nearby."

My cheeks grow hot and I turn away so Kal won't see me blushing. "You're welcome," I murmur more to the scribes sitting at the table next to us than to Kal. Luckily, they're too engrossed in their work to notice.

"I'm sorry, I didn't mean to embarrass you." Kal starts to pull his hand away, but I hold on tight.

"It's alright." I face him, not caring if I'm as red as a baboon's ass. "I don't mind."

Kal smiles and my heart races. Then he leans close, so close I can feel his breath on my cheek. My own breath stills, but my thoughts are a jumble. Is he going to kiss me? Every nerve in my body sparks. I close my eyes...

And he brushes the stray hairs away from my face and tucks them behind my ear.

A mixture of disappointment and relief floods my senses and all I can do is open my eyes.

"Oh," I say as I release my breath, not able to utter more than that.

A cheeky grin spreads across his face. "Did you think I was going to kiss you?"

My mouth drops and I quickly close it. "No, of course not. No." I've obviously misread the situation and Kal doesn't feel the same way about me as I do about him. Embarrassed, I try to pull my hand away, but he wraps both of his hands around mine and scoots closer to me.

"Don't worry, I will. Not now, though. When the time is right." He lifts my hand and kisses the back of it. Tingles race down my forearm, prickling the hairs and making them stand on end while an electrifying rush spreads from the base of my skull, across the back of my neck, and down my spine.

If that's what a kiss from Kal on my hand feels like, I can't imagine what will happen if he ever tries to kiss me for real.

I fight back a grin and furrow my brows.

"Don't bother," I say, my pride still wounded.

Kal laughs. "You're pretty when you're flustered, Naira Khoum."

And there it is. My name on his lips. I want to sit next to Kal holding his hand, with him smiling at me and telling me I'm pretty, until the skies turn dark and the sun ceases to shine, but Basheera returns and shoos our hands away so she can place a small wooden box the size of her palm on the table.

"What's in the box?" Kal asks.

"Something your father gave us before he died. To prove his claim." Basheera opens the latch and lifts the lid, revealing a golden clasp in the shape of a hand holding on to a sword.

"I've seen that before." Kal takes the clasp and unhooks the hand from the sword. "The woman who came to fight my father. She wore one like this on her cloak. I remember because the tip of the sword broke off during the fight. I searched the whole ship for it, but I never found it. After a while, I forgot about it."

"Every Hand is issued a sword forged in the godfire and a gray cloak with this clasp," Basheera says. "If a Hand leaves the order, he must turn in his sword, but he keeps the clasp. Did your father carry a sword with lots of strange markings on the blade and a hilt wrapped in gold wire?"

"No, I never saw anything like that." Kal turns the clasp over. There are markings engraved on the palm.

I lean closer to read the words, but they're written in another language. "What do these symbols mean?"

Basheera reaches for the clasp. Kal hooks the two pieces together and gives them to her. "I'm still working on the translation, but it goes something like this: *One must die so the other can live. And as long as one lives, the other will never die.*"

"What language was that?" Kal asks.

I assume he's joking, but he looks completely serious. When I'm about to blurt out *Merzan*, Basheera speaks.

"Ancient Volsgarian. Many of our modern languages have roots in Volsgarian. For instance—"

"Wait, can you say it again?" I ask. "In Volsgarian?"

Basheera pushes her glasses up her nose and repeats the prophecy and once again I understand every word as if Basheera is speaking Merzan.

"And that was Volsgarian?" I ask.

"Are you doubting me?" Basheera looks offended.

"No, it's just…" I need a moment to collect my thoughts. The Mistress claimed I spoke Waldyrian that night in the tomb. I dismissed that as nonsense, but now I have no trouble understanding a dead language without even realizing it. Can it be true—am I able to speak languages I never learned? "It just sounded so strange."

"What does it mean?"

Basheera translates the words for Kal and they are exactly as I heard them.

"It sounds like a riddle," Kal says.

"It's from a series of texts called *The Foretold* written in Old Volsgarian by the prophet Gamikal," Basheera says. "Scholars have spent centuries trying to make meaning of his prophecies. *The Foretold* does not give up its secrets easily."

"Who's Gamikal?" I ask.

Expecting a huff from Basheera at my lack of knowledge, I'm surprised when she excitedly leans forward. "Now that's a good question!" She flips through some papers and pulls out a sheet crammed with notes. "I was researching him before, well, you know—" she gestures at the scrolls and books about the Hands of God crowding the table "—and he's simply fascinating. He first appears during the Volsgarian War. Some say he was the brother of the Righteous Heir, some say he was a pawn of the Bastard King, and some say he *'appeared from the mists.'*" Basheera skims her notes, her face lighting up when she finds the next interesting tidbit. "He's been sighted dozens of times in the five centuries after the war, most often in the Kilmare Mountains. The last sighting was about twenty years ago."

Kal holds up a hand and Basheera pauses. "Wait—are you saying the Gamikal from the Volsgarian War is the same Gamikal seen twenty years ago?"

"Yes! Isn't that interesting?" Basheera places her notes in

front of us, but her writing is so cramped I can barely read it. She points at a section near the middle of the page. "These are the sources for the sightings. Most of them are credible, a few are dubious, but they're still relevant because it means people have never forgotten him, even after all this time. That *has* to mean something, doesn't it?"

There aren't many records from before the war that tore Volsgaria apart, since many libraries from that time were destroyed in the fighting. After the war ended with the deaths of the Bastard King and the Rightful Heir, chaos ruled the lands for nearly 150 years as anyone with the ability to raise an army fought for control of the Volsgarian throne. Eventually, the remaining leaders agreed to break up Volsgaria and form four distinct countries: the islands of Nauvia in the west, Waldyria in the frigid north, the vast lands in the east ringed by mountains became Johtan, and finally Merza in the south. To have so many references over the centuries about one person is rare.

"Is he some kind of god?" I ask, wondering how someone could live for so long.

Basheera shakes her head. "He specifically states in *The Foretold* that he is as human as you or I. That's one of the few statements where the meaning is clear. He is an immortal being, filled with wisdom gleaned from communicating with the gods. Or so some say. How and why he became that way is not known."

"Is that why his prophecy is engraved on my father's clasp?"

"The connection between the Hands of God and Gamikal is not clear. As you know, they are a very secretive organization and Gamikal hasn't written anything else besides

The Foretold. But since he seems to spend a lot of time in the Kilmare Mountains where the Hands also live, it makes sense that they would have contact with each other." Basheera places the clasp back in the wooden box and shuts the lid. She pushes the box across the table toward Kal. "You should keep this. It belonged to your father, after all."

"Thank you." Kal holds the box with both hands.

A bell rings and Basheera gets to her feet. Scribes at the other tables put down their writing instruments, roll up their scrolls, and rise.

"I have to attend the daily constitutional," Basheera huffs. "It's the price I pay to be surrounded by so much knowledge."

I stand as well. "But—" I need to ask more questions, find out why I can understand languages besides the only one I was taught, but Basheera cuts me off.

"We'll talk more later," she assures me, grabbing the scroll where she wrote Kal's account. "I can't miss another devotion or I'll lose my access to the restricted areas."

Kal thanks Basheera one more time, then we leave through the heavy wooden doors, the scribes filing past us in a rush.

"I can't believe they're still following their routines." I hold the door open for a scribe. "With all that's going on, you'd think they wouldn't have time."

"When things get chaotic, you have to make time for calm," Kal says. "It's what keeps you grounded when it seems as if the world is falling away beneath your feet."

"That sounds like something my father would say. I don't know how, but he always seemed to be in control. No matter what was happening around him." I'm trying to be more like him, but it's not easy.

"I learned it in the camps," Kal says. "We never knew what each day would bring. My oldest brother taught me to focus on the things that didn't change: our mother's smile, Baba's strong hands, our other brother's laugh. So I worked hard to make my mother smile and my brothers laugh and held on tight to my father's hand as we marched from one day to the next."

We enter the main Temple, where the scribes join with the Mother, the Daughters, and other devout laypeople. They exit through the doors on the north wall and head out to the plaza, where the giant statues of the thirteen dragon gods wait for them to offer prayers and praise.

"You survived by focusing on those you love," I say.

"Yes, but all my family's gone." His eyes are on the floor, his voice thick with unshed tears. My heart breaks for all that he's lost. "Who do I focus on now?"

"Nez and I, we're your family now," I say. "Focus on us."

Kal looks up and laughs. "I've never met anyone like you. Not many people would call a stranger family."

Grinning, I brush away his words with a wave of my hand. "We're not strangers. We've faced danger together, shared a meal, survived Basheera's scrutiny. We're practically best pals."

Another laugh from Kal and then he smiles. "Alright, best pal, we'd better find the others and figure out what's next."

In lighter spirits, Kal and I make our way to the alcove, where we find Nez and Rima.

"Sure took you two a long time." Nez is lounging on an even bigger pile of cushions than before. "Did you stop off somewhere for a kiss?"

My stomach drops and I pray for a hole to open up in the

floor and swallow me. I don't know how to respond, so I stand there, stiff as the wooden sparring dummy in our jirkana, in silence. Kal walks up beside me and bumps my shoulder with his own.

"Your brother's quite the handful, isn't he?"

I can only nod.

This time it's Rima who throws a pillow at Nez, hitting him squarely in the face. Beneath the fabric, Nez laughs.

"Thank you," I say to Rima, finally getting control of my senses.

"Of course," Rima replies with a knowing look.

I give Nez's cushions a swift kick as I pass by and he howls in fake pain.

"I was only joking," Nez says as he emerges from his mound of cushions. "Besides, you should be thanking me instead of kicking me. I found a runner to take a note to Omma. I let her know we're safe and in the Temple."

I sit down with a sigh of relief. "Well, at least you're not completely useless."

"What's in the box?" Rima asks as Kal joins us on the floor. He crosses his legs and places the box on his lap.

"It's my father's." He opens the lid, takes out the gold clasp, and recounts the conversation we had with Basheera for Rima and Nez. When he gets to the part about the prophecy, I tense. I debate whether to tell them I understand that ancient language, but I decide to keep it to myself until I can figure out why.

"So your father was definitely a Hand of God?" Nez asks and Kal nods. "Whew, that's tough."

"Nez!" I admonish.

"What?" He throws up his hands and shrugs. "I'm just saying, we all know what the Hands did… Finding out your father was one of them can't be easy."

I narrow my eyes at my rude brother but Kal doesn't seem to mind.

"Nez is right." He fiddles with the clasp, his eyes on the golden object. "The Hands betrayed the Asim. They're cowards. But my father wasn't like that. He was the bravest, most honorable man I've ever known."

"Maybe that's why he left," Nez says. "Because he *wasn't* like them."

"Maybe," Kal says, his voice unconvinced. "But then why did he survive the Hakkuen Trial? And why did he say the Hands are coming? Why are they honoring their promise to the Asim now when she's been dead for sixteen years?"

We all fall silent, none of us able to provide the answers that Kal seeks.

"May I see the clasp?" Rima leans forward.

Kal hands her the gold object. "Sure."

"That's some fine craftsmanship," Nez says in appreciation, peering over Rima's shoulder.

"What are you going to do with it?" Rima asks, handing it back to Kal.

"I think I want to wear it." Kal studies the hand and sword one more time before placing it in the box. "Even though it's a symbol of the Hands of God, it's one of the few things I have left that belonged to my father, and I don't want to lose it."

"That's a great idea." Rima rises to her feet and motions for Kal to do the same. "Come with me. I know someone who can sew that on for you."

"Really?" Kal's face brightens into a smile and he turns to me. "I'll be back in a bit." Then he gets on his feet and follows Rima across the Temple.

Once Rima and Kal are well enough away, Nez props his head up on his hand and stares at me.

"So, how long has this been going on?"

"What are you talking about?" I snap. I'm still angry with Nez for embarrassing me in front of Kal.

"You know what I mean." Nez is undeterred by my attitude. "You and handsome over there."

"What?" I try to sound incredulous but it comes out as a squeak. I never expected my oblivious brother to notice I was developing feelings for someone before I even knew the extent of those feelings. I had no idea he was paying such close attention to me.

"Nothing's going on. He's just a friend."

Nez sits up. "As your brother and your *best* friend, I'm telling you to be careful. Just because someone has broad shoulders and a winning smile doesn't mean you have to fall head over heels for him after only a week."

I scoff. "Oh, you're one to talk. You can barely contain your excitement now that Rima's back. When we were little, I could tell you had a crush on her. I bet you still do."

"Have you met Rima? Who wouldn't have a crush on her?"

"You really have no shame," I say with a laugh. When Nez teased me for liking Kal, I thought my heart would stop right then and there, yet when I do the same thing to him, he owns up to it, not caring if everyone knows the feelings he cradles in his heart. I wish I was more open like Nez. It's probably why he makes friends so easily while I struggle to make even one.

"Look, I'm going to be serious for a moment," Nez says and my eyes widen in surprise. "Don't worry. It won't be long." We both laugh. "I just feel like I need to look after you even more than before," Nez continues, his expression solemn. "With Obba gone, I have to step up as your big brother. We can't depend on Obba to protect us. So, I'm going to give you and handsome a hard time. If he's the right one, he can take it."

I reach across the mound of cushions and hug Nez. A couple of tears spill out of my eyes and drip onto his tunic.

"Thanks, Nez." I pull away and wipe my eyes. I glance at my brother and for the first time see Obba's strength residing deep within him. I hope Nez sees the same in me. "And don't worry. I'll do the same for you. I'll always be there to pick you up because we both know you're gonna fall."

"Oh, ha ha." Nez whacks me on the side of the head with a pillow. All I can do is laugh. "I was trying to have a moment and you ruined it."

"Sorry," I giggle.

Nez rolls his eyes but he's smiling.

"Come on, let's go see where Rima and Kal went off to." He crawls off the pile of cushions and gets on his feet.

As I stand, the front doors of the Temple are flung open and two rangers rush inside. Conversations cease, practicing fighters stop midattack, and even the children hush.

"Vra Gool Dambi," one of the rangers yells. "A pack of them coming up the steps! If you can fight, we need you out here now!"

I glance at Nez and he grabs his bow and arrows, slings them over his shoulder, and we both run to the front of the Temple.

My eyes on my brother's back, only one thought crosses my mind as we join the Lagusans ready to fight back a Dambi horde: I will set the world on fire if I lose another family member to the Dambi, and the Mistress will be the kindling.

CHAPTER SIXTEEN

OUTSIDE, IT TAKES MY EYES A MOMENT TO ADJUST TO the blinding sun. Barricades made of wood and stone fill the front plaza, blocking off the entrance to the Temple. Sentries posted on top of the battlements point their arrows at the oncoming horde. The smell of death permeates the air, and many of the fighters cover their noses and mouths with scarves to block the stench.

Nez and I run forward to join them, but a burly ranger grabs us both by the arm with his meaty hands.

"What're you doing out here?" he yells in our faces.

"We're here to fight!" I yell back.

"*You're* the ones we're trying to protect!" The ranger shoves us back toward the Temple. "Get inside, hide with the other children, and stay there until it's all clear!"

I try to argue but the ranger won't budge.

"Come on, Naira." Nez pulls me through the entrance. "Samir Shouty isn't going to let us through, so we have to find another way."

Back in the Temple, Daughters are herding all the children through the hidden door that leads to the catacombs.

"This way," one of them urges us. "Hurry."

"We're not hiding—we want to fight," I say, but the Daughter pays my words no mind as she pushes me toward the group.

We're quickly swallowed up by panicking children, some of the younger ones openly crying, the rush of bodies preventing us from standing our ground.

But before we enter the catacombs, I hear Rima call our names. Craning my neck, I spot her and Kal standing by the doors leading to the library. I grab Nez's arm and push my way against the crowd until we're free.

"What's going on?" Rima asks when we reach them.

"A horde of Dambi are coming up the steps, and they won't let us go outside to help fight them," Nez replies. "The Daughters tried to send us into hiding with the others."

"The back is being guarded as well," Kal says. "They wouldn't let us out that way either."

"I'm not one for hiding," I say. "I don't like sitting back while others fight for me."

"Me neither," Nez joins in.

"Well then, we'd better do something," Kal adds.

"I know where we can go." Rima opens the door to the library. "There's a terrace up a hidden flight of stairs. We can at least see what's happening from there."

Rima leads the way through the now-empty library. The scrolls and papers are strewn about as if the scribes gathered what they could before hiding in the catacombs with everyone else. I wonder if Basheera is with them, and if she's upset that her sister isn't with her.

We follow Rima down a few aisles and then behind a folding screen. A staircase waits on the other side, most of the arched entryway boarded up. Kal uses his sword to bash through the boards, and once the way is clear, we climb the crumbling steps.

"Basheera used to let me play up here after school on the days she had to work late. They eventually closed off the entrance, but by then, I was too old to care."

"You'd think they'd be using the terrace as part of the defenses," Nez says as we make our way up the narrow staircase. "I wonder why they aren't."

At the top, a tattered curtain covers the exit. I push it aside and reveal a sand-covered terrace. The railing long ago fell apart and lies in pieces on the pockmarked stone floor.

Nez steps onto the stone slab—and the terrace responds with a creak and a groan as it tips forward.

"Oh." Nez quickly hops backward, the rest of us grabbing him by his arms and the fabric of his tunic to hold him steady. "That's why."

With the terrace too fragile to support our weight, all I can do is stand in the doorway with the others, straining my ears to hear what's going on. Beyond the barricades, a horde of Dambi twenty strong are climbing up the stone steps carved into the hillside.

Even though we have almost ten times as many fighters in the Temple, twenty Dambi is a lot. The damage a handful of Dambi can do against trained rangers and watchguards is staggering—and many of our fighters are ordinary men and women who probably picked up a weapon for the first time when they joined the resistance. A full-on assault by this many Dambi will be a slaughter.

That doesn't stop me from wishing I was down there, in the thick of it.

"Who's that?" Nez points at a figure in white leading the Dambi.

"Isn't that one of the Subaans?" Rima squints her eyes at the woman whose arms are raised to show she comes under the guise of peace. "Subaan Ledisi, I think."

My breath catches. Subaan Ledisi was part of the attack outside of the gate—the same attack that killed Obba.

If one Subaan is still alive, does this mean Obba might be as well?

"Are you thinking what I'm thinking?" Nez whispers to me and I nod.

Determined more than ever to confront the Mistress, I grab the hilts of my daggers and hold tight. If there is even the slightest chance Obba is alive, I will do whatever it takes to save him.

Shouts from below draw my attention. Archers have their bows trained on the Subaan and the Dambi, but a man I recognize as Captain Farouk orders them to hold steady. The Mother joins the fighters on the battlements, her back hunched and her hair white.

"If you are here only to relay a message, then may the Fires burn me in their flames if harm comes to you," the Mother says. "Tell us why you have come."

"The Mistress sent me," Subaan Ledisi shouts. Behind her, the Dambi stand still as statues. But I know how quickly that can change, so I keep my hands on my daggers. "I've been her captive," the Subaan continues, "surrounded by these things—" she motions to the Dambi "—for days on end. I had no choice but to deliver her request for a meeting. Please do not think I serve her—I only want to be free."

"A meeting?" Captain Farouk calls out. "Where? And with whom?"

"Not here," the Mother says, her voice carrying on the wind up to the terrace. "I will not have that woman and her abominations defiling the sanctity of the Temple."

"She wants to meet with our Mother," Subaan Ledisi replies. "At the meeting house tomorrow morning."

"What does she want to meet about?" Captain Farouk yells.

"She didn't say," Subaan Ledisi replies.

"How do we know we can trust her? How do we know she isn't trying to lure our Mother into the meeting house so that she can incapacitate her?"

Tears stream down Subaan Ledisi's face. "She says me being alive should be all the proof you need that she won't hurt our Mother. Please, I'm afraid if you don't come, she *will* kill me."

"We must discuss this among ourselves," the Mother calls down. "We will give you our answer in half a hand."

Slowly, the Mother descends the battlement, one hand on the wooden railings, the other holding on to a Daughter's arm. As she disappears from view, her voice grows faint and I can't hear what is being said.

"We have to get back down there," I tell the others and they agree. One by one, we head back down the stairs, through the library, and into the Temple.

"Should we try going out the front doors again?" Nez asks.

"I don't see what else we can do if we want to know what's going on," I reply.

The doors at the front of the Temple burst open and a crowd enters, their voices loud and upset. I run toward the commotion, the others close on my heels. In front of us, Captain Farouk and a cluster of heavily armed men and women surround the Mother and some Daughters. Feeble and blind in one eye, the Mother leans on the arm of a Daughter for support.

I hide behind a pillar when I'm close enough to hear the conversation over the din of the Temple. Rima joins me while Kal and Nez find a pillar of their own.

"I will meet with her, if that's what it will take to end this madness," the Mother is saying, raising her voice to be heard over the noise.

"What about the Hands of God?" someone asks. "If they are indeed as powerful as the scribes say, shouldn't we wait until they arrive before—"

"We've been waiting sixteen years for the Hands of God to show up," another person cuts in. "How much longer can we wait while the Mistress steals our children and destroys our village?"

"This meeting is a trap," Captain Farouk says. "She only wants to kill you, hoping that your death will put an end to the resistance."

Murmurs of agreement come from the others, but the Mother waves them away with her free hand. "Nonsense, Captain Farouk. My death at the hands of that woman would only make this resistance stronger."

Now cries of disagreement fill the Temple, and once again, the Mother ignores them.

"I am going to meet with the Mistress," she says, her voice strong as when she leads the prayer to the gods. "Who will be my guard?"

I expect all of the men and women hanging on to the Mother to put their hands up and I'm stunned when they don't. Most plead for the Mother to rethink her decision, while the others back away in fear of being chosen.

"I'll be your guard." I step out from behind the pillar. Rima tugs on my sleeve and Nez motions for me to get back in place, but I ignore them. I glance at Kal and he too leaves his hiding place. Rima and Nez are compelled to do the same.

A hush falls over the adults and the Mother looks out among the people. "Who said that?" she asks. "Come closer to where I can see you."

With my shoulders back and my chin up, I lead the others to the Mother. The crowd surrounding the holy woman parts, and when the Mother and I are face-to-face, she places her hand on my shoulder.

"You are no more than a child, and yet you have a braver heart than men and women twice your age," the Mother says. The crowd grumbles. "You'll make a fine guard—" she pats my shoulder and my chest swells with pride "—but not today. I can't bring a lamb into the wolf's lair."

"I'm not a lamb," I say. I try not to be angry at the Mother's quick dismissal of my offer to help, but I can't stop my fists from clenching. "I fought a Dambi and won. I can take care of myself, and I can protect you."

"I have no doubt you are a capable fighter." The Mother's

voice is gentle. "You are the daughter of Samir Isrof Khoum, are you not? And that is his son behind you. I also recognize you, Samida Okuba." The Mother stares at Kal. "You, I am sorry to say, I do not know."

"I'm a refugee," Kal tells her. "My name is Kal Sayeed, and I also want to do whatever I can to help in the fight against the Mistress."

"Samir Sayeed, another bold warrior," the Mother says. "You all put my designated protectors to shame." Scowls and more grumbles follow her words but she talks over them as if they've said nothing. "They don't want me to meet with the Mistress. What do the four of you say?"

I glance at my brother and friends. They all nod, content to let me speak for all of us.

"Until we know why she is rounding up the children of Lagusa, we are at a disadvantage," I say after some thought. "And until we have the numbers necessary to fight and defeat the Dambi, we have to do whatever it takes to stop the Mistress from achieving her plans, whatever they may be. Her request for a meeting could be a trap, or it could be a way for us to get information that could help us win a battle against the Dambi. I think we have to take the chance. We have to be bold. Our fear only strengthens our enemies."

"Spoken like a true warrior," the Mother says with another pat on my shoulder. "The fire of Crafulgar the Fiend-Slayer shines bright in you. But if that fire is to continue to burn, I cannot bring you with me to meet the Mistress. You must understand."

I understand, though it doesn't make accepting the Mother's

decision any easier. I said everything I could and still she chooses to leave me behind.

I step back and the Mother turns to the crowd. "I have made my decision. I will meet with the Mistress. I will find out what she wants with our children. I ask again, which brave souls among you will join me?"

Captain Farouk steps forward. "I will protect you with my life, Mother." He crosses his arms, his fingertips resting on his shoulders, and bows.

Either through shame or because they finally found their courage, many of the others do the same. Satisfied, the Mother holds out her hands and blesses her people.

"By the Fires you live, by the Fires you are blessed, and by the Fires you die," she says with a voice that begs the gods to listen. "Protect our people with your Fires, and may our enemies perish in your flames."

"By the Fires," the worshippers murmur in response. I do as the others, folding my arms across my chest and bowing, repeating the phrases I learned as a young child. The same phrases I repeated with my father the day he died. Obba was a devout man who prayed to the Thirteen every day—but where was Zulgaron and his shield when he needed him? Why didn't Albedego heal his wounds? Dynago should have showered my father with riches for all of the faith he put in the gods and Nurega should have blessed him with a long and happy life, but that's not what happened.

How do the faithful keep their faith when the gods let people like my father die while creatures like the Dambi live?

When the prayer is finished, the Mother pulls me aside.

"This world is on fire—and Sothpike is the spark." The

Mother leads me deeper into the Temple. "Fires can cleanse, and they can also destroy. Knowing which type of fire you're up against requires you to get burned. It will hurt, but you will come out stronger in the end. Are you ready to face the flames?"

I think back to my time in the tomb, how I used fire to keep the Dambi at bay, and how I saved the maugrab. "Fire doesn't scare me."

The Mother stops in front of the statue of the dragon Galgamex the Peace-Bearer. She smiles, her teeth brown and crooked like the dragon's.

"Right now, the world is facing destruction. There are people who run away from the dangerous fires. And then there are people like you, who rush in headfirst to stamp them out. We need more people like you. The fire-eaters." The old woman places her hand on my shoulder again, and I can't help but be reminded of Obba. "In ancient times, the fallen dragon Ergenegon breathed blue fire, the hottest and most destructive fire of all the dragons. Only Crafulgar could withstand the heat and defeat him. Sothpike and his forces are our Ergenegon. People like you are our Crafulgar. Only those willing to face the fire despite all its dangers can douse the flames. Let the fire draw you in. It is where you belong."

The Mother's hand is heavy on my shoulder and I'm not sure I can carry the weight. The idea that I can take on anything as remotely powerful as Ergenegon is almost too much to fathom. If it's anything like my nightmare in the tombs, Ergenegon's blue-hot flames are too much for me to handle. But the challenge to face him anyway, even though I might fall, inspires me to stand tall beneath the pressure.

After all, I'm the type who jumps into the fire, right?

The Mother smiles, pats my shoulder one last time, and goes back outside to give Subaan Ledisi her response, her new protectors following her to the battlements.

I walk over to the statue of the dragon Crafulgar. Her wings are outstretched, her sword raised high, her mouth open to spew fire. Crafulgar is named the Fiend-Slayer for a reason—she looks ready to take on anything that threatens to harm the humans she protects. I wonder what it would be like to have a dragon at my side, or better yet, to be a dragon myself. The power to vanquish my enemies with a blast of fire, to fly into battle with my flaming sword and emerge triumphant.

Is that what draws in the faithful—the power these dragons possess? The hope that one day soon, another dragon will come to save us?

I touch the base of the statue, my hand drawing warmth from the rough stone. The heat surprises me—it's the first time I've ever felt anything in connection to the gods beyond indifference. Could this be a sign that maybe Crafulgar *is* watching over us? I don't know, but at least now I know what I have to do.

I leave the statue and join my brother and friends as they make their way back to our alcove. Once we're alone, I gather the others around me.

"I'm going to the meeting," I say, my voice hushed. "I don't care what the Mother says, I didn't join the resistance to hide. You don't have to come with me—"

"I was thinking the same thing," Nez cuts in. "About going to the meeting."

"Me too," Kal says.

"Well, if you're all going, then I am too," Rima says.

I grin. "So, how are we going to do it?"

We each grab a pillow and sit in a circle to plan how we're going to get to the meeting house undetected and what we'll do once we're there. While we talk, the Mother's words come back to me.

Only those willing to face the fire despite all its dangers can douse the flames. Let the fire draw you in. It is where you belong.

If sneaking into the meeting house, right into the hands of the woman who is kidnapping children, isn't facing the fire, I don't know what is. The Mother told me to be our Crafulgar, and so I will.

Some flames burn everything, even the brave ones who try to put them out. But even though smoke is dark and thick, fire bright and hot, they both call out to me like nothing else.

CHAPTER SEVENTEEN

MORNING ARRIVES WITH A MESSAGE FROM OMMA.

The runner passes the note to Nez and turns to leave, but Nez calls out to him.

"Wait—how was she? Was she upset?"

"She seemed fine to me," the runner replies. "When I told her you're with the resistance, she didn't seem surprised. She made me stay the night and wouldn't let me leave until after breakfast."

Nez's eyes widen. "Tell me, what did she make for breakfast? Was it good?" With every word, he takes a step closer to the runner until they are nose to nose. "You smell like apricots. Did she make her famous apricot kaavi?"

The runner stumbles back. "I think so."

"It's so good," Nez continues, lost in memories of apricot kaavi, "the way the pudding melts on your tongue and the flaky crust. Did you like it? Don't tell me you didn't like it."

"Well, uh—" the runner stammers.

I snatch the note out of Nez's hand and shove him aside.

"Ignore my brother, please," I say. The runner gives me a grateful look before scampering away.

"Wait!" Nez cries out. "Give me one more whiff!"

I elbow Nez in the ribs. "Cut it out."

"I miss Omma," Nez says, rubbing his side.

"Do you miss Omma," I tease, "or her cooking?"

"Can't I miss both?" Nez laughs as he avoids another jab from my elbow.

I sit on the floor and hold the note in my hands, but I hesitate before opening it. The runner said Omma seemed fine, but he doesn't know her, and she might have been saving her wrath for this letter.

"Are you going to open it?" Kal asks, kneeling next to me.

Knowing I can't avoid my mother forever, I unfold the slip of paper. There is only one sentence, a short one, and I smile when I read it.

"What does it say?" Nez asks. I pass the note to Nez and he reads the words out loud. "'*Make me proud.*'" With a laugh, Nez kisses the note. "Yes, Omma!"

I take a deep breath. I feel stronger knowing I have Omma's support. Doubts that danced around the back of my mind about confronting the Mistress vanish. I'm confident we're doing the right thing. We need information, and the only way to get it is inside the meeting house. We don't have weeks and months to sort through secrets and rumors, and the longer we wait, the more danger we put everyone in the village in.

A bell rings, the deep sound resonating within my chest, and I get on my feet. Scribes exiting the library file past toward the altar on the far side of the Temple.

"It's time," I say to the others, and they rise with me. But before we walk very far, Basheera emerges from the group of scribes.

"Why do you have a spear?" she asks, grabbing her younger sister by the arm. "Where do you think you're going?"

"I'm going with my friends to stand guard when our Mother leaves for the meeting," Rima replies, shaking off her sister. "I told you last night."

"And I told you to sleep on it." Basheera steps in front of Rima. "Which meant, you can't go."

"I'm sixteen," Rima says. "I'm old enough to make my own decisions."

"Not if you're going to make the wrong ones!"

The scribe Mandisa approaches and lays a gentle hand on Basheera's shoulder.

"Yelling at Rima won't make her change her mind," she says. Then she turns to Rima. "Your sister is very worried about you."

"I know," Rima says, "but I have to do this. I can't stay back. You're doing what you can with your research, but I'm not smart like you. I'm not clever, and I'm not brave. All I can do is stand with my friends. So, I'm going. I wish you wouldn't be mad at me."

Basheera looks as if she wants to say something, but all she does is cross her arms and purse her lips. Her glasses slide down her nose and she shoves them back in place.

"Go," Mandisa says, wrapping an arm around Basheera's shoulder and planting a tender kiss on her cheek to pull her out of Rima's path. "I'll take care of her."

"Thank you, Mandisa." Rima offers the scribe a quick bow,

then she leans forward to give Basheera a kiss on the other cheek. I am surprised when Basheera returns the gesture.

Rima is right. For all her bluster, Basheera is a big softy on the inside.

"You'd better come back," Basheera says with another push of her glasses. Rima nods and Basheera huffs. "Fine, you can go."

Mandisa leads Basheera toward the altar, where they take their places among the other scribes while Rima lets out a big sigh. "Well, the Mistress isn't going to come to us." She adjusts her grip on the spear. "Let's go join the others."

"Are you sure?" I ask. "Your sister was pretty upset."

"She's always upset," Rima replies with a forced laugh. "Besides, she has Mandisa. She'll make sure Basheera is alright."

"Maybe Mandisa should come with us," Nez says and Rima gives him a confused look. "She has to be strong to be with someone like Basheera."

"My sister can come off as scary, but that's how she shows she cares."

"I'd love to see how she treats the people she hates," Nez says. "I changed my mind—we should bring Basheera. I bet she could take down the Mistress with one glare." He mimics Basheera's posture—crossing his arms, pursing his lips—and laughs.

"Stop joking around," I say. Nez dodges to avoid me slapping the back of his head—which puts him in the perfect spot for a punch to the arm by Rima.

Before Nez can respond, Kal slings an arm around his

shoulder, saying, "How about you and I make our way over to the others?"

When Nez and Kal are gone, I turn to Rima. "Are you sure you want to do this? You and Basheera only have each other."

A smile plays across Rima's face, but it doesn't reach her eyes. "Like I said, Basheera also has Mandisa. She'll be fine."

"But Basheera needs you." I try to look into Rima's eyes, but she avoids my gaze.

"After Omma and Obba died, we had Te-Omma." Rima's eyes are on the stoic statue of Xergas the Strength-Giver. "And after Te-Omma died, all we had were each other. But now, Basheera has Mandisa. Who do I have?"

My heart aches for Rima and I wish I knew the words that would erase her pain, but those words don't exist. Instead, I thread my arm through hers.

"You have me," I say. We begin walking to the altar, where we're to meet the Mother. "And you have Nez. He's definitely not going anywhere."

Rima smiles, a real one this time. "That's true. He's fantastic, isn't he?" She places a hand over her heart like a love-sick heroine.

I pretend to gag. "We're talking about the same Nezra Khoum, right?" I laugh but Rima only lets out an awkward chuckle, as if she doesn't like teasing Nez. When we were little, Rima and I were always a team against Nez. He'd yank our braids, and we'd chase him. He'd knock down the tower we built, and we'd throw the colorful wooden building blocks at him. I've always seen Nez as my goofy slightly older brother and I thought Rima still felt the same, but it seems things have changed.

I quit laughing and examine her face, noticing the sparkle in her eyes. "You really like him, don't you?"

Rima sighs. "I don't know. When we were kids, beating him up was fun. But now, I'd rather wrap my arms around him."

"To squeeze the life out of him?"

"No," Rima laughs and swats at my arm. "To embrace him. Like, a real embrace. Not the kind that ends with a quick pat on the back, but the kind you read about in storybooks, where the lovers are finally reunited after years of being apart and they wrap their arms around each other, their bodies pressed against each other, and flowers bloom at their feet and the stars shine and—"

"I think I get it," I say, cutting off Rima's romantic soliloquy before she moves beyond hugging. Rima's always been in love with love—she swooned every time there was a tender moment in the books we read or plays we saw—but I never thought she'd be swooning over Nez.

I'm surprised at how much things have changed. Even though I haven't seen Rima for seven years, I thought we'd all pick up where we left off when we found each other again. But time has that annoying habit of bringing about change, even when you want things to stay the same, and I have to accept that my childhood best friend has feelings for my knucklehead brother.

"Well, Nez will be happy. He's had a crush on you for years, you know."

Rima grins. "I know." She places her hand on mine and squeezes. "I'm glad we're together again. All of us. It's just like the old times. Now I don't feel alone anymore."

"Well, not *just* like the old times," I say. "Not with you and my brother lusting after each other."

"Naira!" Rima tries to push me away but I won't let go of her arm. Then she starts giggling and I start giggling and my heart swells because I have my best friend back.

Still laughing, we approach the crowd waiting near the altar for the Mother. A Daughter tells us to hush and we both fall silent, but only for a moment. Rima covers her mouth as another giggle bursts out and I press my lips together so that I won't do the same. The Daughter frowns, I nod in apology, and pull Rima over to Nez and Kal at the back of the crowd. We stand between them, Nez on Rima's right, Kal on my left, and I pretend not to notice when Nez takes Rima's hand.

Rima presses her cheek against Nez's shoulder and he beams.

I'm sure those two would fall into each other's arms in one of Rima's fantasy hugs right then and there if they weren't surrounded by so many people. It's as if the last seven years apart haven't happened.

I glance over at Kal, his attention on the people around us. I wonder what would happen if I took his hand. Would he whisper my name and call me pretty again? I want to feel my whole body vibrate when his breath brushes my cheek. I want to live in that moment we shared in the library for the rest of my days. Just standing next to him makes me a little light-headed.

I extend my fingers, his palm within my grasp, and then pull away, crossing my arms and placing my hands on the hilts of my daggers where they won't be tempted. It's up to

Kal to make the next move. I wouldn't be able to function if I reached for him and he spurned me.

As we wait, more and more people join us, and quiet conversations turn to shouts and yells. I find myself getting shoved to the back, where I'm too far away to see what's happening at the front. I stand on my toes, but I can barely see over the backs of the people in front of me. Kal's a full head taller, so I tug on his arm and he bends down.

Cupping my hands around my mouth, I shout in his ear. "Let's move closer to the front. I can't see anything."

"Alright." Kal grabs me by the hand to lead me through the mass of bodies packed shoulder to shoulder. His touch is exhilarating. A rush of tingles runs up my arm and down my back, making me shiver. I take Rima's hand and pull her along too, with Nez bringing up the rear. We twist and turn our way nearer to the altar until we find a pocket that isn't as congested as the rest of the Temple.

"Is this better?" Kal yells.

I nod. Kal is still holding my hand, and I don't let go. But now that I've got my wish, I want more. I want my arm around his waist, his arm over my shoulders, pulling me close. I want him to caress my face with more than his breath. By the Fires, I want Rima's fantasy embrace.

I've never had romantic daydreams before, but then I've never met a boy like Kal before.

A hush falls over the congregation as a red curtain parts. I take a deep breath to clear my thoughts so that I can concentrate on what's happening around me.

The Mother appears on the altar, her hand resting on the arm of a Daughter.

"My children," the Mother says, her unclouded eye on those before her, waiting for her guidance. "We walk a path unknown, the light from Thregor's torch barely penetrating the darkness around us. We have only our hearts to guide us. But our hearts have been forged in the Fires. We will prevail. The gods have willed it to be so. We are the righteous ones, for we are born, we live, and we die by the Fires."

"By the Fires," everyone murmurs, making the sign of respect and bowing their heads.

"We know not what this Mistress has planned, but we will fight her with the strength of thirteen dragons!" With her arms and face raised toward the ceiling, the old woman ululates with a voice that pierces the heavens. Loud and strong, she cries out to the dragons, seeking their attention, calling upon them for help.

Behind the Mother, statues of the Thirteen blow jets of fire from their blackened mouths, setting alight a bonfire in the center of the altar.

The Mother turns toward those gathered before her. "By the Fires you live, by the Fires you are blessed, and by the Fires you die."

"By the Fires," the people shout in response.

Ululations erupt from the crowd, many of them invigorated by the prayer that seems to give them hope.

I can't imagine what it must feel like to put all of my hope into the hands of the gods. Is it freeing? Does facing your enemy become easier when you believe there's a god on your side? But what if it's a god you've never seen or heard—why do you keep praying?

I wish my father were here so I could ask him these things.

Maybe he could help me understand. For now, what gives me hope isn't the words of an ancient prayer. It's knowing I'm going to the meeting with the Mistress whether the Mother wants me there or not. Finally, I'll get some answers and maybe even—

I stop myself from finishing that thought. If Obba is still alive—and that is a big *if*—then I will save him. Until then, I can't allow myself to get caught up in the *ifs*. I don't have time for what may be. I have to stay focused on what's happening now.

When the prayer is over, the Mother disappears behind the curtain. The captain jumps onto the altar and waves his hands for silence.

"All of those going to the meeting house, meet our Mother by the front barricades," he says. "The rest of you, get ready for a fight. And if you can't fight, hide the children and keep them safe and quiet. We don't know what the Mistress has planned, but we should be ready for anything. You have your orders. You know what to do. Now, to your stations!"

Kal looks down at me. "Ready?" he asks and I nod. "Then, let our journey into the belly of the beast begin."

As the Mother and her people leave through the front, the children are ushered into the catacombs. This time, we go along with the other kids, allowing ourselves to be herded behind the hidden door in the wall and down the steps to the first level. Armored men and women guard the steps going to the other floors, preventing the children from going deeper into the catacombs.

Some of the younger children are crying. Their weeping echoes around the bodies of the living and the dead.

I turn to Rima. "Alright, you're in charge of getting us out of here. Do you have the notes?"

Rima removes four notes from her waistband that she wrote after talking with Basheera last night.

"Basheera will kill me if she finds out I used her stamp to sign these," Rima says.

"I won't tell her if you won't," I say. A thin smile appears on her face. She takes a deep breath and walks over to a set of guards standing at the top of a flight of stairs. The rest of us follow.

"Hey, let us pass," Rima barks at the guards, sounding like her sister. She waves a slip of paper in her hand. "We're runners. We have to deliver these messages."

One of the guards shakes her head. "No one is allowed past, especially not people your age. We have strict orders to keep all the children safe."

"Tell that to the scribes," Rima replies. "They said it's imperative we deliver these messages now."

"And why did they choose a bunch of children—"

"Because we're the fastest," I say, annoyed with being held up for so long. We need to get going if we're going to make it to the meeting house in time to see what's happening. I grab the notes out of Rima's hand and pass them out to the others, keeping one for myself. "Now are you going to move, or do I have to make you move?"

The guards narrow their eyes at me and I glare right back at them.

"Look, you can stop us from going, but you're going to be the ones to tell Scribe Basheera why her messages weren't delivered," Nez says, stepping between me and the guards.

"Scribe Basheera gave you those notes?" one guard asks.

"Of course," Rima says. "She's going to be furious about this. But what can we do? You won't let us out."

The guards glance at each other, worry and fear clouding their faces.

"Perhaps you should let us pass," Kal says and the guards finally move aside.

"Go," one of the guards says. "And tell the other guards Pemba said to let you through."

"And Aisha!" the second guard yells as we barrel past them.

We race down the steps to the second level, where another group of guards tries to halt our descent. But once they hear about Pemba and Aisha, they let us pass. It's the same on every level until we reach the narrow passage leading to the village. Barricades block the entrance to the passage, and we have to perform our whole charade all over again to convince the guards to let us through.

Time is running out, so I push my way into the captain of the guards' face. "Unless you want Scribe Basheera to come down here, you'd better move out of our way!"

The captain stutters, her eyes wide and her mouth flapping open like a fish. "F-fine," she stammers, composing herself enough to order the barricade open for us to pass through. "You want to get yourselves captured by the Mistress, far be it from me to stop you."

I shoulder past the captain and her guards with the others in tow. Once in the tunnel, we quickly make our way to the door. There, the guards practically shove us outside so they can slide the metal bars back in place to hold the door shut.

As soon as it closes, apprehension sets in. Now that we're

outside the safety of the Temple, I realize how vulnerable we are, how quickly we can be run down, how easily we can be torn apart.

But I can't think about that now. We've made our decision, and we can't go back.

I lead us to the roof of the building. From there, in the glow of the midmorning sun, we can see almost the whole village.

My village. The village my father died to protect. The only home I've ever known.

A strange quiet fills Lagusa. There are no vendors in the market, no customers haggling over prices, no children running around them, no beggars asking for handouts. Dogs don't bark. Even the birds are silent. The streets are also empty of Dambi, but evidence of them is everywhere.

Scratches across stone walls, blood congealing on the dusty streets, flies buzzing around the ripped-apart body of some unknown animal hanging from a tree branch.

I glance at Nez, at Rima, at Kal. Here we are, at the beast's mouth, and I'm leading them into the belly. As I climb over a railing, I hope my rash declaration to kill the Mistress hasn't doomed us all.

CHAPTER EIGHTEEN

AS WE GO UP LADDERS AND ACROSS ROOFTOPS, EACH step drawing us closer to the meeting house, the Dambi stench grows. I swallow to keep the bile from rising in my throat.

"I don't think I'll ever get used to that smell," Nez says between gags.

"I hope I'm not around Dambi enough to ever get used to it," Kal replies.

When we finally reach the roof across the street from the meeting house, I'm not surprised to see scores of Dambi prowling on all fours in front of the dusty-brown, mud-brick building.

The Mother and her retinue are nowhere to be found, and for a moment I think we missed them going inside, but Kal points at movement on his left.

"There they are," he whispers and ducks down. I turn in that direction and see the Mother leading her protectors to the meeting house. I crouch as well and pull on Nez's arm so that he and Rima do the same.

The protectors reach for their weapons once they see the Dambi in front of the meeting house, but the Mother bids them to keep their swords sheathed.

"We have come as guests," she says. "We will not be hurt."

With howls and shrieks that threaten to burst my eardrums, the Dambi part and the Mistress appears from among them, the mark on the back of her hand glowing brightly.

My fingers tighten around the hilts of my daggers. I would give anything to throw one of them right at the center of the Mistress's forehead. But if I do that, nothing would stop the Dambi from killing the Mother and everyone around her. With my jaw clenched, I slowly loosen my grip on the daggers.

"Our Mother speaks truth," the Mistress says. "Come, you will have safe passage."

My lip curls in disgust at the Mistress's words. *Our Mother.* How dare she pretend to have respect for our elders after what she did to the Subaans?

The Mistress turns and withdraws inside the meeting house. The path between the Dambi remains open.

"This feels like a trap," Nez whispers. "As soon as they're in the middle of those creatures, the Dambi are going to attack and kill them all."

"She said they'll have safe passage," Rima counters, but she doesn't sound convinced.

"We won't know until they take the first step." I move closer to the ledge.

As if they heard my words, the Mother and her protectors put aside their fear. The Mother is the first to enter the path between the Dambi, her hand over her mouth and nose to mask the horrid stench emanating from their rotting bodies.

I don't envy the Mother. Even from across the street, the air is so thick with the Dambi's foul odor I can taste it, and they're as frightening as ever with their milky-white eyes, their claws dragging on the ground. But now, as they stand unmoving, I almost feel sorry for them. The humanity they once possessed is gone, ripped away by the transformation Sothpike forced upon them. They should be entombed, their bodies turned to ash, their souls at rest, instead of being controlled by the Mistress.

My heart races from seeing my people among the Dambi, but the monsters keep their distance from those still alive. The doors to the meeting house are wide open, and the Mistress waits on the other side.

"Come in," she says as if she is welcoming guests to a party. "It is much cooler out of the sun."

Once everyone is inside, the doors to the meeting house close, and we have to figure out our next move. It's impossible to approach from the front, as Dambi once again roam the area in front of the building, cutting off access to the entrance.

Still hunched over so that he is hidden by the ledge, Kal motions for the rest of us to get moving. "Let's go."

This time Rima leads the way across rooftops and balconies, through abandoned structures and over planks bridging the gaps between two- and three-story buildings. She stops on the roof of a shop overlooking a closed-off footpath behind the meeting house.

"It was empty the night I found you, just like it is now," Rima says. "I don't think anyone uses it anymore."

"Let's hope they didn't block off the back entrance too," Nez says.

Moving away from the edge, Kal walks over to the trapdoor in the roof. He tugs on the handle, but the door is chained shut on the inside.

"It was open the last time I was here," Rima says, kneeling next to the trapdoor. "I saw one of the runners go through it."

Kal rattles the door one last time but it won't budge. "Well, it's locked now."

"Just break it." Nez stomps on the door, hard, and the wood cracks. He does it again and his foot goes through the splintered wood all the way up to the knee. Before he can move, the door gives way completely and Nez falls through, landing in a heap on the floor below.

I lean into the hole, my heart in my throat. "Nez!"

"I'm alright," he groans and tries to stand. His face pales and he falls back down. "I think I hurt my leg," he says through gritted teeth. "Twisted it or something."

In the distance, a Dambi shrieks. Kal uses his sword to hack at the wood until the hole is wide enough for us to go through without getting scraped by any of the protruding pieces. A ladder is revealed once the trapdoor is cleared away.

Rima is the first one down. She kneels beside Nez to keep him from trying to stand.

"I think it's his ankle," Rima says when I join them. "The right one."

I lift up Nez's pant leg. Already the skin around his ankle is swelling and turning red. "We have to go back."

Nez shakes his head. "No way. We didn't come this far to turn back now."

"He's right," Rima says. "You and Kal keep going. I'll stay with Nez."

I glance at Kal and he nods.

"Alright," I say. "Kal and I will finish this."

With a kiss to Nez's forehead and a promise that I'll be safe, we leave Nez and Rima behind. I can't help but feel like I'm making a mistake—Nez and I do everything together, and it feels wrong to be going off on such a dangerous mission without him. But I still have Kal, and I know Rima will stay with Nez until we return.

We run down the steps to the first floor, where we find a door that leads to the old footpath. We stick to the shadows as we make our way to the back of the meeting house. I search for the crack Nez and I used to crawl through to spy on our father when we were bored or curious.

About halfway down the footpath, I pull aside the overgrown brush clinging to the stone to reveal a hole in the wall.

"This was an old entrance someone bricked up a long time ago," I explain, "but when we were children, Nez discovered this part of the wall was falling down." I motion toward Kal. "You first."

He ducks through and grabs the branches and vines so that I can pass. "You and your brother must've driven your parents crazy growing up."

"I think my parents would say we still do," I reply once I'm on the other side. It isn't until my eyes adjust to the darkness that I realize what I said. *Parents.* As if I still have both of them. I take a deep breath and swallow the lump that's slowly rising in my throat. I have to stay focused.

"Are you alright?" Kal asks.

I nod, not trusting my voice, and glance around.

We find ourselves in an abandoned part of the meeting house, filled with dusty crates and broken chairs. I take the lead, brushing past Kal toward the exit that will take us deeper into the meeting house.

Torchlight at regular intervals guides us out of the storage areas and into the main section of the meeting house. Before entering the assembly room where the Subaans held council, I glance at Kal and put a finger to my lips. Nearby, a Dambi shrieks and I freeze. There is no one and nothing visible. Is it possible a Dambi knows we're inside? Can it smell us, even if it can't see us?

"I heard something scraping the walls behind us," Kal whispers. "We should keep moving."

I wish more than ever Nez hadn't hurt his leg. If I have to fight another Dambi, I want Kal *and* Nez by my side.

We make our way down the hall and up the stairs to a deserted balcony overlooking the assembly room. I duck down and crawl across the floor, coming to a crouch beside the railing with Kal at my side.

We peer over the railing. The Mistress sits in a chair on a dais, her face obscured by the mask. There are three empty chairs on her left, and three more on her right. She is sitting in the seat of the Qal'at Subaan, where Obba should be sitting. My muscles tense and I grip the railing. It physically hurts to be so close to the Mistress, to be near enough to kill her, and not able to do anything about it.

I let go of the railing and listen.

"You still haven't told us what you're doing to our children," the Mother says, "and yet you are asking us to bring you more?"

"I found books from your record-keepers," the Mistress replies. Her strange accent makes it sound as if every word is a struggle. "There are two hundred and thirty-six children between the ages of fifteen and seventeen in this village. I have one hundred and twelve of them. Where are the rest?"

"They are safe," the Mother replies. "And they will remain safe. Tell us why you are here, and maybe we can come to some sort of agreement."

Murmurs erupt from the protectors.

"We can't negotiate with someone who serves Sothpike," someone says. "We should be fighting, not talking."

"Your people are not happy," the Mistress observes. "So, I will tell you why I am here. Perhaps that will appease them. My quest is one that affects your people as well. For I am in search of the child of the last Ur Atum Asim Avari."

I furrow my brows in confusion. Asim Avari's child died upon birth—it's common knowledge. And a few days after the death of her child, Sothpike toppled the great city of Al-Kazar, the capital of Merza, and killed the Asim. Even if Avari's child survived, Sothpike would have surely killed it as well when he stormed the citadel of Al-Kazar.

"I understand your confusion, for even my lord Sothpike believes the child to be dead," the Mistress continues. "But now that I've seen your pretty little village, I believe that it is not. You see, I found something that everyone says doesn't exist: a village beyond the desert. They all think the desert is never-ending, like the Western Sea, but I have always known that every sea has a shore, and every desert an oasis. I found

Lagusa, and I will find the child of the Asim. I believe she lied, that she really sent it away to keep it safe. And what better place to hide a child than in a village that doesn't exist?"

"And what will you do with this child once you find it?" the Mother asks.

"I will offer it to my lord Sothpike as a gift," the Mistress replies. "I am willing to return the children I already have, in exchange for ones I am missing. None of them is the one I am looking for."

"If all she wants is one child," whines a protector, "shouldn't we find the child and give it to her?"

"No," Captain Farouk replies, his voice deep and booming. "We will never *give* Sothpike, or those who serve him, anything. We must fight them over every grain of sand in the Bujarbi Desert!"

Shouts of approval and dissent fill the hall. I wish I could add my voice to those supporting Captain Farouk, but I know I can't do more than shoot looks of disgust at the cowards scared of standing up to the Mistress.

One protector's voice rises above the rest. "Captain Farouk, you would risk the lives of everyone in Lagusa for the sake of one child?"

"Lagusa won't be worth saving if we sacrifice even one child," Captain Farouk answers. "I am surprised to hear such fear from you, Samida Oboro."

"Call it fear if you want, but I say we should let the Mistress have this child," Oboro replies. "Why must we suffer? Let her have it, and maybe she will leave us in peace."

Captain Farouk clutches the hilt of his sword. "If we cannot protect one child, then we do not deserve to live!"

"Captain Farouk, be calm," the Mother admonishes. "This is not the place for such an argument. We must come together and do what's best for the village."

"We will not negotiate with anyone who serves that bastard Sothpike," Captain Farouk shouts. He points his sword at the Mistress. "Give us our children and leave this village, or die where you sit."

In the next breath, the Mistress's hand glows, and the doors to the assembly room burst open. A Dambi races into the room, its claws scratching the tiled floor, and leaps on the captain. It knocks Captain Farouk to the ground, his head hitting the hard floor with a wet smack, and begins shredding his skin, breaking his spine and cracking his ribs. The Dambi pulls out Captain Farouk's still-beating heart and eats it while blood pools on the floor around it.

I stare with my mouth wide open at the carnage. In one moment, Captain Farouk was ready to take on the Mistress with his sword, and in the next, he is being eaten alive by a Dambi. The protectors surround the Mother, their eyes wide with fright, and I ready my daggers. If the Dambi go for the Mother next, I'll have to join the fight. I glance at Kal and he's already unsheathed his sword.

The Mistress twitches her finger and the Dambi shrieks. I cover my ears with my hands. The monster retreats to the side of the room where it skulks, blood dripping from its mouth, its claws leaving red trails on the floor.

"I am a forgiving person," the Mistress says. "But I will not abide blasphemy about my lord Sothpike, the King of Waldyria, Caretaker of Merza, The One Who Will Unite Volsgaria, and He Who Rules All He Sees. Sothpike is greater than all of us, his mission appointed to him by gods older than this earth. He is most holy upon high, and you will serve him as your lord. Now, in the name of my lord Sothpike, bow."

The protectors murmur among themselves, their hushed voices rising and falling. But they do not bow. When no one moves, the Mistress narrows her eyes.

"I said, *bow.*"

The Mother pushes her protectors aside and faces the Mistress. "I will never bow to anyone as foul as your master. I would rather die than serve Sothpike. Be warned: you will burn. The Fires will turn you to ash and send your soul to oblivion."

"Perhaps, our steadfast Mother, perhaps." The hint of a smile plays across the Mistress's lips. "But at least I will not be dying by fire today. Unlike the people in your precious Temple."

Boom boom boom.

Boom boom boom.

Boom boom boom.

The war drum reverberates in my chest. The Dambi are attacking.

The Mother raises a shaking hand to her mouth. "This *was* a trap," she says, "but not for me."

"We have to get back to the Temple," I whisper to Kal. I start to leave, but he grabs my arm.

"Not yet," he whispers back. "They aren't finished yet, and we still don't know what she's going to do to the kids she already captured."

I think of the Daughters and the scribes back at the Temple, the guards and children in the catacombs, and of the Dambi that are probably already tearing them apart. I need to be there—it's why I joined the resistance. Not for honor, not for riches, not for glory. But to do what is right. And what is right is helping the people in the Temple.

But Kal is also right. We need to know what the Mistress has planned, so we can stop her. I have to trust the resistance knows what it is doing. I have to believe that they can protect themselves. I can't be in two places at once. I'm here now, and I need to stay.

With gritted teeth, I return my attention to the scene before us.

"I will have the remaining children," the Mistress says to the Mother. "And you will bow for Sothpike." The Mistress looks beyond the Mother and her protectors, toward the entrance to the hall. "Or they will die."

Expecting more Dambi, I gasp when instead I see one hundred and twelve kids around my age being led into the hall by Subaan Ledisi, their hands bound and tied together, forming one long human chain. Many of them limp, their clothes rip and tattered. They're covered in blood. What has the Mistress been doing to them?

A pack of Dambi prowl alongside the children, snarling and snapping their sharp teeth at them like rabid dogs.

The Mother wrings her hands, her good eye darting from one kid to another, taking in their pain, their suffering.

She turns to the Mistress. "What have you done to our children, our future?"

"Put out the call to your people," the Mistress says to the Mother, ignoring her question. "I want the remaining children brought to me in two days' time, when the sun is six hands in the sky, as you would say. Or I will kill every child in Lagusa, even the little babes still in their cribs. I will set my Dambi loose and command them to eat their bellies and crush their tiny skulls until I find the one I am after."

The Mother faces the Mistress's prisoners once more, tears streaming down her cheeks. One boy stumbles toward the Mother. She stretches out her arms but after only a few steps, he crumples to the floor, too weak to stand. He looks like he could be suffering from exhaustion, hunger, blood loss, or all of them at once. The Mother gasps and covers her mouth with both of her trembling hands.

"Please, do not harm anyone else," the Mother says, dropping to her knees. "I bow to your lord Sothpike."

"Get on your feet," the Mistress says. "And bring me the children."

CHAPTER NINETEEN

I'VE SEEN ENOUGH. I TAP KAL ON THE SHOULDER AND tilt my head toward the exit. He nods, and I lead us out of the building the same way we entered, down the hall, into the junk rooms in the back, and out through the hole covered by brush and vines.

We run back to the building where we left Rima and Nez. I race up the stairs and find Nez standing, one arm across Rima's shoulders, his right leg bent at the knee to keep his foot from touching the ground.

"What happened?" he asks when he sees us.

"We'll tell you on the way back," I say, running toward the ladder.

"Wait," Rima says. "Why were they beating the drums?"

"The Mistress sent her Dambi to attack the Temple," Kal replies.

Nez and Rima's eyes widen with shock but they don't move.

"Come on," I say, my hands on the rungs of the ladder "We have to hurry."

"That crafty witch," Nez says. "She drew us out here, knowing the Mother would bring her best fighters and leave the Temple vulnerable."

"That's why we have to hurry." I start to climb the ladder but stop when Rima calls my name.

"Nez can't use the rooftops," she says when she has my attention. "There's too much jumping, and with his ankle…"

"I'll be fine." Nez reaches for the ladder with his free arm. "Let's go."

"Rima's right," Kal says. "We have to find another way."

"I guess we're taking the streets," Nez says as he hobbles in the other direction.

I admire Nez. He's so good at accepting change and doing what's best for everyone without hesitation.

At the stairs, Kal takes Nez's other arm and he and Rima help Nez hop down. It's slow going, and I want to rush ahead, but I can't leave Nez behind. Not again, not after what the Mistress did to Captain Farouk, and especially not when Nez is injured. I have to stay by his side to protect him.

Outside, people mill about in the middle of the road, their faces turned toward the Temple, hands covering their open mouths, eyes wide with horror. Black smoke pours out of the structure.

"Oh no," I say. "We have to hurry!"

"I am hurrying," Nez replies, his voice filled with frustration as he limps down the street using Kal for support.

A woman my mother's age grabs me by the arm.

"Where are you going, child?" she asks, her voice raspy. "You should be hiding."

"We're going to the Temple," I reply, raising my voice so

that others can hear. "They need our help. If you can fight, then you should come too."

The woman lets go of my arm and backs away. "I will pray for you," she says and crosses her arms over her chest. She bows her head and begins a prayer. "By the Fires, may the gods watch over us and protect us from our enemies. Give us strength, o gods, so that we may—"

Shaking my head, I turn away from the woman. I don't want prayers. I want people with the courage to fight. For sixteen years, people have been praying to the dragon gods to save them from Sothpike, and not once during that time has there been any evidence that the gods are listening. The only protection I can depend on comes from the daggers I wear on my forearms, the training I received from Obba, and my will to survive no matter what.

For too long, the Bujarbi Desert insulated the people of Lagusa from the war happening up north. Now that the war has scaled our wall and beaten down our gates, the time for complacency is over.

"You can pray while the Temple burns," I say to those who join the woman in prayer, "or you can come with us to put out the fire. My brother's ankle is probably broken, but he's still going to the Temple to help. We *can* save our Temple, but it's going to take more than prayers to do it."

"She speaks the truth," says a man brandishing a curved sword like Obba's. He's tall, with glistening black skin, and wears a blue turban. "This is our village, and we must defend it. No one sets fire to my Temple and gets away with it. Who's with me?"

A cheer rises up among the onlookers and the man claps me on the shoulder. "What's your name, samida?"

"Naira Khoum," I reply with a bow, grateful to have someone big and strong on my side to sway the populace. "And you, samir?"

"Bagara Oluweydo." Bagara gives me a wide smile. "Khoum, you say? Any relation to Isrof Khoum?"

"He is—was—my father," I reply.

Bagara's smile drops. "Sorry to hear that. Isrof was a good man. I served with him in Al-Kazar. The best damn Rudan I'd ever met. The Asim was lucky to have him as her guard. Too bad she sent him away before Sothpike arrived. Isrof would have cut him down before that bastard even thought about laying a hand on the Asim."

"I think you must have my father confused with someone else," I say, backing away from Bagara. "Neither of my parents have ever been to Al-Kazar, so there was no way my father could have been a Rudan for the Asim."

"If what you say is true, then I suppose you're right," Bagara says, but he doesn't look as if he believes his own words. I can see the questions forming in his mind from the way he furrows his brow.

I glance over my shoulder. Nez and the others have already gone ahead. "I'd better go. I need to stay with my brother."

"You go, and I'll round up some more fighters." Bagara bows to me, and I do the same. "I'll see you at the Temple, Samida Khoum."

I run ahead and join the others.

"What was that about?" Nez pants, his face screwing up in pain every time his right foot touches the ground.

"There was this guy back there," I reply. "He said he knew our father."

Nez glances over his shoulder. "Really? What did he say?"

"It doesn't matter. He had Obba confused with someone else." I grab Nez's other arm and sling it over my shoulder. "We have to hurry."

With Kal on his right and me on his left, Nez is able to move at a quicker pace. As we move toward the chaos, Kal and I tell Rima and Nez everything we heard while in the meeting house. When we're finished, we're near the building connected to the tunnel that leads to the Temple.

"Should we go in through the catacombs or up the hill?" Rima asks.

"Doesn't matter to me," Nez says. "Either way, it's a lot of stairs."

"I think we should take the tunnel," I say. "Most likely she's attacking because she wants the other kids, so we should find them first and protect them."

"I agree," Kal says. "Let's go up the back way."

But the back way is covered in scratches and blood. Great gashes in the clay walls and unidentifiable body parts cover the floor near the battered entrance to the tunnel. Rima slips on a splatter of blood and would have fallen if I hadn't put out a hand to catch her.

"This is awful," Rima says.

"We can't go this way," Kal says. "What if they're still in the tunnel? If we try to fight them in there, they'll have the advantage in such a tight space, and we'll be killed."

I purse my lips. We'll have to go up the hill, right into the midst of the fighting. We exit the building and follow the main road to the Temple. Soon, the sounds of a battle reach our ears.

As we climb the stairs carved in the hillside, screams from the living and the undead carry on the same wind that chokes our breath and blinds our eyes with dark smoke. The acrid smell of burning flesh almost overpowers the Dambi stench.

By the time we've climbed the last stair, everyone is covered in soot and drenched in sweat from taking turns helping Nez. My eyes burn from the smoke and I cough after almost every breath.

Ahead, shadowy figures clash in the smoke. A Dambi pounces on a man in front of me, a curtain of black smoke obscures my view, then a clawed hand bursts through the smoke and swipes at my face. I jump back, bumping into Nez, who's holding on to Rima, and almost knock them both down.

"Get Nez out of here," I say, my throat scratchy. In the same breath, I grab my daggers.

"I'm not hiding," Nez shouts as the Dambi jumps out of the smoke at him. Kal slices the Dambi across the arm with his sword and it changes direction, charging at Kal instead. Standing on one foot, Nez pulls out his bow and shoots an arrow in the back of the Dambi's head.

The creature stumbles, but keeps going, its steps faltering but not stopping.

"I got this one," Kal yells as he runs into the clouds of fire and ash, leading the Dambi away, taking my heart with him. "Go save the others!"

"Kal!" I scream into the smoke, but he doesn't answer. My hands shake with fear and I drop one of my daggers.

Staring at the fallen weapon, I hear Obba's voice.

A Khoum never drops their weapon, not as long as they have breath in their lungs.

I still have breath, so I pick up my dagger and wrap my fingers tight around the grip. As much as I want to follow Kal, I know he's right. We have to keep moving. I grab Rima with one hand and Nez with the other. "Come on." I drag them out of the worst of the smoke, toward the entrance of the Temple.

The barricades have been destroyed by fire and the doors to the Temple are wide open.

We step over burnt bodies. Human or Dambi, it's hard to tell.

Inside, the screaming is even louder. I quickly hide behind a pillar, pulling Rima and Nez with me. There, I crouch and survey the scene.

Dambi rip apart bodies of the resistance fighters as if they are rag dolls and claw at the wall leading to the catacombs. There's even more fighting happening on the back plaza. It seems like that's where most of the Dambi are concentrated. I guess the fighters drew the Dambi out of the Temple once they made it past the front barricades.

The sliding wall that leads to the catacombs is crumbling. Large chunks of stone litter the floor, but the Dambi haven't broken through. Yet.

"We have to protect that wall," I say. There must be at least a dozen kids my age on the other side, and many more who are even younger. I hope the Dambi that made it to the tunnel have been killed before making it deeper into the catacombs. If we protect that wall, we can still stop the Mistress from capturing those children, but we have to act fast.

As I'm figuring out what to do next, Kal races into the Temple, sees us hiding behind a pillar, and quickly joins us. I let out a sigh of relief and would hug him, but his face is covered in black blood and there are large scratches across his stomach and left arm.

"Are you alright?" I take his face in my hands to check for cuts, but there aren't any. "How'd you get so bloody?"

"Dambi bleed like a stuck pig," Kal says, wiping the blood away with his sleeve. "Especially when they've been stabbed in the gut with their own claws."

Nez stares at Kal with his mouth open. "Your whole life is like one of those fantastic adventure books I used to read when I was a little kid," he says, his voice filled with awe. "Is there anything you can't do?"

Kal shrugs. "I can't think of anything."

I motion toward the Dambi tearing apart the wall. "We have to—"

"Basheera," Rima whispers, her eyes on the busted doors of the library.

Everyone follows Rima's gaze. There are no Dambi by the library. Either they already killed everyone inside or they haven't raided the library yet. I hope for the latter.

But I'm torn. We can check on my friend's sister, or we can stop the Dambi from breaching the wall. I know how much Basheera means to Rima. And I also know we have to do whatever we can to keep the rest of Lagusa's children away from the Mistress. Whatever she plans to do when she finds Avari's child, it won't be good for the people of Merza.

"The most important thing is stopping the Mistress from finding the child she's searching for," I say. "I'm going to stop those Dambi from getting into the catacombs. If you want to check on Basheera, I won't stop you. But I've got to protect those kids."

Rima takes a deep breath. "You're right. We've got to stop the Mistress. It's what Basheera would do, if she knew what we know."

There are only two Dambi still in the Temple. We can handle that.

The creatures prowl in front of the busted wall, occasionally scratching at it with their claws, reminding me of being trapped in the tomb. I push those distressing memories aside to focus on what is happening now.

We have to lure the Dambi away from the catacombs. But with Nez's injury, it isn't going to be easy. I think back to Obba—what he would do if he was with us, what tactics he would use to turn the battle to his advantage. Strategy was as important to the training Obba gave us as was learning how to hold a weapon.

"Alright, Kal and I will go first and draw those two away," I whisper, pointing at the Dambi blocking the entrance to the catacombs. "While we lead them out to the plaza, you two make a break for the wall and stand guard. Kal and I will join you once we've gotten rid of those two."

"Are you sure that's going to work?" Nez asks. "With my sprained ankle and all?"

"Of course it will," I reply. "It's what Obba would do."

Nez smiles. "Good thing one of us was paying attention to Obba's lessons. I was always too busy trying to catch my breath."

I squeeze Nez's shoulder. "Is everyone ready?"

Rima and Nez both murmur in agreement. Kal takes a deep breath and gets into a crouch. He looks me in the eyes, I nod, and he takes off running toward the catacombs. I'm right behind him, my daggers out.

The Dambi shriek when they see us, and as I predicted, they come galloping toward us with that loping gait that always unnerves me with its awkwardness. The human body—even one resurrected from the dead—isn't meant to run on all fours.

One Dambi goes for Kal, the other for me. We both lead our Dambi toward the back of the Temple—where a third Dambi, which was behind a pillar feasting on the entrails of the dead, rears back on its hind legs and screeches, blocking the exit to the plaza.

My plan didn't account for three Dambi.

I need a new plan.

"We have to draw it away," I shout at Kal. "Get its attention, and once it's following us, we'll circle around and try for the plaza again."

Kal picks up a discarded bowl and throws it at the third Dambi, hitting it in the head. The Dambi charges toward us. I motion for Kal to turn left like me, but he misunderstands and goes to the right instead. One Dambi follows Kal; the other two are fixated on me. My Dambi collide with each other on the turn and get tangled up in their too-long limbs. The Dambi screech and claw at each other.

On my left, Nez and Rima hurry toward the catacombs. Kal's made it to the altar, but his Dambi catches sight of Nez and Rima and starts to turn in their direction. Kal lunges at the Dambi, striking it in the abdomen, getting its attention once more. Kal tries to get the Dambi to chase him, but every time he starts running, the Dambi turns back to Nez and Rima. He has no choice but to fight to keep it away from them. The Dambi swipes at Kal's face. Kal dodges and counters, his blade slicing the Dambi's back.

Behind me, the two Dambi regain their footing and pick up speed. One leaps at me. I duck and it sails over my head. The second Dambi swipes at me, clipping me on the shoulder and knocking me to the ground. When the first Dambi pounces on me again, I roll out of the way and drag the blades of my daggers across its belly, releasing a river of blackened blood. The Dambi howls and stumbles.

By now, Rima and Nez are at the catacombs. One of the Dambi chasing me notices them and shrieks as it changes direction, heading straight for them.

"Nez! Watch out!"

Hopping on one foot and wincing in pain, Nez struggles to nock an arrow while Rima holds her spear with one hand, her other arm around Nez's waist to help steady him. The Dambi is almost close enough to claw both of them, so I jump to my feet and throw one of my daggers at the creature. The blade embeds in its back, but the beast keeps charging. Something sharp grazes my back and I fall forward. I roll over as a claw swipes at my face. I go to stab the Dambi with my second dagger, but it knocks the weapon out of my hand. It skitters across the floor, far out of reach.

Crouching over me, the Dambi lowers its face until it's nose to nose with me. It opens its mouth and shrieks, spittle flying everywhere, the inside of its mouth empty except for its long, sharp teeth. It has no tongue.

The Dambi wraps one hand around my throat, its claws

digging into my skin. It squeezes tighter and tighter and I gasp for air. It bangs my head hard on the stone, making me see stars, and drags me across the floor, its fingers tightening with every step. It's trying to take me back to its Mistress. I kick, scratch, and punch the Dambi, but it won't let go.

Nez yells out, Rima screams, and when I turn my head, I see Kal fall to the ground.

This isn't how it was supposed to end, I think as the edges of the world tinge black. *Not like this*.

CHAPTER TWENTY

SHRIEKING AND SHOUTING FILL MY EARS. MY EYELIDS FLY open and color returns to my sight. Gasping for air, I get on my hands and knees and crawl to where I last saw my dagger, the back of my head throbbing with pain, the scratches on my back burning like fire.

It takes a moment for me to understand what is going on inside the Temple. My vision swims as I regain consciousness, and there is so much noise. I shake my head to clear my sight, finally reaching the dagger. With trembling legs, I use a pillar to pull myself onto my feet.

What I see when I can finally make sense of things causes my mouth to fall open in shock.

Nine warriors in dusty gray cloaks wielding long silver swords fight the remaining Dambi alongside the villagers. Layers of cloth wrap around their noses, mouths, and the tops of their heads, leaving only narrow strips for their eyes. One of the warriors holds up a pole with a flag that shows three eyes emblazoned on a palm in front of a gray-green flame.

In the center of all the commotion is a woman on horse-back. She orders her warriors out of the Temple to the back plaza and tells them to kill every Dambi they see. Then she turns her white horse toward the altar, where Bagara Olu-weydo, the man who claimed to have served as a Rudan with my father, helps Kal fight the remaining Dambi. Kal keeps his left arm bent at the elbow and presses it close to his body. He's injured, his face is battered, but he's still standing.

Thundering hoofbeats fill the Temple as the woman charges the Dambi. It turns around and with a single arc of her sword, she slices off its head.

The sword cuts through the Dambi as if it's nothing but air. Its body falls to its knees then slumps to the floor, while the head rolls across the altar, stopping near a dead Dambi that has my second dagger still embedded in its back and a silver-tipped spear jutting through its throat. The woman yanks on the reins of her horse and follows the others out the back to take on the remaining Dambi.

I watch the woman in gray leave, my mind still trying to process what I just saw. Killing the Dambi was like swatting a fly to her. It barely took any effort.

Outside, the battle continues, but now the tide has turned. While every fight I have with the creatures is a life-or-death struggle, the woman and her warriors pick them off easily. One blow from the woman's silver sword is enough to down a Dambi—and keep it down.

But even though the gray warriors are powerful, there are more Dambi than there are warriors, and we're not safe yet. Panic and fear still fill the Temple, and everyone flinches when a Dambi shrieks in the doorway leading to the plaza, its inhuman cries reminding us how close we are to death in their presence.

A group of villagers try to open the hidden entrance to the catacombs, their grunts and groans replacing the Dambi's shrieks and screams.

A ranger by the entrance motions for us to hurry. "Get over here before they snatch you too!" she yells.

"Snatch us?" Rima asks. "Who?"

"The Dambi," a villager responds, his arms straining to move the heavy stone. The wall's been damaged and it no longer slides open with simply a touch. "They took some of the older kids before we could get them all inside. We tried to stop them but..." He shakes his head before putting his back against the heavy stone and pushing against it with his legs. The battered wall scrapes the floor as it slowly moves to the side.

My stomach sinks. We were too late. I glance at the ripped cloth sacks and broken baskets strewn across the Temple, at the streaks of blood coating everyone's possessions. Hamala's family's makeshift enclosure is demolished, their belongings scattered among everyone else's.

"Naira, let's go!"

Nez waves me over to where he and Rima had been guarding the wall. With another push, the villagers manage to open it wide enough for us to squeeze through.

My body aching, I stumble over to the speared Dambi and retrieve my dagger from its back before heading toward the opening. Rima helps Nez hop over the broken hunks of stone and into the catacombs. His arm still bent, Kal enters next, and Bagara Oluweydo waits for me to pass through before following.

Guards grip their weapons and yell at us as we pass through to keep moving, get downstairs, stay together.

We go down to the second level, where we find groups of kids huddled together, their faces stricken with fear. They're scared, but unharmed. There is no shrieking, no Dambi stench in the catacombs. I sigh with relief. We may have been too late for some, but we made it in time for the ones here.

Nez claps Kal on the back. "Can you believe it?"

Kal tries to smile but only grimaces in pain.

"Looks like you hurt your arm," Bagara says.

"It's only dislocated," Kal says. "I'll be fine."

"Let me help you with that." Before Kal can protest, Bagara grabs Kal's bent arm and twists it with one hand while the other presses down on the crook of Kal's elbow. With a series of wet clicks, the shoulder pops back into place. Kal groans, but when it's finished, he's able to move his arm again. He smiles at Bagara.

"Thanks."

"No problem," Bagara says.

My eyes scan our surroundings and land on Hamala's family. Her little sister cries in the elderly man's arms while her mother tries to comfort the young boy. Hamala and her father are both missing.

I don't know what happened to Hamala's father, but I have a good guess where I'll find Hamala.

As much as I want to celebrate with Nez and the others, we weren't able to protect everyone. Even though Hamala and I have fought more times than I can count, I've seen what the Mistress does to her hostages, and nobody deserves that.

I move to the side as more people come down the steps to join us on the second level.

"What's going on outside?" someone asks the newcomers, and other voices join in.

"Where is our Mother?"

"Is she with you?"

Everyone shakes their head.

"No one's seen our Mother since she left for the meeting house," a ranger replies, "and as far as we know, she's still there."

"What about the scribes?" Rima asks. "Are they alright?"

No one has an answer for Rima. She turns to us. "I have to go to the library and find my sister."

"I'll go with you," Nez says, his arm still around Rima's shoulder.

"You need to get your ankle taken care of," Kal says. "I'll go."

"You're not in that great shape yourself, samir." Nez holds on tightly to Rima. "Why don't you get some of those cuts looked at and I'll—"

"How about both of you stop pretending to be invincible and settle down," I say. I remove Nez's arm from around Rima's shoulders and force him to sit. Then I turn to Kal. "You're bleeding everywhere. I wouldn't be surprised if you passed out right now. So why don't you sit down next to Nez and let a Daughter take care of you."

"Yes, samida," Kal says as he follows my orders.

A Daughter comes over and pulls up Nez's trouser leg to

inspect his ankle. Nez opens his mouth to protest but I give him a sharp look and he quickly closes it.

"Now that they're squared away," I say to Rima, "let's go find your sister."

"Hold on, young lady," Bagara says. His booming voice startles me. I forgot he was there. "Have you taken a look at yourself? It looks like a maugrab's been sharpening its claws on your back. If you don't get those looked at, they'll get infected. I've seen what happens to untreated Dambi scratches. It's not pretty."

"It's not that bad," I say, even though throbbing pain radiates from the scratches and my head aches something fierce. I had wanted to push through it, but then I realize that's exactly what Nez and Kal tried to do, and I didn't let them. But Rima needs to find her sister, and she can't go alone.

As if he can read my mind, Bagara says, "I've escorted people in worse situations. We'll be back before you know it." He turns to Rima. "Now, where're we off to?"

"The library." Rima turns to me and the others. "Get better. I'll be back soon." Then she and Bagara rush toward the stairs, Bagara bellowing at the guards to let them through, and they step aside.

A Daughter kneels beside me. "Come with me so I can take a look at your wounds."

I follow the Daughter behind a makeshift curtain where she removes what's left of my tunic. The cloth is ripped to shreds and my back throbs when I twist to look at the damage.

"I'm going to need you to lie down on your stomach," the Daughter says, pointing at a pallet on the floor. I do as she says and watch her open a bottle of firewort and pour the yellow liquid on a cloth.

"I don't suppose you have any bitterroot?" My face screws up in anticipation of the liquid touching my skin.

"No, samida," the Daughter replies as she begins dabbing the antiseptic on my cuts.

"You're always out of bitterroot," I say through clenched teeth. The firewort burns and I breathe in sharply with every application, the pain in my head turning into a dull throb.

"Thank Albedego the Heart-Saver these scratches aren't deep," the Daughter says, "or that Dambi would have done some real damage." She moves the hairs from the back of my neck and applies firewort on the claw marks there, as well.

When she's finished cleaning the wounds, the Daughter makes a poultice and covers my back with the mixture and bandages. Then she finds a new tunic for me to wear.

"We'll need to put on fresh poultices and bandages every day for the next few days," the Daughter says as I dress. "So, be sure to come and see me tomorrow. We don't want you to get an infection."

I stifle a laugh. Who knows what will happen in the next few hours, let alone the next few days? But I keep my composure and gingerly pull the tunic over my head.

"Thank you." I bow to the Daughter and she returns the gesture.

Once I'm free to go, I find Nez. His ankle has been wrapped up tightly and he lies with his foot resting on a stack of pillows.

"I have to keep it elevated," he says when I sit down next

to him. "So…it looks like I'm going to be taking a lot of naps. Daughter's orders."

"Any excuse to laze about." I jab Nez in the shoulder with my elbow playfully.

"I hope Rima comes back soon," Nez says. "I don't like her out there with all that going on."

"Me neither."

Nez lifts himself up on one elbow. "Hey, I was worried about you. If those people hadn't shown up… I hate to think what could have happened."

"Then don't." I also don't want to think about how close I came to having the life squeezed out of me. It scared me how easily that Dambi could have killed me. And there would have been nothing I could do about it. I will do whatever it takes to never be put in a position of helplessness again.

Shouts come down from the top of the stairs and everyone quiets.

"What's going on?" someone asks.

"Did they say it's all clear?"

"Does this mean we can leave now?"

A guard runs down the stairs, shouting, "The Dambi are dead!"

After a moment of shocked silence, a cheer rises up from those hiding in the catacombs. Nez wraps me in a hug, and I flinch when his arms press against the wounds on my back.

"Sorry," he says, then kisses me on the cheek and pumps his fist in the air. "We did it!" But he doesn't celebrate for long before scrambling onto his feet using a wooden crutch one of the Daughters fashioned for him. "Let's go find Rima."

"Wait, where's Kal?" I want to be sure he's heard the good news.

Nez glances around and points toward his right. "See, he's already on his way over."

"Did you hear?" Kal laughs once he's near. "We won!"

I'm about to hug Kal, not caring at all about the pain, when a hush falls over the room. Everyone is watching the stairs, so I turn to follow their gaze.

The warriors in gray are descending, uncovering their faces as they approach. My eyes are drawn to the familiar ones first, the ones who look like my people. Their deep brown skin, thick coily hair, and brown eyes remind me of the people I see every day in Lagusa. The others are definitely foreigners, but I have no idea from where. I've never seen such a mixture of skin tones, hair, eyes. Some have skin paler than mine, skin as light as the statues of the Thirteen. Their eyes are different shades of green and blue, their yellow and red hair hanging loose and limp from their scalps. Others have straight, black hair, their eyes dark like mine.

One of the women stands out from the rest. She walks down the steps first, her shoulders squared and her chin held high. A long, silver sword with gold wire wrapped around the hilt dangles at her side.

"Who is in charge here?" she says with an accent that reminds me of the Mistress's.

"I recognize her." Kal eyes the woman leading the foreign warriors, the same one who rode into the Temple on a white horse and chopped off the head of a Dambi with one slice of her sword. "She's the one who came to fight my father. The Hakkuen Trial, remember? And she's wearing the clasp with the broken sword." Kal points at the golden hand clutching a sword with a broken tip attached to the woman's cloak, holding it closed. My eyes widen at the sight—it looks exactly like his father's clasp, which Kal now wears on his belt.

One of the Daughters steps forward. "I am the First Daughter. I am in charge, until our Mother returns."

"Well then," the woman says, "find your Mother and tell her the Hands of God have arrived."

Shouts of surprise fill the catacombs along with whispers of disbelief. Behind me, an older woman falls on her knees and praises the Thirteen while others glare at the Hands, their fists clenched or gripping their weapons. I'm not surprised by the mixed reaction—many still hate the Hands for abandoning the Asim, but others welcome their presence, hoping they will save us from the Dambi.

All my life I've thought of the Hands as cowards, but after seeing them fight the Dambi, I know how useful they can be in a battle. I want to hear what they have to say for themselves.

But it's not the Hands who speak next. Instead, it's protector Oboro.

"Our Mother is being held captive by the Mistress," the protector says over the din, limping down the stairs behind the Hands. Her face is battered and bloody, as if she fought through a gauntlet to get to the Temple. "The Mistress knows we are not alone, and she refuses to give up our Mother or the captured children until we give her what she wants."

"And what is that?" someone asks.

Oboro places a hand over the gash on her side and slumps onto the steps, her other hand leaving a smear of red on the wall. Blood drips from her lips. "The rest of the children. All of them, no matter what age. She said our future now belongs to Sothpike."

The First Daughter runs over to Oboro's side. "What did they do to you, Samida Oboro?"

Oboro laughs, but the sound is harsh. "Everything."

"What do we do now?" one of the children cries out.

"You burn our dead," Oboro says, her chin falling against her chest. "Then you kill the Mistress."

And with that, protector Oboro breathes her last.

CHAPTER
TWENTY-ONE

NORMALLY, WE BURN OUR DEAD IN TOMBS, BUT THERE are too many bodies and no tomb big enough to hold all of them. The First Daughter decides to do the burning in the back plaza under the statues of the gods the next day when the sun is at its zenith.

I spend the night helping build the pyre. As I worked, I listened to people talking about the Hands—those welcoming their arrival speaking in whispers, while those who want them to pay for not protecting Asim Avari shout their protests.

I understand why people are angry. If the Hands had saved the Asim, it's possible the war would be over already. The Mistress would have never come to Lagusa. My father might still be alive.

I try to stay away from those kinds of thoughts. They're dangerous, bringing up nothing but fury, forcing me to stay in the past where all the hurt and pain weighs me down, when I need to be thinking of tomorrow.

While I can't go so far as the others and praise the Thirteen for the arrival of the Hands, I understand we need them. As long as they are useful in our fight against the Mistress, I'll give them a chance.

After a few hours of sleep, I eat, have my wounds tended to, then help carry the remains from inside the Temple to the pyre.

Some of the bodies are so mangled I feel ill looking at them, but I steel my stomach and keep my eyes on the ground or the other person helping me carry. I leave the disembodied hands and shredded body parts for others. There isn't enough steel in my stomach for that.

When we're finished placing the bodies of our dead on the pyre, the First Daughter enters the plaza rubbing a Maganor figurine dangling from a rope around her waist. She's praying, muttering under her breath, her eyes unfocused. Behind her walk six more Daughters carrying concave metal disks, polished to a mirror-like shine, to light the fire by reflecting the sun's rays at the kindling.

Around and around they walk, the First Daughter with her arms raised and her face turned toward the sky, the other Daughters holding the disks in front of their chests, the metal turning orange like the glow of the dragons as it's warmed by the sun, until the kindling ignites.

The First Daughter ululates and the worshippers surrounding the pyre join her. Then she begins the prayer.

"Glory be to the dragons, our gods, whom we honor with the deaths of our beloveds," she cries out, her voice carrying across the plaza and up to the heavens. "This is a blessed day. This day, your fire consumes our dead. This day, everything we are and everything they once were belong to our gods.

This day, we beg the dragons, who came to bestow their gifts and raise our people out of the mud, to carry the souls of our dead to their next lives."

The First Daughter turns toward the crowd. "By the Fires we live, by the Fires we are blessed, and by the Fires we die."

Everyone repeats the First Daughter's words. Even I feel comfort from the peaceful chanting, reciting the phrasing I grew up speaking. I think of Obba and wish we could have performed the same ceremony for his remains.

Nez leans on my shoulder, my arm wrapped around his waist for extra support, as he wipes away the tears from his eyes. On my other side, Kal holds my hand. Without a free hand to wipe my own tears, I let them flow freely down my cheeks.

Rima stands on Nez's other side, next to her sister and Mandisa, both of them found safe inside the library with the other scribes. Basheera barricaded the entrance with a maze of shelves and tables to keep the Dambi from getting in. It was the sound of her sister's voice that convinced Basheera and the other scribes it was safe to leave. I'm grateful something worked out in our favor for a change.

Basheera is even more grateful for the Hands—she said their arrival proves one of Gamikal's prophecies true, which means there might be more truths hidden in the text. She's eager to translate the rest of *The Foretold* after paying her respects at the burning.

The fire grows into a crackling beast, filling the plaza with smoke and heat. Sweat drips down my brow and pools at my waistband, but I don't mind. The warmth envelops me like a comforting hug, and I can feel it burning away the stress and pain of the previous days.

When the First Daughter finishes, she goes back into the Temple, her shoulders hunched, Daughters holding both of her arms to keep her steady. I know it's more than the ceremony that has worn the First Daughter out. All the fighting over the past few days, all the death, and with no end in sight—it's exhausting.

While the family members of the dead circle the fire, chanting and crying, the rest of us head back inside the Temple. The floors have been mopped, the blood on the walls washed away. But there are still places where the tiles are cracked and broken. Gashes and claw marks rip across pillars and through stone walls. The doors to the library still lie in a heap, the passageway to the catacombs open because we can no longer slide the wall back into place. The wood of the altar is cracked and stained with blood that won't wash off, no matter how many times a Daughter scrubs it.

The Hands of God wait for the First Daughter in the center of the Temple. They kept a respectful distance during the ceremony, but it appears that now they want to talk.

A tall man spits at the feet of the Hands' leader. "I prayed that you were all dead after you betrayed the Ur Atum Asim," he says, his hands on his hips. "Now you show up sixteen years too late. Well, we don't need you!"

The First Daughter pushes the man aside and bows to the Hands.

"Don't show those traitors respect," the man grumbles as his friends pull him away.

"Is there a more private place where we can speak?" the leader of the Hands asks the First Daughter.

"I will not hide from my people," the First Daughter replies. "We are facing terrible times, and we must come together in our decisions on how best to confront them."

"Very well," the woman says, her voice steady and her face expressionless. "I am Sister Cornelia. I lead the Hands of God. We have much to discuss."

"Before we *discuss* anything," the First Daughter says, "we need to know you are who you say you are."

Bagara joins the First Daughter facing Sister Cornelia. "The Hands of God haven't been seen since before the war. We heard that you had abandoned your monastery in the Kilmare Mountains. It's rumored you all had forsaken your vows and disbanded. So how can we believe what you say to us now?"

Sister Cornelia steps onto the stained altar and points at one of the Merzan Hands. He joins her on the wooden platform. Standing behind him, Sister Cornelia unsheathes her sword.

"Behold, the glory of our god."

She drives the sword through his chest. Several people scream and gasp, and I'm riveted to the spectacle before me. Sister Cornelia withdraws the blade slowly as she mutters prayers. The remaining Hands bow their heads and pray with her. When the sword is completely removed, Sister Cornelia steps around the still-standing Merzan Hand, his dusty gray clothes unblemished by blood or even a rip from the sword.

Sister Cornelia holds the clean blade above her head for all to see.

"This sword has been blessed in the godfire of the Kilmare Mountains," she says in stilted Merzan. "The sacred godfire was created by the Three-Faced God, and tended faithfully for these many centuries by their servants. A blade forged in the godfire will never harm a true Hand of God."

I stare at the silver sword, unblinking, not sure what I just witnessed. Beside me, Nez is transfixed as well, his mouth hanging open and his eyes wide.

"Did you see that?" he whispers, his voice full of awe. "I want to learn how to do that!"

"I don't even know what *that* was," I reply, skepticism setting in. "It has to be a trick of some kind. That sword must be fake."

Nez shakes his head. "I saw it pierce through the man completely. It was real. All of it."

There's a long moment of silence before the First Daughter speaks. "They've proven themselves enough for me," she says when she recovers from her shock. "Tell us, Sister Cornelia, why you have come to Lagusa."

Sister Cornelia bows in respect before the crowd, then says, "One of Sothpike's Mistresses has taken over your village."

"One of Sothpike's Mistresses—does that mean there's more of them?" I say aloud.

"He has thousands of Dambi," Kal replies. "He would need many Mistresses to control all of them."

The weight of his words makes my shoulders slump. Thousands of Dambi controlled by who knows how many Mistresses. How can we defeat so many?

I shake my head to clear away those thoughts. There's only one Mistress in Lagusa, and she's the only one I should be worrying about. I can deal with one Mistress.

I turn my attention back to the Hands, where Sister Cornelia continues speaking. "We know why the Mistress is here. Sixteen years ago, a child was born to the Ur Atum Asim Avari—"

"You don't get to say her name," someone in the crowd shouts out. "Not after you betrayed her!"

"Be quiet," another man yells in response. "They came to help us, the least we could do is hear what they have to say."

Sister Cornelia's eyes wash over the crowd and quiet fills the Temple. "One of Sothpike's Mistresses seeks this child. We must find it before she does."

That's the same story the Mistress told the Mother in the meeting house. I'm about to say so, when the First Daughter cuts in.

"That child is dead," she says. "It died during birth."

"That is what we thought," Sister Cornelia replies. "That is what Sothpike thought. But a few weeks ago, the Three-Faced God showed us its three sacred faces, and in them we saw that the child still lives."

"And you think this child is in Lagusa?" the First Daughter asks.

"We *know* this child is in Lagusa," Sister Cornelia responds. "Our god has told us so. The veil separating the Three-Faced God from our world has been lifted. The hunt for this child has brought us here now that we know its death was a ruse."

"What's so special about this child?" Bagara asks.

"According to the vision, this child has the power to defeat Sothpike, or to destroy the world. We must find the child before Sothpike's minion does. Nothing will protect us if the child comes to full power under Sothpike's guidance."

One of the Lagusans scoffs. "Power? What does that mean?"

"It means the Three-Faced God bestowed a gift upon this child. More than that, we cannot say."

"If we are to give you this child, what would you do with it? How do we know you won't use the child to hurt others? To destroy *us*?"

"We will do with the child as the Three-Faced God demands," Sister Cornelia replies. "For the moment, our god demands we procure the child and bring it to the safety of the mountains and our walls."

A chill runs through me as I consider all the meanings behind Sister Cornelia's words. Perhaps the Hands will protect the child, as they say. But there is also the possibility they will kill the child to keep it out of Sothpike's hands if the Three-Faced God tells them to. Does that make them any better than the Mistress? What about what the child wants, whoever they are?

"What's most important right now is rescuing our children and our Mother from the Mistress," Bagara says. "This child, if it even exists, can't protect us from Sothpike or his Mistresses. Making sure our people are safe is our priority, not wasting time and resources scouring the village for one child."

"First Daughter, do you believe what they are saying?" a woman asks. "That the child of the Ur Atum Asim lives?"

"The Mistress said the same thing at the meeting house," Kal says. All eyes turn in his direction.

"And how do you know?" someone asks.

"Because I was there," Kal replies. "I snuck in while the Mother and the Mistress met, and the Mistress told the same tale—that the child of the Asim lives, and she is here in Lagusa to find it."

"Did she say why?"

Kal shakes his head. "Only that she wants to give it to Sothpike."

The First Daughter faces Kal. "If what you say is true—"

"It is true," Kal cuts in.

"—then it means we have heard the same story from the Hands as well as the Mistress," the First Daughter finishes. "In that case, we have a duty as citizens of Merza to return this child to its rightful place—on the throne in Al-Kazar."

For the first time, Sister Cornelia's restrained facade cracks. Her brows furrow—in worry or irritation, I can't tell.

"That would be a mistake," Sister Cornelia says. "This child can do much more than sit upon a chair made of stone."

"Where were you sixteen years ago when the Asim needed you?" I ask, my voice strong and startling me with its clarity. "Even if everything you say is true, why should we trust you? The Asim trusted you, and look what happened to her."

Murmurs of agreement fill the Temple, and Sister Cornelia turns her gaze toward me. Her eyes dart from me to Nez and the others surrounding us, and she raises one eyebrow.

"We did not have to ask," Sister Cornelia replies. "We could have simply taken the child during the fighting, and no one would have been the wiser. Instead, we came to you as a show of respect. We will ask the child to come with us willingly."

Sister Cornelia steps down from the altar. The crowd parts before her and she stands in front of me.

"You ask why we did not save the Asim. It is because she knew her fate. The Three-Faced God showed her Sothpike's true plans, that he would use her child to sow an eternity of destruction. She made the decision to send the child to the bottom of the world instead of abiding by the command of the Three-Faced God. She told everyone the child was dead, when she should have given us the child as the Three-Faced God instructed. The Asim defied our god, and for that she paid a price. For sixteen years, the Hands of God have been vigilant, but directionless, because of her decision. Once the path to Lagusa was revealed to us, we were directionless no longer."

"You let the Asim die because she didn't do what you wanted?" Basheera asks. "Sounds like a case of spitefulness to me. Like something a spoiled child would do."

"You see things in your way," Sister Cornelia responds. "We see things as the will of our god."

The First Daughter claps her hands to gain everyone's attention. "My people have much to discuss," she says to Sister Cornelia. "Please, give us time to—"

"There is no more time," Sister Cornelia says, taking her place back on the altar. "For now, we will leave the child in your care. But you must allow my comrades and me to stay in Lagusa to assist you. Because Sothpike is coming, do not doubt that. The Hands of God and one of his Mistresses have found you, and so will Sothpike. On our trek to Lagusa, we saw evidence of a great army marching across the sands. We saw their tents and heard the shrieks of Dambi from across the dunes. Sothpike is already on his way across the desert, the last barrier protecting you from his all-consuming wrath."

Sister Cornelia chose her words wisely. The proof of Sothpike coming for us is more than enough to make the people eager to accept help from the Hands. After seeing how quickly the Hands cut down the Dambi, we would be fools not to.

It doesn't take long for the First Daughter to agree to Sister Cornelia's terms.

But still, I don't trust her.

All of a sudden, I have the urge to go home. I've been away for too long, and I tell Nez as much.

"We should check on Omma," Nez agrees before turning to the others. "All of you are welcome to come with us. Our mother is a fantastic cook."

"I think Mandisa and I will stay," Basheera says, reaching for her partner's hand.

"There's a lot to be done in the library," Mandisa says. "You know, cleanup and research."

Basheera turns to Rima. "But you should go with your friends. You haven't had a home-cooked meal that you didn't have to cook in a while."

Rima smiles and gives her sister a hug. "Thanks, Basheera."

"Besides," Basheera says, pushing her glasses up her nose and facing the others, "Rima's the only one who got out of that fight unscathed. You all could learn a thing or two from her."

"Yes, samida," Nez says with a bow.

Basheera only huffs and adjusts her glasses again. She and Mandisa make their way over to the library, while the rest of us head toward the front entrance.

I feel eyes on me as I squeeze through the crowd. When I dare to glance over my shoulder, my feeling is confirmed—with a smile that suggests she and I share a terrible secret, Sister Cornelia watches me from atop the altar, her eyes seeming to follow me around every corner, down every street, all the way home.

CHAPTER TWENTY-TWO

THE STREETS GOING HOME ARE EMPTY OF DAMBI, AND I'm grateful. We cut a wide berth around the meeting house, the shrieks coming from that direction letting us know the Mistress is still inside. A few of the more curious villagers venture outside their homes, their eyes on the black smoke coming from the Temple where the bodies of the dead still burn. They ask what happened, what is going on, but we don't linger after answering their questions. I lead the way, eager to be inside familiar walls.

But dread overcomes me when I turn onto our street. Nez, on the other hand, doesn't seem to have any qualms about returning home. He hobbles faster with his crutch, cajoling the rest of us to hurry up.

"Come on," Nez calls, waving us on. "We're almost there."

Rima runs ahead with Nez, while Kal walks a few steps behind with me.

"Nervous?" he asks.

"A little. Even though she told us to make her proud, she's

probably been so worried, and she's already dealing with so much. I honestly don't know how she's going to react."

"There's only one way to find out." Kal takes my hand and pulls me forward.

Tingles radiate from where our skin meets, up my arm and the back of my neck, and I hold on to Kal tightly. I wonder about that kiss he promised me, and I'm tempted to pull him into the abandoned house next door to steal a moment to ourselves. Why can't the right time be now?

I didn't realize I had slowed to a crawl in my daydreaming until Kal glances back at me and tugs on my hand. I smile and break out into a run, joining Rima and Nez at the front door of our house.

Nez grabs the door knocker. "Ready?"

I take a deep breath and Nez bangs on the door. Shuffling footsteps come from the other side, and then Omma's strong voice.

"Who's there?"

"It's us, Omma," Nez says, a great big grin spreading across his face. "We're home!"

"Nez?" A scraping sound lets me know the metal bar is being lifted. I swallow a deep breath, my stomach wrapped around itself like two monkeys wrestling. The latch clicks and the door swings open. Then there's Omma—along with two men behind her with bows, their arrows trained on me and my companions.

"Whoa," Nez says, throwing his hands up. "We come in peace."

I reach for my daggers while Omma motions for the men to put down their bows. "These are my children," she says and they lower their weapons. She opens her arms to me and Nez. "Welcome home."

My stomach unravels and I rush forward to hug Omma, Nez right behind and wrapping us both in his arms, his crutch clattering to the floor.

When we break apart, Omma kisses my cheeks and does the same to Nez. Then she notices our bloodied clothes and Nez's bandaged ankle.

"What happened to you?" Her eyes are wide and her hands tremble as she inspects our injuries.

"We're fine, Omma," I say, taking her hands in my own to steady them. "I promise."

Omma presses her lips together to hold back all the things she wants to say. "You promise?"

"Yes, Omma, we're fine." Nez gives her another hug and that seems to assuage her concern.

"It's only been a few days, but it feels like forever," Omma says when Nez untangles his arms from around her.

"I'm sorry," I say. "For sneaking away like that. But we had to go. We have to protect Lagusa."

"As long as you promise not to leave without telling me again, I'll forgive you," Omma says. "I would never stop you from doing what you think is right. I might try to delay you a little, but that's only to be sure you're ready."

"I'm sorry too, Omma," Nez says, sheepishly rubbing the back of his neck, his other arm resting on my shoulder for support.

Omma waves Nez's words out of the air. "That's in the past. Come in and tell me what's been going on." Then she notices Kal and Rima standing in the doorway and playfully slaps Nez's arm. "Why didn't you tell me you brought guests?"

Nez rubs the sore spot. "Why'd you hit me? Naira didn't say anything about them either!"

Ignoring Nez, Omma invites Kal and Rima inside as I pick up Nez's crutch and hand it to him. Omma tells our guests to take off their shoes and brings over a basin of water for them to wash their feet.

"Clean yourselves up," she says, placing the basin on the floor. "Wash away the outside world and all the troubles trailing behind you."

"This is Kal," I say as Omma gathers his shoes and stores them under the stone bench. "You remember him, don't you?"

"Of course I do." She turns to Kal. "Welcome home."

Kal bows deeply. "Thank you, Samida Khoum."

Then Omma faces Rima. "I remember you as well," she says, holding Rima's hands and giving her a once-over. "I haven't seen you since you were a little thing. My, how you've grown."

"It's nice to see you again, Samida Khoum," Rima says with a bow.

"None of that samida nonsense," Omma says. "Call me Farina, both of you."

"Yes, Sami—" Kal starts then corrects himself. "I mean, Farina."

"You all came home at the perfect time," Omma says, her face all smiles. "We're having a little party tonight for Samir Cheboh. It's his birthday."

"Did you make a cake?" Nez asks, practically drooling just at the thought. "Please tell me you made a cake."

Omma laughs. "Not yet, but I will." She points at Nez's crutch. "So, are you going to tell me what happened to you?"

"I fell through a roof," Nez says, limping toward Omma and wrapping an arm around her shoulder.

Omma's eyes widen and she motions for us to come deeper into the residence. "Well, come inside and tell me what's been happening out there."

I trail behind the rest, locking the latch and putting the metal bar back across the door. I notice a sword leaning against the wall by the front door. Omma must have put it there for protection.

Inside, the remaining sick and wounded Omma had been tending to are on their feet, armed with polearms, bows, and swords from Obba's armory. They bow when I pass, and I return the gesture.

By the time I catch up with the others in the dining room, Nez has already begun to tell Omma about the child the Mistress is searching for.

"She says the Asim's kid is still alive, and hiding somewhere in Lagusa," Nez is saying.

"That's why she has her Dambi stealing children," Rima adds.

Omma pauses, her brows furrowed in concern. "Did anyone believe her?"

"I don't think so," Kal replies. "That is, until the Hands of God showed up and said the same thing."

"You should have seen them, Omma," Nez says. "The Hands are amazing. The one in charge, Sister Cornelia, she—"

"I want you to stay away from the Hands, you hear me?" Omma grabs Nez by the arm. "And stay away from that

Mistress. Both of you," she says, pointing at me. "In fact, I want both of you to stay here. No more gallivanting around town, sticking your noses in places they don't belong. You stay home." Then she turns toward Rima and Kal. "And if I were your mothers, I would tell you two the same thing. Stay home and out of trouble. The more you traipse around the streets, the more likely you'll be caught."

"But we're safe at the Temple," Nez says, squirming out of Omma's grasp.

"Besides, a moment ago you said you wouldn't try to stop us," I add, confused by Omma's abrupt change.

"That was before," Omma says. "Before I knew..." Omma shakes her head as if to clear it. Her expression softens and she takes me by one hand and Nez by the other. "You have to trust me. The less you have to do with that Mistress and those Hands, the better."

"But, Omma—" I start.

Omma cuts me off. "I will not repeat myself. If your father were here, he'd say the same. If Isrof were here—" Omma's voice grows thick and she holds back tears "—he would not want you getting mixed up in that mess. You're children. Leave these battles to the adults."

It pains me to see Omma upset, but I can't give in that easily. I try to interject, but she holds up a hand to stop me.

"That's enough. My mind is made up and I won't discuss it any more." She steers us toward the table. "Now, sit down and I'll bring you dinner." She turns to Rima and Kal, who are both hanging in the doorway as if they wish they could escape this conversation. "You two, come on in. I'm going to fix you a nice meal, and you'll eat well, and there will be no more talk about going back out there, alright?"

"Yes, samida," Kal says as he sits down on a cushion. Nez sits across from him, Rima at his side, and I'm next to Kal.

"Alright," Omma says, clasping her hands together across her belly. "I'll be back soon."

"Well, that was weird," Nez says when she's out of earshot.

"What was that all about?" Rima asks.

"She must be afraid something will happen to us," Nez replies. "Like what happened to Obba. But that was different. We have the Hands of God on our side now. We can't lose."

I'm not so sure that's it. Only a moment ago, Omma was willing to let us fight. But all of the sudden, she forbade us all from leaving the house. The only thing that changed is Omma learning what the Hands and the Mistress want.

But why would that change her mind so drastically? She already knew that the Mistress was gathering the children of Lagusa.

I rise from the table. "I'm going to try talking to her," I say. "See if I can figure out what's really going on."

In the kitchen, I find Omma standing at the stove, her back to the entrance, her shoulders shaking with sobs. I run inside, wrapping my arms around her waist and pressing my cheek against her back.

"Omma, what's wrong?"

"Nothing," she replies, pulling herself together and patting my hands. "I've been so worried about you both, that's all."

"You can tell me," I say, not letting go of her. "You've always been there for me. Now I want to be there for you."

"And you are, my headstrong girl, you are," Omma says.

She takes a deep breath and reaches for a pot. "Now, let me go so I can cook," she adds with a laugh that doesn't feel forced.

"You sure everything's alright?"

"I'm sure." She pats my hands one more time and I let them fall to my side.

"So, what are we cooking?"

Omma wipes the last of the tears from her eyes. "Well, our stores are pretty meager nowadays, so it's mostly rice, beans, and whatever I can get from our garden. Sometimes a vendor comes by with meat or grain. I buy what I can, but the prices are so high…" Then she smiles and pulls back a cloth covering a basket. "I was able to get this for a decent price, though." I peek inside at the leg of lamb. My stomach growls and Omma laughs. "I was going to salt it and save it for something special, but I can't think of anything more special than having my children back home."

"I would have to agree." I grab one of the clay bowls with a laugh of my own. "Should I go fetch some water for the rice?"

Omma nods and I take the bowl through the garden to the spigot. The garden is almost picked clean, the fruit trees bare, and I wonder how much longer we can last. If my family's usually well-stocked reserves have run so low, I can't image how other people who don't have gardens are surviving. We have to get rid of the Mistress—and soon.

The spigot is near the jirkana. Seeing the empty building makes invisible hands clench around my heart and I stop for a moment to catch my breath. I open the door to the dark room, dust floating through the shafts of light that penetrate the darkness, and see that it's empty. All of Obba's weapons, even the practice ones, are gone. But as I look closer, I notice there's actually one weapon left: Obba's sword. It rests on the shelf where it belongs, untouched and unmarred, pristine and shining with the faintest glint of light.

I cross the room and touch the sword, running my finger along the back of the blade, slowly wrapping my hands around the hilt.

"I miss you, Obba."

Every thought I have is of how different things would be if Obba were still with us. He would have found a way to get rid of the Mistress. He would have united the people and driven her out. He would have—

But he isn't still with us. At least not in person. Only the memories of him are still alive. I can't waste time on what Obba would have done. Instead, I need to focus on what *I* can do.

I let go of the sword and back out of the jirkana. I fill the bowl with water and return to the kitchen.

Yet, thinking of Obba reminds me of what Bagara said about him being one of the Asim's Rudans. Even though I'm sure he had Obba mixed up with someone else, I turn to Omma and ask, "Have you ever heard of anyone named Bagara Oluweydo?"

Omma freezes. "How do you know that name?"

"I met someone with that name. He said he used to be a friend of Obba's." I watch Omma, her reaction making me uneasy. "He also said that Obba was a Rudan for the Asim. But that can't be true. You and Obba have never even been to Al-Kazar, so how could he have been a Rudan?"

"That man is someone else you should stay away from." Omma's hands tremble so much she drops the spoon she's holding, the wooden instrument clattering to the table. It takes her two tries to pick it back up.

"At this rate, we won't be able to talk to anyone," I joke, trying to lighten the mood.

But Omma isn't laughing. "I'm serious, Naira."

"Omma, what is going on?" I set the bowl on the table and try to look into her eyes but she avoids my gaze. "I mean, it can't be that bad. It's not like I'm the Asim's missing child, is it?"

Omma narrows her eyes. "Don't even joke about such things," she warns. "You have no idea what you're saying."

For the first time, I see my mother as others must see her: medium height; thick, dark hair that is graying at the edges pulled back in braids; full lips; wide, dark eyes; and dark brown skin. Then I look at myself, at my light skin and brown curly hair that won't stay in a braid no matter how hard I try.

When I was a girl, I asked my mother why her and Obba's skin was the color of the rich brown earth where the plants and flowers grow, while mine was the color of the desert sand. She didn't have an answer.

Instead, she told me a story.

Long ago, a child was born: one whose skin was as pale as the clouds in the sky. The child longed to have rich dark skin like his parents and the people in his village. So every night, the child knelt before his family's mazan and prayed to the gods that he would wake up the next day with skin as dark as his parents'. But every morning, he'd wake up with skin as pale as the moon, and he would cry.

For years this went on, until his parents asked their son why he wanted to change his skin color when he was beautiful just as he was. *You are wonderfully made*, his parents told him, *inside and out*. The boy looked at his skin and at his parents' skin and realized that no matter how much he prayed, he could never be anyone else. He could only be himself.

"And that is what I hope for you—that you will learn to stop wondering why you aren't like everyone else and start seeing yourself the way I do: beautiful, smart, and strong," Omma said as she hugged me close. "Sometimes, there is no answer to the question *why*. Sometimes, all we have is what happened. The reason *why* it happened is for the gods to know. You must learn to accept yourself for who you are—this is how the gods made you, and the gods don't make mistakes."

Back then, the surety in Omma's voice was enough to stop me from wondering further. But now I'm older, and I have questions that can't be answered with a fable. I need the truth, and there's something Omma isn't telling me. Something important—and, I fear, something that has to do with everything that has happened recently.

"Omma, please," I beg.

She purses her lips and stares at the table. "I don't want to lose you and your brother as well. I've already lost so much— I couldn't start all over. Not again."

I'm taken aback. I don't know what I expected, but it isn't this. Omma sounds forlorn, like everything she holds dear is slipping away. I feel like the tide is washing away the sand beneath my feet and there is nothing I can do to stop it.

Omma sighs, tears fill her eyes, and another wave rips the sand from the shore. I'm off-balance, my feet on unsteady ground. My head suddenly flares with pain, making me see stars. The world dims.

I put a hand on the table to steady myself while my body lowers itself to the floor. It seems as if everything is moving at half-speed—Omma running around the table to help me stand, shouting my name, my knee slamming on the ground, my shoulder crashing to the floor next.

But it's the voice in my head that startles me the most. The one that crackles like the flames that burned the bodies of the dead. Waves of welcoming fire rush over my body as it speaks clearly for the first time while I'm still conscious.

You will awaken.

CHAPTER TWENTY-THREE

I OPEN MY EYES AND ENTER SOMEONE ELSE'S LIFE. AT least, that's what it feels like.

Like the other times I've passed out, this dream feels as real as if I'm awake. Although I'm in an unfamiliar place—a long passageway with windows on one side and archways on the other—it reminds me of the lavish hall where the shadow people partied in my previous dream.

To my left is a sun-drenched garden full of colorful flowers, topiaries shaped like dragons, and a maze of hedges. The windows on my right reveal richly appointed rooms where thick rugs cover tiled floors and vibrant murals depicting moments in the dragons' lives fill the walls. Tasseled pillows and throws with silver strands in the weave are tossed about on the floor and on benches, while mosaic glass lamps hang from the ceiling on golden chains. A gentle breeze carries the scent of lavender and I inhale deeply.

"Where am I?"

"This is your first memory," a voice says from behind me.

I turn and am blinded by a bright light. I throw up my arms to shield my face and wait for the headache to pounce, but it never strikes. In fact, I don't feel any pain at all.

Slowly, I lower my arms and squint. A swirling orange mass with pinpoints of bright light burns in front of me, reminding me of clouds obscuring the stars in the night sky. The cloud-like mass spreads and morphs, the way a heavy drop of dye travels through a tub of water. It forms a human-like shape, then something resembling a dog, then a creature I have never seen before and hope I never will. As the orange mass continues to shift and change, the lights maintain their positions.

These lights are just like the ones I saw in the other dreams—shining in the distant sky while I chased Ergene-gon and flickering in the woman's eyes at the party filled with shadow people.

"What is this?" I hold out my hand to touch the swirling mass but grasp nothing.

"If I showed you my true self, you would go mad." The voice seems to come from the swirling mass.

"Who are you?" I ask.

"I am Vanusha the Creator," the light replies. "One part of the Three-Faced God."

The Three-Faced God—the same one the Hands pray to. But how can that be? I've only ever prayed to the Thirteen, and that was mostly out of obligation to my father. Why would a god show itself to a nonbeliever who only recently learned about its existence?

But I can't deny the fact that this isn't a regular dream. It feels just as real as those other visions, like I'm peering into a moment in another person's life, a moment in time that existed in the real world.

"I don't understand. I pray to the dragon gods. If a god was going to talk to me, wouldn't it be one of them?"

The lights shine so brightly they blind me, as if Vanusha is angry at me. I shield my eyes and back away.

"My sisters and I are old gods." Vanusha's voice is calm and the lights dim until they no longer hurt my eyes. "We've seen much, and we are the only ones who can protect you. Heed our warnings, accept our guidance, and this world will be righted."

I can't help but think about what Sister Cornelia said: the Asim defied the Three-Faced God, and for that, they abandoned her. And all the while, my people have prayed to the Thirteen to save us from Sothpike, but now his dead army is almost at our doorstep.

I don't know what's worse: believing in old gods who turn their backs on you when you need them most, or putting your faith in dragon gods who never show up. "Where are the other faces?"

"You will meet Kuresh and Uthera in time. For now, I have something to show you."

The light floats ahead of me and a gentle force presses into my back, propelling me forward. But when I turn around, the passageway is empty. I have two options: do nothing and wait for the vision to end, or find out what it is the old god Vanusha wants to show me. Curiosity overcomes my stubbornness and I decide to follow the light. Together, we enter one of the rooms—where a scream rings out that raises the hairs on the back of my neck. Yet, I still see no one.

The light leads me through one room, then another, down airy halls and up a short marble staircase. Loud sounds surround me: the clanging of swords, running footsteps, voices pleading with others to let them go, the crunch of bone breaking from the force of a blunt object, and screaming. Always screaming. Thick, dark smoke envelops me as we walk up the stairs, a rush of heat fans across my face, and I raise my arms to block whatever is coming. The potted plants on each step burst into flames, the white marble blackens with soot and ash, yet I emerge from the invisible fire unscathed.

My heart pounds with the fear of being burned alive, of Ergenegon's fire finding me in this dream. I'm hesitant to keep moving forward, but the light is insistent, and once again the invisible presence pushes me forward, up the stairs.

At the top, the light turns left and enters a palatial chamber. Shadowy figures, like the ones from the party but not dressed as finely, grab statues and small objects off the many tables and shelves, stuffing them into baskets. One shadow runs toward me, arms full of scrolls, and before I can get out of the way, he passes right through me, the sensation nothing more than a gust of air blowing against my skin. I turn around and see the shadow stop short. He drops the scrolls, his hands clutch his gut, and he collapses to the floor. I can't see who struck the killing blow, but the other shadows can. Some try to flee, only to be hit in the back and fall to the ground, while others fight against an unseen enemy, but they too are killed.

"What is this?" The acrid fumes from the fires fill the room and the shadow people disappear from view.

"Your first memory," Vanusha says again.

"Why do you keep saying that?" I ask. "I've never been here in my life. I don't even know what's going on. *What is happening?*"

The previous dreams were straightforward, but this one is chaotic. Some people are shadows; others are completely invisible. Fire and smoke surround me but don't hurt me. And there's a Three-Faced God insisting that this is all a memory of mine.

Vanusha is silent as she moves forward, and again I have no other option but to follow. Even though I don't know where I am or why these people are fighting, I don't doubt that what I am seeing, hearing, even smelling, is real. There's no way I could have imagined any of this. People lived in these rooms once. Until someone murdered them.

The light leads me into the bedchamber of a crying woman. I see her close-cropped, dark hair, the sharp angle of her deep brown nose, her lips cracked to reveal white teeth as she weeps. Like the woman from the party, she's not a shadow, and as I look closer, I realize she's the same person but older.

The woman sits on the edge of a bed, cradling something small in her arms. A shadow tries to take it from her, but the woman hugs the bundle to her chest and shoves the arms of the shadow away.

Something in that gesture—the way the woman holds the bundle close to her chest—makes me think of my own mother and how she tries so hard to protect her children.

"Go," the woman screeches to the shadow. "Before it's too late."

The shadow must have spoken, because the woman quiets and stares at the dark figure.

"I am still the Ur Atum Asim," she says in reply and I gasp. The woman is Avari, the last Ur Atum Asim of Merza. And this must be the day Sothpike invaded Al-Kazar and stormed the citadel.

This is the day the Asim dies.

"And you are still my handmaiden," the Asim continues. "I am ordering you to go. Both of you!" She turns and I notice another shadow, this one tall and thin, standing across the room. It cradles two small bundles in its arms like the one the Asim holds, but these bundles move and squirm.

"Please," she pleads with the second shadow. "You must protect them."

The tall shadow seems to meet the Asim's gaze and nods. The Asim takes a deep breath and wipes away her tears with the heel of her hand.

"Thank you," she says.

Someone bangs on the door. The Asim pulls the bundle close, and the shadows disappear. Fear flashes across her face as she looks toward the door, but it's quickly replaced with resolve. She stands, still holding the bundle, then disappears.

The room—the memory—goes with her.

Everything is gone: the furniture, the walls, the noise of battle, the smell of fire.

I'm in the kitchen, Omma kneeling beside me on the floor.

"Are you alright?" she asks as she helps me get back on my feet.

I nod, the headache nothing but a memory. I don't need the Three-Faced God to tell me what I just witnessed. The last Ur Atum Asim, Avari, taking her final stand against Sothpike. And in Avari's arms, the child he came to collect. I lean against the wall and take a deep breath, my stomach churning. Omma hands me a cup of water and I gladly drink. I'm not ready to speak anyway. My thoughts are still on the vision.

The Three-Faced God said that what I saw was my first memory. But that's impossible. I wasn't even born yet when the Asim died, and I've never been to Al-Kazar. At the start of the war, my parents fled their hometown in the northeast, and Nez and I were born soon after they arrived in Lagusa.

So why did the Three-Faced God show me something about the Asim that everyone already knows?

"Are you alright, Naira?" Omma asks again, brushing the hair out of my face. "Maybe you should go lie down. I'll call you when the food is ready."

I shake my head. "I'm fine. How long was I out?"

"Just a moment or two. No more than a heartbeat, but long enough to make me worry." Omma takes the cup from my trembling hands and sets it on the table. "At least sit down, if you won't go to bed." She pushes me toward a stool.

Noise in the doorway catches my attention and I look up to see Rima lingering there.

"I thought you might need some help with the food," Rima says with a smile, oblivious to all that has just happened.

"You're our guest. You should be resting." Omma starts to shoo Rima away, but Rima ignores her and walks over to the table.

"There's no resting with Nez around." Rima picks up a knife and begins chopping onions. "When I left, he was challenging Kal to arm wrestle. That was after Kal beat him playing ritska."

Omma laughs. "Sounds like Kal is a good sport to put up with Nez like that."

Omma and Rima cook and laugh over the boys' antics, and as hard as I try to join their fun, my thoughts keep returning to that strange vision. I must have had it because of the stories Sister Cornelia and the Mistress told about the Asim's child. After everything I've been through, it would be strange if I *didn't* have a vision after passing out from dehydration.

I pour myself another cup of water from the pitcher and drink deeply.

That's all it was, I tell myself, even as the knot in my stomach contradicts my thoughts. *A weird dream brought on by the excitement of the last few days and thirst.*

There's an explanation for everything. The first time I had a strange dream, I had just been hit in the head. And the second time, I had passed out from the pain of having a wound cauterized. This time, I was sick with dehydration.

But why does it feel like those are just excuses?

Omma opens the oven and the rich smell of roasted leg of lamb fills the kitchen, jolting me out of my thoughts. As Omma slices the meat, I transfer a portion of the mashed beans to a ceramic bowl and place it on a wooden tray, hoping the familiar actions will help to banish my unease. Rima pours half the pot of stewed vegetables into another bowl and places it next to the beans while Omma piles a platter high with meat and puts that on the tray as well. And then the final touch: a bunch of red grapes in a bowl in the very center. While Rima helps me carry the tray into the dining room, Omma finds someone to serve the rest of the food to the boarders.

In the dining room, Nez is in the middle of telling a story to Kal.

"So then I said, 'You're so brainless you'd climb a glass wall to see what's on the other side,'" Nez says and Kal laughs. When Nez notices Rima and me coming into the room, he jumps to his feet, his sore ankle seemingly forgotten at the sight of so much food. "Finally! You guys were taking so long, I thought I was going to have to eat Kal."

"If you wanted to eat sooner, you could have helped cook." I hand my end of the tray to Nez and he takes Rima's side as well.

"You don't want me to cook." Nez sets it in the middle of the table. "The last time I tried, we had to put a new roof on the kitchen and build another mazan."

I roll my eyes and sigh. "You're useless," I joke as I grab some bowls and spoons from a shelf leaning against the wall.

We sit on cushions at the table, me and Kal on one side, Nez and Rima on the other. Nez opens the lid to the beans and I slap his hand.

I point at the empty seat at the head of the table. "Wait for Omma."

Nez crosses his arms and makes a face at me, but his annoyance doesn't last long. Soon Omma joins us and implores everyone to begin eating.

We dig in, our hunger stealing away words and forcing us to fill our mouths with food instead. But I find it difficult to eat. My stomach is already full of knots. That dream wasn't just a dream—it really did happen. I don't know if the other two dreams are based on real events, but Al-Kazar did burn, and even though the Mistress and the Hands believe otherwise, the Asim's child did die. The image of the Asim cradling her stillborn baby while preparing herself to face Sothpike is burned in my memory.

I try to replace the knots in my stomach with real food. I pour some stewed vegetables over my beans and bring the spoon to my mouth.

The sound of something hard and heavy banging on the front door makes us all freeze in place. A man carrying a polearm bursts into the dining room.

"Someone's at the door," he says. "She calls herself Sister Cornelia."

CHAPTER TWENTY-FOUR

"STAY HERE," OMMA TELLS US. "DO NOT LEAVE THIS ROOM, understand?"

"But, Omma—" I begin.

"No buts. For once, will you please do as I say without arguing about it?"

She doesn't give any of us a chance to respond before leaving the dining room, releasing the curtain in the doorway so that it cuts off our view of the courtyard.

I stand. "Well, I can't just sit here."

"But your mother…" Rima's voice trails off as Nez joins me at the entryway.

I pull the curtain aside wide enough for me to see what's happening. Even though she only brought three of her comrades with her, Sister Cornelia and her Hands of God fill the courtyard with their gray cloaks and silver swords. One of the men protecting the house points at Omma as she approaches.

"That is Samida Khoum," he says.

Sister Cornelia bows and the other Hands do the same. Omma does not repeat the gesture.

"I have come to speak to the widow of Qal'at Subaan Isrof Khoum," Sister Cornelia says. "I believe we have much to discuss."

"Not out here." Omma walks toward Obba's study. "Come with me."

Sister Cornelia follows, leaving her brethren outside of the study to guard the entrance. A curtain drops in place over the doorway, blocking the room from view.

I sigh and sit back at the table.

"What happened?" Rima asks.

I shrug. "I don't know. My mother took Sister Cornelia into Obba's study before she could say anything."

"Is there any way to listen in?"

Nez shakes his head as he rejoins the table. "Not with those Hands of God blocking the doorway."

"So, we have to wait?"

I glance at Nez and we both reluctantly nod.

Kal keeps watch at the door while Rima and I pick at our food—Nez resumes devouring his meal as if nothing happened.

"How can you stuff your face at a time like this?" I ask.

"It's better than worrying about something I have no control over on an empty stomach," he says between mouthfuls.

It feels like many hands have passed, but it's probably only one or two, before Kal whispers, "They're coming out."

Nez and I jump up from the table and join him at the door. I peel back the curtain as Sister Cornelia leaves the study first, followed by Omma.

"You will tell them, yes?" Sister Cornelia asks. "Or shall I?"

"Of course I will," Omma replies. "Just give me some time."

"Time is something we do not have to spare," Sister Cornelia says. "It must be done immediately. Sothpike *is* coming, and he'll be here any day now. This cannot wait. Not if you want them—"

Omma glances at the dining room, and Sister Cornelia does the same. She seems to stare right into my eyes.

"Behold, the glory of our god."

I drop the curtain back in place, my heartbeat quickening, as Nez and Kal both jump away from the doorway.

"She looked right at me," Nez says, his hand over his heart.

I'm glad I'm not the only one to feel Sister Cornelia's penetrating gaze. I've just returned to my place at the table when Omma shoves the curtain to the dining room aside.

"Nez and Naira," she says, hands on her hips. "Come with me."

Nez and I share an anxious glance as we rise from the table.

Inside Obba's study, Omma releases the rope holding back the curtain. The length of heavy cloth falls in place, covering the entrance and blocking out the sights and sounds of the courtyard. Then Omma sits on one side of the ebony desk, Nez and I on the other.

The room still smells like Obba, like the scented oil he put in his hair. Though it makes my chest ache, it also comforts me.

"Your father and I knew this day would come," Omma says, her eyes on the broken staff that still lies on the desk. "But we didn't think it would be so soon. We both hoped we would have more time. And I never dreamed that your father wouldn't be here with me when it came."

Omma has never been one to hide her emotions, not like Obba used to, but right now I can't tell if she's angry or sad, tired or scared.

"What day?" I ask.

"The day we—I—finally tell you the truth."

Nez and I share a look of concern, both of our brows drawn together tightly, our lips thin lines across our faces.

"The truth about what?" Nez asks as the knot in my stomach tightens.

In response, Omma takes a deep breath and begins to speak. "Eighteen years ago, a bright young girl was hired in service to the Asim Avari in the citadel. Dependable and loyal, she quickly rose through the ranks and was appointed the Asim's personal handmaiden. The girl was so proud. She wrote home to her parents the same day it was announced and bought herself a new headscarf imported from Johtan—her first silk scarf. This was six months before Sothpike killed the Asim, six months before the handmaiden's life changed forever.

"During those six months, the Asim and the girl grew close as she helped her prepare for her first child. The Daughters couldn't decide if it was to be a boy or a girl, so the Asim and the handmaiden sewed clothes for both. When Asim Avari gave birth, the handmaiden was the only one she allowed in the room, along with a Rudan. The handmaiden was petrified—she had been taught to weave and sew and play music but had never helped anyone deliver a baby—but it was what the Asim wanted, and she was determined to serve her Asim faithfully.

"Soon, the Asim and the handmaiden learned why the Daughters had been in such disagreement. The Asim gave birth to twins—a boy and a girl. The boy was born first, with a smile on his face. Then came the girl, her brows furrowed, her hands clenched into little fists. But the Asim didn't want anyone to know she had given birth to a healthy baby, let alone a set of twins. She knew that Sothpike had a plan for her child, one that must never be realized. She didn't explain how she knew, just that Sothpike would scorch the earth to find her child. So she asked the Rudan to find her a child, a stillborn, which was easy to do with a war going on. When the Rudan returned with what she asked, she presented the stillborn child to Sothpike, and it was this child that got her killed."

"Why are you telling us this?" Nez asks. "We all know the Asim had one child, and it died during childbirth."

"I'm sorry, Nez," Omma says, "but that's the first of many lies you've been told over the years."

Nez's mouth gapes open, but no sound comes out, as if the shock has stolen his voice. He turns to me for help processing what Omma said, his face full of disbelief, confusion, questions—all the things I'm feeling myself—and there's nothing I can say to comfort him.

I think back to the vision, to the shadowy figure holding two squirming bundles in its arms, and understand what Vanusha was trying to show me. It's the same story Omma told, except now I know who the other shadowy figures were.

The one holding the living babies was Obba, and the shadow trying to take the dead baby from the Asim was Omma.

The knot that has been forming in my stomach since I woke up from my vision rips in half. I've always trusted my parents more than I trusted myself. Whenever I was wrong, they were always right.

But they both lied to me.

"But why?" I let Nez ask all the questions. I have so many of my own that I don't know where to start.

Omma takes a deep breath. "Because I was the handmaiden to the Asim," she says. "I was there when you were born."

Nez laughs. "Of course you were. You're our m—"

Watching the moment when the puzzle pieces snap together for Nez is like looking in a mirror. A darkness settles deep in our hearts after realizing our parents are not our parents.

"So, what are you saying? You're not my omma?" Nez's shoulders slump, as if the news is crushing him. "And Obba isn't—wasn't—my obba?"

Omma reaches across the desk and grabs his hand, squeezing it within her own as if trying to pass her strength on to Nez.

"Your mother was the Ur Atum Asim Avari," Omma says. "And your father was the Ur Atum Asimra Yafeu. Those are your birth parents."

Omma takes my hand as well. I stare at her hands, the same hands that rub my back to help me fall asleep when I have nightmares, the same hands that smooth the worries from my brow and wipe away the many tears I've cried over the years. I cling to those same hands, grateful for their familiarity.

"Your mother loved you both so very much. And your father was so excited to meet you. Asimra Yafeu was at the western front, fighting Sothpike's invaders, but he still made sure to send a list of proposed names to the Asim in his final letter. His favorites were Kalari if they had a daughter, and Ghen for a son. But when you were born, the Asim gave you the complementary names Nezra and Naira, as our people do when they have twins."

"Thank the dragons," Nez says, his voice choked. "Kalari is fine, but Ghen? That sound like a name for a goat herder. And you know how I feel about herding. No, thank you."

Normally I'd roll my eyes at Nez's preference for silliness when he should be serious, but this time I laugh and send a silent thank-you to the gods for giving me a brother who tells awful jokes so everyone can break free of the tension clouding the room.

"Isrof hated that name as well," Omma chuckles, which makes us giggle even more.

"As soon as you were born," she continues when we calm down, "the Asim gave you each a kiss and held you in her arms. I still remember her smile the first time she saw you both. But then she told me to take you away, to hide you, and to never tell anyone the truth. Not even you, her children. Here I was, not yet twenty, and the Asim had put the Ur Atums in my care. And I couldn't ask anyone for help."

"What about Obba?" Nez asks. "Why did the Asim choose him?"

"Your father was the youngest Rudan," she replies, "and the most loyal. He would have gladly given his life for the Asim, but she ordered him to take her children away from Al-Kazar. I still remember what she said when she called him to the birthing room: '*I am giving you my children. You must protect them with your life. Raise them as your own, love them as you love me, and never let Sothpike near them.'"*

Omma tears up. A lump rises in my throat, but she quickly wipes her eyes and I swallow it back down. Then she continues her story. "Two days later, Sothpike invaded Al-Kazar. He went straight to the citadel, right to Asim Avari's chambers, and she told him that her child had died during birth. And he killed her for it. Since she failed to deliver him a healthy child, he had no further use for her." Anger flashes across Omma's face, but it is quickly replaced by sadness. "We left Al-Kazar with one last gift from the Asim: a map to Lagusa. We set out across the desert, and along the way we came up with our story. 'We are husband and wife,' we'd tell people, 'parents to twins, who fled to Lagusa to escape Sothpike.' That year, people made the trek to Lagusa in droves." Omma looks tired, as if the memory of those days is enough to wear her down. "We blended in as best we could. Many couldn't understand why we'd risk the journey with two newborns, but what else could we do? We couldn't go back, and Sothpike was everywhere except in Lagusa."

"I can't believe it," Nez says. "You mean to tell me *we're* royalty? I mean, of course I come from good stock. But this one?" Nez lifts my frizzy braid and lets it drop against my back. "Come on."

I shake my head and roll my eyes, grateful to have my jumbled mess of emotions replaced with laughter for a moment.

"Well, as the daughter of the Asim, Naira ranks higher than you," Omma says with a sly grin. "The crown is handed down from mother to daughter. The Asim is the Mother of Merza, after all."

Nez groans. "So now I have to be *nice* to her?"

"That's right." I elbow Nez in the side, glad that knowing we are the children of the last Asim of Merza hasn't changed Nez one bit. I turn to Omma.

"But what about the Hands of God? And Sothpike? Why are they looking for us? Is it because I'm the heir to the throne?" It sounds silly saying that aloud. I've never even dreamed I could be an Asim, not even as a child when Nez and I played pretend. I was always a ranger, never royalty.

Omma shakes her head. "The Hands don't care about restoring the throne of Merza, and Sothpike didn't even know the Asim had a daughter. The last instruction the Asim gave us was to wait for someone named Gamikal. She told us he'll come when the time is right and will know what to do next."

"And who is Gamikal?" Nez asks.

For once, I have the answer instead of countless questions. I tell him what I learned from Basheera, about the prophecy from *The Foretold* and the last recorded sighting of him in the Kilmare Mountains twenty years ago.

"I thought nothing could top finding out that the Asim is our mother, but now you're telling me that we're waiting for some five-hundred-year-old prophet wandering around in the mountains to come help us?" Nez crosses his arms and I can tell he's having trouble accepting all of this new information. Prophecies, immortal beings, old gods and dragon gods, the Hands and our birth parents—it's a lot to take in.

"He probably doesn't even exist," Nez continues. "What if the Asim was confused?"

"No. The Asim knew what she was talking about," Omma replies. "Until today, we thought the Hands of God had faded away into history, just like how, to the rest of the world, the Asim's only child died sixteen years ago. The truth has a way of existing despite everyone believing otherwise."

"So, now what?" Nez asks. "Do we still keep calling you Omma, keep pretending that nothing's changed?"

"Well, things *have* changed," Omma says. "All the pretending in the world won't make the Hands of God or Sothpike or even the Mistress go away. But you can still call me Omma." Her voice wavers. "If you want to."

Nez doesn't need to speak his reply—he stands and wraps Omma in a crushing hug. Then he holds out an arm to me and motions for me to join them. I lean over the desk and put my arms around my mother and brother, both of them crying. A little sob rises in my throat when I think of Obba, and how this moment feels incomplete without him there.

"Is this what Sister Cornelia wanted?" Nez asks when we pull away. "For you to tell us the truth about our birth mother?"

Omma sighs. "That was part of it. The other part was a request. In the days before you were born, the Asim told the Hands of God that she had other plans for her child, that she wasn't going to entrust her child to their care. So they abandoned Al-Kazar. Like Sothpike, they thought the Asim's child was dead. But Sister Cornelia claims their god recently revealed that not only did the Asim's child survive, but there are two of them. They want one of you to join the Hands. The other will remain in my care until Gamikal is found."

I brace myself for what's to come next. With the strange vision and dreams, my ability to understand Volsgarian and Waldyrian even though I've never heard them before, and as heir to the throne, I must be the one the Hands want. But they will be going back to the Kilmare Mountains empty-handed. I will never leave my family behind, not after we've already lost so much.

"So, they want one of us?" Nez asks.

I sit up straight, ready to tell Omma I will never join Sister Cornelia, when Omma takes Nez's hands.

"Yes, my son," she says. "They want you."

CHAPTER TWENTY-FIVE

I'M STUNNED, AND NEZ SEEMS TO BE AS WELL. THEN I feel ridiculous for even thinking I could be the one the Hands came to Lagusa for. Of course it's Nez.

He's always the favorite.

And he's my only brother. No matter what, I refuse to let the Hands take him.

"You have to say no," I say to Nez. "We're all we have. We have to stay together." When Nez doesn't respond, I turn to my mother. "Right, Omma? Tell him he can't leave us."

"Nez told me how easily the Hands of God cut down the Vra Gool Dambi," Omma says, still holding Nez's hand. She reaches for mine, but I pull away. I suspect where this conversation is going and I don't like it. "And Sister Cornelia promised to protect Nez with her life. I asked her if she would take you both, but she said Naira needs to go on a different path, one to find Gamikal."

"Fine, then we'll all go to the mountains," I say. "That's where Gamikal is anyway, right?"

Omma shakes her head. "Not anymore. Sister Cornelia said he now spends his time among the Haltayi on the Rocky Plains."

I let out a frustrated sigh. Of course Gamikal isn't where he's supposed to be. It feels like some powerful unseen force is determined to split my family apart.

"The Rocky Plains—that's just on the other side of the river," Nez says. "If he's so close, why didn't he come to us like the Asim said he would?"

"I asked Sister Cornelia the same question and she didn't know. So now Naira must go to him. Their god wills it so."

But I don't serve Vanusha, Kuresh, Uthera, or any other god, especially ones that want to tear my family apart.

"If Nez goes with the Hands, then we go too," I reply, my eyes on Omma. "You and I, we *have* to go with him. He's our family, and we have to protect him."

"It doesn't work that way, Naira," Omma replies. "Sister Cornelia made it clear—"

"Well, tell Sister Cornelia the answer is no," I say, crossing my arms over my chest. "Right, Nez?"

"Don't I get a say in what happens in my own life?" Nez stands and looks down at me and Omma, his face contorted in frustration. "You two are talking like I'm not even here, like I'm not old enough to make my own decisions. What if I want to join the Hands? What if I think they're amazing and I want to be like them? What if that's what I want?"

For a moment I can't speak. It never crossed my mind Nez would want something different than what I want.

That he would want to leave me.

"You can't," is all I can say.

"I can," Nez replies. "And I do."

I turn to Omma for help. "Omma, tell him he can't—"

"I've already made up my mind," Nez says. "I'm going with the Hands." He sits back down in his chair, looking to our mother. "What do I have to do?"

Before she can respond, I jump to my feet and tower over my brother for the first time in years. "I can't believe this! You're abandoning your family when we need you the most. Stop being so selfish!"

"*I'm* being selfish?" Nez snaps, rising again and forcing me to step back. At his full height, he's at least a head taller than me. "You're the one trying to force me to give up something I want because it's not what *you* want. Well, guess what, Naira, we're not the same person! I *will* go with the Hands and I *don't* need your permission to do it."

Omma steps in the middle and pushes us apart. "That's enough! Sit back down." When neither of us moves, Omma pushes us toward the chairs. "Both of you, sit!"

"Why are you doing this, Nez?" I demand, still standing. "Are you trying to prove something?"

"I already told you, Naira," Nez says, sitting back down. "I'm doing it because I want to."

Omma tries to calm me with a hand on my shoulder, but I wrench out of her grasp. "I'm done talking. If you join the Hands of God, then you're no brother of mine." I jab a finger at him. "Because my brother would *never* abandon his family like that." I turn to Omma. "I need to leave before I say something I regret."

"Kind of too late for that, isn't it?" Nez says with a sad laugh.

I snatch a heavy bunch of grapes from a bowl on top of the desk and throw them at Nez.

"Naira!" Omma admonishes.

"Grow up, Nez," I say, ignoring her.

"Says the girl throwing the temper tantrum *and* grapes." Nez snatches what's left of the bunch off the floor and stuffs a handful of grapes in his mouth. "Thank you," he says, his words muffled by the food.

I cross my arms and fume in silence, unable to even look at Nez. Omma opens her mouth to speak when a cry of pain from the courtyard pierces through the tension in the room, startling me and the others. All eyes turn toward the doorway.

On the other side of the curtain, someone clears their throat.

"Excuse me, but Shantar hurt herself practicing with the polearm," a man's voice says. "I think she broke her arm. Can you come take a look?"

"Of course." Omma rises from the desk. She shoots me and Nez one last paralyzing look before leaving. "You two need to come together. All this fighting isn't helping anyone. Neither of you can leave this room until you've made up. Understand?" Then she exits, the curtain swaying shut in the breeze she leaves behind.

We sit in silence for a long time. It's as if we both know that whatever we say will upset the other, and neither wants to be the one to start the next argument.

But I can't stay silent forever.

"I don't want you to go, Nez. How do you know the Hands aren't using us? Separating us, sending me in one direction and you in the other. They could be working for Sothpike for all we know!"

"You can't live your life thinking that way," Nez says. "You have to trust some people sometimes."

"We trusted Omma and Obba, and look how that turned out." As soon as the words leave my mouth, I regret them.

Nez looks at me out of the side of his eye. "That's not fair and you know it. Omma and Obba lied to save our lives. And if the Hands think that I need to go with them and you need to find that guy, we have to believe in them. Because what else do we have? If we only hold on to each other, we risk losing our grip on everything else we care about. All those people—Omma, Rima, *Kal*—are depending on us."

"Then I'm going with you," I say.

"Didn't you hear what I just said?" Nez asks with a tired laugh. "Besides, someone has to take care of Omma. You can't leave her alone. She needs you."

"What are you talking about? You're her favorite."

Nez pops a grape in his mouth. "I know, right? Can't blame her."

Another wave of silence fills the room.

All I can think about is how much it will hurt if Nez leaves. He's been by my side since birth, helping me keep my temper in check when I'm so angry I can't see straight. And when I do lose my temper, he defends me without hesitation. He's *always* been there. He understands me like no one else.

I thought losing Obba was the worst thing that could ever happen—but that's only because I never thought I'd lose my twin. My rock.

What am I going to do without him?

A lump forms in my throat and I work hard to keep myself from crying. Even though I still feel like Nez is making the wrong decision, I don't want to argue with him anymore. I want things between us to be normal—easy and fun, each of us looking out for the other.

So I take a deep breath, pretend like I'm not being torn in half, and ignore every urge I have that tells me to hold on to my brother and never let him go. "You're really going, then?"

"Anything to get away from you." Nez jabs me in the side with his elbow and makes a funny face.

Isn't this what I wanted, for things to go back to normal again? Then why do I still feel like crying?

"Oh Naira." Nez must be able to tell I'm upset because he scoots close, gently places my head on his shoulder, and wraps his arm around me. "It's not like we'll never see each other again."

I sniffle. "You don't know that. Anything could happen."

"True." I tense—I don't want to think about everything that could go wrong when I still haven't gotten used to the idea of him leaving—and he rubs my arm to calm me. "But I promise I will do everything I can, fight every Dambi in the world, even kill Sothpike myself, to see you again."

"Promise?"

Nez nods. "You can count on me." He ruffles the loose hairs on top of my head. "Besides, you're leaving too. You have to search the Rocky Plains to find that old guy. They're almost as vast as the Bujarbi Desert. So good luck with that!"

We both laugh.

"But at least you'll have Omma with you," Nez continues. "I'll be with the Hands."

"They're so strange," I say. "I've never heard any of them talk except that Sister Cornelia, and she's the strangest one of all." I remember her uncomfortable stare back in the Temple.

"Behold the glory of our god," Nez mimics, his tone flat and emotionless.

"Good luck with *that*."

Nez chuckles. "So, are we made up?" I nod and Nez throws open his arms. "Come here, little sis."

I hug him and squirm out of his grasp when he tries to give me a wet, grape-y kiss on the cheek, but deep down I'm still troubled. If the Hands came for Nez, does that mean the Mistress is looking for him as well? Why did all those strange things happen to me if I'm not the one they're looking for? And now that the truth is revealed, when will we be forced to go on our separate ways? When will I lose my other half?

"You think it's safe to leave?" Nez peeks through the curtain.

My stomach drops—Nez is leaving already?—and I almost start to panic until I realize he's talking about leaving Obba's study.

"Where are you running off to?" I hope my steady voice belies the tremors I feel inside.

"I wanted to freshen up." Nez tries to smooth down his curls with his hands but they spring back up and out in all directions. "You know, for the party."

"For Rima, you mean."

"Yeah, her too." He looks me up and down and scrunches his nose. "You should clean yourself up. You look like you haven't had a decent night's sleep in days."

"That's because I haven't." I slug Nez on the shoulder and

he fake winces in pain. He's right, though. I must look terrible after spending so much time at the Temple. I leave Obba's study first, then head across the courtyard to my room.

Once there, I sit on the floor, light a lamp, and pick up the mirror from my dressing table. The old mirror tinges my reflection orange, but the image is clear enough for me to see. I stare at myself, comparing my features to what I remember of the Asim from the visions.

Like the Asim, my eyes are wide and dark, my nose sharply defined, and we have the same full cheeks. Nez, I decide, must look more like Yafeu, with his light brown eyes and high cheekbones.

Both of our skin color is nothing like the Asim's, who was dark like our parents. I think back to the story Omma told me about the pale-skinned boy who prayed for his skin to darken so that he looked more like everyone else. Perhaps our skin color was a surprise to the Asim as well, or perhaps we got it from the Asimra Yafeu, who hailed from the coast like Kal.

I recall the dream of the party, of the Asim kissing the shadowy man behind the screens, and wonder if he was Yafeu. Could he be our father?

I put the mirror down, disturbing the clay pots and jars of face paint next to my brushes and combs and scented oils. A long, tapered needle poking out of one of the clay pots is knocked aside. One end is shaped like a tiny spoon and blackened with kohl while the other narrows to a dull point. The end with the kohl dumps all over my lap, leaving a mess on my clothes.

"By the Fires!" I exclaim as I try to scoop up the kohl with the needle and put it back in the pot. But my hand shakes holding the delicate instrument, and I end up spreading the kohl more than cleaning it up.

In my haste, I bump the night table holding a pitcher of water, sending it crashing to the floor, spilling water everywhere. Suddenly, my breathing feels tight and my eyes are swimming with tears.

Everything's falling apart.

Obba's gone, Nez is leaving, and I'm going to lose the only home I've ever known to go on a journey that I don't want to take.

I thought getting rid of the Mistress would fix everything, but now my brother is abandoning me, I found out my parents aren't really my parents, and Sothpike is crossing the desert.

Everything's falling apart and there's nothing I can do to put it back together.

The curtain to my room parts and Rima rushes inside.

"What are you doing?" Rima asks, her eyes widening as she takes in the scene.

"I was trying to get rid of this stupid powder but it won't come off and now there's water everywhere and I don't know what to do!"

I'm not really upset about the kohl or the water. It's everything else. I thought I was fine—I even laughed with Nez before leaving Obba's study—but now I'm crying and can't stop.

Rima rushes over and kneels beside me.

"It's alright," she says as she wipes the tears from my eyes with her sleeve. She finds a clean towel and makes quick work of mopping up the floor. "Everything's going to be alright."

Ugly, gasping sobs burst out of me and I don't try to stop them. "How could they do this to me?"

"Who? What did they do?"

"All of them." I brush the remnants of the kohl off my lap and onto the floor. "They're all liars and it makes me so angry I could scream!"

Rima looks confused. "What are you talking about?"

"My parents lied to me! They lied, and I know why they did it, but it still hurts, and there's nothing I can do about it. Nothing will make this...this...pain inside of me go away. Nothing they say or do can make me whole again."

"Naira, you're going to have to start making some sense." Rima gets on her feet, pulls me up, and walks me over to the cushion in the corner. We sit down, leaning against the wall and each other.

"Do you still keep sweets in here?" Rima asks as she grabs a box off my nightstand and flips open the lid. Inside are colorful, tart candies—our favorite when we were children. Rima takes one and hands the box to me, then lights the lamp on the night table.

"Now," Rima continues, her cheek swollen from the round candy, "tell me everything. From the beginning."

I take a candy, but I don't eat it. My mouth is already full of all the things I need to say, the words I need to get out before they fester and poison my thoughts even further.

"My parents aren't my real parents," I say.

Rima's eyes widen. "What?"

The shock on Rima's face makes me hesitate. Should I be telling all of this to her? But now that I've started, I don't want to stop. I need to talk about this, with someone who isn't Nez or Omma. So, I tell Rima the story Omma told me.

"That means you're the Ur Atum Asim," Rima says slowly, trying to make sense of it all. "Right?"

"No," I say, shaking my head. "The last Ur Atum Asim of Merza is dead. I'm Naira—" I let out a tired laugh and stare at my lap, the orange glow from the oil lamp casting long shadows across my folded hands, making them seem unfamiliar, as if they belong to someone else. "But I'm not Naira Khoum, am I? I don't know who I am."

Rima places her hand over mine and squeezes tight. "I know who you are. You're my friend. You're hotheaded and stubborn, but you're also loyal, and I know if I was ever in trouble, you would be there for me. You're still the same person. It doesn't matter who your parents are, you're still you."

Rima's words help, but only a little. There's more to the story, and it's even more difficult to share.

"You know what this means, right?" I ask. "Nez and I are the reason the Mistress and the Hands are here. Everyone who's died fighting the Dambi has died because of us." I don't say what I'm really thinking—that Obba is dead because of us. If I say that out loud, I'll start crying again, and I don't think I'll ever stop.

"But why?" Rima asks. "Why do the Mistress and the Hands want you and Nez?"

I shrug. "I don't know. The Hands might be able to answer that question. *Nez* is the reason they came here. Their god told them to come get him, but I don't want him to go. *I'm* supposed to search the Rocky Plains for some old man named Gamikal to tell me what happens next."

"The Hands are here for Nez?" Rima asks, concern filling her face.

"That's what they told my mother."

"I see," Rima says. She looks as if she's going to say more, but then she changes the subject. "Who's Gamikal?"

"You're going to love this," I say with a roll of my eyes. "His story is more unbelievable than me being the daughter of the Asim."

I repeat everything I've learned about him, from what Basheera told me to what Sister Cornelia told my mother.

"Did anyone ever consider that maybe this Gamikal fellow isn't who everyone thinks he is? I mean, you've been waiting for him for sixteen years, and now you have to go find *him*?"

I stuff the candy in my mouth and lean against the wall to think. Rima is voicing my own doubts, but I have to believe the Asim told my parents about Gamikal for a reason. I only wish the Asim had told them what that reason was.

"Even if I don't go looking for him, I still can't go with the Hands," I say. Thinking about Sister Cornelia and the way she looked at me sends shivers down my spine. There's nothing altruistic about the Hands wanting to take Nez away. "They only want Nez—and only their god knows why."

"The Hands said Sothpike is crossing the desert. Does this mean he knows the Asim's child didn't die? Does he know there are two of you?"

I sit up and shake my head mindlessly. "I don't know. I don't know what to do. Tell me, Rima. Tell me what I can do to make this all stop." A tear trickles down my cheek. I'm not full of anger anymore. That has passed, and now I know why.

I'm scared.

"Tell me, please," I beg before breaking down again in Rima's arms. "I can't lose my brother too."

Rima rubs my back. "It's going to be alright," she says, pulling me close. "We'll figure it out. I promise."

I cling to Rima as though she's the only star in the night sky, the only thing guiding me home, and if I lose sight of her light for one beat of my heart, if I let go even a little, I'll be lost in the darkness forever. "All these awful things keep happening to us and I don't know what to do. I hate it. I want everything to go back to the way it was before my father died."

"Me too," Rima says. She lifts me up and once again wipes away my tears with her sleeve before rubbing the heel of her hand over her face.

We sit in silence for a while, leaning on each other, eating the hard candies. Rima is quiet for so long, I worry she fell asleep, until she finally stirs.

"So, is Nez joining the Hands?" She speaks as if she's scared to say the words out loud, as if simply asking the question will make it come true.

"I didn't think..." I slump against the wall. I was so caught up in my feelings, I didn't consider Rima's. "You shouldn't have found out this way. I'm sorry."

Rima looks up at the ceiling and blinks a few times before responding.

"It's fine," she says, her voice thick. She clears her throat. "It doesn't sound like he has much of a choice anyway. And we haven't been together long."

"I know, but..."

"If it's meant to be, it will be," she says.

"It will be," I say, squeezing Rima's hand. She gives me a half-hearted grin in response.

CHAPTER TWENTY-SIX

BY THE TIME WE LEAVE MY ROOM, THE SUN IS BEGINNING to set and many of the boarders are getting ready for the birthday party, save those who patrol the premises. The partiers pass around a bottle of wine, their laughter carrying on the wind. To keep away the approaching night, others light oil lamps hanging from wooden poles around the perimeter of the courtyard. A man holds a small drum against his hip and taps the taut skin with a small mallet. Beside him, musicians pluck the strings of eukalah and blow into kitars to produce a lilting melody to the beat of the drum.

It seems a strange time for a party, but I understand why one is needed. We can't be afraid all the time. Besides, my parents like to entertain. After all the arguing in Obba's study, Omma probably encouraged the party even more as a way to cleanse the air of our harsh words.

I find the man for whom the party is being thrown sitting on a bench near the center of the courtyard. Samir Cheboh has a little monkey that sits on his shoulder named Bous-Bous who hates everyone except her owner, and she only seems to tolerate him because he feeds her a constant stream of grapes.

When I come near to wish Samir Cheboh a happy birthday, the little creature screeches at me before hiding behind the bearded old man.

"She gets greedy when she has grapes," Samir Cheboh explains to me with a shrug as if to say, *What can you do?*

I bow and say happy birthday from afar. Then, I find Rima among the revelers, laughing and twirling around in a circle, with a colorful fabric trailing from her hands as she spins. Nez grabs one of the pieces of cloth and joins Rima in her hypnotic dance.

As I cross the courtyard, Nez takes my hands and spins me around in time with the music. I twirl round and round, my movements whirling like my thoughts. I hold on tightly to Nez's hands, glad to have an anchor to keep me from flying out of control.

The musicians switch to a slower tune, and Nez finally lets me go as he returns to Rima. Out of breath and laughing despite the day's events still clouding my thoughts, I exit the party and go to the jirkana. As I make my way there, the faint sounds of the celebration carry on the breeze like a childhood memory.

Inside the jirkana, I stare at Obba's sword, wanting to touch it, but not daring to. What if it feels different, now that I know Obba isn't my real father?

I don't want to be angry at my parents, but why did they keep it from us for so long? I feel like I'm standing on the edge of a cliff, the future a deep black void in front of me, because everything behind me—my past, who I am, everything I thought to be true—is a lie. I don't know who I am anymore if I'm not the daughter of Isrof and Farina Khoum.

"I thought I'd find you here," Kal says from the doorway.

Grateful to have someone else to occupy my tortured thoughts, I walk over to him and he takes me by the hand.

"Is everything alright?" he asks. "You look like you've been crying."

I take a deep breath. I don't want to cry again, especially not in front of Kal. "I was a little upset earlier, but I'm fine now."

Kal looks like he doesn't believe me, like he wants to ask more questions, but I don't want to talk about it anymore.

"I'm okay, I promise," I insist, and when he nods in acceptance, I'm grateful he didn't try to pressure me into speaking before I'm ready.

I smile. "Were you looking for me?"

His face breaks out into a grin. "Come on," he says, "or we'll miss it."

He hurries through the garden to a storage room surrounded by wooden crates and I have to run to keep up with him. He climbs the crates until he's on the roof of the small room. From where he stands, he's higher than most of the buildings surrounding us.

I follow, watching as Kal kneels on the roof and opens a wooden case. The inside is lined with soft velvet, and he pulls out a long, cylindrical object wrapped in cloth. He carefully unwraps the cloth to reveal a silver telescope.

Obba had a telescope, but it wasn't nearly as large or as fancy as Kal's. The metal is etched with images from the sea: waves and fish, strange creatures emerging from the water, islands with palm trees and dancing maidens. The largest image is a boat with billowing sails, and I wonder if that's Kal's father's boat.

"Hold this," he says, passing the telescope to me. It's much heavier than it looks and I hold it with both hands to ensure I don't drop the precious object. Kal lifts the velvet padding and pulls out three sticks of metal that he links together to create a tripod for the telescope to rest upon. Once assembled, he points it west toward the setting sun and lies on his stomach. I watch, fascinated as he peers through the glass while squinting one eye, then making some adjustments, and finally motioning for me to lie down beside him.

"Here," he says, scooting out of my way so I can put my eye to the lens. "Look at this."

I do as instructed, but see nothing except an evening sky streaked with red, orange, and pink.

"What am I supposed to be looking at?"

"You can't see it?" He hovers near me, the heat from his body making my skin tingle. "Let me take a look."

I lean to the right, and Kal presses even closer to see through the lens. He points the telescope slightly nearer to the horizon, then moves back so I can take another look. I put my eye to the lens and gasp. All along the horizon, little flashes of green light dance as the sun drops out of the sky.

"It's beautiful," I say. The flashes disappear as the sky darkens, so I move the telescope to the left, closer to the remnants of the sun. Kal grabs hold of the instrument, though.

"You don't want to stare directly at the sun," he says, nudging the telescope away from the orange globe of light. "You'll hurt your eyes."

When the sun finishes its work for the day, I pull away from the telescope and turn to Kal.

"What was that?"

"Sailors say it's good luck," he says. Behind him, the first stars appear in the sky. "*'Keep your eye on the sky when the sun goes to bed / if you wish to have fair weather ahead / For strong winds at your back on your journey 'cross the sea / catch the green lady and she'll sail with thee.'*"

"I like that," I say, my voice hushed. Kal is only a breath away.

"Of course, others say seeing the green lights means you'll never go wrong in matters of the heart." His brown-and-green eyes lock with mine, and I couldn't look away even if I wanted to.

And I don't want to.

"Really? And which do you believe?"

Kal answers my question by leaning forward and kissing me. Surprised, my whole body stiffens, but I quickly melt in his arms as his soft gentleness becomes hungry, growing in such intensity that I cling to him. If we were standing, I'm sure my legs would have given out and he'd have to hold me steady. Instead, we lie on the rooftop side by side, with Kal's lips pressed against mine and his hand on my back, keeping me close but somehow not close enough. I shiver as he trails kisses across my cheek, down my neck. My breath comes out in gasps as I run my fingers through his thick curls. Music drifts over from the party in the courtyard, swelling strings and pounding rhythms matching my heart. Here with him, so entwined, I've never felt more sure that this is exactly where I'm supposed to be.

I can't think of a more perfect moment.

Kal pulls away first and rests his forehead against mine, his chest against my shoulder, his hand on the small of my back, my body vibrating with heat wherever we touch.

"I probably should have asked first, but I did warn you I was going to kiss you." He lies on his side and props himself up with an arm, using his free hand to tuck an errant curl behind my ear.

This time, I kiss him. We're both smiling as our lips meet. "There. Now we're even."

Kal leans forward to kiss me again. I close my eyes, hungry for more, when—

"Kal, where are you?" Nez shouts from the garden below.

I startle, knocking the tripod over. Only Kal's quick reflexes keep the telescope from crashing to the ground.

"I'm so sorry," I say as I pick up the dismantled tripod.

"It's fine." Kal laughs as he lifts the padding for me to put the tripod in the case. He folds the cloth around the telescope, places it on the padding, and snaps the lid closed.

"What are you doing up there?" Nez yells, his eyes on the roof of the shed.

"Hi, Nez." Kal waves. "We'll be down in a second."

"Can't you tell him to go away?" I mutter, making Kal laugh again. He hops down on the crates then helps me do the same.

"What were you guys doing up there?" Nez asks.

"None of your business," I snap, grateful for the darkness, which hides my red face.

"We were looking at the horizon," Kal replies at the same time, holding up the wooden case. "With my telescope."

Nez looks at both of us, his eyes narrowing. "Alright," he says slowly. Then he fixes his attention on Kal. "My mother was looking for you. She moved all of your things into my room. She thought we could bunk together for the night. That is, if you want to stay?"

Kal glances at me and bumps my shoulder with his own. "Of course I'll stay." He turns to Nez. "I suppose I'd better go thank your mother. Where can I find her?"

"She's at the party," Nez says.

"Thanks." Kal bows and we leave the garden, Nez trailing behind us. Back at the festivities, Kal kisses my cheek before going off to search for Omma.

I watch him disappear into the crowd, feeling Nez's eyes on me. When I glance back at him, he's staring at me with one brow raised.

Before he can say what I know he's thinking, I hook my arm through his and drag him into the middle of the dancing. The thought of Nez leaving terrifies me, and I want to cling to him forever, but I know I can't keep my brother at my side for the rest of our lives. I pass Nez off to Rima and throw myself into dancing until my feet are aching and my breath comes in short spurts and sweat drips down my back. I dance until I think of nothing else except moving to the music instead of the pain coursing through my heart.

Later that night, Rima sleeps quietly beside me, but my thoughts won't calm down long enough for me to fall asleep as well. I flop onto my side and sigh. I try to let my mind drift into nothingness, but it keeps taking me back to the rooftop.

The way Kal pulled me close. The way he pressed his lips against mine. How I can't wait to do it again.

I must have fallen asleep eventually because the next thing I know, sunlight is streaming through the curtains and Rima is gone.

I get out of bed and make my way to the kitchen, where I pour myself a cup of water and gulp it down. All that crying yesterday made me thirsty. As I finish my second cup, Omma enters the kitchen.

"I take it you and Nez made up?"

"Yes, Omma." I light the stove and put on a pot of water to cook the rice.

"That's good," she says, sitting at the table. "Change is difficult, but you have to learn to adapt. If things don't go your way, don't waste your time arguing about it. You figure out a new way. Your brother is leaving us. I don't want him to go either, but I realize he has to. I tried to think of what your father would have done. And I believe he would have let Nez go. This is the path for Nez. You have to find yours."

"Why can't my path be to stay here with you?" I place a lid on the simmering pot of rice, hoping that the familiarity of cooking something that we eat almost every day will ease my anxiety, but it doesn't.

Omma rises from the table and places a comforting hand on my shoulder.

"That's not a path, my headstrong girl," she says, resting her cheek against my back. "That's a stop, a pause in your great journey. You are destined for more than watching your Omma grow old. And when the time comes, when your path reveals itself, you'll be ready to face it, won't you?"

I say yes because I know that's what Omma wants to hear, but I'm not so sure. What if I don't like the path set out before me? Am I still supposed to go along with it? Why can't I forge my own path? Why do I have to rely on the mysterious Gamikal to show me where to go next? Why can't Nez stay home where he belongs? Why, why, why?

"I'd better fetch more water." I grab the wooden bucket and run out of the kitchen before Omma notices the tears welling in my eyes.

When I return, others have joined Omma in making breakfast for everyone. There's not much for me to do, so I sit by the pool in the courtyard and let my fingers drift in the water. I'm lost in the ripples when the first rock lands in the water beside me, then another.

I look up and see a face peering down at me from the roof. Jumping to my feet, I go for my daggers but they're gone. I took them off to sleep and didn't put them back on.

"I'm looking for Rima Okuba," the person says. He holds out a note. "It's from her sister, the scribe Basheera."

My heart slows down. "Are you a runner from the Temple?"

He nods. "Can you get this to her?"

I hold out my hand. "Of course."

I watch the note drift down on the breeze and land on my palm. When I look back up, the runner is gone.

I head back to the kitchen and pull Rima outside. In the garden, where it's quiet, I hand her the note and wait while she reads it.

"Basheera says they're not going to deliver the rest of the children to the Mistress," she says. "Instead, they're going to attack the meeting house."

"When?"

Rima glances at the sun. "Now."

CHAPTER TWENTY-SEVEN

"HOW ARE THEY GOING TO DO IT?" I ASK AS WE RUN back to my room to gather our weapons. "A full-on assault?"

"The note doesn't say," Rima answers. "But I heard Basheera talking to the others as they pored over the maps. She thinks we can use the rooftops to our advantage. They didn't use her idea before, but I guess with the Hands helping, they must think we have a chance."

It makes sense to attack now, while we have the Hands on our side and before the Mistress has time to gather reinforcements.

Or worse, before Sothpike himself arrives.

I sheathe my daggers and strap on my leather gauntlets as Rima grabs her spear. We hurry to Nez's room next door and find him still asleep. I leave Rima to wake him while I search for Kal.

When I don't find him in the jirkana, I head back out to the garden. A glint of light above the storage shed catches my eye. Kal's up there with his telescope trained on something in the distance, the sun reflecting off the lens. I scramble up the crates and join him.

"What are you looking at?"

Kal scoots over so I can peer into the glass eyepiece. In the distance, I see hundreds of people running along the rooftops toward the meeting house.

"Something's happening out there," Kal says, his breath tickling my ear and making me shiver.

"I know. That's why we have to leave now." I start to jump down but Kal places a hand on my arm to stop me.

"Wait," he says. "I have to tell you something."

Wary, I sit back down, both of us cross-legged and facing each other. Kal reaches for my hand and I let him take it.

"I'd heard stories about Lagusa," he says. "A 'desert paradise,' they said. I assumed they were talking about the village, but the true paradise is you." My heart stills. "Being near you is like taking a drink of water after nearly dying of thirst. I feel so alive, like I can do anything, and now I have a reason to keep fighting."

"What is it?"

He brushes his hand against my cheek. "You." My heart thunders back to life, racing and leaping in my chest. I want to ask him if he can hear it, if he knows how I feel, but he drops his hand and holds both of mine. "That's why it's so difficult for me to tell you this."

Now I can't breathe. First he steals my heart, and then my breath. "What are you saying?"

"I'm joining the Hands of God."

I shake my head. "What? No. Why would you do that? I don't understand."

"My father was one of them. I want to follow in his footsteps and learn more about his past. Since I can't ask him about it, the next best thing I can do is join the Hands and ask *them*."

"But you don't have to join to do that," I say. "We can ask Sister Cornelia. She's the one who fought your father all those years ago. I'm sure she can tell you what you want to know."

"I have to do this. For my mother, my brothers. My father. For me."

"I don't want you to go." I wish I could beg and plead for him to stay. But I remember what Nez said the night before, about me trying to force him to do what I want. I know pressuring Kal to change his mind simply because I don't want him to follow his own path is wrong. I don't even notice I'm crying until Kal wipes a tear from my cheek.

"I'll be back." He pulls me close, wrapping his strong arms around me. "I promise."

He smooths my hair and rests his chin on the top of my head. I press my cheek against his chest, my ear by his heart. We remain there, holding each other, for so long that our bodies seem to meld together. I wish we could fuse ourselves together so we could never be apart. In the distance, Nez calls my name, but I ignore him.

"Nez is joining the Hands too," I say into Kal's tunic.

"I know. He told me last night. I had been thinking about it ever since Basheera gave me the clasp, but when he told me he was going, I decided to join him." As Kal speaks, his words rumble through his chest and into my thoughts, where I hope the sound lingers forever.

I don't want to forget what Kal's voice sounds like.

"At least you two will be together." I reluctantly pull out of the embrace. "Will you do me a favor?"

Kal grins. "If you asked me to bring you the moon, I'd do it."

I can't help but smile back. "Nothing that grand. Just... promise me you'll watch out for my brother. He's a numbskull, but he's the only brother I have."

Kal touches his forehead against mine, a silent vow.

"We'd better get going," I say but I don't make an effort to move. I don't want to be the first one to break contact this time. Not when this might be the last time.

"Naira! Kal!"

Nez's shout startles us apart.

"On second thought, maybe I *don't* want you looking out for him," I joke as I help Kal put the telescope back in the case. When we're done, we jump down from the shed and find Nez in the garden, his bow slung across his shoulder.

"Is it time to go?" I ask and Nez nods.

"Is everyone ready?" Kal asks.

Nez adjusts his bow and quiver. "I've been ready. I was born ready." Then he rubs the back of his neck. "But first, someone's gotta tell Omma we're going back out there. And I volunteer you!" He points at me.

"No way," I say, backing up. "You're Omma's favorite. *You* tell her."

"Rima already told me," Omma says, entering the garden with Rima right behind her. "At least one of you has the guts to let me know what you're planning."

"So—is it alright if we go?" Nez asks.

"I'd rather all of you stayed here with me where I can watch you," Omma replies. "But I won't stop you. If you feel like this is what you need to do, then I won't stand in your way."

I give my mother a kiss on the cheek. "Thank you, Omma."

"As soon as one of you gets injured, even if it's just a stubbed toe, you come right back, understand?"

We all nod our heads in agreement. One by one, Omma gives us her blessing with a kiss on the cheek and a hug. When it's my turn, I don't let go of her right away.

"My headstrong girl," she says, giving me another kiss on the cheek before gently pulling away.

Omma walks us to the front door and opens it herself.

"Be safe," she says as we head out into the turbulent world.

Our going is slower than when we snuck out the first time and ended up joining the resistance. Nez's ankle still bothers him, my sore back limits the mobility of my arms and torso, and even though Kal's dislocated shoulder is set in place, the muscles seem to be tender—I catch him rubbing his bicep and rotating his shoulder every once in a while. We're bruised, but not broken.

As we make our way to the meeting house, we keep our eyes peeled for a way onto the rooftops with everyone else. When Nez finds an open doorway to an abandoned apartment building, we dash inside, climb the steps, and burst onto the rooftop. A few buildings away, we see a large group of resistance fighters, so we hurry over boards connecting the buildings and vault over railings to join them.

I'm amazed by all the activity on the roof. The energy is a bit frantic, and I feed off it, the revelations from the previous day fading to the back of my mind as I let myself get excited for what's coming next.

Most of the resistance fighters are huddled around a large table covered with maps of the village, with Basheera presiding over them with a decorated ranger and a high-ranking watchguard.

"Scribe Okuba has formulated a plan—" the ranger says.

"A good plan," Basheera cuts in.

The ranger clears his throat. "Yes, a good plan, and we'd be wise to follow it." He turns to the watchguard beside him.

"If Captain Farouk were here," the watchguard says, "he'd tell you that this is our only chance. If we do this right, then we'll be done with the Mistress and her Dambi for good. So I want you all to listen up, because we won't get another shot."

The watchguard nods at Basheera, and she steps in front of the maps, using a stylus to scratch off certain roads and draw arrows down others.

"We'll corral them down Honey Street—it's a dead end and all of the buildings are at least two stories high," Basheera says. "We'll use our knowledge of *our* village—knowledge they don't have—to turn the tides in our favor. We only have to keep them busy long enough for the Hands to pick off the stragglers in front of the meeting house. Once the Hands have cleared the plaza, the rest of you go in. We don't know where she's holding our Mother and the children, but they're in there, and we have to find them. We'll keep the majority of the Dambi away for as long as we can, so be quick. Understand?"

Basheera stares down the people surrounding her and they all respond with quick bows.

"Then what are you waiting for?" she barks as she pushes her glasses up the bridge of her nose. "Take your places!"

Everyone breaks away at a run. As the crowd thins, Basheera notices Rima and the rest of us. She frowns when Rima steps closer.

"I was hoping you wouldn't come."

"No, you weren't," Rima says with a grin, "or you wouldn't've sent the note."

Basheera rolls her eyes as her younger sister hugs her.

"What are the rest of you doing here? Are you looking to get killed?"

"We want to help," I say.

"Well, you can help by keeping out of the way. I'll let you stay, but you have to promise to do whatever I tell you. Understood?"

She gives the four of us the same withering gaze she gave the fighters and I find myself nodding even though I don't plan on simply watching. But at least she didn't try to send us away.

I have to be grateful for that.

We join Basheera at the roof's ledge where we have a view of Honey Street on our left and the meeting house on our right. Honey Street is empty, but the meeting house is crawling with Dambi. There's so many I can't even count them. They pace in front of the building, swiping at each other when they get too close, sometimes raising their faces to the sky and screeching.

Seeing them now, so many creatures who were resurrected solely to kill, I just hope Basheera's plan works.

Resistance fighters scatter across the roofs in all directions, but most of them go toward Honey Street. I notice a few fighters on the ground heading straight for the meeting house, and I realize they're the bait. One of the fighters on the ground nocks an arrow and lets it loose, right into the skull of one of the Dambi prowling in front of the meeting house. The creature shrieks. After a moment of silence, the rest of the sixty-odd Dambi do the same.

I cover my ears with my hands and even still, the sound reverberates between my ears. My face scrunches up in pain as the noise grows louder before finally fading. The fighters taunt the Dambi, but all the creatures do is pace back and forth, as if some unseen force is holding them back from chasing them.

I recall the mark on the Mistress's hand. She's probably controlling them right now, preventing them from running off.

"Come on, come on," Nez whispers beside me. "Take the bait."

Just when it seems like Basheera will have to come up with a new plan, a handful of Dambi break away and chase after the fighters. But that isn't enough—there are too many Dambi still in front of the meeting house. Even though the Hands are impressive fighters, there are only nine of them, and they won't last long against a horde.

As the fighters run, they turn to fire more arrows into the swarm of waiting Dambi. Suddenly, as if their chains were finally broken, the Dambi charge forward, their hands and feet thundering on the dirt-packed road, sending up clouds of dust. The people on the rooftops cheer and hit the Dambi with more arrows, enraging the creatures and ensuring they keep up the chase, heading right into the trap.

As soon as most of the Dambi are diverted to Honey Street, barricades are shoved across the entrance to the street and set on fire, preventing the Dambi from escaping. Next come vats of hot oil and boiling water poured down from the rooftops lining Honey Street. I appreciate Basheera's plan even more. Not only is Honey Street a dead end, but it's where people go to have their skin oiled and luxuriate in steam baths, so the area was already equipped with all the hot water and oil Basheera needed. She simply used the village's resources against the Dambi.

Screams of pain erupt from Honey Street, but this time, I don't cover my ears.

Commotion on my right gets my attention. The Hands of God swoop into the plaza, their swords catching the sun and shooting off sparks of light as they cut down the remaining Dambi. Once they're dead, fighters carrying a battering ram enter the plaza.

Before I can celebrate, human screams draw my attention back to Honey Street. A second round of hot oil and water rains down on the Dambi, but that isn't enough to kill them. Some have broken through the barrier, their skin melting away to reveal blackened bones. They're still able to fight, to kill. My hands tighten around my daggers.

"We have to help them," I whisper to Nez.

"I know. But how will we get away from Basheera?"

"We just go," Rima says, pulling on Nez's arm.

She drags him to a set of planks stretching from our roof to the building next door. Rima is halfway across before Basheera notices.

"Hey! Get down from there!"

"Sorry, Basheera, but we can't stay," Rima calls back as she jumps onto the roof across the alley. Nez climbs onto the planks next and makes his way over, his slight limp barely slowing him down, with Kal right behind.

"Naira Khoum, don't you dare—"

"I'm sorry," is all I can say before scrambling onto the planks myself and joining the others.

"You better not let anything happen to my sister!" Basheera calls after us as we race across the roof. "Or I will hunt you down! I swear by the Fires!"

"Yes, samida!" Nez yells over his shoulder.

When we're far enough away from Basheera, I slow down and turn my attention to the meeting house. The fighters are having trouble bashing in the door, and random Dambi keep the Hands too busy to help.

"That's where we should be going," I say to the others. They stop and follow my gaze.

"But what about the people on Honey Street?" Nez asks. "They're going to be killed."

"Naira's right," Kal says. "Finding and stopping the Mistress is the most important thing. She can control the Dambi, which means she can also stop them from killing."

"I guess it's back to the meeting house," Nez says, still favoring his right ankle from when he fell through the trapdoor. Even now, he stands with most of his weight resting on his left leg.

"It's time to end this," I say, leading the way.

We continue across the rooftops, to the building behind the meeting house where Nez twisted his ankle. Three Dambi roam the footpath between the two buildings.

"We're going to have to take them out to get inside," I tell the others.

"Well, what are you waiting for?" Nez asks, jumping down through the still-broken trapdoor.

"By the Fires, I hope he didn't twist his other ankle!" Rima exclaims as she runs over to peer inside.

Luckily, Nez is fine and waiting for us, looking more pleased with himself than he has any right to.

We hurry down the steps to the first floor. Kal puts his shoulder against the back door to shove it open, but Nez places a hand on his arm to stop him.

"Last chance," he says. "If anyone wants to back out, do it now. We're going after the Mistress and she won't let us retreat. This is it."

"We have a saying where I come from," Kal says, facing us. "*'We sailors have to ride the wind together, or we drown together.'* As long as we go into this together, watching out for each other, we'll make it through."

We can do this. I know we can. I look into Nez's eyes. "We can't fail. And we won't."

Rima strikes the end of her spear on the ground. "I'm ready to kill a Mistress."

CHAPTER TWENTY-EIGHT

TWO OF THE DAMBI IN FRONT OF US ARE ATTACKING each other at the far end of the footpath. If we're quiet, we can sneak into the building without them knowing. The third Dambi blocks the entrance to the meeting house. It paces and clutches at its eyes, but the sockets are empty black holes.

"I think that's the Dambi you blinded with your arrows," I whisper to Nez as we huddle in the open doorway.

"Of course," he groans. "What would my day be like if there wasn't an indestructible Dambi blocking my path who probably wants my blood? Well, nothing to do now but put it out of its misery."

Nez nocks two arrows and lets them fly. One embeds in the creature's forehead, the other in its chest. The Dambi opens its mouth to shriek but Nez plunges another arrow into its throat, stopping all sound.

The last arrow knocks the Dambi back against the wall, causing some of the bricks to crumble, revealing the hidden entrance and drawing the attention of the other two. They come tearing down the footpath and descend upon the injured Dambi, biting its flesh and ripping it apart with their claws. While they feast, we creep toward the widened opening.

We're quiet, but not quiet enough. Someone kicks a loose brick, and the faint sound it makes when it scrapes the ground is all it takes for the Dambi to whirl around and spot us.

Nez pushes Rima toward the meeting house. "Hurry up!"

She scrambles through the crack in the wall with Nez and Kal right behind her. But I'm not so lucky. A Dambi jumps in my way and snarls while the other stalks in front of the entrance.

With no other options, I run back in the building across the footpath and slam the door shut. Wood splinters as I race up the stairs, both Dambi bursting through the door and scrambling behind me, the stairwell too narrow for more than one of us at a time.

I have the advantage, a very small one, and I'm determined to use it.

When I turn the corner to go up the next flight of stairs, I stop and press my back against the wall, my breath coming in quick bursts. As soon as a Dambi comes around the corner, I throw my dagger and it lands in the creature's forehead. Avoiding its claws, I jab the second dagger in as well. When I pull out both daggers, the Dambi topples back down the stairs.

The next Dambi tramples over the injured one and I swing at one of its grasping arms, miss, then connect with the bones of the other arm. The Dambi howls and I ram the daggers through its guts.

But it isn't dead yet.

I race up the next flight of stairs, back to the trapdoor lead-

ing to the roof. Heaving for air, I climb up the ladder, hoping
the Dambi won't be able to follow. But the creature jumps
through the broken trapdoor, bursting through the remaining shafts of wood as if they're nothing more than sheets of
paper. I dodge out of the creature's way as it tries to tackle me.

There isn't anywhere to hide on the big, empty roof, so
all I can do is stay out of its way and try to get in a good jab
when I can. I'm too close to the edge for my liking so I roll
out of the way as the Dambi lunges at me. The monster tee-
ters on the edge of the roof and just when it seems to regain
its balance, an arrow embeds in its back, sending it over the
edge onto the footpath below.

The Dambi screams as it falls and crashes with a sicken-
ing thud.

"Let's try this again, shall we?" Nez says, holding out a
hand to help me onto my feet.

Inside the building, Kal is about to climb the ladder to the
roof. He smiles when he sees I'm safe and sound.

"Don't go running off like that again," he says, helping me
down the ladder.

"I won't," I reply, unable to stop myself from smiling at
him, despite the danger we're in.

We go back down the stairs, this time stepping over the
body of the Dambi I stabbed in the head. Kal and Nez finished it off with their sword and bow. Rima waits for us at
the bottom, the tip of her spear pointed at the door.

"I didn't know what to expect when you ran back into
the building," she says, "but it wasn't for a Dambi to fall off
the roof."

Splatters of black blood and steaming guts cover the footpath. The stench makes me gag. The Dambi smell even worse when they die for the second time.

One by one, we crawl through the hole in the wall and enter the meeting house. The sound of the battering ram bashing the front doors echoes throughout the building at regular intervals and grows louder as we make our way to the front of the building, like the footsteps of a giant coming closer and closer. Howls and screeches answer every bash of the ram, and I try to guess how many Dambi are inside. A dozen? Maybe more? Will we be able to fend off that many to give those outside the chance to break in?

My fingers curl around the hilts of my daggers and I hold my breath with every step. The element of surprise is our biggest advantage, and we'll need all the help we can get if we're going to attack the Dambi.

When we reach the main entrance, we discover why the resistance fighters are having a hard time bashing inside. Scores of dead bodies, Dambi and human, are pressed against the door, and I count ten more Dambi prowling among and over them. With all that weight against the doors, it will take ages for the others to get through.

And once they do, more Dambi will be waiting to kill them.

"We could take out a few of those Dambi," Nez suggests as screams and cries for help erupt from our right.

"I bet that's the hostages," Kal whispers.

"We have to help them," Rima says.

I know our first priority is finding the Mistress, but I can't turn my back on these people in need. There are kids in there, some of them younger than me, and they can't defend

themselves against Dambi like the Hands of God and the resistance fighters. I lead us away from the main entrance. We
follow the sounds to a set of double doors leading to a chamber room where the Subaans would normally discuss matters
in private. A metal bar across the doors keeps them closed.

A dead body is slumped against one of the doors, its guts
spilled out on the floor. One hand still holds a bloody knife.

"That's Subaan Ledisi," Rima says.

"She must have locked them in there," I say. "And then
killed herself in shame."

"Then we'd better free them," Kal says as he lifts the metal
bar and shoves the doors open.

Inside, the Mother's remaining protectors keep two Dambi
at bay on one end of the room while the Mother herds all
of the kids to the other side. Blood and body parts litter the
floor, the smell of death strong and metallic.

The kids are mangled, their bodies scratched and bruised,
many of them missing a limb or two, their stumps bandaged
just enough to keep them from bleeding out. It's as if the
Mistress has been using them to keep her creatures satiated.

My stomach turns and rage blossoms in my chest and the
urge to kill is so strong I shudder.

"That witch has to die," I mutter.

Any hope I carried that Obba was somehow still alive fades
away. If this is what the Mistress does to children, she'd never
let someone like Obba, someone who openly defied her, live.

As soon as the Mother notices the doors are open, she starts
grabbing kids and pointing them toward the escape. We stand
aside and help usher them out while cautioning them to keep

quiet so that we don't alert the Dambi prowling around the entrance.

As everyone rushes out of the room, I spot Hamala among them. I'm relieved to know she's alive, but she looks ill. Her left hand is mangled—only bits of skin and muscle hang from her wrist, the bones gone. Last time I saw her she was braiding her sister's hair.

When Hamala sees me, tears fill her eyes, but she quickly wipes them away with her uninjured hand.

"I knew you'd show up," she says in that annoyed tone, but this time the sharp edge is softened. "I can always depend on you to stick your nose in my business."

"Like you said at the Temple, everywhere you go, there's Naira Khoum."

As she files past, she lowers her head into a bow. That's as close to a thank-you as I'll ever get from Hamala, and I return the gesture.

When she's gone, I run inside with Nez and Kal to help the protectors with the Dambi while Rima beckons the rest of the kids on.

Nez sends two arrows flying, one into the chest of each Dambi. One of them screeches and claws at the arrow protruding from its chest. The protectors use this distraction to gang up on the creature, hacking away at it with their swords until it's a bloody mess of cuts and slashes, finally unable to move.

The second Dambi isn't felled so easily. It ignores the arrow and instead grabs one of the protectors, digging its claws into his face, ripping the skin off. Kal plunges his sword in the Dambi's stomach and yanks down, rending the creature's torso in half. Nez lets loose more arrows, this time at the back of the Dambi's head, while I slide across the bloody floor, beneath the Dambi's clawing grasp, and spring up right in front of the foul beast, plunging my daggers into the top of its skull.

The Dambi stumbles and falls on one knee, but it still claws and scratches at anyone who comes near. Kal dodges its attacks and with a perfectly timed blow, stabs the Dambi in the heart.

Black blood spews out of the wound, coating Kal's blade. The Dambi drops to its knees and he kicks it in the shoulder causing it to fall back with a crash, releasing his sword.

"That's five," Nez says, leaning against a wall to give his sore ankle a rest. "Just another hundred or so to go."

"Five is better than none," I say, and he shrugs in half agreement.

Now that the Dambi are dead, all eyes turn to me and my friends.

"Where did you come from?" one of the protectors asks, her face bloody.

"What's going on out there?" asks another.

"Is this a rescue?"

"Who are you?"

"We snuck in; the resistance is attacking the meeting house; yes, we're rescuing you; and we're a band of amazing fighters who are going to save the world from evil scum like Sothpike," Nez says, holding up a finger as he answers each question. "I think that's everything."

"And then some," Kal says.

"You're children," a protector says with awe in her voice. "How did you…? It doesn't matter. Let's get out of here."

"Wait," I say. "Where's the Mistress? We have to find her and kill her."

One of the protectors wheezes a weary laugh. "That's what the resistance is for," he says. "You should be helping us protect our Mother and those children. Now come on, we don't have time to dally."

"We're not leaving without making sure the Mistress is dead," I say.

"You're serious?"

Nez stands next to me. "Completely."

"Last we saw, she was in the assembly room," a protector says. "That's where she commands her creatures. Now, if you aren't coming with us, then tell us how you got in, so we can get out."

"Through a back way," Nez says.

"I'll lead you," Rima volunteers.

Nez shakes his head and pulls Rima aside. "What are you doing? You have to stay with us!"

"They need me," Rima says, looking to the crying kids. "I can help them. I'm not a great fighter like you, but I can lead."

"Then I'm going with you," Nez says.

"No." Now Rima shakes her head. "You have to do this. Go with the others. I'll be fine."

"Be safe," Nez says.

"I will." Rima starts to hug him, but he surprises her, and me, with a kiss to her lips.

Kal nudges me with his shoulder and smiles. I can't stop myself from grinning too.

When Rima and Nez pull apart, he smiles briefly before worry tinges his expression. "I'll see you soon," he promises.

With one last lingering look at Nez, she turns to join the children and the Mother.

"May the Fires guide you," the protectors tell us as they leave the hall.

What's guiding me is my desire to kill the Mistress, not the Fires nor the dragon gods nor even the Three-Faced God. Until the gods step in to help, I would do better praying to my blades, because at least I know they will protect me.

While Rima leads her group left, the rest of us go right, toward the assembly room. The doors there are locked, a metal bar on the other side preventing them from opening.

"We'll have to try the balcony." I guide us to the same spiral staircase Kal and I used to gain access to the balcony, where we spied on the Mistress's conversation with the Mother. Nez limps up the stairs, his ankle bothering him, but he puts on a brave face and keeps going. Halfway up the stairs, a shriek rises from behind us.

"Hurry," Kal says, grabbing Nez's arm and slinging it over his shoulder to help him move faster.

I race up the steps and the Dambi screeches again, this time louder than before. Closer. Looking back, I glimpse its claws on the steps below. Kal releases Nez's arm and gives him a shove up the stairs.

"Go, go, go," he yells. Then he brandishes his sword and starts back down toward the Dambi. "No matter what, just keep going!"

"Kal!" I scream. I want to follow him, to fight alongside him, but Nez grabs me. When I try to wrench my arm out of Nez's grasp, he holds tight.

"Come on," he grunts, pulling me up the stairs. "He knows what he's doing."

I know Nez is right, but that doesn't stop my heart from tearing into pieces with every step leading me away from Kal.

CHAPTER TWENTY-NINE

THE SOUNDS OF KAL'S BATTLE DOWN BELOW CARRY UP the stairwell—sword clanging against stone, the Dambi shrieking, claws scraping the stairs and ripping cloth. Kal cries out and I struggle against Nez to go help him, but Nez won't let go.

I'm reminded of Nez pulling me away from our father being struck down, preventing me from joining the fight.

"Come *on*," he says, yanking me up the stairs. "We have to stop the Mistress."

He's right. I have to keep moving. We finally reach the door to the balcony when a Dambi jumps out from the entryway.

Nez skids on a pool of blood on the floor. I grab his arm to keep him from crashing into the creature, which lunges at us, and I press myself and Nez against the wall to avoid its claws. I grab a torch off the wall and shove it in the Dambi's face, and it screams as the fire eats its skin. Nez shoots arrow after arrow at its flailing arms, pinning it to the wall. I slit the Dambi's throat, silencing it, and warm blood coats my arm. I jab the daggers into the monster's stomach, heart, under its rib cage.

The beast shudders and then stills, the fire now consuming its torso and filling the hallway with the acrid smoke of burning flesh that makes my nose wrinkle in disgust.

"I hope that's the last of the Dambi surprises," Nez says, a hand covering a stitch in his side. "I don't know if I can take much more."

"You can," I say, this time pulling Nez along, "and you will."

We run onto the balcony to find the Mistress sitting in our father's chair on the dais with almost a dozen Dambi standing before her, waiting for her command.

The Mistress fingers a strange necklace, lifting a handful of shriveled, black objects dangling from the chain around her neck to her mouth. She clamps her teeth around one of the objects, then another, her eyes clouding over each time she bites down. She lets the objects fall against her chest, then lifts another bunch and starts biting them.

"What *are* those things?" Nez asks.

A Dambi screeches its bone-shattering call. I think about how their mouths are black and empty, and realize what those dangling objects are.

"Vra Gool Dambi tongues," I say.

Nez gags and I have the urge to do the same, but I tamp it down.

"Shh," I warn him.

Too late.

"Did you think I didn't see you coming?" the Mistress asks,

dropping the tongues and turning her eyes to the balcony. "I see everything. My children give me hundreds of eyes."

The Dambi all turn in our direction and stare at us with their cloudy eyes. I take a step back from the railing, but it's too late to hide.

The Mistress stands. "Come closer," she says, motioning for us to join her downstairs. "My children will not hurt you if you behave."

Nez shakes his head. "It's a trap. She only wants us to go down there so she can kill us. We should leave and come back with reinforcements."

"Everyone is too busy fighting outside," I say. "We're here. We need to deal with her." I sheathe my daggers. "Come on."

I walk over to the stairwell connecting the balcony to the assembly room and take it to the ground floor, where all the Dambi and their Mistress are waiting. Nez is right behind me, but he still has his bow out with an arrow trained on the Mistress's forehead.

"That's right, come closer," the Mistress says as her children part to let us through. I can only hope that she'll keep her word and prevent her Dambi from attacking.

Maybe I've been around Vra Gool Dambi for too long, but the stench emanating from these ones is almost bearable. As we make our way through the crowd, it dawns on me why—they aren't as rotted as the other ones. Their skin is dry and brittle, crumbling away to reveal white bone, like the ones in the catacombs. That night her Dambi chased me in the tombs, she must have been plundering bodies, finding some still buried in their dilapidated tombs from the years before our village started burning our dead.

This is why Sothpike always wins—a dead soldier is a chance to create another Dambi. He takes his dead, and the bodies of those he's killed, and resurrects them into a new army that's even more powerful than before.

Up close and in the light, the intricate patterns of swirls and lines are visible on the Mistress's black mask. I stare directly into her eyes, and she stares back.

"I remember you," she says, stepping down from the dais. "You are the girl from the tombs, the one who got away." Her voice drops. "The one who hurt my children."

I take a step back and reach for my daggers.

"No, you don't want to do that," she says and points behind me, her hand glowing.

I spin around to find a Dambi holding Nez by the neck, its claws digging into his skin and trickles of blood running down his throat.

"You said you wouldn't hurt us," I say to the Mistress. "Let him go!"

The Mistress only smiles at me from behind the mask.

"Bring him to me," she says to her Dambi.

The creature obeys her command and drags Nez by the throat toward the dais. As they approach, the Mistress's eyes widen and she lowers her arms.

"You..." she stammers. "You are the one. You look so much like him. How did I not see it before?"

"Screw you," Nez says with a grimace. The Dambi tightens its grip around his neck and he chokes for air.

"Stop hurting him!" I exclaim.

The Mistress flicks one of her fingers and the Dambi loosens its hold. She reaches into her robes and pulls out a shiny metal disk.

"Look at the fire, and tell me what you see," she says, holding the disk up to Nez's face.

"What fire?" he asks, squirming under the Dambi's grip.

"The fire inside! Don't you see it? You *must* see it. You must!"

"Leave him alone," I say, rushing forward and snatching the disk out of the Mistress's hands before she can hurt him. "It's just a piece of...metal..."

But it is so much more than that.

A fire dances in the center of the disk, one that glows bright blue, and as I watch, it grows stronger and stronger until it explodes out of the disk and latches on to my hands, my clothes, racing up my arms, engulfing my entire body.

My skin crackles under the searing-hot pain and memories of a dragon's flames flash through my thoughts, the same flames from my first vision.

This is Ergenegon's fire, somehow trapped in a metal disk.

The fallen dragon appears from behind the flames, his wings tattered and torn, his mouth open wide to unleash another onslaught of heat and blue fire. The wall of heat knocks me down and I curl up in a ball on the ground, covering my face with my arms, as the fire pours over me. I scream, the hungry flames stealing the breath out of my mouth, ripping the air from my lungs. My skin and hair burn as the black dragon hovers over me, his lips pulled back in a cruel smile revealing sharp, yellow teeth, his tail snaking through the air.

When I think I can't take more of the pain, the flames dissipate and I find myself in a throne room. Smoke and fire pour through the windows; the sound of screams and metal swords clanging fills the room.

Before me are two figures: one of them a shadow sitting upon the throne of Merza, the other the Ur Atum Asim. Avari kneels on the ground before the shadow, the dead baby in her arms, her face stoic.

"I killed my child so that you could never have it," she says to the figure, and it howls in fury.

After a moment, the shadow speaks, but I can't hear what it says. Tears trickle from Avari's eyes. Despite her sorrow, she remains steadfast and glares at the figure.

"Kill me then, and be done with it! You've taken everything else. Why not take my life as well?"

"No!" I yell, but they can't hear me. Even though I know the Asim is fated to die by Sothpike's hands, I don't want to witness it. Avari is the mother I never knew, and from the little I saw of her, I want to know more. But I'm not going to get that chance.

The shadow—Sothpike—plunges a sword through Avari's heart and she collapses on the ground, the dead baby rolling out of her arms. Her body convulses once, twice, and then stills. Sothpike kneels beside her, cradling her head in his hands, wiping the blood from her mouth. He speaks words I can't hear and don't want to, then closes Avari's eyes.

They sit there, still as a painting, for so long I think the vision is over, but the scene doesn't disappear. I notice Sothpike's lips moving and his fingers trace a pattern on the back of Avari's right hand. The mark shines dimly at first, but its light intensifies when he pulls something heavy out of his cloak.

It's a mask, like the one the Mistress wears. He places it on

Avari's face and, though she's dead, her eyes fly open. She sits up with a jolt and sucks in a deep breath. She turns to me, and I stare into the cold eyes of the Mistress.

The woman who killed Obba.

Sothpike stands and holds out his hand to his new Mistress. She takes it and follows him out of the throne room, leaving the dead baby and the throne of Merza behind her as if they mean nothing.

I blink and find myself back in the meeting house, the Mistress staring at me expectantly.

"What did you see? Tell me!"

"I saw…" I drop the disk on the floor, my hands trembling too much to hold on to it. I face the Mistress and realize why the visible part of her face looks familiar. "I saw you."

"What?" Nez says, his voice breaking through my scrambled thoughts. "But I didn't see anything—"

"Because you are not the one." The Mistress steps closer to me. I move back, my heart racing as I put my thoughts in order.

The Mistress is the Asim Avari. Asim Avari is my mother. Which means…the Mistress is my mother.

My *real* mother.

I shake my head. "That can't be true. No. I refuse to believe it."

"Believe what?" Nez asks, still struggling against the Dambi.

"Tell me what you saw." The Mistress takes another step toward me. "Tell me!"

I'm not sure what to say. Whatever ritual Sothpike conducted to raise the Asim from the dead and turn her into his

Mistress must be why she became so twisted. Because the Avari from my dreams, the Avari Omma and Obba loved, would never serve someone like Sothpike.

"Did you see him?" the Mistress asks, her dark eyes filled with excitement. "Did you see my master?"

"I saw his shadow," I say, deciding to tell the truth. It may be the only way to get the truth in return. "And I saw you. I saw when he killed you and put that mask on your face. I saw you defy him, then I saw you follow him."

"Kill me?" The Mistress laughs but there is no humor to it. "You are mistaken. My master would never hurt me."

"You asked me what I saw and I'm telling you," I say. "I saw who you really are—the Ur Atum Asim Avari."

Nez's mouth falls open in shock and the Dambi finally lets him go. He drops to the floor, scrambling to pick up the metal disk, staring into it as if he can see what I saw if only he looks hard enough.

With a snarl, the Mistress snatches the disk from his hands and holds it up to her face. Slowly, she removes her mask and drops it on the floor, where it shatters into pieces.

Everything in her expression changes when she sees her true face reflected in the shiny disk. Her eyes widen, her mouth softens, and she looks more like herself.

More like Avari.

More like me.

But Avari is dead. I saw her die. And somehow, looking into the mirror, she seems to see it herself.

"No," she whispers, tracing her image in the metal. "I don't believe…"

"*That's* our mother?" Nez asks as I help him stand. All of

the Dambi pace around us but don't attack, as if the Mistress still has a hold over them even though she isn't paying attention to them.

I nod. Sothpike turned her into something cruel and twisted, and I'm overwhelmed with a sense of pity. He stole her life. No one deserves what she's been through, despite everything she's done since.

I reach a hand toward her.

"I don't believe it!" The Mistress throws the disk at me, hitting me square in the chest, and I cry out in pain. "I was going to bring you to my lord Sothpike whole, but I will not abide such talk about my master!" She twitches her finger, and a Dambi charges toward Nez and I push him aside.

The Dambi swipes at me and I dodge under its unnervingly long arm while keeping an eye on the Mistress. She sidles toward Nez, who is getting on his feet, and an angry fire burns in my core.

I will do anything to protect my brother, and I will kill anyone who threatens him. Even the woman who brought us into this world.

CHAPTER THIRTY

THREE DAMBI CHARGE AT ME AND I DODGE THEM ALL.
With my daggers, I take a swipe here, stab another one there,
and plunge my blades into the back of the third one.

The rest of the Dambi surround their Mistress, breaking
off a few at a time to attack me or Nez.

"I've got the Dambi," I tell Nez, "you go for the Mistress."

He lets an arrow fly at her, but one of the Dambi jumps
into its path and it embeds in its neck. He nocks another
arrow, this one aimed at the Mistress's chest, but she sweeps
her robes out in front of her, deflecting that arrow as well.

She uses her robes as a shield, sometimes whipping the cloth
around to swat the arrows out of the air, other times catching
the arrows within the heavy fabric and snapping them in half.
Her movements are fluid and strong, almost mesmerizing in
their precision, as she blocks every attempt.

Meanwhile, I'm leading the Dambi on a chase away from
my brother and the Mistress. I drag a dagger across the belly
of one Dambi, jump over a stack of pillows, then take a swipe

at the heels of another. The creatures are eager to get me, snarling and screeching in frustration whenever they miss me with their stretched arms.

My eyes are on the battle between the Mistress and Nez, so I don't see the Dambi that knocks me into the oil-filled lantern hanging from a low chain attached to the ceiling. Fire and oil spill all over my body, coating my arms and legs, and I scream.

My breath comes in hot and fast as the flames roar, my movements wild and frantic as I slap at the fire burning my hair, coating my chest, dripping down my legs. I stumble and fall to one knee as the oily blaze consumes me, my thoughts racing between confusion at how this can be happening to me to the terrifying realization that I'm not going to survive. But even though the fire is burning my clothes, my skin doesn't seem to be affected. The panic within me dies down the longer I stare at the flames dancing on my skin.

An exquisite surge of energy sears through my veins, flooding my body with heat to match the flames on my skin. A power I've never felt before courses through me and I feel strong, unstoppable, like a comet racing across the sky.

You are awakened.

The words echo in my head once again, but now I understand. I've always had a fire within me, but it's been dormant. Waiting. But now it's alive, powerful. Like my heart is an inferno. I can't help but feel scared of it, this new part of me that I don't understand yet.

But understand it or not, I'm going to use this fire.

All of the Dambi have backed away from me. For once,

there is something in their cloudy eyes besides death as they gaze at the blaze on my skin: fear.

I barrel right into the chest of the nearest Dambi, fiery shoulder first.

When our skin makes contact, the creature lets out a pained howl. Heat flares up where we connect, and when I shove the Dambi aside, there are scorch marks on its chest, the skin there blistered. Flames spread from the point of contact, eating the Dambi's dried-up flesh and tattered clothes. The monster skitters away from me like a wounded animal, the fire it carries keeping the others at bay, and I plow into the next one.

We collide in a mess of limbs and fire, the husk of the creature instantaneously lighting up in flames. I kick it into a pack of scared Dambi and they scream when the flames touch their skin.

By now, more than half of the Dambi that were protecting the Mistress are either dead or on fire. The flames on my skin are slowly dying down and Nez is still squaring off against the Mistress, her robes in tatters from the onslaught of arrows. But Nez's supply is running low. He fires his last arrow and it sinks deep into the Mistress's shoulder. She stumbles backward and he charges toward her.

The mark on her right hand glows—and the remaining Dambi turn their attention to my brother.

"Nez, watch out!"

He turns toward the sound of my voice, eyes widening when he sees all the Dambi coming toward him. I still have a little fire left on my forearms, so I use it to light up a few Dambi as I make my way toward him.

Nez uses his bow to whack a Dambi across the jaw, then

jabs one end of it in the creature's throat. My fire is gone, but hot blood still courses through my veins. Clutching my daggers, I stab and slash everything that moves.

I look up from the carnage to see the Mistress trying to open the doors to the hall. Dambi shriek on the other side. I have to break her control over the creatures before she gets those doors open.

I race across the room, a Dambi on my heels, and barrel right into the Mistress. My daggers entangle in her robes, and I have no choice but to release my grip on the blades and grab her hand. As soon as our skin touches, she screams, thrashing and trying to wrench her hand out of mine. But I hold on tight, concentrating the fire within me to where my skin meets hers.

Smoke pours out of our joined hands. When I finally let go, the mark is gone and her skin is red and puckered.

"What have you done?" The Mistress stares at her mangled hand, her face contorted with pain.

I'm as surprised as her. I don't know what I've done, or how.

"Naira, behind you!"

I glance over my shoulder. A Dambi is bearing down on me, moments away from striking a killing blow.

I grab the Mistress and spin around, putting her between me and the monster. The creature impales her chest with its claws.

For the second time, the Ur Atum Asim Avari dies from a stab to the heart.

She crumples to the floor and the Dambi begins ripping her apart. Without the Mistress controlling it, it's wild and savage. While the Dambi is distracted with its kill, I step closer.

"Naira, what are you doing?" Nez asks, his face ashen as he leans against the wall, his hand pressed against a bleeding wound on his thigh. "The Mistress is dead. The rest of the Dambi are dead. Forget that one and let's go."

I shake my head and take another step toward the Dambi, my hand outstretched as if it's drawn to the creature. I place my hand on its forehead, and the Dambi shrieks beneath my touch, but I hold steady. Streams of black smoke engulf the Dambi's face, and when I let go, the creature convulses on the floor once, twice, and then stills.

"What did you do?" Nez asks, his eyes wide and his voice filled with confusion.

"I don't know." I'm staring at my hand. My palm fades from bright red back to its normal color. Now that the Mistress and her Dambi are dead, my skin cools as the fire within me fades from all-consuming to smoldering embers.

I gather my daggers and go to Nez. When I reach for him, he shies away from my touch and stares at me as if I'm one of Sothpike's abominations.

It's the same look I used to get from Hamala, but I never imagined I'd see it from my brother. It wounds me as if he had sunk one of his arrows in my heart.

"Don't look at me like that." My voice breaks and I drop my hand. "I didn't ask for this."

Nez blinks and furrows his brow after a moment, like he's confused. "Look at you like what? Like my amazing sister who can fell a Dambi with a single touch?" He's trying so hard to sound normal, but I know my brother. Something's changed between us. An easy grin spreads across his face, but

I can't laugh off what I saw. "Well, are you going to help me or just stand there glowering?"

He motions for me to come closer and he wraps his arm across my shoulder and leans against me, his eyes filled with relief. But the memory of his horrified expression lingers like a splinter between us. And like a splinter, I can't ignore it. It's unfair how something so small, a look so fleeting, can cause such pain.

We haven't gone far when a familiar shiver runs up my spine.

I smell the Dambi before I see it.

I turn around and there it is, lurking in a doorway behind the dais. I can't tell if it's seen us or not, and I try to shuffle Nez along faster.

"Hurry," I say, practically dragging him.

He sucks in a sharp breath through clenched teeth. "I'm going as fast as I can."

But it's not fast enough. The Dambi shrieks—sounding like it's right behind us—and when I glance over my shoulder, I freeze.

Nez yells for me to move, keep going, but I can't. I'm frozen to the ground, my feet lead, my eyes stuck wide open, staring at the creature running toward us, its claws tearing into the stone floor.

Because I know that Dambi like I know my own reflection.

CHAPTER THIRTY-ONE

"OBBA?" MY MOUTH FORMS THE WORD BUT NO SOUND comes out. Everything inside me is hollow. Now I know why Obba once warned us that a killing blow can come in many forms, from any direction, at any time.

I wished Obba was still alive, but never like this. To be transformed into a Dambi is a fate worse than death. I'd rather be dead than see him this way.

I watch him run on all fours, a snarl on his blackened lips. I can't move. I know I have to do something or this monster will rip me to shreds, but I can't kill the man who gave his life protecting mine.

He rears back, claws glistening, and Nez slams into my chest, knocking me out of the way. We both land hard on the floor. He gets up first and drags me because my movements are sluggish, as if my body is finally processing what my broken heart already knows.

Obba is one of Sothpike's Vra Gool Dambi.

Obba, my protector, the one whose praise lifted me higher

than the sun, whose disapproval brought me crashing back to the earth. The man who taught me to fight and how to show compassion. I will always crave his wisdom and guidance and still can't imagine a future without his strength, his voice, his comforting hand.

"What's wrong with you?" Nez asks as he tries to pull me out of the Dambi's grasp.

"It's Obba," I say, tears streaming down my face.

"What?" Nez looks at the creature and his eyes widen. "Obba?"

Obba shrieks in response, a sound so inhuman it's hard for me to believe it came out of his mouth. He stalks toward me and I search his face, hoping to see some sort of recognition, hoping that the man I cherish is still inside. Obba's the strongest person I know—there must be some part of him still in there.

"Obba, it's me, Naira!"

Nez joins in, calling Obba's name, begging him to answer. He pauses as if he's heard us and a flicker of hope ignites in my chest. I take a step forward.

"Obba, we missed you."

My father responds by lunging at me. I scramble to the side, and he scrapes his claws on the stone floor as he turns before charging at me again. I try to run, but I can barely see where I'm going, my eyes filled with hot tears.

With a screech, Obba leaps at me. I stumble over a dead Dambi and Obba knocks me down with a blow to my back. I fall hard on the stone floor and barely dodge a claw to the face by rolling to the side.

"Please, Obba," I cry as I get on my feet. "Please."

"Remember us!" Nez shouts, and Obba turns toward him. He shrieks, his attention fully on Nez, and I know he's going to attack him.

I have to make a choice—either kill my father, or let my brother die. Either way, I'm going to lose someone I love.

I wipe away my tears and unsheathe my daggers.

I may not be able to save my father, but I can save my brother.

The Dambi darts toward Nez and I'm right on his heels.

"Nez, move!"

The Dambi stands upright to strike Nez, I plunge my daggers into its back, and Nez finally sees what our father has become.

Obba's eyes are the color of chalk, his hair patchy, and his too-long arms end with sharp black claws. He shrieks and screeches, and his mouth is empty inside, his tongue cut out like the others.

Our father is dead. He died protecting us outside the city gates.

Whatever this creature is, it is not Isrof Khoum.

Nez ducks under the Dambi's arms and limps out of the way. Enraged, the creature writhes, and I struggle to pull my daggers out of its back. The right one tugs free, but I lose my hold on the left one. Frustrated and feeling off-balance with only one dagger, I run to Nez's side.

"Get out of here," I shout at my brother. He's on the ground, picking up any usable arrows. "I'll hold it off, you just get somewhere safe!"

Behind me, the Dambi screeches. I turn to face it and it's so close I don't have time to react. But Nez grabs my arm, yanks me to the ground, and fires an arrow right into the Dambi's mouth. The creature stumbles back before toppling over.

"Never turn your back on your foe." Nez's voice is stern and commanding, sounding exactly like Obba when he trained us in the jirkana. He grabs another arrow off the floor. "Now help me up."

I scramble to my feet and help Nez stand.

I've got one dagger, and he has a dozen arrows. It's not much against a Dambi, but we have each other and everything our father taught us.

Back on its feet, the Dambi claws at the arrow in its mouth. Nez looses another one, landing deep into its skull. The Dambi shrieks but doesn't fall. Nez readies a third arrow— he doesn't have many left—and I race toward the monster.

Another arrow embeds in its neck just as I jump on the Dambi's back. I free my left dagger, then slide them both across its throat. Thick, black blood pours out of its wounds, my hands are covered in it, and the Dambi lurches to one side, throwing me off its back. I land on the floor, my head cracking on the hard stone. Pain shatters my skull and I'm too stunned to move.

In front of me, Nez keeps the Dambi busy with his arrows while I slowly get back on my feet. The dizziness intensifies as I rise, and by the time I'm fully upright, the floor sways beneath me.

The Dambi is closing in on Nez and he lets another arrow fly, this one lodging in its chest. It falters but doesn't stop.

I have to protect my brother. I stagger over to a pillar, both hands outstretched, grabbing on to anything that will keep me steady. I grasp on to the corner of a table, the back of a chair, a length of fabric hanging from the ceiling as I make my way to Nez.

"Naira, I'm out!" Nez wields his bow like a club, ready to go down fighting.

The Dambi is riddled with arrows but still standing. With a deafening screech, it plows through a pile of dead Dambi to get to Nez. The monster raises its claws, Nez drops down into a fighting stance, and I lurch forward and push my brother aside.

The Dambi who once was my father plunges its claws into my stomach, ripping the skin apart.

Obba is killing me the same way he died.

I land on my back, the wind completely knocked out of me, with the Dambi hovering over me. When I catch my breath, all I can do is scream out in pain. The Dambi rears back to attack me again—but this time it's stopped by Nez's bow striking it across the face, knocking it aside.

"Leave my sister alone!"

My broken, injured brother is a whirlwind. With one arm, he wraps the string of his bow around the Dambi's neck and pulls, choking the creature, the string cutting into the Dambi's skin and drawing blood. The Dambi's eyes bulge and it claws at Nez, but he doesn't seem to feel it.

I can't do anything but watch, my breath coming in sharp bursts, my mouth filling with blood. I press my hands against my stomach, trying to stop my life from pouring out of me. I'm so cold. My hands tremble, and the floor around me is slick with my blood.

My eyelids flutter. Within the haze that clouds my vision, I see another shape in the room. Thinking it's another Dambi,

I try to get up to protect Nez, but intense pain pulsates from the gashes across my stomach.

There's shouting—all I can make out is *"Help her"*—and then there's someone kneeling beside me.

"Naira, can you hear me?"

It's Kal. I'm so relieved but all I can do is touch his arm to let him know I'm alive. I try to tell him to go help Nez, but I don't have the strength for words.

"I need to get you to a Daughter," he says, picking me up in his arms. I groan in pain and try to protest—I don't want to leave Nez behind—but I'm too weak. I've lost so much blood already and the pain is excruciating, clouding all my thoughts until there is nothing left but begging for the pain to go away.

A loud thud gets my attention. The Dambi is on the ground, dead, its head pulled off its neck by the bowstring. Nez is covered in blood and scratches, but he's alive. His bow is splintered in half, his arm broken from when he and the Dambi crashed to the ground, and the deep scratch across his thigh is still bleeding, but Nez is alive and that is all that matters.

"Let's go," he says to Kal, limping and clutching his broken arm, the bodies of the Mistress and her Dambi sprawled on the floor behind him.

Suddenly, the doors to the assembly room fly open. Nez and Kal turn toward the sound, both of them tense. Expecting more Dambi, I almost weep when I see the Hands of God instead.

"What has happened here?" Sister Cornelia asks, her horse dancing wildly beneath her.

"The Mistress is dead," Nez says, "and my sister will be, too, if we don't get her some help."

Sister Cornelia commands one of the Hands to fetch a Daughter and he runs off. Kal puts me on the floor and I'm grateful, because the world was starting to spin. My eyelids grow heavy. Nez and Kal call my name, but the sweet relief of darkness is too strong and I let it overcome me.

CHAPTER THIRTY-TWO

TIME PASSES, BUT I CAN'T MAKE MUCH SENSE OF IT. MY dreams flow into wakefulness so that I can't tell the difference between one and the other. People kneel over me. Sometimes it's a Daughter, sometimes Omma, sometimes people I don't recognize. Once, I think I see the Mistress and I jolt up, looking for my daggers, but strong arms push me back down.

Then, I'm back in the royal palace in Al-Kazar, seated upon the same throne where Sothpike killed Avari. This time, Avari, dressed as the Ur Atum Asim, not the Mistress, kneels at my feet.

My first impulse is to go for my daggers, but I'm not wearing them.

"Please, daughter, forgive me," Avari says, holding up her hands in supplication. "I never wanted to hurt you or your brother."

So many emotions flood my senses. Pity for the monster she became, sadness for the mother I will never know. But the strongest emotion is anger. I hate her for what she did to Obba, turning him into one of Sothpike's creatures.

"I am not your daughter," I say through gritted teeth. "You killed my father and then turned him into a Dambi. I will never forgive you."

Avari hangs her head in shame. "I am sorry for what I have done. For what had to be done." Wet spots appear on the floor, but her tears do nothing to diminish my wrath.

"What do you mean, *'what had to be done'*?"

"Everything, from the moment you were conceived, has happened as it was supposed to, in order to make you who you are at this moment," Avari says, lifting her eyes to mine. I can't stand to look at her, but I don't break away. I want her to see my hatred. She flinches under my gaze.

"You don't know anything about me, so how do you know who I am?"

"I know your heart is surrounded by flames," Avari replies. "You have an unquenchable fire that burns in you, one that is stoked by your strongest emotions. Right now, that emotion is anger, and it makes you burn hotter than the sun."

I look at my hands and recall the way they burned the Mistress when I touched her. I was so angry, *so afraid* she'd kill my brother. My desire to protect Nez exploded in me like a cask of oil thrown onto a bonfire.

The Three-Faced God said I was awakened—is this what it meant? Does this mean I'll have to keep my emotions in check lest they burn the people closest to me, friend or foe?

"Your fire is what will defeat the greatest threat this world has ever known," Avari continues. "Keep it, hold on to it, and never let it die out. You and your brother are all that stand between the world and oblivion."

"How do you know all this?"

"I have been visited by the Three-Faced God as well," she says. "We all have a part to play, and though I never asked for it, the Mistress was my role. Your role is to take your fire of vengeance and be a beacon of light against the darkness."

I don't know what to say. Was Obba's death merely a ploy to ignite the fire in my heart and fuel it with rage? The thought is an insult to every memory I have of him.

But Obba would not want me to wallow in fury or let hatred guide my actions. I know he would advise me to forgive Avari and let her move on to the next life in peace, but I can't let the anger go. It's a part of me now, filling the hole Obba once occupied.

But that doesn't mean I have to be ruled by it.

I look at Avari with eyes unclouded by hate and join her at the base of the throne. I don't like sitting on that glorified chair anyway.

"I saw you when you gave Nez and me to our parents. You were trying to protect us, only to hunt us down years later for *him*."

Avari wipes tears from her eyes. "When Sothpike put that mask on me, I didn't know who I was, only that I was to serve him. But even still, that is no excuse. I sought you out, and I found you both. It took me sixteen years, but I did it."

It's difficult being so close to the person who took Obba from me and not give in to the urge to rip her heart out like she did mine. I clasp my hands together to keep them from acting out on their own accord.

"Why did you come after us? Why couldn't you leave us alone?"

"It would be so easy to blame Sothpike for everything," Avari says, "but some part of me must have wanted to find you. Because even though Sothpike believed you were dead, something inside me knew that you were not. I am ashamed that the part of me that wanted to protect you was weaker than the part of me that wanted to please him."

My stomach curdles at the thought of wanting to please Sothpike, but I try not to let my disgust show. I have so many questions, and she has the answers.

"The Hands of God said Sothpike is crossing the desert. Why now?"

"Because I used my scrying disk to tell him what I found," Avari replies. "A secluded village at the bottom of the world. The perfect place to hide until you and your brother were ready to be found."

Another wave of fury crashes through me. Avari notices my shudder and puts more distance between herself and me.

"You have a temper," she says. "Just like your father. Your birth father."

"Tell me about him," I say. I don't want to hear more about Sothpike. I'm afraid the flames inside will consume me if they burn any brighter.

"He was full of passion and fire," Avari says with a smile, and I see myself in the way her nostrils flare, in the crinkles in the corners of her eyes. "Just like you."

As far back as I can remember, I looked for physical similarities between myself and Omma and found none. Even though Omma is my mother, and always will be, I can't deny there is a connection between me and Avari—a bond through blood that has given me her mouth and eyes. Her smile.

"The early days were some of the happiest of my life," she continues, her smile fading. "I loved Yafeu with everything in me, and I know that he loved me the same. But then Soth-pike tricked him, he tricked everyone, and my love was killed. I lost everything—"

Avari stops, overcome with emotion. I want to ask her to tell me more about Yafeu, but I don't get a chance. She reaches out a hand toward me, as if to caress my cheek, and I flinch. She quickly pulls away.

"I'm sorry," she says. "I just… You are even more beautiful than I remember. You've grown into a strong young woman."

I think about my parents—Farina and Isrof—picking me up when I fell, rubbing my back when I cried, holding my hand when I was scared. They were there to calm me down when my temper spun out of control and to rescue me at my lowest. Their love and guidance formed me into the person I am now.

"My parents raised me well."

"I knew they would," Avari says. "I chose them for their compassion, strength, and loyalty. I knew they would love you as I loved you. They were good friends to me, and good parents to you."

My eyes well with tears. "I never got to say goodbye to my father."

Avari winces as if my words have wounded her. "I am truly sorry. Can you ever forgive me?"

I could lie, tell her what she wants to hear, but that won't help anything.

"No," I say as I blink away the tears and swallow the lump in my throat. "You took my father from me. I know you were under Sothpike's control, but that doesn't change the fact that Obba is dead and you were the one who gave the order to kill him."

Avari looks crestfallen and I almost wish I hadn't been so truthful. Then she wipes away the last of her tears, takes a deep breath, and squares her shoulders.

"Yes," she says. "It is right that you hold on to your anger. It is what fuels the fire that burns within. But I hope that, with time, you will come to see that the Mistress who brought you so much pain is truly dead, and your fire can feed off something even greater than your hatred of me."

Avari stands and I do the same.

"I want you to know I will do everything I can from this side to protect you and your brother." Her gaze penetrates mine, her dark eyes captivating in their strength. "Tell Nezra I'll be waiting for him. He will never be alone."

"What does that mean?"

"Please tell him," Avari says. "When the time is right, he will understand." She disappears, taking the throne room with her.

I'm alone in my bedroom, the sun pouring through the open curtains. Slowly, I sit up, my stomach wound pulling with every movement and causing me to breathe in sharply. Waves of pain and heat radiate from the injury, and when I pull down the blanket to take a look, another shot of agony spreads across my stomach. Red and ragged and covered with zigzagging stitches, the scar throbs and shines with ointment.

But at least I'm still alive to feel it.

I close my eyes and I'm back in the meeting house, Obba ripping apart my skin—

No. Not Obba. A Dambi. I can't let what that creature did taint the memories I have of my father.

The simple act of sitting up tires me out and I rest my head back down on the pillow. The curtain to my room parts, revealing Nez standing in the entryway, one arm in a sling, his ankle still bandaged.

"You're awake," he says with a grin. He leans back out into the courtyard and is about to shout for Omma when I stop him.

"Wait, Nez. I have to tell you something," I say, my throat scratchy from disuse.

Nez hurries to my side and pours me a drink of water from the pitcher on my night table. I notice it's a new one to replace the one I broke so many nights ago.

After I drink, I tell Nez about the dream I had about Avari. When I'm done, I wait for him to comment, but he's silent.

"Well?" I ask.

"Well, what?"

"Well, what do you make of what she said? That she'd be waiting for you?"

Nez shrugs. "She said I'd know when the time comes. Maybe it's not the right time yet." He sits on a cushion next to me. "Besides, it was a dream, right?"

"Yes, but I've had other dreams like this that seem so real. Like I was witnessing events as they actually happened." I tell him about chasing Ergenegon through the skies and his blue fire, the same fire that engulfed me when I looked into the scrying disk. I tell him about the party with the shadow people, and then about seeing Avari command our parents to escape Al-Kazar and protect her children.

"Why does all the interesting stuff happen to you?" Nez asks. "My dreams are all about green fire and dark creatures that lurk in the shadows." He leans back against the wall and sighs, his eyes on the ceiling. "Especially after I killed...you know..."

"Obba," I say, my voice a whisper.

"Yes."

"Our father was already dead." I'm trying to reassure myself as much as Nez. "He just didn't know it. You put his body to rest. He was suffering, and you freed him from it."

"I know, but..." He looks down at his hands. "Why does it still feel like murder?" He glances up at me. "How about you? You killed the Mistress. Avari. Our mother. Our *real* mother."

"I had to," I say, staring at my own hands as I remember how I burned her and shoved her into the Dambi's claws. I swallow hard and look at Nez. "I didn't have a choice. She would have killed us if I hadn't."

"We did the right thing."

"And I'd do it again. I'd kill every Dambi and Mistress a thousand times to keep you safe."

"That's a lot of killing," Nez laughs, but his face is serious. "You don't want all that blood on your hands."

"No. But I don't want you to die either. I'll do whatever I can to prevent that from happening."

Nez fiddles with his fingers. "I wish you could promise me you'd live forever. I hated seeing you so close to death."

"I can't promise that."

"I know." Nez takes a deep breath and lifts his head. "So,

the Hands want me, but the Mistress and Sothpike wanted you. Who knew you are so popular?"

I try to hold back a laugh, but that hurts almost as much as letting it escape. I take in a few sharp breaths and sigh.

"Are you still joining the Hands of God?"

"I believe in them," he says. "I think they can help win this battle against Sothpike for good."

"How can you be so sure?" Nez has never been this serious about anything before. He always finds a way to make a joke, but when it comes to the Hands, he's completely sincere in his devotion to them.

"They have something powerful guiding their steps," Nez replies. "You said it yourself, the Three-Faced God came to you in your dreams. When have you ever dreamed about Maganor or Nurega or any of the other Thirteen? The Hands have so many secrets to teach me, and I know they will."

"Admit it, you just want to learn how to put on a magic show where you stab someone and they walk away unhurt," I joke and Nez laughs.

"I think Rima would be really impressed by that."

"I think she's already impressed by you."

"Not as much as I'm impressed by her," Nez says with pride in his voice. "Unlike the rest of us, she's never set foot in a jirkana and yet she didn't hesitate to fight. She's amazing."

"You're going to miss her when you're stuck in the mountains."

"Don't I know it." He rubs the back of his neck. "I'm going to miss you too, little sister."

"You don't have to go. You can stay here with me."

Half a smile appears on Nez's face. "Sometimes I wish we

could go back. Back to before all this started, before Obba died. But then other times I'm excited about what's going to happen next. I want to go to the mountains with the Hands. Does that make me selfish?"

I shake my head. "No, of course not. We can't live in the past. It's a fine place to visit every once in a while, but we can't stay there forever. We have to keep moving forward."

"I don't want to leave you." Nez takes my hand, squeezing it tightly. I return the gesture.

"It's not like we're never going to see each other again," I say. "You'll have to come out of the mountains eventually, even if it's just to show off your new magic tricks."

"Ha ha," Nez says with a smile. "You've got all the jokes today. Usually, I'm the one making you laugh."

As much as I'm trying to be excited for Nez to go off on his own adventures, my heart is heavy at the thought of being separated for who knows how long. I think of all the coming days when I'll be without Nez's easy laugh. I need him to keep from becoming too serious, too angry, too upset.

What am I going to do without my twin?

A tear creeps out of the corner of my eye and I'm glad it's from the side facing the wall, where Nez can't see it. I want him to leave without worrying about me. I'll survive without him—it won't be easy, but I'll survive.

At least, that's what I hope. I don't know for sure. We've never been apart.

I want this moment with my brother to last forever, but my eyelids are getting heavy and I lean back on the pillows. I sigh and close my eyes.

"I'm tired," I say as Omma enters the room.

"Oh, my headstrong girl," she says as she sits on the edge of my pallet and holds my hand. "My beautiful, headstrong girl."

"Omma," I whisper with a smile and then fall back asleep.

CHAPTER THIRTY-THREE

THE NEXT TIME I WAKE, I FEEL EVEN BETTER AND AM ABLE to sit up without nearly as much pain. A cool nighttime breeze drifts through the open curtains. I crawl out of bed, doing my best not to disturb Omma sleeping beside me, and step out of my room, my hand on the wound to help ease the ache that comes with using my stomach muscles to walk.

The courtyard is empty for the first time in weeks. I suppose the refugees that were staying with us have finally been able to find residences of their own. Now that the Mistress is dead, there is no reason for them to hide in our house any longer.

I carefully make my way to the back of the house and enter the jirkana. The room is completely empty except for Obba's sword, still sitting on the shelf where I left it.

The last time I saw the sword, I learned my parents were not my real parents. I was scared to touch the hilt out of fear that it would feel different with that new knowledge weighing down my thoughts. But this time I don't hesitate to grab the weapon.

Long ago, when I was still a little girl, Obba knelt beside me and held my hand to help me grasp the string of a kite, whispering instructions in my ear on how to make the sticks and fabric soar in the sky like a bird.

That's what I miss most: Obba's hands guiding me, his voice soothing and strong.

I place the curved sword back on the shelf. Everything else in the jirkana might be gone, but the memory of Obba will never be forgotten.

Back outside, a glint of light from the garden catches my attention and I make my way to the shed. Kal must be up there using his telescope.

As I approach the wooden structure, my stomach flutters and my cheeks flush with the memory of the moments I shared with Kal. My heart beats faster just thinking about every kiss.

"Naira, you're awake," Kal says when he sees me. He puts the telescope in the box and jumps down from the shed. A fading scar across his right brow reminds me of all we've been through together.

"Can I hug you?" he asks, his arms already open.

"We'll never know until you try," I say with a laugh that gives me twinges of pain, but I don't mind.

Kal gently wraps his arms around my shoulders and pulls me as close as he dares, which isn't very close at all. I put my arms around his waist and embrace him tightly.

"I missed you," he says, his breath ruffling my hair.

"I missed you, too."

We stay like that for a long time, in each other's arms, letting the rest of the world fall away.

"I don't want this night to end," I say.

"Me neither," Kal replies. "But look, it's almost morning."

I pull away and see that he's right. The sky is whitish blue, the sun just about to peek over the horizon.

"I have to leave soon," Kal says, his voice a whisper.

"Do you still have to go?" I ask. "The Mistress is dead."

Kal shakes his head. "Sothpike is still coming. While you were recuperating, there was a skirmish between his troops and some of our people in the desert."

"A skirmish? What happened?"

"The rangers expanded the perimeter," Kal explains. "They came across some of Sothpike's scouts and it turned into a battle. Luckily, we won, but we still suffered some losses. We don't have the numbers to fend off Sothpike for long. He has the living and the dead fighting for him."

"So it's true. Sothpike is coming."

"He's close," Kal says. "Really close."

"But that doesn't mean you have to join the Hands," I say, hating the whine that accompanies every word, but unable to stop it.

"This is the only way to learn more about my father."

I know that, but it doesn't make Kal leaving any easier for me. "I don't want you to leave."

"I don't want to either," Kal says. "But I'm not the only one. Hundreds of others have left Lagusa already. You and your mother will be setting out for the Rocky Plains soon to find the prophet Gamikal. We were waiting..."

"For me to wake up?"

Kal nods.

"I wish I was still asleep."

"I don't," Kal says. "Because then I wouldn't be able to do this." He presses his lips to mine, gently but firmly. I run my fingers through his hair, over his broad shoulders, trace the hairs on the nape of his neck. Kal leaves a trail of kisses on my neck, nibbles on my ear, sending shivers down my spine, before returning to my mouth for more.

I can hardly breathe but I don't want to stop. Kal is so warm and strong. I press my body against his, ignoring my tender wound, and he wraps his arms around my waist, pulling me close. I gasp in pain. Something cold and hard stabs me in the stomach, threatening to pierce my wound. We pull apart, Kal offering apologies for his Hands of God buckle causing me discomfort.

His brows furrow in concern. "Are you alright? Did I hurt you?"

I shake my head. "I'm fine. The Hands of God don't want us to be together, do they?" He cracks half a smile and I place a hand on my sore stomach. "I should get some rest."

Taking me by the other hand, Kal walks me back to my room. Even though I already slept so much, I can't wait to lie back down and close my eyes.

But rest won't come. My heart is overwhelmed with emotions. It's possible I'll never see Nez or Kal again. How will I survive without them? I already lost Obba; I can't lose them forever as well. Soon it will be only me and Omma. Our family, which had already been small, is getting smaller. It's up to me to keep Omma safe. But am I ready for the task?

And Sothpike is closer than he's ever been. The lives of my

family are in jeopardy because of me. They've been waiting for me to heal far past the time they should have left, risking their lives to ensure mine. I can't afford to be weak because I don't doubt Sothpike will hit Lagusa with everything he has. He's already destroyed an entire country; one little village at the bottom of the world will barely make him break a sweat. My home—everything I know—will be gone.

I shake my head to clear my thoughts. I can't spend my nights worrying. It isn't going to help anything. I have to get better, and to do that, I need to rest.

I close my eyes and will myself to sleep. When my thoughts and my heart quiet enough for me to drift off, I hope I'll dream of Obba as I dreamed of Avari, but I don't get my wish.

Obba exists now only in memories.

I wake a few hours later to find Omma packing my belongings.

"Are we leaving?" I ask as I rub my eyes.

"It's time," Omma says. "Sister Cornelia received word that Gamikal was spotted in a Haltayi village out on the Rocky Plains." She folds a stack of tunics and stuffs them into a bag.

"Do we have to go find him?"

A tired smile crosses Omma's face. "I wish we didn't, but if he can help us figure out what to do about Sothpike, then we must."

I offer to help but Omma shoos away my efforts and tells me to go get something to eat. I slowly make my way across the courtyard and find not only Nez and Kal at the dining room table, but Rima, Basheera, and Mandisa as well. They're laughing and when I fully pull back the curtain, all eyes turn toward me and a hush falls over the room.

"Well, don't just stare!" Rima jumps up to help me. "Move over so Naira can sit." She nudges Nez and he scoots to make space for me at the table. He bumps shoulders with Basheera, who glares at him over her glasses.

"Sorry, samida," Nez says with a bow.

"Will you tell your boyfriend to stop calling me that?" Basheera complains to her sister. "I'm not *that* scary, am I?"

I laugh—even I'm scared of Basheera and I've faced Ergenegon's flames twice—and my tender stomach muscles clench painfully. I gasp and laugh again, which causes me to gasp once more.

"Is she broken?" Basheera asks, genuinely concerned.

Basheera's words only make me laugh harder, rocking back and forth, clutching my aching stomach.

"Are you alright?" Rima rubs my back as if I need comfort.

"Stop making me laugh," I finally manage to get out, causing everyone to chuckle with relief.

Omma joins us, the space so crowded that everyone bumps elbows, but I'm glad everyone I care about is squeezed in at one table.

I look around at all the people who matter to me the most and want to engrave their faces in my mind forever. I never want to forget the delicate way brash Basheera strokes the back of Mandisa's hand, or how my mother's eyes shine when they land on her children. My heart bursts upon seeing Rima lean against Nez and clutch his arm. The way he looks at her—as if she's the sun after a long, cold night—makes me hope they'll stay together through Nez's journey to the Kilmare Mountains with the Hands and for many years thereafter.

And then there is Kal, smiling with the others, letting Nez

jab him in the side with his elbow in an effort to make him laugh at a corny joke, and grabbing my hand under the table in a quiet show of his affection. He knows I'm easily embarrassed and doesn't want to make me uncomfortable while showing me he cares.

This will be our final meal together for a long time, and I don't want the laughter to end.

Amid the joking and the laughing, Omma hands me a bowl of rice and I eat skewers of chicken and onions, vegetables simmering in a rich tomato sauce, fried pastries dipped in sweet syrup, and the last of our dates with the others. I feel a change coming, and I'm grateful to have this moment with everyone, this last memory before we all depart for separate horizons.

Afterward, Rima and Mandisa start to clean up, but Omma tells them to leave it.

"This is our last meal at this table," she says. "I want this house and anyone who comes after to know that we were here."

"If I had known we're supposed to leave messes behind, I wouldn't have straightened up my room," Nez jokes, which earns him a swat to his good arm from Omma.

A knock on the front door sends Nez scurrying to the entrance, his limp barely noticeable.

"Omma, the wagon is here!" he yells back into the house.

Slowly, I rise from the table and join my family in the courtyard. Satchels and baskets fill one corner—our lives packed up and ready to leave Lagusa behind.

Kal and Nez pile our belongings onto the wagon, Nez's broken arm making it difficult for him to pick up the baskets and trunks, so he leaves those for Kal. Rima, Basheera, and Mandisa pitch in too, but when I try to help, everyone shoos me away.

"What if you rip your stitches?" Rima admonishes as she steers me toward a bench in the main entrance.

While they're busy, I go back to the jirkana and grab Obba's sword. I carry it to the front and tuck it into one of my bags.

"I put what remained of his staff in that basket," Omma says, hugging me close and pointing at a basket Kal and Basheera are lifting onto the wagon. "We don't have his ashes to take with us, but we have his spirit."

"I miss Obba so much," I say.

Omma wipes her eyes. "He was everything to me. When we left Al-Kazar, all we had were each other and two squalling babies. I had to depend on him to survive, and he had no one else but me. We grew close during those years, and one day I realized I was in love. We had just moved into this house and your father was teaching Nez how to walk over there in the courtyard. He was being so patient, even though he was a tough soldier, trained to kill in a hundred different ways. But with you two, he became soft and gentle and I thought, *That is the kind of man I want to marry.* Luckily for me, we already were."

My heart swells. My parents gave up their lives and families in Al-Kazar to raise two children with a partner they barely knew, but somehow they did it. Not only that, but they thrived, and showed their children what true love looks like.

"I want to hear more about you and Obba," I say.

"Now that there are no more secrets between us, there's so

much I want to tell you." Omma smiles. "But first, we have to say goodbye to our home."

I call Nez over and together we walk to the family mazan, where wooden icons of the Thirteen rest on an altar. We cross our arms, our fingertips resting on our shoulders, and bow our heads. Nez can only cross one arm, but he performs the rest of the gesture.

"We've had many good years in this house," Omma says. "May we have more wherever our road takes us. May the Fires of the Thirteen guide us on this new journey."

We finish the prayer in unison: "By the Fires we live, by the Fires we are blessed, and by the Fires we die."

I don't know if praying to the Thirteen helps, but it was something Obba would have done, and I'm glad to speak the words one last time as a family.

When we're finished, Omma packs up the mazan and we meet everyone at the wagon. Omma and I climb up next to the driver. Nez and the others ride in the back.

"Where are we going?" I ask Omma.

"To the river. I've booked us passage on a boat that will take us to the other shore. Then we'll venture to the Rocky Plains, where we'll find Gamikal and be far away from Sothpike."

"It's good you're getting out now," the wagon driver says around the hay stalk sticking out of his mouth. "They say Sothpike's army is getting closer every day."

"Aren't you going to leave too?" I ask.

The driver shakes his head. "I was born here, and I'm gonna die here. I'm old, not like you young things. I can't start all over. There's nothing for me on the other side of the Bujarbi Desert. My life's in Lagusa. And so's my death, I suppose."

The streets are empty and quiet, but dread hangs in the air. Everyone knows Sothpike is coming, and those who remain in the village have drenched the streets in frightened anticipation.

The closer we get to the river, the more people we see. When we reach the docks, the roads are teeming with wagons and people carrying bundles on their heads, families trying to buy passage on boats and captains calling to the crowd, trying to gain the attention of those who are desperate to leave the village. Merchants have set up shops to sell whatever they can to those fleeing Lagusa while others offer to buy family heirlooms and extra goods from those who need the rubes.

The Mugabe family are among those trying to book passage. Hamala catches my eye and bows. I return the gesture, a breeze from the river tousling my hair.

Barges filled with horses and crates, passengers and crew pull away from the shore, the crew using long poles to push the crafts into the current. There are a few remaining two- and three-masted ships for those with enough rubes to pay for the exorbitant fares, and I wonder which boat we'll be taking.

I look to my right at the domed Temple atop the highest hill, protecting gods who never answer prayers. The scorched building reflects the damage done to the village. A ribbon of black smoke rises from the plaza where the statues of the Thirteen sleep peacefully while their believers flee certain death.

"What about the Mother and the Daughters?" I ask Omma.

"They chose to stay," she says. "As long as the village needs them, they will be there."

Amid the shouts, mobs of people, and other wagons, Omma directs the driver toward the Hands of God, their gray cloaks and stony expressions making them stand out. When we pull up, Sister Cornelia stares at me with her piercing blue eyes.

"Behold, the glory of our god," she says. "You're alive and well." Then she turns to Omma, who is helping me down from the wagon. "Sothpike's army is less than a day's ride from here. If you are to be going, you must leave now."

Every fiber of my being wants to stay in Lagusa, my only home. I think about how hard it was for my parents to start over after they left Al-Kazar and I don't want Omma to go through that again.

But Sothpike isn't giving us a choice. We have to leave, which means Nez and I are going to be separated for the first time.

A sob rises in my throat and I lean against the wagon until it passes, blinking my eyes to hold back the tears. I have to be strong. I don't want Nez's last memory of me to be of a weeping mess.

With the Hands' help, all of our belongings are passed to the captain of the *Terebi*, a single-mast ship that's going to take us across the river. From there, we'll trek through the mountains to the Rocky Plains to that Haltayi village where Gamikal was spotted. Rima and her family are joining us, so at least Omma and I won't be alone. I take my time boarding the ship, the vessel swaying beneath my feet, until Sister Cornelia grows impatient.

"We must be going if we are to get away as well," she says from the shore. "We have our own boat to catch."

"I understand," Omma says. "Let us say our goodbyes." With tears in her eyes, she hugs Nez close and kisses his cheeks. "Be safe, my love."

Nez sniffles but doesn't let the tears fall. We give each other gentle hugs, both of us aware of the other's injuries.

"Don't do anything stupid," I whisper in his ear, choking back tears.

"You know I will," Nez says with a laugh. "And so will you."

"And we'll tell each other all about it when we're together again."

"You're going to have some amazing stories when we're reunited. I just know it."

Nez gives me one last grin before pulling Rima aside. They talk quietly to each other, and he wipes tears from her eyes before giving her a lingering kiss. I turn away to give them privacy...

And lock eyes with Kal in front of me. He rests his chin on the top of my head when he pulls me in for a hug, and suddenly it feels as if I can't breathe.

"Don't worry, I'll keep him safe."

"Thank you." A single tear escapes my eye and leaves a wet spot on his tunic. "Are you sure you have to go?"

"I wish I could stay," he says. "But this is my path."

"I know." And I truly do, but it doesn't make this parting any easier.

"We'll be together again. I promise. This isn't forever."

"I'm going to hold you to that." I look into his many-colored eyes for what could possibly be the last time. But I don't want to think about that. I want to believe—I *have* to believe—we will see each other again. I force myself to imagine what it will be like when Kal and I see each other again.

We'll both smile, and hug each other close, and I'll smell

the sea on him, and he'll feel the fire that burns within me, and we'll be together. Nothing will tear us apart again.

That's what I think about when Kal kisses me one last time.

With a final reminder from Omma to be safe, Nez walks down the gangway back onto the docks, his limp giving him a swagger, with Kal following. Nez grabs his bow from the wagon, a new one, and slings it over his shoulder along with his satchel while Kal gathers his own things, at his hip the sword he chose from our jirkana in what feels like another life. I watch as they make their way over to Sister Cornelia, her arms crossed, her face expressionless. She greets them, her voice lost in the distance between our boat and the shore, but I don't need to hear her words to know what she said: *Behold, the glory of our god.*

Then the captain of the *Terebi* pulls up the gangplanks, unfurls the sails, and the boat drifts away from the dock.

I wave goodbye to Nez and Kal and to the village Obba gave his life for.

"What happens next?"

Omma puts an arm around me and I lean my head on her shoulder. I want to jump overboard, swim to the shore, and hold tight to my brother, but I remember his words: *If we only hold on to each other, we risk losing our grip on everything else.*

"We face whatever comes next with strength and pride," Omma says.

Rima takes my other hand. "We stand together, even though we are apart."

"And we kick Sothpike's ass," Basheera says, pushing her glasses up her nose with one hand and holding Mandisa's with the other.

I smile and glance over my shoulder at the far shore. In a few hours, we'll reach the other side, where we'll have to cross a prairie before venturing through the mountains using the Sharafi Yazul Pass. On the other side of the mountains are the Rocky Plains, an area even more barren than the desert, filled with salt pans, nomads called the Haltayi, giant furry beasts called maugrabs, and a mythical man named Gamikal who's going to show me how to defeat Sothpike.

Sothpike is coming, but he'll have to trek long and hard to find me. And while he searches, I'll continue to heal. When we finally meet, I vow to myself that I'll be far stronger than before.

I will defeat him—not for honor, not for riches, not for glory. For what is right.

A fire burns within me, one that has been awakened by the Three-Faced God, one that can't be stamped out. There is more the Three-Faced God wants to show me: I feel the first hints of a headache that signals we will speak again, and I welcome it.

I am the type who jumps into the fire, after all.

★ ★ ★ ★ ★

ACKNOWLEDGMENTS

This book wouldn't be possible without my family, who have always supported my dream of becoming a published author, who read my stories even in the early days of my writing journey when I'm sure it was torture, who brainstormed and summarized and shared ideas with me, and who are as excited about this book as I am. Sara and Barbra: Does this good news mean our family curse is finally broken? Special shout-out to Amya who drew the first map of Naira's world! And to Shyla: you got your printed copy—no more excuses.

I can't forget my writing group: Hannah, Danielle, Adelle, Denise, and Miranda—thank you! Each of you has given me feedback and advice and cheered me on, and I am so glad that I can count on you to steer me in the right direction.

A very special thanks to my very special friend Hannah—this book would not be possible without you. You have no idea how much I appreciate you and how often I think about how your sending me an Instagram post led to my dream coming true.

I must thank everyone at Inkyard Press, from my editor, Claire Stetzer, to cover designer Kathleen Oudit to cover artist Hillary Wilson to everyone else who worked on my book and made this all possible!

Of course, I have to thank Claire Friedman at Inkwell for being my champion throughout this process! When I realized my agent and editor have the same first name and that they work at similar-sounding companies, I knew this was kismet.

And to Little Cat, Grady, Stripe, Rocky, Bully, and now Martha—thank you for all the purrs.